Praise for

T.M. LO[...]

'Logan belongs in the top echelons of British thriller writers'
Sunday Express

'Logan is the master of the everyman thriller . . . be prepared to sacrifice sleep'
Gillian McAllister

'Thriller of the year? This is the thriller of the decade'
My Weekly

'Clever, taut and twisty . . . full of tension and gasp-out-loud moments'
Claire Douglas

'An irresistible premise, a nerve-shredding nightmare . . .
T.M. Logan has done it again'
Chris Whitaker

'Absorbing and tense, fuelled by a very real sense of jeopardy'
Adele Parks

'Assured, compelling, and hypnotically readable – with a twist
at the end I guarantee you won't see coming'
Lee Child

'A truly addictive thriller'
Louise Candlish

'Logan is undoubtedly the master of the all-too-believable,
it-could-happen-to-me story'
B.A. Paris

'Darkly gripping and addictive . . . T.M. Logan at his absolute best'
Sarah Pearse

'Even the cleverest second-guesser is unlikely to arrive at the truth
until it's much, much too late'
The Times

THE DAUGHTER

T.M. Logan is a *Sunday Times* bestseller whose thrillers have sold more than two million copies in the UK and are published in 22 countries around the world. *The Holiday* was a Richard and Judy Book Club pick and was adapted into a four-part TV drama, as was *The Catch*. Formerly a national newspaper journalist, he writes full time and lives in Nottinghamshire with his wife and two children.

THE DAUGHTER

T.M. LOGAN

ZAFFRE

First published in the UK in 2025 by
ZAFFRE
An imprint of Bonnier Books UK
5th Floor, HYLO, 103-105 Bunhill Row,
London, EC1Y 8LZ
Owned by Bonnier Books
Sveavägen 56, Stockholm, Sweden

A CIP catalogue record for this book is
available from the British Library.

Hardback ISBN: 978-1-80418-514-8
Trade paperback ISBN: 978-1-80418-515-5

Also available as an ebook and an audiobook

1 3 5 7 9 10 8 6 4 2

Typeset by IDSUK (Data Connection) Ltd
Printed and bound in Great Britain by Clays Ltd, Elcograf S.p.A.

www.bonnierbooks.co.uk

For my Dad, Mike,
who was the first to read me a story

You may give them [your children] your love but not your thoughts, for they have their own thoughts. You may house their bodies but not their souls, for their souls dwell in the house of tomorrow, which you cannot visit, not even in your dreams.

—Kahlil Gibran, *The Prophet*

PART I

1

SATURDAY

Ten weeks. It is the longest time we've ever been apart.

Longer than all the rest of the time put together. All the teenage sleepovers and festivals, her holidays with friends, the trips away with school.

A long time to be apart from my eldest child, though Evie had been so excited to leave. So excited to start this next phase of her life, to enjoy her first real freedom. I was happy for her, as her mother of course I was, full of hopes and dreams like any parent. But anxious too, as the summer had ebbed away. As Evie got her grades and her place was confirmed. As she'd marked her departure date on our kitchen calendar, in big happy capitals with three exclamation marks.

Wanting to keep her close for just a little while longer. But knowing I had to let her go. That she would be OK. She was ready for university: safe, shallow waters before the open ocean.

And now, finally, the endless first term is over.

I'd woken before my alarm this morning, eager to get on the road, everything laid out and ready to go. A packed lunch of tuna mayo sandwiches – Evie's favourite – water bottles for the journey, bags for gathering washing and a roll of bin liners for anything else. A cold bag so she could empty her fridge, a few sprays and wipes to give her room a freshen up. Certain I'd forgotten something, but not sure what it was.

Traffic grinds to a steady crawl when I hit the M25. A watery winter sun glows cold behind drifting clouds, but there is a warm buzz of anticipation in my chest at the thought of seeing Evie again. Of wrapping my arms around this wonderful, big-hearted, stubborn, beautiful daughter of mine for the first time in ten weeks.

By the time I'm turning onto the leafy parkland campus it's almost 11 a.m. and there is a long line of traffic snaking slowly along the main access road. New Orchard Hall is a sixties-built accommodation block, four red-brick storeys encircled by footpaths. The roads are lined with parked cars half-up the pavement, boots open, roof boxes revealed, parents hefting suitcases and bags and boxes of every shape and size to load up for the journey home.

Evie had wanted to catch a train, but I had insisted on picking her up.

It was a peace offering, a chance for us to talk on the drive home from London, to *really* talk. To draw a line under what had gone before, the constant tension of teenage boundaries being pushed and pushed until they buckled and broke. To say: *things between us can be different this time.*

I park in a spot just vacated by a Mercedes four-by-four and check my phone. I'd messaged Evie when I set off from Reading to give her at least an hour's warning that I was on the way. She'd not replied, but that wasn't unusual for her: she was probably still asleep. I take a couple of folded blue Ikea bags for laundry and head up to the main door, where a heavily laden dad trails behind a teenager chatting on her phone. I head upstairs to the third floor and turn left out of the stairwell, following the signs. It's vaguely familiar from the only other time I've been here.

Each floor of the hall is divided into six flats, each of which has eight single rooms. A *lot* of teenagers packed into a relatively small space. I check the Notes app on my phone: Evie is on the third floor, flat F, room number eight.

The door to the flat is wedged open with a single grubby trainer. Inside I'm greeted with a heavy odour that's so thick I can almost touch it: sweaty feet, burned toast, damp clothes. The first door on the left is a shared kitchen, the table a mess of bottles, half-empty glasses and crushed cans, spilled alcohol dried to a dull sheen on the plastic. The sink is worse and there are more bottles clustered in ranks three-deep around the overflowing bin, greasy pizza boxes crammed into the top.

I guess there was some kind of end-of-term party here last night, or pre-drinks, or whatever they call it when they are getting ready for a big night. I feel a momentary pang of pity for the cleaner and remember that I have a roll of black bin bags in the car. I'll make a start on some of this mess while Evie finishes packing. If I know my daughter, she'll have left everything until the last minute.

I knock gently on her door and wait. There is no answer; only silence from within the room.

I knock again.

'Evie?' I say. 'It's Mum.'

The silence is disturbed by the first faint sounds of movement, a creak of springs, mumbled words, a yawn, a sniff.

Just as I'm raising my hand to knock again, the lock clicks and the door opens a few inches. I rearrange my face into a smile, determined that we won't start today off with another row.

The door opens a little more, a face appearing in the small gap. A skinny boy in a sleeveless black T-shirt, hair flattened to his head. His skin is puffy and creased, his eyes still heavy with sleep. A few wispy hairs sprout from his chin.

Ah. OK. This is . . . slightly awkward, but probably more for him than me. And for Evie most of all. Although I can't help thinking that she could do better than this lad. She hasn't mentioned a boyfriend, but maybe this explains why contact has been intermittent over the last few weeks. Or perhaps . . . it was just a one-night thing? They are freshers. It's what freshers do.

The skinny boy blinks at me, squinting against the bright strip light.

'Hi,' I say brightly. 'Sorry to wake you. I'm Evie's mum.'

He looks at me as if he's grappling with a tough piece of algebra, a test he wasn't expecting. He frowns, turns to look back into the room for a second, before his bloodshot eyes return to me.

'Huh?'

It seems I'd been a bit naive to hope my daughter would be packed and ready to jump in the car. She's not even awake yet.

'Evie,' I say, putting my hands in the pockets of my jeans. 'Is she . . . decent? We're heading home today, just want to get her things packed up.'

He rubs a nail-bitten finger at the corner of his eye. It's possible, I suppose, that he's still drunk from last night. He peers over my shoulder, cranes his head around the door frame as if someone's holding up a phone, recording this awkward interaction. As if this might be some kind of prank that will end up on social media.

His answer, when it finally comes, catches me off guard.

'Who's Evie?'

2

There is a girl's voice inside the room, muffled and indistinct behind the half-open door.

I shake off the momentary feeling of alarm. Of course Evie's here. Where else would she be?

'She's my daughter,' I say slowly, indicating the number next to the door. 'Evie Wingfield. This is her room.'

The boy – young man – shakes his head, tries to speak. But it comes out as a hungover grunt. He clears his throat and tries again.

'S'mine.'

'What?'

'My room.'

There is a glow of embarrassment in his cheeks now, perhaps for her, for himself, or for this situation. Evie and I will laugh about it on the way home, I'm sure. Or if not on the way home, in a few days' time when she's had a chance to rest and recharge and eat some good home-cooked food. Without wanting to make this moment any more awkward than it already is, I nod towards the side of the room where my daughter must be, still in the narrow single bed they presumably shared last night.

'Evie?' I raise my voice a little, so she can hear me through the door. 'Shall I make us all a cup of tea in the kitchen while you sort yourself out?'

The young guy shakes his head again. 'Think you might have the wrong room.'

Before I can reply, he pushes the door softly shut and I'm left standing there in the empty corridor. The hushed tones of an urgent conversation from inside, only the words 'Mum' and 'Evie' and various swear words audible through the scratched wooden door.

Explanations push through my confusion. Maybe she's just dying with embarrassment that I've caught her with a boy. That she's overslept and is hungover and this sleepy-eyed teenager is just covering for her, stumbling into some foolish lie in the moments after he wakes up. Or . . . maybe he is someone *else's* boyfriend. Some poor girl who had already headed home for Christmas, who had only been gone for a day or two before he hopped into bed with someone else.

But that was none of my business. They were adults – technically, at least.

I glance at the metal panel next to the door again to confirm my eyes aren't playing tricks on me. *3F8.* Check the Notes app on my phone again. This was *definitely* the room number I'd noted down when I dropped Evie off in September. Unless . . . I'd got one of the digits wrong? It had been a chaotic day, after all.

I remember our hug before I left, of not wanting to let her go. Slowly backing out of her room, trying to think of reasons to stay a little longer while I tried to ignore the vibe Evie was giving off. Her body language was clear: *I'm OK, Mum, you don't have to hang around, you can go now.* Humouring me while I made excuses to stay five minutes longer, then another five. Then another.

Finally – after one more quick hug – I let the door close between us, heading for the stairs, determined not to look back, not to cry. She didn't need that on her first day here, she needed me to be happy for her. And I *was* happy, amid the swirl of all the other emotions. Evie had worked hard to get here and it was a new phase of her life. A new step. A new phase of my life, too.

The tears had come when I was halfway home, alone in the corner of a service station car park. A quick cry as I cradled a coffee, the hollow feeling in my chest, the sobs that I had held down deep all day suddenly rising up, one after another. A strange, sad-happy ache that eased after I'd finally let the tears out. But there would be no tears on the journey home today: I had my daughter back for three whole weeks.

The Notes app on my phone says 'New Orchard Hall third floor flat F room 8'.

I knock on the door of room 3F8 again. More hushed voices before it's pulled open for a second time.

'Yes?' The lad looks slightly more awake and annoyed than a moment ago. 'Look, what is this?'

'I'm really sorry,' I say. 'But I do need to get Evie moving and get her stuff packed. Could you give her a nudge for me?'

'Like I *said*.' He puts a heavy emphasis on the word. 'You've got the wrong room.'

'No, I'm pretty sure I'm in the right place, I made a note on my phone when I brought her in September. Look.' I hold up the phone as if this is incontrovertible proof that he is somehow mistaken, or lying, or perhaps both.

He exhales dramatically.

'There's no Evie, OK? This is *my* room.'

He moves to push the door closed but I put my boot in it before he can shut it on me a second time.

'Hang on,' I say. 'What?'

'I told you,' he says. 'Now can you move your foot, please?'

A new thought occurs to me: perhaps she'd not got on with her flatmates and had asked to move. Maybe that was it.

'Were you here right from the start of term?'

'Eh?'

'Did you move in here from a different hall? Or were you a late-starter?'

'What's that got to do with you?'

'But was there a girl here before you?' I remove my boot from the door, hoping we can just have a conversation like two adults. 'Do you know where she went?'

'Sorry, can't help you.' The slam of the door is followed by a solid *click* as the lock is engaged from the other side.

3

I stand for a moment in the corridor, straining to hear muffled voices on the other side of the door.

This whole strange interlude feels like some kind of practical joke, and I'm half expecting Evie will burst out at any moment and shout, 'Gotcha!' with a big mischievous grin on her face.

Another door opens a little way up the shared corridor. But it's not Evie, instead it's a pale young woman in a long purple hoodie with QAU and the university's logo across it, hair wrapped in a towel, her legs bare. She's barefoot, brushing her teeth and studiously avoiding eye contact. She steps around me and heads for the kitchen without acknowledgement.

'Excuse me,' I say. 'Hi. This is New Orchard Hall, right?'

The young woman turns and stops brushing her teeth for a moment.

'Huh?'

'This hall,' I say. 'What's it called?'

'Hang on,' she says out of the corner of a mouth filled with toothpaste. She slips into the kitchen from where I hear the *splat* as she spits into the sink. She returns carrying an almost-empty pint of milk and a bag of sugar.

'Sorry,' she says. 'New Orchard, yeah. Which one are you looking for? There's, like, Maynard over towards the union building, then going the other way you've got Lodge, Chesney, the thing is they all look identical except for—'

'But this is New Orchard?'

'Yah,' she says again. She has a self-assured private school drawl, an easy confidence that belies her age. 'So you're Sam's mum, are you?'

I feel another unpleasant flicker of unease low down in my stomach. The far-off echo sounding again.

'Who?'

She indicates room 3F8. 'Good luck waking that reprobate up though, he was *so* smashed last night. Hope you don't mind me saying so but that boy is an absolute liability when he's had a few pints.'

'No, I'm . . . listen, there was a girl here, Evie, I dropped her off myself in the first week. She was doing law, she's got shoulder-length brown hair, brown eyes, about this tall.' I hold a hand up a little above my own eyeline. 'Do you remember her?'

She looks blank. 'The thing is, you meet so many new people in first term that it's virtually impossible to keep track. It's all a bit of a blur, to be honest, union bar was doing five shots for a fiver for the whole of Welcome Week. Absolute *carnage.*'

I take my phone out and show her the screensaver, a rare picture of Evie and her brother together, smiling in the sunny back garden of a country pub.

The young woman studies it for a moment, gives a brief shake of her head.

'No,' she says. 'Sorry. I can like, *sort of* remember that Sam joined us in the flat in week two, but it's super-vague and so long ago. I thought the room was just vacant before he arrived.'

'She's supposed to be here,' I say, hating how uncertain I sound. 'I'm supposed to be taking her home today. How does it work, can you ask to move rooms, move halls? Is that something you're able to do?'

'My friend Johnny had to move in week three,' she says in a matter-of-fact tone. 'His original flatmates in Selincourt were, like, absolute *animals*. It was so grim, you wouldn't believe what one of them left in the kitchen sink, it was—'

'That must be it,' I say. 'She must have moved rooms. Do you know where she went, the girl who was here before Sam?'

She shrugs. 'She didn't tell you?'

'I don't . . . think so.'

'Savage,' she says absently. 'Did you have, like, a huge row or something?'

I try to think back, to the intermittent conversations we'd had on the phone. The desultory messages, brief replies to my enquiries about student life and how she was finding it. My friend Nathalie's daughter had been back home almost every other weekend in the first term and while I knew Evie wouldn't be *that* desperate for some home comforts I'd assumed she'd come back at least once, since Reading was barely fifty miles away. I'd thought at the time that she was too busy having a good time, making friends and discovering London – maybe even doing some studying. But now I wonder if it was something else.

'Maybe she did tell me back then and I've just forgotten.'

'Most likely,' she says with a nod of sincerity. 'Look I'm really sorry, my dad's going to be here in, like, two minutes and I've not even started packing yet and he's going to go *ballistic*.' She flashes me a practised smile. 'It was nice to meet you though.'

She turns and disappears back into her room, 3F4, the door swinging heavily shut behind her with a slam.

That must be it. Evie had just not got on with her flatmates for some reason, had asked to move and was somewhere else on campus. There must be a procedure for that, a process – it probably happened all the time in the first few weeks of term as so many freshers settled in. She must have told me, mentioned it at some point and I'd just forgotten. I take my phone out and call her number, but it just goes to voicemail so I leave a message asking her to call me back.

In the kitchen, I clear one of the chairs of a pizza crust and a muddy T-shirt, before sitting down to scroll back through all her messages, flicking from one app to another. There were texts, a few replies to our little family group on WhatsApp, an occasional conversation on Messenger and some on Snapchat – which I had joined just to stay in touch with my children – but I can't find anything that mentions a change of accommodation.

I don't even have anything official, any notification from the university itself – all of the university correspondence had been sent direct to her. She had insisted on dealing with everything herself right from the beginning, and everything was electronic in any case, done through the student portal. I scroll back through my own emails, although Evie had never been a big user and didn't even bother checking her inbox half the time. It was an older technology that seemed to have little interest for her generation – too formal, too slow. I scroll through my inbox, through half a dozen archived folders, with that nagging feeling of searching for something I know I'm not going to find.

I admit defeat and send Evie a text instead.

Hi, it's me, I'm here. What's your room number again? X

Pushing the phone back into my pocket, I head downstairs. In the main lobby by the front door, there is a long row of old-style wooden pigeonholes along the wall. The one for 3F8 looks as if it's not been emptied in a while, crammed with fast food flyers, leaflets and assorted other junk mail. I take everything out anyway, examining it all piece by piece. There is a single piece of official-looking mail, a white envelope bearing the university's crest and the name *Samuel Beaufort-Raines* behind the clear window. Without quite knowing why, I take out my phone and snap a picture of his name.

I go through everything in the pigeonholes on either side of the one designated 3F8, and those above and below it too, in case something has been misplaced. Something official put into the wrong slot by mistake. But it's only more of the same. Nothing with my daughter's name on it.

The phone buzzes in my hand with what I assume is a reply from Evie, but when I check the display it says something else instead. I read it, frowning, read it again. Just two words in grey italics.

Message failed

My text sits above it, undelivered. *Hi, it's me, I'm here. What's your room number again? x* But there is no green tick to show it's been received. What did *message failed* even mean? That her phone's out of charge, or broken, or somehow not connected to a network? It can't be because it's switched off – it would just show as pending or unread or whatever.

I send her another.

Evie please reply when you get this x

After a moment, the same response appears beneath it.

Message failed

Perhaps she'd run out of credit, or there was some problem with her phone contract?

I pull open the main door, holding it for another mum who gives me a grateful smile as she squeezes through with a bulging black bin liner in each hand. Outside, the sky is darkening with heavy clouds that threaten rain, the December air sharp against my cheeks after the stuffy warmth of the hall. Wherever she is on campus, I hope Evie is somewhere inside, somewhere warm. A chilly gust of rain sends parents and their offspring hurrying to their cars as they finish loading up and start to head home. All of them together, reunited after a temporary separation: fathers, daughters, mothers, sons. I am the exception here, the odd one out. The outlier, left behind. Still on my own as I select Evie's number on the phone again and press *dial*.

This time it doesn't even ring. Doesn't even let me leave a message. Instead, just a computerised female voice.

I'm sorry, the robotic response says evenly. *That number is not recognised.*

4

The first stirrings of panic begin to roll in my stomach: the sick, unmoored feeling of the world shifting on its axis.

I try calling my daughter twice more, greeted each time by the same robotic message. Evie's phone number seems to be unavailable. I call my mum instead, trying to keep my voice steady, to hold at bay all the dark thoughts that are circling closer and closer, like wolves around a dying campfire.

But she hasn't heard from Evie either.

'Is everything all right, Lauren?' The background noise fades at her end of the line as she turns down Classic FM. 'You're picking her up this weekend, aren't you?'

'Yes.' My hand, gripping the phone, is damp with sweat. 'It's fine. Just . . . I'll let you know when we're home.'

I ring off and call my son, who is spending the day at his friend Isaac's house and is deep into a marathon videogames session when he picks up. Lucas is distracted, his mind on a game of Quidditch Champions, our conversation interspersed with various cries of triumph or frustration as he tells me that he's not been in touch with his sister this week. A brief, awkward conversation with the mother of Evie's best friend, Millie, yields the same result.

None of them know anything, have heard anything, that might help me track down my daughter.

I make my way to the Students' Union building, a high-sided slab of pebble-dashed concrete, asking at reception where I'm told the accommodation office is closed on weekends but there might still be someone around in the School of Law, a five-minute walk down the hill. Evie would know this campus like the back of her hand by now, I think, with a twinge of irony. She would know where I need to go.

Sliding glass doors into the School of Law open slowly to reveal a small reception area devoid of people. A small, sad-looking plastic Christmas tree stands in the corner, hung with purple baubles. I check a listing of room numbers next to the lift and take it up to the second floor, following signs to the left through a heavy double door. The corridors are empty and still, motion-activated lights flicking on as I walk beneath them; the only sound the echo of my heels on the parquet wooden floor.

I finally find room C-44 but there is no answer when I knock. The sign beside it says it belongs to Professor Carl Henbrandt CBE FRS, Head of School, a printed note Blu-tacked below his title that reads '*Office hours for student consultation Tues/Weds 11–12, Thurs 1–2 p.m.*' I knock again and try the handle, but it's locked. I knock on the next door down the corridor, then the door opposite. There is no answer at either. The whole department feels like a ghost town, fully wound down for Christmas already.

Frustration rising, I approach a passing student outside and he points towards the social sciences faculty hub in the modern building next door. I'm starting to feel as if I've entered some endless maze of acronyms and empty offices, a hall of mirrors that will keep me going around in circles until I give up.

Inside the lofty atrium of the faculty hub next door, a bright yellow helpdesk is manned by a single beanie-wearing teenager who seems barely older than Evie herself. He too seems stumped when I ask him who I need to speak to.

'Saturday today.' He barely glances up from his phone. 'Teaching's finished, end of term.'

Everyone I meet, I show Evie's picture in the hope that it might dislodge a memory or yield a spark of recognition.

Nothing.

'This is Evie.' I hold my phone up in front of his face, so he has to look at the picture on the screen. 'My name's Lauren, I'm her mum. Evie's not where she's supposed to be – how do I find her?'

He looks blankly at me, as if it might be a trick question.

'Like, I don't know, you could ring her?'

I bite back a sarcastic reply and ask again, feeling my temper starting to fray. A cleaner passing by overhears our conversation. He suggests I try the basement of another brutalist concrete building nearby – the main administration block – where the security office is located.

Security's front desk seems deserted, the hinged section at the end raised and resting against the wall. I call *hello* a couple of times and I'm about to walk in when a door opens and a nondescript man emerges in a pale grey suit, his top shirt button undone above a festively patterned tie. He's in his late fifties, with a neat white beard and a paunch stretching his shirt.

'Hello there,' he says. 'Can I help you, madam?'

'I hope so – I've been all over the campus trying to find *someone* who can help.' I feel the painful lump in my throat as I put it into words for another stranger. 'This is going to sound odd but . . . I can't find my daughter. I came here to pick her up like everyone else is doing, but she's not here, she's not in her room like she was supposed to be. I can't get through to her on the phone. She must have moved rooms and I need to know where she is.'

'I see,' he says, his brow creasing with concern. 'Why don't you come through to my office and have a seat for a minute while we get this sorted out? Let me get you some water first.'

My instinct is to snap at him, *I don't want a drink! I just want to take my daughter home*, but he's already turning and heading to the water cooler at the other end of the office. He returns a moment later with two plastic cups, ushering me through to his small office and gesturing to a battered plastic chair against the wall. He sits down behind the desk and introduces himself as the deputy head of security, a lanyard around his neck identifying him as Craig Farley.

I take him through the events of the last half an hour, from the moment I knocked on Evie's door and the strange conversation with Sam. Every time I say it out loud, it becomes more real, less like a strange fever dream.

Farley nods and scribbles a few notes on an A4 pad. He asks me for photo ID to verify I'm Evie's mum and I slide my driver's licence across the desk. Next, he takes down her full name, date of birth and the academic course she's studying. While he writes I notice a framed photograph of two teenagers at the edge of his desk, a boy and a girl, with a woman standing between them, blue sky above them and the sun-baked depths of the Grand Canyon in the background.

For the first time since I knocked on Evie's door, I feel as if I'm returning to something like normality. Farley's voice, the picture of his children, the holly-and-ivy pattern on his tie, seems to calm the churn of uncertainty that has kept me off balance for the better part of an hour.

'I'm sorry,' I say. 'To bother you with all this, Mr Farley. I should have double-checked with Evie before today, it just never occurred to me that she wouldn't be there, where she was supposed to be.'

'Please call me Craig,' he says, waving my apology away. 'Listen, this kind of mix-up happens more often than you might think, and there's almost always a perfectly reasonable explanation – normally to do with our ancient IT system.' He taps at his keyboard with a heavy two-fingered peck. 'We have twenty-two thousand students all told, including just over five thousand first-years who live in halls of residence, like your daughter. Those first-years are allocated across thirteen halls of residence spread across two different campuses.' He gives me a small smile, his eyes crinkling with a careful kindness. 'So as you can imagine, there's plenty of room for confusion on a day like today.'

'Of course.' I take a long drink of water from the plastic cup. I've not had anything since leaving the house this morning and hadn't realised how thirsty I was.

'Let me just get into the system here.' He moves his right hand to the mouse, click-clicking through something I can't see on the screen. 'And then we can get this all sorted out for you. I'm just logging into SRS – our Student Records System – and we'll see what we can see on this year's active roll.'

While he types, I check my phone again, tapping out a third, hopeful text that is stacked on top of the last two.

Evie where are you? Please message me back x

And the same automated response in grey beneath it, dropping in a moment later.

Message failed

When I look up again, Farley is frowning, fingers drumming softly on his A4 pad. He frowns, checks his handwritten note.

'Sorry, I think I've got the name wrong, must be my terrible handwriting. Can you spell your surname out for me again?'

I spell our family name out letter by letter as he checks against his note. Types it in again and hits the return key with a decisive stab of his index finger, his deep-set eyes narrowing slightly. He makes a *hmm* noise in his throat and starts clicking the mouse again.

'Forgive me,' he says. 'Looks like the network's on a go-slow today.' He drums his fingers impatiently on the desk, staring at the screen. 'Computer system is older than most of our students. Sorry.'

'It's fine,' I say. 'I'm used to it. Sounds like where I work.'

He clicks the mouse again. 'A university, is it?'

'The Driver and Vehicle Standards Agency. Counter-fraud unit, there's a regional hub near Reading.'

'Small world,' he says. 'My wife used to work for that lot. So . . . you're an investigator, are you?'

'More of a manager now,' I say. 'For the last few years, anyway.'

There is another awkward beat of silence between us, as he mashes the return button on his keyboard once, twice, three times.

Finally, his computer beeps.

'Ah,' Farley says. 'Here we are. OK. That's . . . curious.'

'What?'

'Have you been in contact with your daughter recently?'

I glance down at the phone in my hand with its string of unanswered messages still on the screen.

'Yes.'

'When was the last time, if you don't mind me asking?'

'I don't know, earlier this week? She messaged me yesterday, but there's some problem with her phone today, things aren't going through. Why do you ask that question?'

He gives me a strange look.

'Well, the good news is that I've found her student record on the system.'

'And what's the bad news?'

'I'm not really supposed to do this,' he says, with a glance towards the main office. 'But since you're here in person and this might be a slightly unusual situation . . .'

He angles the monitor of his computer towards me, the display on the screen split into two sections. My heart clenches at the first thing I see: a head-and-shoulders picture of Evie against a white background, her beautiful brown eyes staring thoughtfully into the camera, the kind of photo you might find on an ID card. She looks so serious, so grown up, so *adult*. My impulsive, free-spirited daughter who saw the best in everyone. My girl.

I tear my eyes away from the picture to look at the panel of information beside it which has her basic details and then her course codes, mode of study, nationality, address and so on. On the right is a smaller box with the heading 'SAO/restricted'.

'SAO is the Student Administration Office,' Farley explains. 'They log all the more detailed information about each student including any additional needs, exam scores, fee status, disciplinary issues and so on.'

'Are you saying she's in some kind of trouble?'

'No,' he says quickly. 'But look here.'

His finger guides me to a single entry at the bottom of the screen, the text in red rather than black. Three letters and six numbers.

VWS 061124

'What does that mean?'

'It means . . . well, it's a code that we use. Everything is done with three-letter acronyms in this place, it's just the way that—'

'But what does it actually *mean*?' I can feel my awkwardness and embarrassment curdling into something else. Frustration turning it into something darker. 'What does VWS stand for?'

He gives me an apologetic look.

'It means she's not here anymore, Mrs Wingfield.' His voice softens. 'She dropped out.'

5

Evie's not here.

She hadn't asked to switch from one room to another in a different hall, hadn't just forgotten to tell me. It wasn't a crossed wire.

VWS, Farley explained, stands for Voluntary Withdrawal from Study.

Evie had left more than a month ago.

A *month*. She had dropped out, walked away from it all. And gone . . . where? I had no idea.

I stare at the screen, my heart free-falling like an elevator plunging to the bottom of the shaft.

'You're telling me she dropped out on November the sixth?'

'That's what her record says.'

'That doesn't make sense.' My voice rises in exasperation. 'She's a first-year law student, she worked bloody hard to get the grades and she's been here for more than two months. I dropped her off myself at the beginning of term and I've been in touch with her, talked to her on the phone, she's sent pictures of herself on nights out, told me about essays and tutors and hall food, that sort of thing. She *has* to be here.'

He shakes his head. 'I'm sorry, I'm just giving you the information we have, the student records are—'

'But your IT system is ancient – you said it yourself – so maybe it's some kind of glitch, maybe that's what's happened here? Her file has somehow been mixed up with someone else's? Corrupted or something?'

'The system crashes quite regularly,' he says. 'It's been patched so many times that there are fixes on top of old fixes. It's twenty-year-old software held together with gaffer tape and bits of string, basically, but I can't remember a time when it's actually merged two student profiles together.'

'Human error, then. Someone has entered the wrong code on her record.'

Farley looks apologetic, as if he doesn't know what to say.

'There's no new hall address to suggest she moved,' he says. 'No file note to say alternative accommodation was arranged.'

'Perhaps she's living off campus, in a shared house?'

'Perhaps,' he says. 'But she's withdrawn from her course so she's not technically a Queen Anne's student anymore.'

Questions crowd my mind, too many of them all at once. Why had she dropped out? Why hadn't she told me? All of them fading into irrelevance beside the one question that loomed above them all, more important than anything else. The only question that really mattered.

Where was Evie now?

I raise both hands from my lap. 'Surely you have a duty of care to all the students? You're ... what's that phrase? You're *in loco parentis*, right? You take the place of the parent for all these kids when their own parents are a long way away?'

He nods slowly. 'Yes, that's true up to a point – while they're here. But not if they've withdrawn.'

'But surely you have a responsibility to inform the parents if they do that? To inform someone?'

'That's ... not within our remit.'

'Your *remit*?' I lean forward across the desk. 'These are children!'

'They're adults in the eyes of the law, Mrs Wingfield. They're over eighteen, they have a right to privacy, a right to make their own decisions – including who they decide to inform if they with-draw from their course. I'm sorry, but that's how the law stands. We're no different from any other UK university in that respect.'

'But . . .' I stop, momentarily at a loss. How could it be that Evie had simply walked out of this place one day, while I was completely oblivious? 'It just seems crazy that I wouldn't even be notified. That the first I know of it is more than a month later.'

'You had no inkling at all that she was having second thoughts about pursuing a degree?'

'It doesn't make any sense,' I say again. 'She worked so hard to get here, harder than I've ever seen her work for anything. She looked forward to it all summer. She had it all planned, she'd been saving money from her part-time job at the theatre, doing extra shifts just so she wouldn't have to work during term time. So she could concentrate on her studies.'

'Look,' Farley says, lacing his fingers together on the desk. 'There are certain procedures that should have been triggered by a prolonged period of absence – if a student misses a cer-tain number of lectures or contact hours with their personal tutor, the department should carry out a welfare check. There should have been something logged when that took place. I'm pretty sure the director of undergraduate studies in the School of Law will still be in her office, let me give her a ring. See if she can shed any light on things.'

He picks up his mobile from a wireless charger on the desk, taps the screen a few times and holds it to his ear. I feel like I've entered some parallel reality, a twilight zone where everything I thought I knew has been turned on its head.

'Laura?' he says briskly into his mobile. 'Hi, yeah, I'm good thanks, how are you?' He doesn't wait long for a reply. 'Listen, are you still on campus? I've got a parent here with me, could we swing by your office for a brief chat about one of your first-years? Easier to do it face to face.'

Five minutes later, I'm trying to keep up with his brisk stride as we walk past the main library and some other blocky concrete buildings. The place is still busy with young people saying their goodbyes to new friends and rejoining their parents. A small rite of passage that must happen a million times a year all over the country, without a hitch. A rite of passage that for me – for us, for Evie – had somehow gone horribly, inexplicably wrong.

'Forgive me for asking the obvious,' Farley says as we turn onto an access road still busy with parked cars. 'But I take it that you've tried ringing your daughter?'

'Calls aren't going through to her number. It won't even let me leave a message.'

He frowns. 'As of when?'

'This morning.'

'And you've been in contact with her before then?'

'Of course.'

He lets the obvious implication go unsaid: that Evie had been leading me a merry dance all this time. Lying to me.

We pass the rest of the short walk in silence.

For the second time today, I find myself walking through the sliding glass doors of the School of Law, past the sad little fake Christmas tree once more. I follow him up to the second floor, into a maze of corridors and a double door opened with his security pass.

Professor Laura Gray is around forty-five, with a pale complexion and auburn hair tied back in a loose ponytail. She's wearing a cream sweater and dark suit trousers, with clear-framed glasses that give her a thoughtful, bookish air. Her desk is crowded with two screens plus an open laptop, textbooks and stacks of paperwork jostling for what little space remains.

Farley does the introductions and explains that we're looking for any more information about Evie.

'So you're enquiring about a refund of fees?' Gray says, turning to face one of the other monitors on her desk. 'Because we'd normally need to be notified within fourteen working days of the start of term for a—'

'I'm not asking for a refund,' I say. 'At least not yet. Right now I just want to find out where my daughter is. And I can't actually believe that she dropped out.'

Gray takes her glasses off and lays them on the desk. Rubs her eyes with a thumb and forefinger.

'Law is a tough degree,' she says, her tone softening a little. 'A very demanding course. And the step up from A level can be a struggle for some of our students. Our first-year drop-out rate averages around six or seven per cent, so with a cohort of this size you're usually talking between twelve and twenty students in any given year who decide that law is not for them.'

'How many students on her course overall?'

'This cohort? Just over two hundred and fifty.'

So many. An easy place to fade into the background. To be invisible. To disappear.

'As I say, some students find the step up quite a challenge; it can be a shock in the first few weeks in particular when they start to grasp how much work they'll need to put in.'

'Not Evie,' I say. 'She was straight As at A level, in the top third of the LNAT for her year.'

She had spent months preparing for the LNAT – the Law National Aptitude Test – knowing that good A-level results alone would not be enough to get her onto the course she wanted. She had needed to ace this additional, gruelling test – and she had.

Gray clicks her mouse, narrowing her eyes at the screen.

'We did . . . do a welfare check on the twenty-fourth of October. An email followed by a call four days later.'

'And?'

'I'm not really allowed to divulge—'

'Please? Surely I'm listed as her next of kin.'

The professor scrolls further down the screen. 'Actually, no.'

'Well it must be me.' For a moment I wonder whether she has listed her grandma in this role, but that was ridiculous. Mum would have told me. 'There isn't really anyone else.'

Gray exchanges a glance with Farley.

'Under her emergency contact details,' she says reluctantly. 'The NCP box is ticked.'

I look from one of them to the other, beads of cold, clammy sweat gathering at the back of my neck.

'What is that?' I say, frowning at yet another three-letter acronym. 'What does NCP mean?'

The professor is silent for a moment. 'It stands for "no contact with parents".'

I feel a sharp stab of confusion, a needle sliding into my heart.

'But . . . that can't be right. I don't understand.'

'It's an option available to our students.'

'Why would her record say that?'

'The student can amend their own emergency contact details on the system.'

'So who *is* the emergency contact?'

'I'm not allowed to say.'

'You have a record of where she went, though? A forwarding address, contact details?'

'We would never discuss a student's status without their explicit consent to do so.'

A painful tension is building in my chest, as if all the air is being squeezed from my lungs.

'Surely this is an exception? My daughter is missing.'

She exchanges a glance with Farley, who gives a small nod before her eyes return to the computer screen.

'She said she'd returned to the family address on Selby Road, Reading.'

I open my mouth to reply but nothing comes out, paralysis creeping up my throat with the sudden random thought that Evie might have headed home to Reading weeks ago, but something had happened to her on the way. Something that had cut that journey short. Then I remember that we've been in contact in the last few days and a new idea starts to takes hold. An idea that grows stronger with every breath: that maybe the distance that has grown between my daughter and I was far, far greater than I've ever imagined.

That perhaps I don't know her at all anymore.

EVIE

Nine months earlier

It started with a lost dog.

Evie was shopping in Windsor High Street with her friend Millie, a rare Saturday break from A-level revision. They had gone from one charity shop to the next, aiming to pick up a few bargains that the people of the town had thrown out after one season. It was unbelievable, the kind of stuff you found on the shelves at Barnardo's, the Shelter shop, the Cancer Research place. She'd already got a sleeveless Zara top that looked virtually new and Millie had picked up a Prada jacket and ballet pumps for almost nothing.

They were outside Oxfam comparing bargains when she first heard the dog, a rapid clicking of paws against the pavement. She turned to find a chocolate-brown Labrador by her side, tail wagging furiously, pink tongue hanging out as it panted with exertion.

The dog sat down on the pavement next to her.

'Hello,' Evie said. 'Where did you come from?'

She looked around, stroking the dog's smooth head. But she couldn't see anyone who seemed to be looking for a stray pet, no one whistling or calling it to heel.

Millie knelt down, scratching under the Labrador's chin.

'Oh he's *so* cute. He's *gorgeous*. Aren't you? Yes you *are*.'

Evie continued stroking the animal's head, the fur smooth and silky under her palm. It was clearly a well-cared-for dog.

'Who's a good boy then?' Millie said. 'You're *such* a good boy, aren't you? Did you wander off? Where's your owner?'

The dog panted, licking her hand. Gazing up at them both with bright amber eyes.

'She's a girl,' Evie said, peering at the heart-shaped silver tag on the Labrador's collar. 'Lulu. She's Lulu.'

The dog gave a single, enthusiastic bark at the sound of her own name.

Evie turned the tag over to see a phone number engraved on the other side.

Millie stood up. 'What are we supposed to do? Call the RSPCA or something?'

'Maybe we should just call the owner?' She held the tag up so her friend could see.

'Really?'

'They can't be far away.'

Evie tapped the digits into her phone, raised it to her ear.

Even as it started to ring, she heard running feet and turned to see a guy hurrying across the street towards them. He was puffing and panting and holding a black lead in one hand, a small green dog waste bag swinging from the other.

'God,' he said. 'I'm so sorry. Was she bothering you?'

'She was no trouble,' Evie said. 'She's very sweet.'

The second thing she noticed was: he was the hottest guy she'd ever seen.

Bar none.

Including on TV, or Instagram, or anywhere else. Mid-twenties, in a crisp white shirt and blazer, smart jeans and brown brogues. Chiselled cheekbones, a dimpled square jaw and deep blue eyes the colour of a tropical ocean. Dark blond hair brushed back from his forehead and cut razor short at the sides.

THE DAUGHTER | 33

He was so beautiful that – to her huge embarrassment – Evie found she couldn't actually speak. She could barely take her eyes off him.

'Thank you,' he said again, still breathing hard. 'She slipped the lead while I was picking up the . . .' He held up the small green bag, tied at the top. 'God, sorry, you don't need to know about that. Ignore me, I'm just glad to have her back safe. You're a bit naughty, aren't you, Lou?'

Evie hooked two fingers under Lulu's collar while he clipped the lead back on, their hands brushing for one electrifying moment before he pulled away.

'She's beautiful,' Evie said, finally finding her voice again. 'I've always wanted a chocolate Lab.'

'Best dogs in the world.' He gave them both a grin.

'I'd love to get one when I have my own place.'

'Me too,' said Millie, although Evie couldn't remember her ever saying anything about dogs, let alone about this particular breed.

'I'm Scott, by the way.' He patted the dog's flank. 'And you've already met Lulu. We're actually in Windsor to see this dog trainer I heard about. Anyway, it was nice to meet you. I'll, erm, let you get on with your shopping and—'

'I'm Millie,' Evie's friend said quickly. 'Nice to meet you too.'

Scott smiled at them both, then he clicked his tongue at the dog, waved a quick goodbye, and headed off back down the high street with Lulu trotting happily beside him.

6

Evie had led me to believe she was still at university. She had told the university she was with me, at home.

She had played us off against each other.

After giving both Farley and Gray my phone number and asking them to call me if they find out anything else, I spend another hour wandering around the campus. The throb of a painful headache building as I check every floor of the library, the cavernous student union building with its cafés, bars and event spaces. Unwilling to believe the evidence of my eyes and ears, wanting to delay the moment when I climb back into my car, alone, for the silent drive home. But everywhere is shuttered and deserted, going into hibernation for the winter break.

I even go back to New Orchard Hall again, but by the time I get there it's late afternoon and the hustle and bustle of departing first-years has died down to almost nothing. There is no one to let me in the main doors, no cars parked outside, only a handful of lights on in the windows above me. The place is eerily quiet now.

Just me and my questions and a desperate, gnawing fear. Reality settling its weight across my shoulders like the straps of an impossibly heavy pack.

It's fully dark and the rain is getting harder when I finally get back to my car, unlock it and slump into the driver's seat. I stare at the Tupperware box of tuna and sweetcorn sandwiches on the passenger side next to me, unopened and untouched. I pull off the lid, but my appetite has disappeared.

I sit for a minute, staring at the raindrops rolling down the windscreen instead, the box of sandwiches in my lap. This was not *right*. It was not how today was supposed to go. I was fully prepared for my daughter to be tired, or hungover or uncommunicative on the drive home, for her to be reticent or defensive or just plain exhausted. For there to be silence between us while I extended an olive branch. Perhaps for her to stare at her phone or – more likely – to sleep all the way home.

But there was no script for this, for her absence, and I didn't know what I was supposed to do next. It had never occurred to me that I would be in this situation, even after all the ups and downs of the last few challenging years with her. And I keep thinking back to the words of the student I'd met on Evie's corridor in New Orchard Hall, the girl in the purple hoodie.

Did you have, like, a huge row or something?

It's a constant echo, like a song I can't get out of my head.

Had there been a row? Some kind of new fracture in our relationship, a fault line so deep I had not even seen it? Evie had always been bright, inquisitive, and she had been a challenging teenager. *Not* a child, I keep reminding myself – an adult now, with adult freedoms and the autonomy to do whatever she wanted. But the truth was, there had been more rows than I could count over the past few years. Even before she'd hit her teens. In fact, not long after she'd started at secondary school with its endless merry-go-round of shifting friendship groups, of puberty arriving in the toxic glare of social media, which meant that everything was recorded, compared, judged, out there online for all to see. And then of boys and parties and alcohol, with a constant kicking against any kind of boundary I tried to enforce. There had been that huge blow-up on her seventeenth birthday, the worst we'd ever had, after which I'd grounded her for a month and she'd barely spoken to me for the first fortnight.

Never mind the academic pressure of getting the perfect grades.

Yes, there had been rows, of course there had – what parent of a teenager could say otherwise? And perhaps with Evie there had been more than most. But not recently. Not since she'd gone to uni. Come to think of it, not since she'd got her A-level results in August.

I needed to talk to people who knew her like I did, who were close to her. Perhaps I was missing something obvious, and she had just gone to stay with one of them? Or they'd forgotten to pass on a message about a holiday, a trip, a visit to relatives up north?

I dig out an old WhatsApp group of mums and daughters set up to offer babysitting jobs a few years ago and send a message to Millie and Amber, Evie's two closest friends, trying to keep the tone light.

Hi, have you heard from Evie today or this week? Can't get through on her phone. Thanks x

Both girls are – like Evie – attached to their phones all day long, so I sit and stare at the screen for a minute assuming they will come straight back to me.

Neither of them reply.

My mum, on the other hand, answers my call after two rings with the sound of her TV blaring in the background. After a few brief pleasantries, I cut her off to tell her about Evie.

'What do you mean, gone?' The sound of the TV at her end is abruptly cut off. 'Gone where?'

'That's just it, Mum. I don't know. Are you sure she hasn't been in touch with you today, this week?'

'Not for . . . a couple of weeks. I thought you were getting her from that university tomorrow?'

'It's today, Mum. Today.' I hear the wobble in my voice. 'But she's not here. Can you remember the last time you actually spoke to her? Not just a message.'

There is a moment of silence on the other end of the line.

'Around the start of December? When I asked her what she'd like for Christmas.'

When she was younger, Evie had always taken time to write up and illustrate a detailed Christmas wish list in her best handwriting, asking for games and arty-crafty things, colouring sets, books, gadgets, dolls, Disney princess outfits. Always more than I could afford but never complaining when a particular gift didn't turn up on Christmas morning. And once into her teens, the items on the list had got smaller and smaller while going up in price, mostly electronics, jewellery and vouchers until the last year or two when she mostly asked for gift certificates for Urban Outfitters, BooHoo or Missguided.

'Vouchers for clothes?' I ask my mother.

'No,' she replies. 'Not this year. She said not to worry about getting expensive presents, she didn't want me spending money on her. Which is silly because I *love* buying her nice things, always have. It was actually rather odd. I was going to ask you for some ideas of things to get her.'

It *was* odd – it was completely out of character for Evie. But then so was dropping out of uni and not telling anyone. I explain to my mother as quickly as I can about Evie's phone, about her withdrawal from the law course and her room in the hall of residence.

'I don't know what's going on, Mum. She should *be* here. You're sure she didn't say anything to you about going off somewhere else before Christmas?'

'Quite sure, love. I don't suppose she's posted anything on one of her apps, has she? She lives her life on that phone, on Instagram and Backchat.'

'Snapchat.'

'That's what I meant. Have you had a look on there?'

She offers to drive over to mine from her bungalow in New-bury but I ask her to stay put on the off chance that Evie might appear on her doorstep. However unlikely that possibility might be. We ring off after she's promised to let me know if she hears anything.

Fighting down the steady creep of panic, I go through my phone to see the intermittent contact with Evie since that cold day in September when we had said goodbye. Searching for any hint of where she might have gone, or why. Was there some subtle clue that I had missed, some indication that she was unhappy here, that she was struggling, that she was lonely or depressed or over-whelmed by the workload?

She had always been one for messaging rather than having an old-fashioned conversation on the phone. Our contact had been intermittent, often prompted by me after I'd not heard from her for a few days. Mostly perfunctory updates, a couple of lines, *All good here, yes having fun, course is hard but good, met some nice girls on my corridor.* A FaceTime video call the week she'd moved in, then another a couple of weeks later.

I scroll back through my call log to find the date of our last phone conversation, the last time I'd actually heard her voice. It's more than two weeks ago, a call of less than five minutes. She had been . . . walking at night, that was it. She'd wanted to have some-one on the other end of the phone line while she walked, someone to talk to, to discourage unwanted attention.

I didn't want to point out to her at the time that it didn't really lessen the chances of some random attacker jumping out of the shadows, that being on the phone to her mum was no defence at all.

The call is logged at 10.43 p.m., 30th November. At the time I'd assumed she was on campus – walking back to her hall of residence after a night out.

But it was weeks after she'd dropped out. *Weeks* after she'd already left this place.

Her Instagram posts are predictable, at least on the account where she's allowed me to follow her. They are also fairly infrequent. A few nights out in what looks like the student union, a selfie of Evie with a multicoloured cocktail in hand, the bar crowded six deep behind her. A band on stage. A post in the library: another selfie with lots of hashtags – #studyhard #law #QAU. Another night out in a crowded bar somewhere, another drink, another selfie.

I stare out of the window. My car is the last one here. Across the road in the student union building, the last three lighted windows blink out as I watch, one by one, until the whole place is in darkness.

All at once the silence inside my car is too much to bear and I stab a button on the dashboard to turn the radio on. The four o'clock news has just started, the presenter's deep baritone voice relaying a story about hospital waiting lists and NHS funding. But the words are just background noise, flowing over me without really making any sense.

The next item on the bulletin is about flooding in Somerset, rivers bursting their banks after weeks of rain, a seven-year-old boy missing after being swept away by fast-flowing water near Taunton. A reporter on the ground gives details of a search by the police and fire brigade to find the boy, who had been playing with his siblings near a swollen river when he slipped and fell. *The current just took him*, a witness says. *It swept him away. One minute he was there, the next he was gone.*

The story hits me with horrible clarity, snapping my thoughts into focus. A child snatched away from his family. An unfolding emergency. A police search.

I swallow the bile rising up my throat. *The current just took him.*

With shaking hands, I scroll to the newest contact in my phone and hit dial. To my surprise, the call is answered after two rings.

'Mrs Wingfield,' Farley says. His voice is muffled, as if he's chewing a mouthful of food. 'How are you—'

'When we talked earlier about Evie leaving the uni, how can you be so sure she wanted to go?'

'I'm sorry?'

'How can you be sure that she left of her own free will?'

He clears his throat. 'Well . . . she's formally withdrawn from her course of study. She's gone through the process on the student system, and presumably cleared out her room.'

'You said that before,' I say. 'But we don't even know if it's true, do we?'

'How do you mean?'

'What if she didn't leave of her own free will? What if she was coerced, forced, pressured into it somehow? What if someone else got access to her student record and altered it without her permission?'

'We don't have any evidence of that.'

'But it could be? I mean, what if something's happened to her?' I swallow hard. 'What if she was . . . taken?'

Farley considers this for a moment. 'I understand that you're worried, Mrs Wingfield. I've got kids and I get it, honestly I do. But there's nothing to suggest Evie didn't leave under her own steam.'

'What about CCTV?'

'I'm working on that. But I still honestly believe that there's a reasonable explanation for this and I'm not just saying that because I work here. Every year we have a handful of young people who just don't get on with student life, who have a lot of expectations on their shoulders, a lot of pressure, and when they arrive they realise that university just isn't for them. Sometimes that can be a very hard thing to admit to parents, to family, friends. Even to themselves.'

But even as he's saying it, even as the call ends, I know in my heart there's more to it than that. I'm her mother, I just *know*.

I know Evie would not have just disappeared from her life. Would not have missed a family Christmas, her little brother's birthday, a chance to catch up with friends from home.

Sitting alone in the gathering dark, on a rainswept parkland campus out on the northern edge of London, I raise my phone again with a trembling hand and dial the police.

7

The 101 call handler takes an age to put me through to someone willing to take my details.

After ten minutes on hold, of giving my name and the nature of my call three times, eventually I'm connected to a young guy who doesn't sound much older than Evie. He tells me his name is Joseph and I report the events of the day, listening to the rapid *click-clack* of his keyboard as he types up the details.

'So, I want to make a missing person's report,' I say finally. 'For my daughter.'

'OK,' he says slowly, stringing the two letters out. 'And how long has she been missing?'

'Well, I was supposed to pick her up at lunchtime today, so, I suppose, about five hours or so. But she's not been there since November the sixth, which is, what, five weeks ago now?'

The *click-clack* of his typing stops. 'So is it five hours, madam, or five weeks?'

I hadn't thought about it like that. 'Well, five weeks, I suppose.'

'She's been missing five weeks but you're only reporting it today?'

'I didn't know until today.'

'So . . . you're estranged from your daughter?'

'No!' It comes out a little too forcefully. 'No, but I've not seen her since the start of term. Just spoken to her on the phone, exchanged messages.'

'I see,' he says. 'And do you believe your daughter to be at imme-
diate risk of serious harm, from herself or from others?'

'I hope not.'

'Would you say she was a danger to others?'

'No,' I say. 'Not at all.'

'And does your daughter have ongoing mental health issues
that we should know about?'

'No.'

'How about medication?' he says, typing again now. He sounds as
if he's reading from a checklist of standard questions. 'Is she taking
any prescription medication that she may not have access to?'

'No,' I say. 'None.'

'And what about her father?' he says carefully. 'Is it possible that
he's been in contact with your daughter?'

I take a steadying breath. 'He's no longer around.'

'Right, so you're separated, or—'

'He passed away.'

'Oh. I see.' He clears his throat. 'I'm sorry to hear that, Mrs
Wingfield.'

'She was young, it was a long time ago. She barely remembers him.'

'I see,' he says again. There is a long moment of awkward silence,
broken only when he asks me about her mobile and I explain to
him that Evie's phone seems to have been disconnected, messages
bouncing back undelivered.

She had insisted on taking out her own phone contract when
she'd turned eighteen, paying for it herself and opting to become
the named contract holder without any suggestion from me. And I
hadn't discouraged her – I thought it showed encouraging signs of
independence, of wanting to take responsibility for her life. When
friends bemoaned the fact that their teenage children barely knew
how much their monthly bill was, never mind paying for it, I'd feel
a warm glow of smug satisfaction – somehow my daughter was
the exception.

But now it meant I had no way of checking her account, of logging in to see if there was a problem with her contract or maybe an unpaid bill. No way of seeing who she might have been in contact with, who she'd been calling.

It seemed like too much of a coincidence for the phone to have been disconnected on the very day I was due to pick her up.

Emails to her Gmail account had started bouncing back too, I had discovered this afternoon. Each one yielding the same automated response: *Delivery status notification – failure. There was a problem delivering your message to evie.wingfield18@gmail.com, the recipient server did not accept our requests to connect.*

Every time I look at the message I feel winded all over again, as if I've been punched in the stomach. I had no idea exactly what it meant, but assumed it was because her email had been deactivated. Either by Evie – or someone else trying to cut off all possible methods of communication with my daughter. Both possibilities are terrifying in their own way.

Joseph finally stops typing, his young voice coming back on the line.

'And has Eve—'

'Evie.'

'Right. Has Evie done anything like this before?'

I hesitate. 'Once. But it was a few years ago.'

Which wasn't *strictly* true. The first time she'd not run away, exactly, she'd just gone to Reading music festival with her friends despite the fact that I'd explicitly told her she needed to stay home for her grandmother's birthday celebrations. We'd had an almighty row about it and then Evie had gone anyway without telling me, camping overnight with some other kids from her year. I'd simply returned from work on Friday evening and found my fifteen-year-old missing, no message, no note, nothing to say where she was until after midnight when she finally replied to my increasingly desperate texts and calls.

The fact that the festival was only a few miles away, in her own hometown, meant she couldn't understand why I was, in her words, *making such a big deal of it*. Why I was *totally freaking out and blowing up her phone* when she was just having a laugh with her mates. Cue another row when she returned the next day, hungry, tired and still defiant. I had grounded her for a week.

The second time – six months later – was a two-night jaunt to London with Millie and Amber, to stay in a flat that belonged to Millie's aunt and uncle. Each of the girls had used the other as a cover story, in the naive teenage hope that none of the parents would ask questions. And it had *almost* worked, until I had bumped into Amber's mother in Asda and asked how the sleepover had gone.

Again I'd grounded Evie and stopped her allowance for a month, taken away her phone for a fortnight and barred her from contact with Millie and Amber until the end of the school term. Things had been difficult between us for months afterwards – but I thought she'd learned her lesson.

Joseph clears his throat. 'So she's run away before?'

'This is not *running away*,' I say. 'She's disappeared. She's missing and no one knows where she is. *I* have no idea where she is.'

'Or from another perspective,' he says, 'and I'm just playing devil's advocate here, you might also say that rather than being missing she's just not told you where she is. And the good news is that ninety-nine per cent of missing people are found safe and well within the first week.'

I can feel the heat rising to my face, my grip around the phone white-knuckle tight. It feels like it's been a long day and I'm already getting tired of people treating me like I'm some hysterical helicopter parent.

'Are you a detective, Joseph?'

'No, madam,' he says. 'I'm a civilian. But I will certainly pass your information along.'

'Well then, I'd like to talk to an actual detective, please. Can you transfer me?'

He doesn't miss a beat. 'I'm afraid all of my colleagues in CID are tied up at the moment. Weekends in December are always a busy time, as I'm sure you can imagine.'

'So when?'

'When what?'

'When will you pass on the information about Evie?'

'The report will be logged for the duty sergeant, and when he comes on shift tomorrow morning, he'll go through everything and take a view on allocating resources according to priority.'

'*This* is a high priority.'

'Of course, Mrs Wingfield. Someone will be in touch – and if you hear from your daughter in the meantime, please do let us know as soon as possible.'

We go around the houses for another five minutes as he double-checks all the information I've given him, repeating what he's already said. He reads my mobile number back to me and gives me an incident number and a phone number for Enfield police station which I scribble on the back of an envelope.

When the call is over, I sit in my car for a few more minutes, reliving the memories I had described to Joseph in outline. Half an hour ago I had wondered whether Evie might have been taken from the campus against her will. But being reminded of those times when she was fifteen, sixteen, and had disappeared for a day or two, something else stirs in my memory. The rows in the unhappy days and weeks that had followed, the sanctions I'd imposed to punish her – for her own good – to show that she couldn't just disappear, that she shouldn't lie to her mother, at the very least she had to tell me where she was going and who she was going there with.

I had thought, at the time, that she had learned her lesson.

But perhaps it had been a very different lesson from the one I'd thought.

8

Saturday night traffic is bad on the way home.

It's barely fifty miles according to Google Maps but it takes more than two hours, curving south around the top of London, picking up the M4 and heading further away from the capital and westward into Berkshire. According to the car's dashboard display, it's only just above freezing outside and even though I have the heaters turned up high, I can't seem to keep the chill from my bones. What if Evie is out in this weather right now? Lost in this bitter cold without a proper coat, without anywhere to go, anywhere to get warm? Every so often I glance across at the empty passenger seat beside me, a fist of anguish closing around my heart. Each time, the queuing red lights of traffic in front of me blurring with tears. Perhaps this was what grieving expectant mothers felt like when they returned home from the hospital empty-handed.

At one point I'm sobbing in stationary traffic right next to another solo driver, my cheeks wet. When I glance around he catches my eye, sees me crying, and quickly looks away.

* * *

I pick up my son from his friend's house. But it's not until we're home and he's in his pyjamas, next to me on the sofa, giggling at an old episode of *Taskmaster* that he realises something is amiss. I'm scrolling through results on Google about what to do if a loved one goes missing.

Lucas is focused on the TV, eyes smiling behind his glasses, a spoon in one hand halfway to a bowl on the arm of the sofa. Through a mouthful of ice cream he says, still half distracted: 'Where's Evie?'

For a moment, I think about telling him a white lie – I don't want him worrying too. He tries to put on a front around his friends but I know that deep down, my twelve-year-old is one of life's worriers. He's an over-thinker with a vivid imagination – not always the best mix – the son of a father snatched away before he could even remember. I don't want him to jump to any conclusions.

But I also need to find out if he knows anything about his sister's disappearance – perhaps without even realising it.

His face pales as I explain what happened today, his brow lowering as if he can't understand what I'm saying.

'But . . . what do you mean, she wasn't there?' He stabs the *mute* button on the TV remote, puts his bowl of ice cream down on the side table. 'Where is she, Mum? Who is she staying with?'

'I don't know, Lucas. But it'll just be for a few days.' I force a smile, wondering if he can see through it. 'She'll be back before Christmas, I'm sure.'

He has a million questions and I'm painfully aware that I don't have any good answers. While we talk, and I try to reassure him, he pulls his phone from the pocket of his dressing gown and starts to flick from one app to the next. I can't imagine his big sister has allowed him to follow many of her social media accounts, but he studies the pictures, posts, comments and replies, convinced that the answer must lie somewhere in the small glowing screen in the palm of his hand.

'She must have posted something about where she is,' he says, scrolling furiously. 'She *must* have.'

I do the same and we compare notes, dates, places, trying to make a connection that has so far eluded me. Both my children have grown up with this technology and it seems inconceivable that she hasn't left some kind of clue.

I refuse to think about the alternative.

Finally, in a small voice Lucas says: 'Have you phoned the police?'

I nod and smile and tell him not to worry. 'Just as a precaution though.'

'So is it like before?' he says. 'When she went away to London with her friends?'

'Probably, yes.' I skirt around the fact that her absence this time is not just a matter of days but weeks. 'So she never said anything to you about going away somewhere? Anything about uni, or how she was getting on?'

'To *me*?' He gives me an exaggerated frown, shakes his head. 'No. She wouldn't tell me, Mum. She never tells me anything anymore.'

I give him a hug and tell him everything will be OK, biting back my own tears. He doesn't need his mother crying in front of him. When he's gone up to bed, I text Amber and Millie again. Both have blanked my earlier text. Then I sit for a while longer in my silent lounge, replying to messages from my mum and combing through a thread on Reddit about people searching for missing loved ones. There are so many stories, so much desperation. So many unanswered questions.

At some point Bella, our small tortoiseshell cat, wanders into the room with a small chirp of greeting and settles beside me on the sofa.

She was Evie's cat really, adopted from an RSPCA shelter when my daughter was six and *all she wanted in the whole wide world* was a kitten. I feel a sudden powerful pang of longing for those days, for a time when I could be the parent that she wanted me to be. I could give her what she needed and see her face light up, see that beautiful smile and feel the warmth of her when she hugged me so tight.

And all I had to do that year was bring Bella home from the rescue shelter.

The thought of Christmas Day without Evie hits me like a hammer, snapping me back to the here and now. She would have known I'd come to pick her up, that she couldn't pretend to be staying on campus over Christmas. So she would have known she had until mid-December before I found out she was gone – unless I'd just turned up unannounced. But with my work and looking after her brother she would also have known I was unlikely to make a hundred mile round trip and just *drop in* without warning. Until then a weekly phone call, a handful of texts, a few photos would probably be enough.

All these weeks, via intermittent texts and occasional phone calls, I had believed my daughter was safe. Enjoying a new stage of life away from home – enjoying the freedom of being able to spread her wings. Evie's brother had believed it too.

I scroll back through her Instagram posts once more, clicking into each one in turn, studying my daughter's beautiful face for any signs that she was depressed, or withdrawn, or having a tougher time than she was letting on. Because I should have seen it, shouldn't I? I should have been able to tell. I know her better than anyone else on this earth.

But she doesn't look sad, or lonely, or overwhelmed. With her dark hair loose around her shoulders, she smiles into the camera wearing the silver necklace I bought her for her eighteenth birthday. More than a hundred likes on the post but only a handful of comments, mostly emojis of hearts and flames or kisses from strangers.

It's only when I start to look at the rest of the pictures, at the next one and the next, that I finally spot something that catches my eye.

In a picture posted more than a month after she arrived at Queen Anne's, she's wearing a black V-neck top. I guess she must like this top as it features several times in the grid of pictures. This one also seems to have been taken on a night out, in a bar with lots of people in the background, the messy smiles and shot glasses of a Friday or Saturday night. The neon pink lettering of a poster is cut off on the right-hand side of the image, only the first three letters visible: WEL—

I stop. Press the back button to return me to her grid of pictures until I find what I'm looking for. Flick back and forth between the two images.

It was a shot from Welcome Week, from the first week of October, only the first three letters visible of the bright pink welcome poster. Right at the beginning of term. Her hair is tied back in this one, but she's wearing the same top. The exact same outfit, in fact, same earrings, same necklace, same smoky eye makeup, same combination of bracelets around her right wrist. I screenshot both pictures, save them into a collage so I can compare them side by side. A chill tapping at the back of my neck despite the warmth of the room.

Evie wasn't wearing the same outfit on different nights.

They were pictures from the *same* night, posted six weeks apart.

A picture from Welcome Week, just after she'd first arrived at the beginning of October. But posted to her Instagram account on 23rd November.

I had been stupid not to see it. Blinded by my own wishful thinking that she was safe and happy, that she didn't want to come home for a weekend because she was too busy having a good time. She knew I followed her on this account. She *knew*. And so she had shown me what she thought I wanted to see.

Which meant one of two things: either she had put a lot of thought into convincing me she was OK in her first term.

Or someone was trying to cover up the fact that she was not.

9

I jolt awake before dawn feeling as if I haven't slept at all, my eyes gritty and sore. I'd kept my phone on all night, rolling over to the bedside table every hour or so in case there is a message from Evie, from the university, the police, from anyone.

There is nothing.

My mind had been churning with worry, conjuring images of the very worst things that could have happened to my daughter. Trying to make sense of what little I knew, of her small dishonesty on Instagram and how it slotted into the much larger deception of the last ten weeks. At least I could be sure I'd spoken to her *after* that second picture had been posted on 23rd November – I had talked to her on the phone perhaps four or five times. Had I actually *seen* her on a video call though, on FaceTime? I check the app and see there had been a few FaceTime calls in the early part of term, but none after the middle of November. It was easier, Evie had said, just to talk on the phone because she always seemed to be walking somewhere, going to a lecture, getting ready for a night out or getting food from the local Tesco Express.

I hadn't questioned it at the time, it was just nice to hear her voice.

Lucas comes down in his Avengers dressing gown while I'm making a cup of tea – which is not like him as he's started sleeping in more at the weekends – his dark hair sticking up at random angles. He doesn't look as if he slept much either.

'Have you heard from Evie?' It's the first thing he says, before he's even sat down at the breakfast bar next to me.

I shake my head and pull him into a hug.

'Not yet,' I say, rubbing his back. 'I'm going to see some of her friends this morning, see if any of them can help. I'll drop you at Grandma's house on the way.'

'Why can't I come with you?'

'You can, but it'll probably be boring.'

He shrugs. 'Maybe I can help.'

* * *

After we've eaten and dressed, I drive the mile to Northcourt Avenue, trying to remember the house number of one of Evie's best friends. But there is no car on the drive at the Burrows house and no answer at the front door, even after I ring the doorbell enough times to elicit an embarrassed stage whisper from Lucas behind me on the porch – 'Mum, you can't just keep on ringing it, they're obviously not in so can we go?' It occurs to me that Amber might still be in bed, enjoying the kind of coma-tose teenage lie-in that defies all disturbance. I text her mum, Beverley, instead and give her a very short version of what's happened since yesterday, asking for Amber to call me urgently.

A few streets away, all the curtains are still closed on the big bay windows of Isobel Hawley-Sands' house, even though it's nearly 11 a.m. But there are three cars on the drive and the faint twinkle of Christmas icicle lights hanging above the front door, presum-ably left on twenty-four hours a day. I ring the doorbell twice and knock, twice, until finally a tinny, disembodied voice takes me by surprise.

'Yes?'

I look around for the source of the voice until Lucas points to the small circular lens of a Ring doorbell on the door frame, the discreet speaker beneath it from where the voice is coming. I guess we're on camera.

'Isobel,' I say, looking into the lens. 'Hi, it's Lauren. Really sorry to bother you on a Sunday morning. I was wondering if I could have a quick chat with Millie?'

There is a pause before her voice comes back, scratchy and metallic sounding.

'Oh,' she says. 'Now? What about?'

I explain the reason for my visit, feeling awkward and self-conscious as I talk into the small rectangle of plastic with its electronic eye. She doesn't reply for a minute and I'm starting to think she's cut me off when the big double front door swings silently open a few inches and her puffy face appears in the gap. Isobel is wrapped up in a huge, fluffy white dressing gown, with fluffy white slippers on her feet and her expensively streaked blonde hair pulled back into a hurried ponytail. Her eyes are hidden by huge Jackie O style sunglasses.

'My God, Lauren,' she says. 'That's awful, I'm so sorry. I'd invite you in but the place is a bit of a bombsite.' She gestures vaguely over her shoulder towards the open-plan kitchen-diner down the hall. 'We had friends over last night and I've just been cleaning up.'

'I just need to know that Evie is safe so I wanted to have a quick word with Millie. Is she up yet?'

Our daughters had been best friends since the start of secondary school, since their first day at the big comprehensive when they'd sat next to each other in maths and bonded over a shared dislike of Mr McClintock's corny jokes and terrible shirts.

'Can't help you there, I'm afraid,' Isobel says. 'She's away at the moment working a ski season as a chalet girl, a chalet worker or whatever you're supposed to call them now. Her flight back isn't until Christmas Eve. *Really* sorry.'

There is something in her tone that is a little forced, a little *too* apologetic, but I can't work out whether it's because I've interrupted her Sunday or for a different reason.

A small white poodle appears by her feet on the welcome mat, barks once, stubby tail wagging madly.

'Raffy!' she says sharply. 'Behave yourself.'

The dog sits obediently with its tongue hanging out. Lucas reaches out a tentative hand and strokes his head, getting an enthusiastic lick in return.

My son scratches under the dog's chin. 'He's very cute.'

'He's an absolute prima donna, but we all love him,' Isobel says. 'Especially Millie.'

'I messaged her yesterday,' I say. 'But I've not had a reply yet.'

'Well, they've got her doing twelve-hour days by the sound of it, up at the crack of dawn to make breakfast for all these city types and then working late to wash up at the end of the day. And she's trying to fit in skiing, partying and sightseeing on top of that, so she might not respond straightaway. But I'm due to FaceTime her this evening so I'll tell her to reply to your message.'

'Thanks, Isobel, I appreciate it.'

She waves a manicured hand. 'Not at all. You really have no idea where Evie might be?'

An idea comes to me. 'I don't suppose she might have kept a key to your brother's flat in London, or copied a key? Where the girls stayed together when they did that weekend trip without telling us?'

'She might have, I suppose, but she's not staying there now – I've got rellys from South Africa using it for the whole of December – Tony's family, he spoke to them last night.' She seems to register the look of disappointment on my face. 'Look, sweetie, I'm sure she's fine, she's probably just staying with friends and she's lost track of the date. You know what eighteen-year-olds are like. Me, I was terrible at that age. I was an absolute *nightmare* for my parents. I shudder to think about it now.'

I muster a weak smile. 'If Evie's talked to anyone about this, about where she's gone, she must have talked to Millie about it.'

'It's possible, I suppose.'

But there is doubt in her voice now, a new edge of uncertainty.

I frown. 'You don't think so?'

'The thing is . . .' She tails off with a sigh. 'God, I swore off getting mixed up in the girls' friendship stuff years ago. Fingers burned too many times.'

'What friendship stuff?' I say. 'What do you mean, Isobel? Tell me.'

She looks over her shoulder, back into the house, but there is still no sign of her husband Tony or their other two daughters.

'It's probably not my place to say,' she says, her voice dropping a little. 'But Millie might not be the best person to ask.'

'I get it,' I say. 'I know they're super-loyal to each other and Evie's probably sworn her to secrecy. But if I can explain it to Millie, talk to her face to face, I'm sure she'll understand it's gone beyond that now. I just need to know that Evie is OK.'

'Of course.' Isobel gives me a tight smile, her eyes still hidden behind the big sunglasses. 'But that wasn't quite what I meant.'

'You don't think she'll tell me?'

'It's not that. I'm just not sure how much . . . contact they've had with each other recently.'

'Since Evie started at uni and Millie went to work in France?'

'Well, yes and no.' She wraps the thick dressing gown more tightly around herself, crosses her arms over it. 'Like I said, it's probably not my place to say. I try to stay out of M's business. But between you and me, Lauren, I don't think they've been close for quite a while now.'

10

I stand on the doorstep of Isobel's impressive double-fronted house with its big bay windows and immaculate block-paved driveway.

'What do you mean?' I say. 'I thought they were best friends?'

Isobel gives me a slow, awkward shrug.

'They're not . . . like they were. Not anymore.'

'Since when?'

'Since . . . I don't know, exactly. Maybe in the summer?'

'Six *months* ago?'

She turns and closes the inner door completely, so we can't be overheard by her family.

'Or it could have been before that,' she says. 'I mean it wasn't like Millie came downstairs one day and announced it to everyone. You know what girls are like. We were just talking one day and she was saying about some summer trip she was organising, driving down to Brighton for the day when their exams were all finished. I asked her who was going and telling her she'd struggle to fit five into her little Fiat all the way to the south coast and back, and she says, "No, Mum, there's only four of us." Evie wasn't included – she'd not been invited. Millie wouldn't tell me what it was about. Just changed the subject.'

I shake my head, another certainty *gone* just like that, like a tooth ripped out by the root. There's no memory of any falling-out with Millie, of arguments about a trip to Brighton or anything else.

'Was it one thing in particular? An argument or a boy or something that happened at school?'

'Like I said, Millie never really went into detail,' she says. 'At the time I thought it was just a temporary thing and they'd sort it out, but I don't think they did. Sorry – I assumed you already knew.'

There had been a few years when Evie had seemed to spend more time at Millie's house than she had at home, when they had lived in each other's pockets in that burningly intense way that teenage girls did. Doing everything together, choosing the same GCSE options so they could sit together, first experiments with makeup, first parties, first drink, first boyfriends, first break-up – they had gone through it all together. Not to mention that jaunt to London that had got them both grounded for a month. I knew that some friendships drifted over time, or fractured over some teenage drama, but not this one. Evie and Millie had been *solid*. As solid as they come.

How had I not noticed they had drifted apart? More to the point, why had Evie not told me? Although, as I discovered yesterday, this was clearly not the only secret she had been keeping.

I make sure Isobel has my number and my mum's number too, in case she hears anything. Then Lucas and I return to the car to head back the way we came.

*　*　*

Tyler Maxwell is in the tinned foods aisle when I find him, unloading a pallet of soups onto the shelf. Even in the bland, shapeless green Waitrose uniform he's a good-looking lad, with his dark eyes and strong jaw, floppy hair tucked back behind his ears. At six foot two he's at least half a head taller than me, muscular arms shifting the weight with ease, the bottom of a swirling Celtic tattoo just visible beneath the sleeve of his polo shirt. He has his back to me and I watch him for a moment as he works, taking tins from an open-sided trolley cage and stacking them quickly and efficiently on the shelf.

He'd first got involved with Evie at the school prom to cele-brate the end of their GCSEs more than two years ago, and it had been an on–off relationship all through their two years of A levels. She'd fallen hard for him and he'd been to our house a lot – but to be honest, I'd always known he would break her heart sooner or later. He was one of those boys who had matured early and didn't have to work very hard for female attention, with a certain cool that he'd grown into. He was sporty, played for several of the school's first teams, and smart too, securing the grades to study medicine.

So when Evie had told me Tyler wanted them to 'take a break' before she headed off to university, I wasn't entirely surprised. She had been upset and hadn't wanted to talk much to me about it, but I'd tried to give her space while making sure she knew I was there for her, willing to listen if she changed her mind. Barely a week later I had been driving her to university, the car full of bags and boxes, but she'd still not wanted to open up.

I think back to that conversation now.

'So,' I'd said, merging onto the M4 as we headed for London. 'How have you left it then, with Tyler?'

'I told you, Mum,' she'd said, not looking up from her phone. 'He wants us to take a step back from things while I'm away. He said he didn't want to do a long-distance relationship anyway because they never work.'

Reading to north London is not exactly long-distance, I'd thought at the time. But it was one of those observations best kept to yourself.

'Did you get a chance to say goodbye to him this week?'

'Why would I want to say goodbye to him?'

'I mean, you're still friends, right? You might want to leave that door open.'

'Maybe.' She'd looked up from her phone then, to stare out of the car's side window at trees flashing past. 'Can we talk about something else, Mum?'

She'd been defensive about it but I guessed that made sense. It must have still been quite raw back then, the pain still fresh, and she didn't want me raking it all up again. But I wonder now, as I stand in this supermarket aisle watching my daughter's ex-boyfriend, whether her disappearance had something to do with their break-up. Whether heartbreak at home meant she didn't want to return.

Whether it was more than a coincidence. But why would she have dropped out, if that was the case?

As far as I could remember now, Tyler's plan was to take a gap year, working every supermarket shift he could get for six months to build up some savings, then to go travelling for six months, before going north to start at Manchester University medical school next year.

'Tyler?'

He turns as if I'm a customer, ready to help. But his smile falters when he sees that it's me.

'Oh, hi.' He raises a hand to my son. 'Hey, Lucas.'

'Hi,' Lucas says in a small voice, close beside me.

I muster a smile. 'How have you been?'

'Fine. Busy, you know.'

'Have you got a minute?'

'Sure.' He puts the last of the tins of tomato soup onto the shelf, straightens up. 'What is it you need?'

'I'm not looking for anything here, just need to ask you a couple of questions. About Evie.'

His smile disappears. 'Questions?'

'I need to know when you last heard from her.'

'What? Why?'

'Has she been in touch with you recently?'

He frowns. 'Is she all right?'

'Why do you ask that?'

'No reason.' He finally seems to notice that I'm empty-handed. No basket, no trolley. 'What's going on?'

Lucas jumps in before I can reply, his voice low as if he's imparting a closely guarded secret.

'She's gone missing,' he says. 'From her uni.'

'*What?*' Tyler looks both ways down the aisle, perhaps checking that his supervisor has not suddenly appeared. 'What do you mean?'

I give him an abbreviated version of the last twenty-four hours. He listens, blinking fast, as I explain that I *really* need to know if Evie had ever talked about friends in London, or anywhere she might have gone to stay.

He's already shaking his head. 'No. Sorry.'

'She's cut off contact, Tyler. Is there *anything* she might have said to you? Even something that seemed unimportant at the time, like a place she really wanted to visit?'

'Look, I'm really sorry but I can't help you.' He turns to go. 'I've not heard from her in ages.'

'Please.' I put a hand on his arm and he looks at it, then at me, as if this is a gross violation of his personal space. 'No one on her uni campus even remembers her name, no one recognises her picture, no one knows where she's gone. She's vanished.'

'And you thought I might know where she is?'

'You know her pretty well. You used to be close, didn't you?' And then I can't resist adding: 'Until you broke up with her.'

He stares at me for a moment then looks at his watch, starts to push the trolley cage towards the back of the store.

'I'm sorry,' he says over his shoulder. 'I wish I could help you but I can't, Lauren.'

'Please,' Lucas says. 'You can't just walk away.'

'I'm going on my break.'

My daughter's ex-boyfriend keeps going with the empty trolley cage, manoeuvring around a toddler as he heads for a pair of swing doors marked *Staff Only* in neat green lettering.

With a *follow me* nod of my head to Lucas, I set off after him.

11

Tyler pushes through the double swing doors and disappears. With Lucas scurrying to keep up beside me, I stroll casually up to the same doors and – with a quick check that no one's watching – push through them and follow. Something about the way he spoke to us doesn't quite ring true. Doing the kind of work I do day to day, investigating cheats and scammers trying to play the system, you get a nose for dishonesty. A sense for when someone is trying to bend the truth. The irony of being deceived by my own child is not lost on me.

Beyond the doors the soft muzak of the shop is replaced by the clatter of pallets and the hum of big refrigerated units. It's a large open-plan warehouse space, bare concrete on the floor and metal racks that reach all the way to the ceiling. The strip lighting is bright and harsh, the temperature several degrees cooler than the shop floor, the smell an odd mixture of diesel, dirt and disinfectant.

'Mum,' Lucas says in a stage whisper, tugging my hand. 'We're not supposed to be in here, are we?'

'We'll only be a minute.'

'*Mum.*'

His hand slips out of mine but he keeps up with me as we walk deeper into the warehouse. For a second I think we've lost Tyler but then I spot his tall frame pushing the empty trolley into a bay full of dozens more. He pats his pocket absently and heads away in the opposite direction.

'Come on,' I say softly to Lucas. 'We'll just pretend we're lost.'

We walk quickly down the aisle, racks of shrink-wrapped cardboard boxes towering above us on both sides. Rounding the corner there are more of the same, the insistent *beep-beep* of a forklift lifting down a pallet in another aisle to our left. Thankfully there are not many staff around and the handful we do see are too busy working, carrying, unpacking, loading boxes to notice us as we hurry past. Going through another doorway we emerge into a loading bay, with a cavernous entrance open to the outside.

I spot Tyler leaning against the frame of the big rear entrance where another articulated lorry is just backing in, to the piercing accompaniment of its reversing alarm. He's wreathed in vape smoke, thumb-typing furiously on his phone, dark hair falling across his fine cheekbones.

The noise of the reversing truck hides our approach until we're only a few feet away.

He looks up from his phone, startled. 'You can't come back here. It's staff only, the shift supervisor will go ape—'

'Then talk to me, Tyler.'

'I've already told you.' He hits the power button on his phone and the screen goes black. 'I can't help you. Haven't heard from Evie in ages and that is the honest truth.'

'It's all right, Tyler. I understand.'

He frowns. 'What do you mean?'

'Look, I get it, OK? I'm not blaming you for breaking up with her. I'm not here to have a go at you about that, I think it was probably for the best with her going away. I get it.'

He snorts, shakes his head. 'No, you don't.'

'Trust me, I've been there. It's better to have your freedom when you're nineteen, enjoy yourself, explore the world.'

I want to tell him the rest as well, the exchange I'd had with Evie a hundred times: that she had arrived when I was only nineteen and while I wouldn't wish her away for all the world, I also wished I'd been a little older before I took on all the responsibilities of motherhood. Rather than being forced to drop out of university and having to start life all over again when she'd gone to primary school.

But now doesn't seem like the time or the place for this kind of confession.

He puts the small black vape to his lips, inhaling deeply and blowing a thick stream of sickly sweet smoke towards the entrance. Considering Lucas and me for a moment, he seems to come to a decision.

'I'm sorry to hear about Evie,' he says finally. 'But . . . when do you think we split up?'

I frown. 'Mid-September. A few weeks before she was due to start at Queen Anne's.'

He shakes his head. 'It was ages before that.'

'Mum.' Lucas is tapping urgently on my arm. 'Mum. *Look.*'

I'd almost forgotten my son was there. I look around to where he's pointing, to a round-faced man in green overalls striding towards us across the loading bay.

Tyler mutters a curse under his breath.

The man comes up close enough for me to smell the sharp tang of his body odour and gives me a humourless smile. He's not much older than Tyler, with the ghost of a moustache so pale it's almost invisible, and the general air of someone given a scintilla of authority that had gone straight to his head.

'I'm afraid customers aren't allowed in the warehouse area, madam.' He holds up a hand. 'It's strictly staff only, I'm going to have to ask you to—'

'I'm *so* sorry,' I say in an apologetic tone, indicating my handbag. 'But my son Tyler forgot his medication *again*, if he doesn't take it he's prone to having seizures. Happened in his last job, banged his head and there was blood *everywhere*, a million forms to fill out and all kinds of disclaimers and whatnot. Absolutely awful.'

He gives me a sceptical look. 'I see.'

'Thanks *so* much.'

He glares at Tyler, who takes another puff on his vape but says nothing, as if he's trying to pretend I'm not there. Lucas looks absolutely mortified, shrinking back as if he'd like the ground to swallow him up.

The round-faced guy is pointing his short index finger back towards the main part of the shop. 'All the same, madam, I'm going to have to ask you to leave the warehouse area. Tyler will walk you back.'

'Of course,' I say, giving him my best maternal smile. 'We won't be a minute.'

With a final glare at his more junior colleague, the man turns and stalks away.

When he's out of earshot, Tyler says quietly: 'You're going to drop me right in the shit with him.'

'So talk to me. Then I'll be gone.'

'I've told you everything already. Not heard from Evie in ages.'

'When did you break up? In the summer?'

'Spring term, like, I don't remember exactly. Maybe Easter?'

'So it wasn't because you didn't want a long-distance relationship.'

'No,' he says. 'She just went weird on me.'

'Weird in what way?'

'She just . . . she was different. Detached, like, her head was in a different place. I thought maybe it was the pressure of exams, mocks and all the revision, worrying about getting the grades she needed for her course.'

I cast my mind back to the spring, seven or eight months ago. Trying to identify a time when Evie had been especially upset about her on–off relationship with Tyler coming to an end. But nothing comes to mind – I'd been crazy busy at work and she'd been focusing hard on her exams, applying herself in a way that she'd not done for her GCSEs two years earlier. At the time

I'd been proud of her work ethic, her discipline, of how she'd matured.

But maybe I had just seen what I wanted to see. Maybe she had thrown herself into her revision to block out the heartbreak.

'And anyway,' he adds. 'You've got it backwards.'

'In what way?'

'I didn't break up with her.' He takes another puff on his vape. 'It was the other way around. She finished with me.'

EVIE

Eight months earlier

Evie watched him across the café as he carried the drinks over. He was even better looking than she remembered and she could see other women staring at him as he navigated a path between the tables. She glanced up and caught the eye of one thirty-something woman in expensive leisurewear, her gaze falling on Evie with a mixture of jealousy and admiration.

Scott, though, seemed oblivious to their attention.

She had messaged him in the end. After two weeks of thinking about him in class, on the bus, brushing her teeth in the morning and falling asleep at night, thinking about the number from the dog's collar she'd tapped into her phone that day in Windsor, she had given in and sent him a text asking how the dog training was going. He had replied the following day, and they'd got to talking – on text, at least. First about Lulu, then about other stuff. That was how it started. A couple of weeks after that, he'd told her he was visiting Windsor again – just on the off chance, in case she was planning another shopping trip.

She hadn't been. But she didn't tell him that.

So now here they were, in a gorgeous little coffee shop on Windsor High Street just around the corner from where they'd had their first brief encounter. Lulu dozed on the floor, her chin resting on Evie's shoe as if they'd known each other for years. Evie hadn't told Millie that she was coming back here to meet him. She wasn't quite sure why. Maybe because she didn't want to answer a million questions about Scott. Maybe because she knew Millie would probably tell her mum, and her mum would end up telling someone else who would end up telling Evie's mum. And she knew how that would go: *Who is this guy? How did you meet him? He's a total stranger and he's a lot older than you. What does he do for a living?* And on, and on, and on.

Scott was a secret she wanted to keep to herself. At least for now.

And he was interesting to talk to, smart, funny, charming. He'd *done* things with his life, been places, met people – pretty much the opposite of the lads at school. He was everything that Tyler wasn't. Not that it was Tyler's fault, of course not, he was just so . . . immature. They all were.

Scott didn't like talking about himself. He said he was more interested in her, but there was something else there too: something deep beneath the surface that was cautious, careful, almost reticent, a vulnerability that she saw only in flashes before he hid it again.

It was irresistible.

12

'She'd go absolutely mad,' my son says quietly, 'if she knew we were doing this.'

The two of us are in Evie's bedroom, like a couple of forensic investigators examining a crime scene. The room is relatively tidy by Evie's standards – mainly because she's not been here for months. All the same, Lucas drops down onto his stomach to fish out the various items under the queen-sized bed: a pair of old trainers, a few odd socks, plastic bags, various small fluffy cat toys that Bella must have brought up here and forgotten about, a plate that has been there so long the red smears of jam have dried as hard as concrete. There is nothing beneath the mattress, no secret notes, no cash, no diary.

Lucas blows dust off one of the cat toys. 'What are we even looking for, anyway?'

'I don't know exactly,' I say. 'Anything that might give us a clue. Maybe a train ticket, a receipt, a bank statement?'

'But all that will be on her phone, Mum.'

'Probably,' I concede. 'But you never know what she might have left behind.'

'There is a metal box,' he says. 'Where she keeps her cash from babysitting and from birthdays and Christmas. Other stuff like that.'

'How do you know?'

He shrugs, looks down at the carpet. 'Just do.'

'And do you know where it is?'

He drags the desk chair over to the fitted wardrobe, using the extra height to lean in and pull a mass of bags and old shoeboxes out of the way. Leaning up on tiptoes, he retrieves something right from the back of the wardrobe's top shelf. It's a small metal tin covered in the colourful overlapping stickers Evie had loved as a young girl, of animals and cartoon characters, rainbows and flowers. Lucas hands it to me and climbs down off the chair.

Pointing up to the top of the door frame, he says: 'Key's up there.'

It's my turn to reach up on tiptoes and – sure enough – my fingers find a small silver key on top of the frame. Sliding the key into the slot, the mechanism turns easily as I lift the lid up.

It's empty.

'Do you know how much money she had in here?' He shrugs again as if he doesn't want to incriminate himself any further. 'It's OK, Lucas. I won't tell her, I don't care if you looked before. All I'm bothered about is making sure your sister is safe.'

He crosses his arms over his small chest. 'Last time I looked there was, like, two hundred and fifty pounds in notes. But that was ages ago, before she went away.'

'And you didn't take any of it, did you?'

'No!' His eyes flash with indignation. 'I would never steal.'

'I know, love.' I put a hand on his shoulder. 'Just wanted to hear it from you.'

We put the lockbox and the key back where we found them. I pick up a small, framed photograph on the dresser. It's a composite of four images, of Evie and Tyler in one of those old-style photo booths, laughing in the first two shots, kissing in another, both sticking their tongues out at the camera in the last one. On the wall beside the mirror is a heart-shaped picture frame, this one a montage of half a dozen shots featuring Evie and Millie, her best friend of seven years. Who *had* been her best friend but was now . . . what?

In the pictures, the two of them are laughing, pouting, blowing kisses at the camera, arms around each other, dressed up to the nines for their post-GCSEs prom.

At some point between then and this year, it seemed, Evie had disengaged with everyone.

She had drifted away from her best friend. She had split from her boyfriend. Tyler had been evasive about what exactly had happened between them – probably because she was the first girl ever to split up with him. It must have dented his ego.

And she had kept it from me. All of it.

In the bottom drawer of her desk are a stack of old diaries, all different sizes and colours, some going back to her primary school days. Under normal circumstances I would never look at them – but this weekend has been anything but normal. I pick one of the more recent-looking ones and open to a random page near the middle, the lines full of Evie's neat, rounded handwriting, pages crinkling with blue biro ink.

M. came to ours for a sleepover and so we stayed up till 3 a.m. watching films with some vodka she smuggled in from home lol. Slept in till lunch felt SO hungover then we were talking about doing a Halloween thing here, got the invite list planned and everything, I asked Mum if I could have a small GATHERING at home not even a party and she just straight out said NO and didn't really want to talk about it because of what happened last time plus she's still pissed off about Reading festival because she made SUCH a big deal out of that and won't let me forget it and OH MY GOD I HATE HER!

The word *hate* is underlined twice. A dull twinge of sadness thickens my throat.

I don't remember any kind of argument or specific falling-out about a party – there had been so many over the years that they all tended to blend into one. I flick forward: the last entry is in December 2021, the remaining few dozen pages all blank. The half-dozen diaries below it in the drawer are all for previous years. Nothing since.

Her Austin Butler calendar is still on the wall. It's still stuck on September. The day denoting the 29th is circled in red pen, with a single word underlined: UNI. Like the rest of the room, everything is how she left it on that date and I have a sudden, sickening vision that I'm one of those parents who loses a child and keeps their bedroom exactly as it was left. Preserving it, forever, as a memorial to the lost – or in the hope that one day the child will come back to them.

A shiver flashes through me and I slam the drawer shut. *That's not Evie*. But I feel winded, like I've been kicked in the chest.

She's in danger. I know she is. I *feel* it.

'Mum?' Lucas says, concern in his voice. 'Are you all right?'

'I'm OK.' I straighten up, turn to face him. 'I'm fine. Did you find anything?'

He's sitting cross-legged next to the small bookcase, taking each book out in turn and flicking through all the pages in case anything is tucked inside. He puts each one back in the same place, in the same order as he found it, even now not wanting to risk the wrath of his big sister for messing with her things.

'A few old bookmarks and a picture of Tyler,' he says. 'Nothing else.'

'You know, you're probably right about the useful stuff, there probably won't be hard copies. But if we could access a couple of her apps maybe it would help see where she's been.'

'You mean, like, hacking into her accounts?'

'Just to have a peek at email receipts or maybe debit card trans-actions.' I take my phone out of the pocket of my jeans. 'If I log out,

I could try to log back in as her? She might have written down her passwords somewhere.'

Lucas makes a face. 'Only old people do that.'

'I do it.'

He looks at me with an expression that says: *Exactly*.

'And anyway,' he says. 'She does the thumbprint thing for her bank, iCloud and all the rest. I've seen her do it.'

'But there must be a standard log-in method too, right? The old school way with email and password?'

We sit side by side at the end of Evie's bed and try to guess the passwords for her email, then her Instagram and Snapchat accounts and her iCloud storage. Lucas sits beside me suggesting passwords, his reticence tempered with a measure of excitement at being encouraged to cross an obvious red line in his sibling relationship.

In any case, the effort gets us nowhere: we can't access even a single one of her accounts.

Lucas returns to the bookcase, shaking out each of the remaining paperbacks to see if there is anything tucked inside the pages. I look through her half-empty wardrobe, a few dozen empty hangers alongside Evie's most summery clothes, all the thinnest tops, a couple of lightweight jackets and the stunning backless dress she'd worn to the school leavers' prom this summer. I'd assumed it would be a good option for her first end-of-term bash at university too – but after the last twenty-four hours I'm no longer surprised to see it here, left behind.

'Here's another bookmark,' Lucas says, holding something out to me. 'I swear half the books on her shelf she's not even finished.'

'It's a postcard,' I say. 'Where did you find it?'

He indicates a novel on the floor by his feet. *Ghosts* by Dolly Alderton.

'Nothing else?' I say. 'Just this?'

He nods and I take the card from him. It's a painting, a front cover of *The New Yorker* magazine, a couple in silhouette kissing at the entrance to a subway station. A pink sunset sky darkens to swirls of dusky blue behind them.

I turn it over. There is no date or address – just a single hand-written line, black ink from a fountain pen.

Let me count the ways . . .

There is no name either, just a single letter – a flourishing capital *S*.

The words seem familiar somehow and it only takes Google a second to tell me they belong to Elizabeth Barrett Browning. *How do I love thee? Let me count the ways. I love thee to the depth and breadth and height my soul can reach.* I look at the painting on the other side again. *The New Yorker, Price $4.50, Sept 15, 2008.* New York was one of those places that I'd promised to take the kids – inspired partly by Evie's teenage bingeing of *Suits* and *Gossip Girl* – but we just hadn't quite got around to it. As I study the image, it strikes me that there's something else I haven't looked for since I discovered she was gone.

I go into the master bedroom to check my bedside drawer, where I keep all of our important documents. But it's definitely not there where it should be, with the others. And nowhere in Evie's room either.

It's not just the cash that she's taken from its secret hiding place.

Her passport is gone too.

13

The afternoon slides into evening as I move around the house, stripping beds, putting on two loads of washing, ironing Lucas's weekly complement of school shirts on autopilot. It's almost the shortest day of the year, dark shadows of the evening crowding out the day before it's even really got going. Eventually Lucas drifts off to his room to play on his Xbox and I'm glad he has something to take his mind off things, even if only for a short while.

Evie's friend Amber sends me a long apologetic text full of emojis that basically says she has no idea where Evie might be but she promises to ask around her other friends and had I asked Millie? I take pictures of *The New Yorker* postcard, front and back, and send them to Amber asking if she'd ever seen it before and if she knows who it's from. It's a horrible violation of Evie's privacy but I'm getting to the point where such concerns barely even register.

But Amber knows nothing about the card or the mysterious 'S'.

I make Lucas's packed lunch for tomorrow and call the police station in Enfield, quoting the reference number and waiting on hold until a female voice answers.

We go through the same Q&A as yesterday and she listens while I give her the minor updates I have.

'She's in danger,' I say. 'I know she is.'

'And have you had any contact with your daughter since you spoke to my colleague yesterday?'

'No, but I know something's wrong – she wouldn't have left it this long with no contact. And I'm pretty sure her passport is gone.'

While I'm on the call my phone buzzes with a message and I hurry to check it, my heart clenching with the hope that it might be Evie, almost cutting off the connection by accident.

Hi, my mum said you came around earlier about Evie but I haven't heard from her in a while sorry. Have you talked to Amber?

Millie. Essentially it was the same message as Amber had sent: each girl suggesting I try the other. For a second I'm reminded of their escape to London a few years ago, when the three of them had each told parents they were staying with one of the others.

No. I was being ridiculous. Paranoid.

The police call handler tells me – again – that there are no detectives for me to speak to at the moment but says they will be in touch if there are any updates. She also urges me to let them know when Evie comes home or gets back in touch, as if this is somehow a foregone conclusion.

Lucas does his homework at the dining table while I cook our favourite Sunday dinner – roast chicken with all the trimmings – even though there's far too much for just the two of us. It was supposed to be a special family meal to welcome Evie home, but my appetite has disappeared. I save half the chicken to use tomorrow night and then, over a pudding of apple crumble and custard, I ask Lucas about school and his friends, about Christmas, about what he's been playing on his Xbox. Anything to take his mind off the reality that there are only two of us sitting at our small kitchen table when there should be three. Perhaps to take my mind off it too.

But eventually he puts his spoon down and pushes the bowl of crumble away, only half finished.

'What are you going to do, Mum?' His voice is low as if he's worried these words should not be spoken aloud, or he's frightened of being overheard. 'About Evie?'

I swallow a last mouthful and put my own spoon down too.

'I'm going to find her, Lucas.'

'But . . . how? London is massive and there's so many people, like, *millions* of them.'

'I'll ring the police every day if I have to.' I give him a confident smile. 'You know, it's actually really hard to disappear nowadays. It's so hard not to leave an electronic footprint through your bank, or CCTV cameras or your phone records. There are a hundred ways you can leave a trace even without realising it.'

'You said her phone was disconnected.'

'Yes, but I'm assuming she's got a new one.'

He pushes his glasses up his nose. 'How does that help though, if we don't know her new number?'

'Well, she might call one of her friends or log back into one of her apps and start using it again. She might call you or me, or send a text. And that would give the police a trail to follow.'

But even to me, it sounds like I'm clutching at straws.

'Was it really boring when you were young?' Lucas's tone implies that I grew up in the Middle Ages. 'Before there were phones?'

'We had phones when I was Evie's age, they just weren't smart. And you could get by without one whereas now I don't think you can, especially if you're nineteen like your sister.' I give his arm a playful poke. 'And for the record I'm not *that* old, you cheeky so-and-so.'

He rewards me with a shy smile, but it fades quickly.

'What if you can't, though?' He won't look at me. 'Find her, I mean? How will she get home in time for Christmas?'

I relate what the police call handler had told me yesterday, about 99 per cent of missing people being found within a few days. Trying for a confident tone that I don't feel; to silence the voice inside my head that says, *What about the other 1 per cent? What happens to them?* Then I give him a long hug and he carries our bowls to the sink, telling me he has more homework to finish. My mum calls me for an update, reassuring me that Evie will be fine while I try not to break down in tears again. She has no idea about the postcard or who might have given it to Evie. When we say our goodbyes and hang up the wave of emptiness, of being helpless, is almost crippling – so I do what I always do, when life threatens to overwhelm me. I find a lined A4 pad and lay it out on the kitchen table, write *TOMORROW* at the top of the page and start to make a plan.

Police – need to escalate/detective?
Uni – who is Evie's emergency contact?
Postcard – who is S?
Amber/Millie – covering for each other?
Tyler – why did E break up with him?

When the phone rings a few minutes later I've not progressed beyond this handful of words at the top of the page. I assume it's Mum calling back but the caller ID tells me it's the security man from the university instead.

'Hello, Mrs Wingfield,' Craig Farley says. 'Hope I've not caught you at a bad time?'

'No,' I say. 'No, it's fine.' We exchange brief pleasantries and I tell him there is no news from my end.

'I was going to call you tomorrow morning,' he says. 'But I didn't think you'd want to wait.'

A painful ache throbs in my throat, as if a stone is lodged in my windpipe.

'What is it? Has Evie been in contact?'

'No, sorry,' he says quickly. 'Not that. But I have found something I think you'll want to see.'

14

Everywhere I turn, everywhere I look, every TV channel, every ad break, every commentator, podcast, poster and radio station are all shouting about one thing only – *Christmas* – as if the regular year has already finished and all normal cares and worries are done with too, put away in a box until next year. In the end I have to turn the TV off and find a London radio station to listen for the 8 a.m. bulletin, both hands around a cup of strong black coffee at the kitchen table and praying with all my heart not to hear the words *Police are appealing for witnesses after the body of a young woman was found . . .*

But there is no such story today, nothing about a nineteen-year-old woman – in any case, Evie wasn't even officially a missing person according to the police.

For the first time in forty-eight hours, I'm glad *not* to hear anything about my daughter.

The news presenter hands over to traffic and travel and I switch the radio off. I phone into the office, using my best *at-death's-door* voice to tell them I'm coming down with the flu and probably won't be in for a couple of days, then set about filling a backpack with a bottle of water, snacks, my phone charger and an extra power pack. I've already printed out two dozen colour pictures of Evie – a recent one that was taken at her end-of-school prom – sliding them into a plastic wallet to go into the bag with everything else. My mobile number is printed on every sheet in thick, black marker.

Without thinking too much about it, I grab the small red first aid kit from the kitchen cupboard and shove that in as well.

Last night had been another endless, sleepless descent into every worst-case scenario my mind could conjure up. Evie had been kidnapped. She had been trafficked by a gang. She had turned to drugs or fallen into a life of crime. She was homeless on the bitterly cold streets of London. She was living rough. She had got on a train or a plane headed for some unknown destination and was now hundreds or even thousands of miles away; friendless, vulnerable, at the mercy of the very worst people the world had to offer.

I pour the rest of the freshly brewed coffee into a flask and stow it in my backpack.

Lucas finally appears at the bottom of the stairs. He's fully dressed – but not in school uniform. Instead, he's in jeans and his favourite Warhammer sweatshirt plus bobble hat and gloves, his parka already on.

'Is it non-uniform day today?' I put two more pieces of toast into the toaster. 'You'd better get a move on or you're going to miss the bus.'

'I'm not going,' he says flatly.

'Why?'

'I'm coming with you.'

'You want a lift instead?'

'To London, I mean.' He thrusts his hands into his coat pockets. 'I'm coming to London, to help you find Evie.'

I put the raspberry jam and margarine down on the kitchen worktop and turn to look at him. He's not hit his teenage growth spurt yet and he's still a few inches shorter than me, but he's standing with his shoulders back, chin up, as if he wants to appear older than his twelve years.

'That's very thoughtful of you,' I say. 'But you need to go to school, Lucas. I'll be fine on my own and I've arranged with Yusuf's mum for you to go to his for tea after chess club, in case I'm late back.'

He's already shaking his head.

'I won't be able to concentrate anyway.' He produces his phone from a coat pocket. 'And people at school are already saying things. Posting stuff.'

'What stuff?'

'About Evie.' He frowns. 'I've been getting messages from people asking me where Evie has gone, if she's been kidnapped or if she's not really missing at all and it's just a stunt for Christmas.'

'A *stunt*?'

'That's what one of the Year Twelves said.' He scrolls hurriedly on his phone, holds it out to show me a string of messages he's received overnight. 'Jacob Jackson made a TikTok video saying she's just copying what this girl in America did a few years ago, pretending to disappear to get loads of likes and followers and people being all sympathetic when she finally comes home.'

'This Jacob Jackson kid sounds like an idiot.'

'I know,' he says gloomily. 'But he's the most popular boy in school. And he's got, like, twenty thousand followers on TikTok because he's always posting all these funny takes on the news and music and teenage true crime.'

He taps his phone screen a few more times, holds it up again. The screen shows a fresh-faced boy in a white Armani hoodie talking into the camera, his delivery unnervingly calm, claiming to have the inside scoop on what he's calling 'The Christmas Mystery of Evie Wingfield'. He's weirdly articulate and seems to talk without notes, without hesitation, with a confidence that I assume is born of growing up with a smartphone glued to your hand.

I don't need to ask how the news has got out – presumably it started with Amber and Millie and went viral across the school community.

'Does this lad even know Evie?'

Lucas shrugs. 'I don't think so. He's two years below her, he wouldn't have had anything to do with her at school.'

Although it doesn't really matter – because this video is out there now. Without a single scrap of evidence, this freckled teen-ager, this *child*, was throwing out theories to anyone who would listen that maybe Evie wasn't *really* missing. And by extension, that maybe people didn't really need to look for her.

His final flourish in the video is a none-too-subtle suggestion that Lucas and I might be a part of the deception, a part of the plan, and only going around asking about her to add a sense of realism to the whole thing. I'm shaking my head as he signs off, promising his viewers 'more exclusive news on this unfolding mystery' as soon as he has it.

The view count is almost at a thousand already. On another day, another time, I'd like to pay Jacob Jackson a visit and give him a piece of my mind.

But not today.

Lucas slips the phone into his coat pocket. 'Don't make me go in,' he says. 'I don't want to have everyone whispering behind my back all day, talking crap about my sister like it's some big joke.'

'I understand, Lucas, but school is important. Your studies are important.'

'We're not even really doing proper lessons any more anyway, it's all Christmas quizzes and stuff. *Please*, Mum.'

This is not like him at all. Unlike his sister, he's a rule follower. He's never been one to feign illness or exaggerate symptoms to get time off school. I can't even remember the last time he missed a day.

'It'll probably be very boring, lots of driving and talking to people.'

'I don't mind,' he says. 'And I won't get in the way. I can be the navigator, I can help. I *want* to help.'

I look down into his hazel-brown eyes – his father's eyes – and see the genuine concern there. The shadow of tiredness too.

'OK,' I say. 'Go and get your other backpack from upstairs. I'll call the school and put some things out for you to bring while you eat your toast.'

Ten minutes later we're driving down Wokingham Road in my old Volkswagen Golf, Lucas in the passenger seat beside me. He's plugged the university's postcode into Google Maps on his phone. I've only just got used to having him in the front – for years his sister claimed this seat as a firstborn birthright – and it's another new experience to have him calling out directions and warning me about traffic jams on the M25.

Mostly we talk about Evie. About places she liked to go in London, places we'd visited in the past and where she might have been drawn back to. I can't escape the gnawing feeling that her trail is growing colder with every hour that passes. We're already so far behind her, the last sighting of her already weeks old.

'Mum?' Lucas says as we turn onto a roundabout. 'What if we find Evie and—'

'There's no if,' I say gently. 'We're *going* to find her. Together.'

He considers this for a moment.

'But what if we do find her and ... she doesn't want to come home? Then what?'

'Well, then at least we know she's safe. And we'll know where she is, and we'll tell her that we love her and we'll be ready for her whenever she wants to come back. To celebrate Christmas with us, hopefully.'

'Oh,' he says in a small voice. 'OK.'

He falls silent after that and I press a little harder on the accelerator. We pass a blue and white sign that I must have seen a thousand times over the years.

London, 21 miles.

Ahead of us, to the east, the sky is unnaturally dark despite the morning hour. A mass of heavy winter cloud stretches from one side of the horizon to the other, blotting out the sun and threatening to unleash thunder and lightning on the capital. It seems to me that London has always exerted a powerful draw on the surrounding Home Counties – and I feel it now, the gravitational pull of a dark star drawing us in. As we merge onto the dual carriageway that will take us to the M4, the rain erupts and a sudden torrent of drops batters the windscreen like a spray of shrapnel, the VW's old wipers struggling to push the water aside.

I switch on my headlights and accelerate towards the motorway.

PART II

15

Farley is not alone when I meet him for the second time. Seated at the small table in the corner of his office is a smartly dressed blonde woman who stands when we arrive. He gestures to an extra chair for Lucas as he's doing the introductions.

'This is my colleague, Bryony McKenzie,' the security man says. 'She's here to help.'

Bryony is in her mid-thirties, with a dark checked jacket over a white blouse, her highlighted hair cut into a stylish blunt bob.

She offers me a manicured handshake.

'It's nice to meet you,' she says. 'Thanks for coming in.'

'Do you know Evie? Did you teach her?'

'Oh, I'm not an academic,' she says. 'I run the university's public affairs and advocacy team. We typically handle the public-facing side of any incidents on campus that have the potential to attract wider interest.'

'You handle the media.'

'That's right. Amongst other things.'

'You think they'd be interested in Evie?'

'We can certainly look into that, perhaps a little further down the line.' She gestures to the two chairs on the other side of the desk. 'Have a seat, please. Let's just say we like to be prepared for all eventualities. It's better to have all the facts ahead of time.'

'Of course.' I glance at Farley, then back to her. 'Could you do a press release or something? An appeal?'

'I don't think that would be appropriate at this stage, but it's something we could consider when we're in possession of more of the facts.'

'But that's the whole point, isn't it? We need more facts to find Evie.'

She gives me a careful smile. 'We'll do everything we can, Mrs Wingfield.'

I'm about to reply, and then it clicks: she's not here to publicise my daughter's disappearance. She's here to keep it *out* of the news.

Farley shifts awkwardly in his seat, tapping absently on his keyboard. I wonder whether it was his choice, bringing this woman into the conversation. Whether it might actually be helpful to have her involved, or if this is already turning into one of those situations where everyone simply wants to cover their back. Whatever the truth is, I need to keep them both onside, for now at least. All the same, it feels like a small betrayal by Farley.

I glance at the security boss, but he still won't meet my eye.

'Anyway,' he says, clicking his mouse now. 'The main thing is, we want to help you in any way we can. As I mentioned on the phone, I had time yesterday to gather more information that might be useful.'

'I appreciate it,' I say. 'Thank you. What have you found?'

'So, when a student leaves unexpectedly their room is cleared out to make it ready for the next occupant. We don't return items in the post as that would be prohibitively expensive. But we don't dispose of the contents either, at least not for ninety days – it's put in storage in the intervening period. So I thought I'd check if there's anything still there that would help you get in touch with her.' He looks up. 'As I suspected, when Evie left her room in the hall of residence she didn't take everything with her.'

'Can I see it?'

He nods slowly. 'Everything your daughter left behind, I've brought down to our meeting room and you're welcome to go through it, take it away. But first I want to show you something else. I only found it this morning.'

Every time a student uses their ID card to open a door, he explains, it's logged on the database. Also when it's used to borrow a book from the library or pay for a meal in the refectory. He had found the last dates that Evie's card had been used, and then started checking the CCTV logs around that time and date.

'Most of the main camera footage is only stored for thirty days before it's overwritten with new content,' he says, typing on his keyboard. 'But there are a few others out in the halls and faculties that don't reset until the end of each term.'

He turns his computer monitor to face me, swivelling it on his desk. The screen is split into six rectangular boxes, bird's-eye views of corridors, doors, walkways and roads around campus.

'OK,' he says, pointing to the image at the top left. 'Look at this. It's the main door of New Orchard Hall, where she was allocated a room.'

The screen shows a lobby area, the row of pigeonholes for mail down one side. A figure emerges and even though the image is in grainy black and white from an awkward angle I recognise her immediately: her walk, the shape of her head, the slight swing of her arms. I know everything about her, this first child of mine, this beautiful, clever girl. This young woman who has grown somehow into a stranger.

My heart contracts painfully in my chest, as if it's being squeezed by an unseen fist.

In a very quiet voice next to me, my son says a single word. 'Evie.'

In the video she's wearing jeans, a dark quilted jacket over a pale hoodie, and she has a rucksack on her back that I've never seen before. As we watch, she pushes through the door to the outside, appearing on a different camera for just a few seconds before she stops, turns, and heads back inside. She touches a card to the reader and pushes through the door into the reception area.

'There,' Farley says, pointing at the screen. 'That was the last time her ID card was logged on the system. When she opened the door to go back inside.'

'You found this footage since Saturday?'

He shrugs. 'I was on shift both days of the weekend. Campus has emptied out, there wasn't much else to do.'

On the first screen, Evie goes quickly to her pigeonhole, gathers a few envelopes and tucks them into her jacket pocket. Then for the second time in this short sequence of film, she leaves through the main door but this time she doesn't hesitate or look back. Instead she turns right and walks quickly along the path, disappearing out of shot.

Watching the video I have a sudden, swooping sense of helplessness, a horrible premonition that perhaps these grainy images might be the last time I ever set eyes on my daughter. The last confirmed sighting before she walked beyond the lens of some CCTV camera and disappeared off the face of the earth.

I shake the thought away.

Farley points to the third box on the screen, a wide-angle view taken from a different place, which shows Evie moving left to right across an open square between two buildings. Despite the loaded rucksack on her back she walks quickly, confidently, as if she knows where she's going and doesn't want to be late. There are a few other figures around – other students walking, vaping, chatting in small groups – but none of them pay her any particular attention.

Except one.

16

In the CCTV footage, Evie is checking her phone as she walks when another individual enters the video from the top left. He's behind but angling towards her, hurrying to catch up. A male, in grey sweatpants and a light-coloured sweatshirt with some kind of logo on it. I lean a little closer to the screen. It's not easy to tell in the black-and-white video but it looks as if he has blond hair, tied up in a short topknot at the crown of his head. Evie seems oblivious to his approach, and again she disappears off the edge of the screen.

'Where does she go next?' I say to Farley. 'Do you have another camera? Another angle?'

He points to the next one in the sequence and Evie appears again, still moving from left to right, the figure with the topknot hurrying after her in an awkward half-jog. He's short and very stocky, not a natural runner, but he's still gaining on her and seems to shout something in Evie's direction. She doesn't respond.

'Who's that following her?'

Farley holds a hand up. 'Just watch this for a second.'

The figure jogs the last few paces to catch up and puts a hand on Evie's arm. She pivots towards him, turning her back to the camera. But the face of the guy with the top knot is now clearly visible, thick with stubble and sporting a pair of small round glasses that are somehow incongruous with his muscular frame. He's talking at

Evie in an animated fashion, gesticulating with both hands, shaking his head.

On one hand I'm glad there's someone on campus who seems to know her, who recognises her. But he's also invading her personal space in a way that makes it uncomfortable to watch. I can't tell if she's responding to him but the tension in her posture is obvious, a small step away from him, then another, a glance at her watch.

They talk for perhaps twenty seconds. Then she shakes her head and walks away.

'I assume there's no audio on this?'

Farley shakes his head.

He rewinds the clip and we watch it again.

'Can you zoom in on their faces?' I say. 'Give us an idea what they're talking about?'

'I've already tried but the resolution's not good enough. Sorry.'

As Evie walks away on screen, Farley clicks his mouse and stops the footage, freezing on a shot of the stocky young man staring after her. His body language is aggressive, frustrated, fists clenched at his sides. From the front, the logo on his sweatshirt is visible for the first time, a black-and-white graphic of a shield, with letters in the top half and something else too fuzzy to make out beneath them.

My son murmurs something under his breath.

'What's that, Lucas?' Amid the intensity of seeing Evie, I'd almost forgotten her brother is sitting right here beside me.

'LA Kings,' he says. 'The team on his sweatshirt.'

'You can *see* that?'

He shrugs. 'Recognised the shape of the logo from playing NHL on my Xbox. Is the date right on this video, by the way? I thought you said Evie left on the sixth of November.'

I look at the top right-hand corner of the screen, and see what he means. A time stamp that states the footage was captured at 2.14 p.m., six more digits displaying the date.

'Is that correct?' I say to Farley. 'The twenty-third of October?'

'Yes, the CCTV system is linked up and synchronised with the central database.'

The university's minimum baseline for intervention, he explains, is two weeks of zero engagement without a documented reason. In other words, a fortnight in which any student had zero contact with staff should trigger someone reaching out to check they were OK. But Evie could have circumvented this, Farley admits, by logging into the student learning network, StudyHub, at least once a week – and she could do that from anywhere with an internet connection.

'Each time they log in, it resets the intervention clock back to zero,' he says. 'So the date she officially withdrew might *not* have been the last time she was physically here on campus. It might have been long after.'

'If she knew how it worked,' I say. 'She could have played the system for weeks? Is that what you're telling me?'

He looks at me. 'It's possible.'

'So by the time she formally dropped out, she'd already been gone more than two weeks?'

He nods gravely. 'That's what it looks like. October twenty-third is the last time her ID card is logged on the system.'

He clicks his mouse again and starts the footage on the bottom right of his screen, of Evie walking up to a taxi, a dark-coloured saloon parked at the kerb. As she approaches, the driver pops the boot and she hoists her rucksack in before climbing into the back seat. The car pulls smoothly away and moves out of shot, the guy with the topknot belatedly appearing at the kerb to stare after the departing car. I can just make out the BMW logo above the numberplate.

'That's it,' Farley says. 'That's all of it, all the footage we've got of her on that day. Her card hasn't been used on campus since.'

He rewinds the clip and we watch it again. I frown. Evie doesn't talk to the driver, doesn't greet them through the passenger side window to check if they're available and not booked for anyone else. And the driver opens the boot for her as she approaches, also before they've spoken. Almost as if he knows her – or they've done this before.

A discreet panel on the BMW's passenger door says *Excalibur*. I write the name into the Notes app on my phone.

'It's a north London company,' Farley says. 'Based in Finsbury Park, as far as I could tell from a quick Google search. We have some local taxi firms around here that have cars on campus for students all the time, picking up and dropping off. But Excalibur is not one of them – it's not a company I'm familiar with.'

Lucas is holding out his phone, taking a picture of Topknot on the computer monitor. But Bryony seeing this rises out of her seat a little, her voice stern.

'Er, young man? You can't do that. You can't just go taking pictures like that without consent.'

His face falls. 'Oh, sorry. Didn't realise. I'll delete it.' He taps his screen. 'Gone.'

'So who is he?' I say to Farley. 'The guy with the topknot?'

'I believe he's one of our international students, he's been—'

Bryony cuts him off. 'I'm afraid,' she says, 'we're not legally allowed to divulge *any* information about members of our student body to third parties. As we discussed, Craig.'

Farley reddens slightly. 'Well . . . yes. Strictly speaking, that's true.'

I look from Bryony to him, and back again. 'You can at least give me his name, can't you? Looks like he was the last person on campus that Evie spoke to, perhaps he was a friend.'

'As I said, handing out students' names willy-nilly would be a breach of data protection *and* a breach of that individual's privacy.' Her hands are clasped tightly in her lap. 'Sorry.'

'But clearly you can see this is a special case?' My voice rises with exasperation. 'He might have known where she was going that day when she left. She might have told him her plans, who she was going with, how she was getting there. Anything.'

'We don't make the rules,' Bryony says with a faux brightness that sets my teeth on edge. 'We just have to follow them, I'm afraid.'

'So why are you even bloody showing me this footage? For all we know, this man might be involved somehow in Evie's disappearance.'

'That would be incredibly unlikely.'

'Why?'

'Look, Mrs Wingfield. We want to give as much help as we're allowed to give, up to the limit of the law. And in any case, in terms of our purposes here he's not *actually* been identified. We have more than twenty thousand students on campus at any given time and it would be almost impossible to identify one individual from an image as poor quality as this.'

For the first time I notice a poster on the wall behind her. An advert for the university with the slogan 'Join the QAU family' beneath a sunny group of students, all white-teeth smiles, all beautiful, a perfectly diverse group of genders, ethnicities, sizes, strolling through the central quad as if they're having the time of their lives. Bryony is wearing a pin badge on her lapel, the same motto below a small coat of arms.

'So even if you did know this guy's name,' I say. 'You still wouldn't tell me? How about the police – you'd tell them, right?'

I feel my anger rising, bubbling like a kettle coming to the boil.

She raises her hands.

'Listen, Mrs Wingfield, trust me when I say we really and truly want the same thing. We'd like to be clear for the record that the university has been as helpful as it can be and has provided you with all possible assistance. We want to make sure Evie is safe and sound just as much as you do—'

'I doubt that very much.'

'All the same,' she says without missing a beat, 'I think it's important that we don't jump to any conclusions, there are lots of potential factors at play here and we need to keep an open mind to make sure we don't overlook something obvious. The fact remains that we have one of the lowest dropout rates in the country for law and one of the highest student satisfaction scores of any London university. For all we know, Evie's departure from campus could be entirely unrelated to the academic provision here, or to student life in general.'

With an effort of will, I resist the urge to grab her by the lapels of her expensive jacket and shake some sense into her.

'All I know,' I say instead, 'is that my daughter was able to walk out of here almost two months ago and no one cared. No one batted an eyelid. No one even noticed. And no one thought to notify me. I only found out the day I turned up on campus to take her home.' I stand up and put the strap of my handbag across my shoulder. 'Why don't you put *that* on one of your bloody posters?'

17

Farley ushers Lucas and me into a meeting room. Laid out on the table are three bulging black bin liners, a clear plastic bag of toiletries and a battered green suitcase I recognise as one of ours. These were the contents of Evie's room, he explains.

'It's been in storage,' he says. 'Was due for disposal end of this week.'

'Thank you for keeping it,' I say. 'We can take everything?'

'Yes,' he says. 'But I thought you might want to look at it here first. Let me know when you're finished and I'll help you carry it to your car. Take as long as you need.' He hesitates in the doorway, lowering his voice. 'Sorry about . . . all that with the video. But I thought you'd want to see it all the same.'

With that, he ducks out, leaving Lucas and me with the meagre collection. We go through each bag in turn, emptying them onto the table. The first one is full of winter clothes, sweatshirts, jeans, a scarf, a handful of paperback books. A khaki denim jacket tumbles out of the second one. I pick it up and hold it in both hands.

Lucas looks up from the old suitcase, which he's rooting through like an overzealous customs officer. 'She liked that one, didn't she?'

I nod, lifting the collar of the denim jacket to my face and breathing in deeply. Her Marc Jacobs perfume is still there. In that moment, it feels like she's here in the room with us. Maybe getting ready for a night out, trying on new clothes or unwrapping gifts on her birthday, spritzing us both with a new spray.

She's there for the span of a few heartbeats, and then she's gone. Tears prick at the corners of my eyes.

Lucas pauses next to me. 'She'd hate it if she knew I was going through her stuff.' He lifts the last of the clothes out of the old suit-case, sliding a hand into the zipped pocket beneath. 'Although I wouldn't mind if she *was* having a massive go at me, as long as she was here. With us.'

I pull him in for a quick hug, kissing the top of his head. 'Never thought you'd miss your sister having one of her moods, did you?'

The last bin liner is heavy, half torn already. There are a handful of creased photos from home, pictures of Amber and Millie taken on nights out in Reading that she'd previously had on her dresser. Discarded, just left behind. It also holds a couple of blank note-books and law textbooks.

I guess she isn't continuing her studies somewhere else, then.

Lucas flicks through one of the notebooks, empty pages zipping past under his thumb.

'What is it that's *not* here, though?' he says. 'The things she took with her. Is that maybe more important to figure out, rather than what she left behind?'

I survey the belongings spread across the table.

'Her laptop's not here,' I say. 'Her phone, passport, driver's licence aren't either. Some of her nicer clothes, her going-out clothes, and most of her makeup is missing too.'

'So she's taken her best clothes, her newest stuff?'

I nod. 'Whatever she could fit into that rucksack, I suppose.'

After ten more minutes of sifting and checking pockets, we shove everything back into the bags as best we can. The main office door is ajar and I push it open. They're both still there, Farley behind his desk and Bryony at the side table, talking in low voices. Their conversation comes to an abrupt halt when they see me.

'We're done,' I say. 'With Evie's things.'

Farley rises from his seat. 'Find anything useful?'

'Nothing that jumps out, but it was worth a look. We'll check through it all again later when we get home.'

'Let me give you a hand.'

He follows me back into the meeting room and picks up the heaviest bag with ease, Lucas and I taking another one each.

Bryony is by the front desk when we emerge. She holds out a business card.

'Please do get in touch if there's anything else we can do from our end,' she says coolly. 'And feel free to route any media enquiries onto us, we'd be more than happy to deal with them.'

Spin them a certain way or bury them, more like. I give her a nod and take the card, reminding myself that I need to keep people like her onside no matter how obstructive she tries to be.

'Thanks,' I say. 'And sorry about earlier, I'm just . . . worried sick about Evie.'

'I quite understand, Mrs Wingfield.'

'If there is any media interest, please give them my number and ask them to get in touch.'

'Absolutely.'

She gives me the briefest of nods, and I pretty much know that she'll do nothing of the sort.

Farley holds the outer door open, crisp December air pushing through the gap.

'I'll walk you out,' he says. 'Make sure you haven't got a parking ticket from one of my lads.'

Outside at the kerb, I open the boot of my Golf and swing a bin liner inside. Glancing back at the security office I notice Bryony observing us, phone clamped to her ear, her sleek blonde bob just visible through the ground-floor window.

'So,' Farley says, his breath steaming. 'What's next? Have you tried the police?'

'They don't regard her as a priority.'

He grunts as if he's not surprised at all, hefting another of the black bags into the boot.

'Look, I couldn't say anything in there because of Bryony.' He shifts position so he has his back to the security office window. 'Sorry about her. She reports directly to the registrar, who also happens to be my boss's boss and a man absolutely paranoid about bad publicity. We had a . . . situation a few years back with one of our senior professors, there was a major scandal and he ended up in jail.' Still with his back to the window, he takes a folded slip of paper from his pocket and surreptitiously reaches into the bag, tucking it into the denim jacket before folding the bin liner closed over it. He sees me watching him and we lock eyes for a moment. 'But that being said, I also have a seventeen-year-old daughter, so I get where you're coming from. She's applying to go to uni next year.'

I give him the smallest nod to show him I understand.

'What's your daughter's name?'

'Rosie. She wants to do history of art, for some reason.'

'Well, I hope she gets the place she wants.'

He closes the boot. 'And I hope you find your daughter.'

He reaches out a hand and we shake, a weirdly formal gesture.

'Thank you, Craig.'

'You've got my number,' he says. 'Call me if you think there's anything else I can help with.'

Lucas and I get into the car and I start the engine, then turn the heating up to maximum to clear the windscreen. I'm about to pull away when Farley taps on the driver's side window. I buzz it down.

'One more thing,' he says, leaning over with his hands on his knees. 'From what I understand, the best place to find a King this time of year is in the library.'

I turn down the blast of hot air from the blowers. 'Sorry, I didn't quite catch that, what—'

'The library,' he says again, breath steaming in the cold air. 'If not there, then you might try the gym, which is further down the hill towards the east gate. But mostly, the library, since the King is not going home for Christmas, with it being such a long way.'

I'm still not really following him.

'A King,' he says again. 'The ice hockey kind.'

Then it clicks. *LA Kings.*

'So you *do* know who he is?'

'Let's just say I've crossed paths with him once or twice before. Not to do with your daughter, though. A different . . . situation.'

'Have you talked to him about Evie?'

'Not yet. And he hasn't done anything to merit an intervention from me, as far as I can tell. But I understand why you might want to talk to him.' He straightens up, takes a step away from the car. 'Obviously we haven't had this conversation. But good luck.'

EVIE

Seven months earlier

She could talk to him about anything.

It was like she'd known him for years, but at the same time it was so new, so fresh and exciting, like tasting a beautiful cocktail for the first time and knowing it's going to become your favourite drink.

She was, in fact, drinking a beautiful cocktail that he had recommended: a blueberry mojito which he'd promised she would enjoy – and he'd been absolutely right. She'd met him for an early drink at this fancy bar near Paddington, so she could jump back on the train and be home by seven before anyone got suspicious. As far as her mum knew, Evie was doing some last-minute cramming at Reading central library surrounded by her textbooks.

Scott clinked his glass gently against hers and they both took a drink.

'So how are the exams going?' He smiled. 'Or am I not allowed to ask?'

Evie waved the question away. 'Only two more left, thank God. If I do any more revision, I think my head might actually explode.'

'Well, I'm sure you've done brilliantly,' he said. 'And I'm also sure you're going to make a brilliant lawyer.'

'Maybe.'

'*Definitely.*'

She didn't answer that. Instead, she took another sip of the mojito, savoured the subtle kick of rum and mint. Still not quite believing that instead of being stuck in the library she was *here*, in a posh London bar, whiling away a Friday afternoon drinking cocktails with this amazing guy. His unbearably cute chocolate Labrador slumbering by her feet.

Scott gave her a thoughtful look. 'Did I say the wrong thing?'

'No, it's not that.'

'You need to tell me when I put my foot in it.' He grinned. 'It's kind of my speciality.'

'I . . . don't actually want to be a lawyer.'

There. She'd said it. A sentence she'd never said to anyone – not to Tyler, not to her best friends, her teachers, her mum. God, *definitely* not her mum.

'OK.' He didn't sound surprised at all. Or judgemental, or patronising or anything like that. 'So what is it you want to do?'

'I want to act.'

He shrugged. 'Then you should act.'

'I wish it was as simple as that.'

'Who says it can't be?'

'The thing is . . . all through school, the teachers were always talking about making the right choices, getting the right grades, doing a degree that'll lead to a job with a decent salary. But now I'm almost there and it feels like I've been chasing the wrong thing all along – I'm not even sure why I'm doing it anymore, to be honest. Being a lawyer, it was never really what I wanted to *do* with my life but it just seemed like the smart choice. Head over heart. Because acting is a pipe dream and most people who study drama never make it, right?'

'Some do,' Scott said. 'Why not you? Maybe sometimes you should go with your heart rather than your head.'

'Tell that to my mum.'

'She pushed you to do law?'

'Not exactly. I mean . . . she's never said it in as many words but there's always been this unspoken thing from her that I shouldn't mess up my uni years like she did, shouldn't waste any time and *definitely* shouldn't end up pregnant at nineteen. It was tough for her at my age. She had to rely on herself after my dad died, had to be totally independent and she wants the same for me, so I let her steer me down a path towards some big high-earning career in law. For years I told myself it was all my choice, but slogging through my A levels I realised she was always a part of it too.'

It felt cathartic to say it, like a release of pressure that she'd been holding inside for months, or years.

'If I get the grades in these exams,' she said, 'I'll go to uni and see what happens. Maybe I'll like studying law. Who knows? The most important thing is I'll be away from everyone's expectations: school, teachers, friends. Away from my mum. Then I'll do what *I* want to do. My choice, my way.'

Scott nodded. 'I know exactly how you feel, Evie.'

18

It's a phone number.

The slip of paper Farley put into Evie's jacket has no words written on it, just the eleven digits of a mobile phone number. Presumably he'd taken this from Evie's student record. I don't recognise the number and a quick scan of my own contacts list says it's not my mum, not another family member, not Amber or Millie. A quick Google search doesn't yield anything either.

I'm tempted to call it right now, but I want to check the library first.

The library café is closed and there is only a single member of staff behind the counter near the entrance, a scattering of students here and there. From a brief wander around the ground floor, listening to the hushed conversations of small groups, I guess that most are international students who have opted to stay on over the Christmas break rather than making the long journey back home. So while the library's five floors would presumably have been packed during regular term time, now it is almost empty.

'We could split up?' Lucas asks quietly. 'I'll take the top floor and work my way down. You start down here and I'll meet you in the middle.'

I feel a twinge of anxiety at letting him out of my sight even as I remind myself that he wants to help, wants to be involved.

'Probably better if we stick together, Lucas.'

'It'll be fine, Mum. It's a library, and there's hardly anyone here anyway.'

'OK, but stay in the building,' I say. 'And text me. You think you'll recognise him?'

He holds up his phone with a grin: the photo he snapped of the guy on CCTV. It's grainy black and white, a picture of a picture, but better than nothing.

I smile back – he'd not deleted it after all. 'Clever boy. Send me the picture.'

He gives me a thumbs up and presses the lift button marked '5'.

I cover the ground floor, moving between the shelves and checking each of the study cubicles for any stocky young guys with blond hair. The library is uncomfortably warm after the sharp cold of the air outside, a crinkled, woody smell of old paper and long-stored documents.

I unzip my jacket and take the stairs to the first floor. More long lines of shelving, more study cubicles, a couple of glass-fronted seminar rooms – both empty and dark. My phone buzzes with a WhatsApp from Lucas, the picture of Topknot Guy. I pinch the screen to zoom in on his face, twisted in an angry scowl, his broad chest puffed out beneath the sweatshirt.

Walking slowly and trying to be inconspicuous, I do a full circuit of the floor, scanning the handful of students. There aren't many, and most of them are female. All with a few things in common: headphones, laptops, water flasks, backpacks, big coats. No sign of Topknot Guy.

I'm heading up to the second floor when my phone buzzes with another message from Lucas.

3rd floor near the back

I hurry up another flight of stairs and find my son loitering on the other side of the swing doors, a pleased look on his face. He leads me past more ceiling-high racks of dark leather-bound books and a door marked SPECIAL COLLECTIONS ARCHIVE – AUTHORISED ACCESS ONLY. On the far side, pairs of study cubicles line the wall under the window. Each one has a wide desk, a chair, a dividing wall and a privacy screen facing the rest of the room.

'In the corner,' Lucas says, turning as if to look at one of the old tomes on the shelf. 'Over my left shoulder. What do you think?'

I glance over to the corner, where only one of the study cubicles is occupied. 'I think you're right. Well spotted.'

Farley had been right too. The young guy from the CCTV footage is here, headphones on, hunched over a laptop in the last cubicle. His hair is even gathered up into the same neat topknot, the same thick stubble, although today he's wearing pale-rimmed glasses and a maroon hoodie bearing the name 'Stanford University'. Spread out on the table in front of him are thick books that look older than everything else in this place. A half-finished protein shake and a metal water flask stand next to them on the desk.

He's so absorbed in his work that he doesn't even notice us until we're a few feet away.

'Hi,' I say brightly. 'Have you got a minute?'

He flinches, irritation creasing his forehead. He stares at me, then at Lucas, then points up to a sign on the wall. NO TALKING. NO PHONES. SILENCE PLEASE.

I look around. There's no one else nearby, no one within earshot.

'Sorry to disturb.' I lower my voice. 'But I need to talk to you. Just for a minute.'

Sensing that I'm not going to leave him alone, he slips the headphones off and around his neck and I catch a ferocious blast of screeching guitars before he taps his phone and the music stops abruptly. Close up, he's more substantial than he seemed on the screen in Farley's office, muscular shoulders curving into a thick neck.

'Help you?' His tone implies he'd prefer to do anything but.

'I really hope so. I think—'

"Cause I'm kind of in the middle of something here.' He gestures towards the laptop, the textbooks, an A4 pad packed with tight, slanting handwriting. 'Unless you're interrupting me because you want to help me write my dissertation? How's your knowledge of Norse mythology?'

'Pretty sketchy, I'm afraid.'

'You're not faculty.' He has an abrupt, slightly nasal American accent and there is an intensity to him, a spiky energy that his muscle-taut skin can only just contain. Coupled with the blond beard and topknot that give him the look of a modern-day Viking, he puts me immediately on edge. 'I've never seen you on campus before.' He jerks a thumb towards Lucas. 'And FYI: under-eighteens aren't permitted in this library.'

'I think you might know my daughter.'

His eyes narrow slightly.

'So?'

'Evie Wingfield? I'm Lauren, her mum, and this is her brother, Lucas.'

His belligerent demeanour dissolves before my eyes. He turns in his seat to face me, sitting up a little straighter.

'Wait, what?' He takes his glasses off to get a better look at me. 'What's happened? Is Evie OK?'

'I don't know, that's why we're here. I thought you might be able to help us.' I run over the last forty-eight hours, Evie's disappearance, the CCTV footage of her leaving campus. Glossing over the details of how I'd tracked him down. 'I think you might have been the last person to see her when she left the university that final time. Do you know her well?'

He shrugs. 'Not as well as I wanted to. First met her, like, last year when she came to an open day here. I was the campus guide assigned to her and we hit it off straightaway – you know? Like when you have a real connection with someone? So I stayed in touch over the summer. We didn't really get long enough together this semester but I knew there could have been ... something more, if we'd had a little more time.' He extends a hand and we shake, his large palm grabbing mine in a too-firm grip that is only one notch below uncomfortable. 'I'm Colton Ryczek, by the way.'

Scenes from the CCTV footage return to me, of him spotting Evie striding away as if she couldn't wait to leave, then running to catch up with her. His strong hand on her arm. *Hey, where are you going? When are you coming back? Maybe we could get together for that drink?* A brief, intense conversation that had ended with her marching off without him. Colton stalking after her, rebuffed again, reduced to staring after her taxi as it drove away. And I can see how it might have played out: this intense American, with his gym-bro confidence and his piercing stare, pursuing Evie in those first few weeks of term. Not taking no for an answer. Unable to accept the fact that she was not interested in a relationship.

Could this be the reason she'd left? To get away from him?

19

But surely if Colton had been the problem, Evie would have told me about it, perhaps asked to move rooms. Not just walked away from her course, from her whole degree, from everything.

'But you and Evie were friends?' I say instead. 'For those first few weeks?'

'Yeah.' He's staring at me now, intense blue eyes drilling into mine. The sudden gearshift – from his annoyance to having his full attention – is unnerving. 'She was a special girl, not like most of the assholes here. I guess she probably mentioned me?'

I make a split-second decision to lie.

'Yes. She said she hadn't made many friends yet but she had hung out with a nice American guy, got on really well with him.'

He considers this for a moment, the small flicker of a smile beneath the thick blond covering of his beard. 'Huh. Is that right?'

'You weren't on her course, then? I did wonder if she might have struggled with her studies and that was why she left.'

'Nah,' he says, still staring at me. 'I'm a PhD in the School of History. My final year in this place, hence staying on over Christmas to get a few thousand words of this pain-in-the-ass dissertation done.'

He and Evie had 'reconnected', he says, at a Welcome Week event in the Students' Union and had seen each other frequently over the following month.

'I kept saying to her, she should come to visit me in Santa Monica, we could go out to my dad's ranch in the mountains, do a little hiking, hunting, fishing, you know? It's an awesome place.' He turns to Lucas. 'So you're her kid brother, huh? You like fishing?'

Beside me, Lucas shrugs. 'Never tried it.'

'You sure don't look like her,' Colton says. 'I guess your sister was a one-of-a-kind.'

Was. His use of the past tense sends a shiver of alarm through me.

But I need to get him back on track. 'The truth is, Colton, I'm worried sick about her. We both are. We're here today because we need to find out where she went that day. We need to talk to her friends, her *real* friends. Like you.'

He leans closer and I get a waft of unwashed sweat, the smell dull and sharp at the same time.

'The weird thing is, she didn't seem to *have* many other friends. Most girls go around in groups, right, they're incapable of going *anywhere* unless there's like a whole gang of them all together. To classes, to the pub, even to the bathroom. But Evie wasn't like that. There wasn't like, a group of girls or guys she would hang out with from her course, or even from her flat in New Orchard.'

'You went to her hall? To her room?'

He shrugs. 'Not, like, *in* her room but I often gave her a knock. When I figured she might want to hang out.'

I wonder how he might have discovered her flat, her room number in the hall of residence. Whether she gave it to him – or whether he just followed her one day.

'So she was there for a bit, living in that room?'

'Yeah. To begin with, anyways.'

I show him the slip of paper from Farley but he doesn't recognise the number.

'And the day in October that she left campus,' I say. 'The twenty-third. You talked to her, didn't you? You saw her as she was leaving with that big rucksack.'

'Couldn't tell you for sure what day it was,' he says. 'But I guess we had a few words. I'm like, "Hey Evie where are you going on a Monday morning?" – 'cos I knew she had a bunch of classes back to back on Monday, it was her second-busiest day of the whole week – and "What's up with you not returning my messages?"'

'Anything else?'

'I probably said . . . how about we grab a coffee and chill for a bit. You know. Just normal stuff.'

'And how did she seem?'

He frowns. 'Seem?'

'In herself. Did she look worried, or stressed or upset?'

'Nah.' He thinks for a moment. 'She was in kind of a hurry. Excited, maybe.'

In a small voice, Lucas says: 'Did you ask her where she was going?'

Colton glances at my son. 'She wouldn't say.'

'She didn't give you any idea?' I say. 'Any hint at all?'

'Nope. Nada. She said it was her life, her choice and she'd do what she wanted to.'

It was a line I'd heard from my daughter before but still, I lower my eyes, feeling the sag of disappointment. I'd really thought we were getting somewhere, starting to unpick Evie's last days on campus.

'Damn,' I say under my breath. 'I was so glad that we found you here today. I was hoping Evie might have said something back then. Confided in you.'

'Didn't matter anyway,' Colton says dismissively.

'Why?' Lucas says.

''Cos I already had a pretty good idea where she was going.'

'What?' I look up. 'How?'

'Because she'd done it before. Always the same taxi firm, Excalibur, and it always took her to the same place.'

'Where?' Lucas says. 'Where was it going—'

'Hang on,' I say, cutting him off. 'How do you know where it would take her, Colton?'

He shrugs. 'Well, like I said, I was worried about her. It was messed up, her cutting all her classes and skipping campus twice a week. I thought there was maybe something going on that I could help her with. Like maybe drugs, or whatever, and I wouldn't have judged her for that 'cos we've all been there, right? Not that she'd actually talk to me about it.'

'So you followed her?'

He smooths his beard absently but says nothing.

'You did, didn't you?' I hold both hands up to show I'm not judging him. 'I don't care if you did, I'm just glad you cared enough to look out for her.'

He looks away, down the line of shelves as if to check no one else is in earshot.

'I was worried about her, it was weird how she kept on just vanishing for days at a time. At first I figured she was just super homesick. I was out on my dirt bike anyway and I was curious to see where she lived.'

'She's not been home since September.'

'Yeah,' he says. 'I know that now.'

I'm getting the distinct impression that he's enjoying making us wait, enjoying stringing this out while he has our complete attention. He looks me up and down.

'Are you rich?' he says. 'No offence, Lauren, but you don't *look* rich.'

'It's not a way I've ever been described, no.'

'See, my dad's rich. He's an asshole too, although that's a whole other story. But even he probably wouldn't stay in that kind of place.' He hesitates. 'Hey, maybe you could give Evie my number again? 'Cos I've been messaging her over and over and she's just not replying. I figure she lost her cell.'

'Sure,' I say. 'Of course. I'll pass it on as soon as I find her. So where did she go?'

He pulls up a browser page on his MacBook, types something rapidly into the Google search box and clicks on the first result. Then turns the laptop towards us so we can see the glossy image that fills screen.

The Royal Pearl, Kensington.

'This place,' he says with a flourish. 'That's where the taxi took her. It's one of the most expensive hotels in London.'

20

Lucas reads from the hotel's website as we speed southwards towards central London.

'"A truly five-star experience",' he recites, '"The Royal Pearl is synonymous with rich heritage and uncompromising luxury on a level that ranks it among the very best in Europe. Enjoy fine dining in our Michelin-starred restaurant, swim in the twenty-four-hour pool or sip a cocktail among the sculptures on our award-winning roof terrace, with breathtaking views across Holland Park and the heart of London beyond."'

We had extracted ourselves from Colton's presence with some difficulty, after he had offered to come with us to help find Evie and then made a series of increasingly grandiose offers to call his dad, the vice-chancellor of the university, the Metropolitan Police and the US Embassy to enlist their help. His father, he claimed, was some business mogul who had made a substantial donation to Queen Anne's fund-raising efforts and that gave him influence at the university's top table. I wasn't sure how much of it was bluster and bullshit, but I asked him to hold fire for the time being.

In the end I'd asked Colton to be my eyes and ears on campus in case Evie came back. We'd swapped mobile numbers and he'd promised to let me know if he heard anything.

Even after a conversation lasting barely ten minutes it's a relief to get away from him, to put some space between us and his suffocating intensity. I suspected that in his own mind, he didn't feel like he'd done anything wrong or unusual in pursuing Evie, following her, badgering her when she clearly wasn't interested.

'So what did you make of him?' I say to Lucas as we weave through lunchtime traffic.

My son lowers his phone for a minute. 'Reminded me of some of the boys at school. The sporty ones, who think they're brilliant at everything.'

'You'll come across his type more often than you might like. Avoid them, if you can.'

'The way he talked about Evie,' he says quietly. 'As if she owed him something. I didn't like it.'

We head down through Edgware and Mill Hill, sticking right on the speed limits. Lucas finds me a number for Excalibur, the taxi company, and taps it into my phone in the hands-free cradle. But even when I give them the date, place and exact time of Evie's pick-up from campus on 23rd October, the operator flatly refuses to tell me anything about the destination or who made the booking, citing data protection and privacy concerns – even when I explain the family connection and the fact that no one has seen Evie since. I had suspected as much but it was worth a try.

'So,' I say to Lucas after ending the call. 'This hotel. How much does it cost to stay there?'

Lucas taps at the screen of his phone, scrolls with his index finger. 'Room prices start at . . . £895. Is that for, like, a week? A month?'

I shake my head. 'The booking rate would be for one night.'

He turns to me, open-mouthed. 'But you could buy a new Xbox *and* a new bike for that. How can Evie even afford it?'

'That's what we need to find out.'

We descend into an underground car park off Kensington High Street and park the VW, making the last few minutes of the journey on foot. Google Maps leads us to a quiet street off the main thoroughfare, lined with huge white houses, a couple of embassies and – at the most exclusive end – The Royal Pearl Hotel.

It's every bit as expensive-looking as the website suggests: a soaring glass frontage, a huge revolving door, marble floors, chrome and gold everywhere. A luxuriously appointed Christmas tree that must have been at least six metres high, plush sofas spread around the cavernous reception area, a doorman and a valet out front, attentive bellboys wheeling luggage to the lifts and sharp-suited staff greeting guests at a huge curving reception desk.

'*Woah,*' Lucas says, a note of awe in his voice.

We stand across the street for a few minutes, hands shoved into the pockets of our coats, watching the smooth efficiency of the staff serving lunch to a handful of guests in a brasserie section that faces onto the street. I had never stayed in a place like this. Nor – to the best of my knowledge before today – had Evie. We had shared a few three-star rooms on family holidays from time to time, and me and Evie had spent the night at a Travelodge last year when we attended the university open day in Edinburgh. But nothing like this. Nothing even close.

'So are we going in then, Mum?' Lucas gives me a gentle nudge with his elbow. 'Now?'

'First, we need to get something to eat,' I say. 'Then we'll make a plan.'

There is a chic little Italian brasserie called Luciani's directly across the street: it's warm and welcoming, with a pleasant smell of fresh dough and ground coffee beans. We find a table in the window and order lunch, keeping an eye on the comings and goings at The Royal Pearl. From his rucksack, Lucas produces a handful of the notebooks Evie had left behind in her room and begins flicking through them, page by page.

I order a couple of paninis, a flat white for me and an orange San Pellegrino for Lucas. As the waiter is scribbling our order on his pad, I pull one of the A4 printed pictures of Evie from my backpack and ask whether he recognises her. But he offers only a shrug and a shake of his head.

Once the waiter is out of earshot, I take out the piece of paper Farley had slipped into the pocket of Evie's denim jacket and lay it out on the table, smoothing the creases. I take out my phone, carefully tapping the eleven digits and selecting the 'loudspeaker' option. I put a finger to my lips and Lucas nods an acknowledgement. Both of us stare at the screen, willing the call to connect.

Please don't be out of service like Evie's number. Please don't be another dead end.

The call clicks as it connects and starts to ring. Once, twice, three times. Another soft *click* – and then silence.

I lean down nearer to the mouthpiece of my phone.

'Hello?' There is only silence on the other end of the line. 'Hello?'

I jab a finger into my left ear to block out the background noise of the brasserie, and I'm about to say it for a third time when a voice cuts in.

A woman's voice.

'Who is this?'

21

A jolt of pure nervous energy makes me sit up straighter, holding the phone closer to my ear.

'My name's Lauren Wingfield,' I say quickly, the words almost falling over each other. 'I'm Evie Wingfield's mum? I think this might be the number Evie had down as her emergency contact and the thing is, she's missing, she left her uni course and—'

'How did you get this number?'

'It was her emergency contact at Queen Anne's University, she's a student there. Or she was. Her phone's been out of service and I just really need to get a message to her, to know that she's OK? I would be so grateful if you could put me in touch with her.'

There is silence on the line, a long moment of dead air, and for a moment I think we've been cut off.

'Hello?' I say. 'Are you still there?'

The voice returns, a little softer now. 'Evie, you said?'

I'm momentarily distracted by a white-aproned waiter arriving at the table with our drinks. 'Yes, could you ask her to—'

'And where did you say you were calling from?'

Lucas raises a hand to catch my attention. He's shaking his head.

I mouth a question to him: *What?* He mouths back: *Don't tell her.*

'I'm ... here on campus at the uni.' I hold the phone a little closer. 'Do you have a new number for Evie, by any chance?'

There is another pause, then a click. I check the screen: she's terminated the call. Reaching for my coffee, I realise my hand is shaking with adrenaline.

'Well, *that* was weird,' Lucas says.

'Why were you shaking your head?' I ask him. 'When she asked where we were?'

'Standard red flag, isn't it?' He shrugs his small shoulders. 'We did it in PSHE at school: any time some randomer starts asking where you are, where you live, it's pretty much always a bad sign. They're probably some weirdo, somewhere, trying to . . . you know. Do whatever weirdos do. Delete, block, do not engage – that's what Miss McGurty says we should do.'

I sip my flat white, struck by this flash of maturity from my twelve-year-old. Evie often accused me of babying her little brother, of spoiling him as the younger sibling, and perhaps I had been guilty of that from time to time. But he was a smart kid, he paid attention, he *listened*.

'PSHE? Just remind me.'

'Personal, social, health and economic education,' he says. 'It's mostly really lame. But some of it's all right.'

Our food arrives and we both tuck in, Lucas tearing into his cheese and ham panini with gusto. Mine is sizzling hot, mingling smells of melted mozzarella, prosciutto and basil pesto rising up from the plate making me realise just how hungry I am.

'Anyway,' I say, swallowing the first bite, 'the lady on that number isn't some random person from the internet. She's a way of getting in touch with Evie.'

'Yeah, but all she did was ask you questions.' He points at my phone. '*Who are you? How did you get this number? Where are you?* She didn't actually *tell* you anything. Like I said: weird. Who even was she? Did you recognise her voice?'

I shake my head. In truth, there had been almost nothing in her voice to distinguish it. A flat Thames Valley accent, not

London but not posh either. Vanilla-plain in a way that gave no clues. She wasn't young, but she wasn't old either, perhaps somewhere between thirty and fifty. There had been no sounds in the background, no ambient noise at her end that might give a clue to where she was. In any case, who was I kidding? She clearly didn't want to help. This woman was the only direct link I had to my missing child – and she was a total stranger.

I call her back twice all the same, ready with a couple of follow-up questions to keep her on the line, my heart sinking as it goes to a robotic voicemail each time. I leave my name and number, more in hope than expectation, before sending the same information by text. Lucas was right – and there was something else strange among the few words the mystery woman had spoken.

Evie, you said?

Almost as if she had to confirm it, as if she wasn't sure. Or as if she knew Evie but not all that well. Common sense suggested that if you called someone's emergency contact – effectively their next of kin – they'd know that person closely. There would be an instant connection, an urgency, at least an acknowledgement of shared concern. But that wasn't the vibe I'd got from the brief conversation with this woman. Quite the opposite, in fact.

We both turn our attention back to The Royal Pearl across the street, where things seem to be quietening down. I can still see more staff than guests through the huge glass frontage: valet, doorman, bellboy, receptionist, waiter, all moving quickly and efficiently to ensure the bubble of Kensington luxury remained intact.

Lucas chews, swallows, takes another huge bite of cheese and ham as if he's not eaten in days. 'Can't we just go in and, like, ask someone what room she's in? Tell them it's an emergency, or something?'

'She probably won't still be there now, with those room rates – not unless she's won the lottery. But they should have a record of when she stayed, and who with and how long for.'

'And they'll tell us that, will they?'

I give him a half-smile. 'If we ask them the right way – I just need to figure out a plan. You remember what I do at work, don't you?'

'Something boring for the government,' he says, his mouth full of panini. 'In an office, like, for the counter . . . something team.'

'Counter-fraud team,' I say. 'And it's not *all* boring. Sometimes we do investigations, to catch people breaking the rules and putting others at risk.'

He nods towards the hotel. 'So, are *they* breaking the rules?'

'I don't know,' I say. 'But there's something very weird about Evie coming here.'

As we watch, a lime-green Lamborghini growls into the pull-in at the front of the hotel and disgorges a paunchy fifty-ish man in a crinkled blazer and jeans who tosses the keys to a waiting valet. From the passenger side, a young woman emerges in a stunning belted camel coat and killer heels. She's tall, slim, beautiful – and less than half his age. The man pats her on the backside and takes her hand, leading her through the huge automatic revolving doors into the lobby. They angle left towards a long shining bank of lifts and are lost to sight.

A pulse of nausea rises up my throat and I put the rest of my panini down on the plate, half eaten.

I remember something I'd read in the paper about those websites, where older wealthy men could hook up with young women. *Sugar daddies.* At the time I'd assumed it was very much a niche thing and been surprised at just how *many* such sites had proliferated in the last few years, operating online in plain sight. Some that specified men with a net worth of over £500,000, others aimed at men who were still married or looking for a 'significant age gap' with their other half. And the young women were referred to as . . . what was it? *Sugar babies.* I suppress a shudder.

Lucas has almost finished his lunch already. 'What's the matter, Mum? Are you all right?'

'Full up.' I push my plate towards him. 'You have the rest.'

One of the sugar daddy websites, I remember with a pang of disgust, specialised in matching female students with men willing to 'support their studies'. Had Evie been particularly short of money? No more than most of her peers – at least I didn't think so. She'd taken out all the usual loans and had some savings from her job, plus a bit of help from her grandma.

'I've been thinking about that Colton guy.' Lucas gives the remains of my panini a suspicious sniff, wrinkles his nose and puts it back down on the plate. He's strictly vanilla when it comes to food and the prosciutto and pesto are probably beyond his comfort zone. 'I know he was a bit of a nob and everything, but maybe that wasn't the only reason she wasn't interested in being his girlfriend or whatever.' He's blushing. 'Maybe it was also because she was already . . . y'know. Attached.'

'Tyler said they'd split up ages ago.'

'Not him. Maybe someone else.'

'Hmm.' There had also been the postcard we'd found in her room. *Let me count the ways . . .* Signed with a single mysterious S. 'I was just thinking that.'

'Assuming Colton was even telling the truth about this hotel.'

'Only one way to find out,' I say, signalling to the waiter for our bill. 'Come on, I've had an idea.'

22

'Let me do the talking, OK?'

My son nods his agreement as we stand on the pavement opposite The Royal Pearl. We wait to let a Bentley saloon with tinted windows pass and then cross over Thurland Street to the hotel, Lucas staying close by my side. A tall, neatly bearded door-man – impeccably dressed in a dark grey suit and tie, a heavy overcoat with a red trim and a top hat – gives us a small nod of greeting as we step into the automatic revolving door. His broad face is impassive, even though I'm keenly aware that we must look rather different to the hotel's usual clientele.

Emerging into the warmth on the other side of the door is like walking into a palace, everything smooth and clean and pol-ished to a high shine, fresh-cut flowers in handsome marble vases on every surface, footsteps echoing, soft classical music playing somewhere high above us. The cavernous reception area is less busy now, which I guess is because last night's guests have gone and there seems to be a post-lunch lull before the mid-afternoon check-ins start to arrive. Fortunately, staff numbers seem to have dipped too. There are only two members of staff on reception now, a woman of about my age having an animated conversation in French with a small group of expensively dressed female guests, and a younger guy typing on a computer at the other end of the long curving desk.

Good. I angle towards the young guy. He's in his early twenties, also dressed in a dark grey suit and perfectly knotted tie, with a waistcoat and a name badge on his lapel that reads 'Mariusz' next to two small flags – one Union Jack and another I don't recognise, a tricolour of yellow, green and red.

'Hello,' I say brightly. 'I wonder if you could help me?'

'Of course, madam.' He stops typing and looks up to give me his full attention. 'Good afternoon and welcome to The Royal Pearl. Checking in?'

'Not today, no.' I smooth out my Berkshire vowels into the poshest accent I can manage. 'My daughter tells me *wonderful* things about your hotel, though. She says it's the best in London.'

He gives me a professional smile. 'Absolutely. Thank you, madam, I'm so pleased your daughter enjoyed her stay.'

'I'm actually here on her behalf.' I return his smile. 'There was one small issue, the last time she stayed.'

'Issue?'

'She mislaid something very precious. A bracelet, very special to her and to me – I suppose you could say it's a family heirloom. I was hoping that it might have been handed in by a member of staff, we'd be *desperately* grateful to have it back.'

Beside me, Lucas helps himself to a mint from a large white bowl on the reception desk, unwrapping the sweet and slipping it into his mouth before anyone can object.

'Of course,' Mariusz says. 'I'm very sorry to hear that. If you could just give me your daughter's name?' His accent is softened with practice but still discernible, something eastern European, perhaps. 'Then I can see if anything is logged on the system from her last visit, anything that has been held for safekeeping by the concierge. If I could just ask you to confirm your ID?'

The concierge. It's a far cry from the bin liners full of Evie's possessions laid out in a basement office at the university. This place is a far cry from anywhere Evie has experienced before. Or me, for that matter.

I spell out Evie's first and second names, sliding my driver's licence across the polished marble reception. He studies it, typing in the surname letter by letter.

'Thank you so much, Mrs Wingfield.'

His fingers tap at the keyboard and then he pauses, frowns, types some more. Pauses again. Peers more closely at my driver's licence and repeats the process.

'Err . . . I'm so sorry Mrs Wingfield but I don't seem to have a record for your daughter on the system. My apologies.'

I hear an echo of Farley's words in his voice. *No record of your daughter on the system.* My firstborn child: the ghost.

'She's definitely been here,' I say a little more forcefully. 'Try October twenty-third, that was one of her last visits.'

But he's shaking his head. 'I've . . . interrogated the last three months but there's no record of this name on the system, I'm afraid. Are you sure your daughter was not a guest at another hotel nearby?'

'I'm *quite* sure.' I give him my best withering gaze. 'She was very specific. All of your guests have to sign in, don't they?'

'That's correct, madam.'

'Then check it again. Please.'

He looks at me, then glances across at his colleague – who is still busy – before returning to his keyboard. More typing, followed by another resigned shake of his head.

'I'm afraid there is no record under that name. My apologies.'

Shit. But this can't be a dead end. It *can't* be. I feel the weight of dread tugging at my limbs, the sense of falling further and further behind, of stumbling down a platform as a train picks up speed and pulls further and further away. There *must* be something here.

'Please check that date I gave you,' I say. 'October twenty-third. You must have a record of her arrival.'

Mariusz shakes his head again, his mouth set in a hard, flat line. 'I'm sorry, the bookings system doesn't let me check that kind of thing, madam. Now if I could ask you to—'

'What about CCTV? You have cameras, yes?'

Lucas, who has remained silent for the whole of this exchange so far, says something beside me. A single word under his breath, too quiet for me to make out.

'What is it, Lucas?'

'Hicks,' he says. 'She might have signed in as Evie Hicks.'

I stare at him for a moment, this surname hanging between us like an unwelcome visitor. A name I'd not thought of for years, since consigning it to the past: their father's name. A father he had never really known, apart from a couple of old photographs.

'How come?' I say quietly. 'What makes you say that?'

'Her notebooks, from that bag of her stuff,' he says, helping himself to another mint. 'In the back of one of them there were loads of signatures, page after page of them, like she'd been prac-tising. But not her real one. Evie Hicks instead.'

I relay the alternative name to Mariusz behind the desk, who returns once again to his keyboard.

'Ah,' he says with a broad smile of relief. 'Yes. Here she is: Evie Hicks. We have several bookings since the end of September.'

The smile fades a little. 'But I'm . . . not seeing a record of any property logged with the concierge. I'm sorry.'

'Do you mind if I have a quick look?' I point at his monitor, the thrill of confirmation buzzing in my chest. 'It would be ever so helpful – I just need to check something.'

He reaches up to his monitor and for a second I think he's going to flip it around and show me the screen. Then he seems to remem-ber something, his hand dropping back to the desk.

'I'm afraid I'm not permitted to—'

'I just need to see the name of the person she was staying with. It's very important.'

'As I said, madam, it is not permitted to divulge the personal information of guests to third parties. Perhaps your daughter would be the best source for these kind of . . . details?'

'The thing is, Mariusz, I can't ask my daughter.' I take one of the A4 printouts from my rucksack and lay it out on the reception desk: a recent picture of Evie with my mobile number beneath it. 'I can't ask her because she's missing. Since staying here, in your hotel.'

It wasn't strictly true, but he wasn't to know that.

His mouth opens, closes again. 'Missing?'

'And there's something else you should know about her. My daughter was brought here by a man significantly older than her, for reasons you can probably imagine. She's been here a number of times over the past three months, as your records show. And she's only fifteen. *Fifteen*. She might look older than that, but she's still a child.'

23

It's another untruth, a bigger one, but it seems to have the desired effect.

He glances hesitantly towards his older colleague at the other end of the long, curving reception desk. She still has her hands full with the trio of highly coiffured French women, and their animated conversation seems to have turned into some kind of disagreement.

'Fifteen,' I say again. 'In the eyes of the law, she's a child. Which means the man who brought her here – your guest – is committing a criminal offence on your premises. And it makes this hotel complicit in that crime.'

The colour is draining from his face. 'I have to ... talk to my manager.'

'No you don't, Mariusz.' I gesture to his monitor. 'Just show me what's on that screen and I'll be gone. I won't involve the police, won't embarrass the hotel or let the media know that it's being used to groom vulnerable teenage girls. I won't get you in trouble with your boss. I just need to know who Evie was here with, name and address, then I'll be gone.'

'If you'll give me a moment, madam?'

'Five seconds,' I say. 'That's all. Turn that screen around for five seconds, then I'll be gone and you'll hear no more about it.'

He picks up his desk phone, hits a number and turns away, speaking quietly into the mouthpiece. Replacing the receiver, a tense silence draws out between us. Neither willing to budge.

'Please,' I say finally. 'Do you have a sister, Mariusz? A girlfriend? Evie is just like them. She's young and she's missing. I'm a mother trying to find her child. Please help me.'

He's about to reply when another member of staff appears from a side door. He's older, with a neatly shaved head, a jet-black goatee and the brisk, confident stride of a manager.

Mariusz signals him over and they have a brief whispered conversation that I can't quite hear.

The manager, whose name badge reads 'Vincenzo', turns to me coolly.

'Madam.' He places both hands palm-down on the reception desk. 'I'm afraid I'm going to have to ask you to leave the premises.'

'Of course,' I say. 'As soon as you tell me what I need to know.'

'I don't wish to involve my colleagues in security, but I will if you don't exit the building voluntarily.'

'Just tell me who's been bringing my daughter here.'

'That's against company policy, madam.'

Three things happen then, in the same moment.

Vincenzo raises his arm to signal to someone behind us – the doorman, presumably – with an impatient flicking of his fingers. I push my home-made 'Missing' poster towards him across the desk. And in that same handful of seconds, Lucas makes a strange noise beside me. Something between a cough and a rasp. Turning, I realise he has one hand on his throat, the other fist opening to reveal two of the green-and-white striped mint wrappers. Before I can say anything, his knees buckle and he flops backwards onto the smooth marble floor, his open hand slapping against the marble with an audible *smack*.

Everything else recedes into the distance. Everything is gone, the hotel, the desk, the staff, even thoughts of Evie. All gone.

Because my son is choking. He can't breathe.

I drop to one knee beside him. 'Lucas, baby, what is it? Something in your throat? Can you speak?'

He gives a weak shake of his head, eyelids already fluttering, his glasses askew. Another horrible, dry, pinhole gasp and suddenly I know what's happening.

An allergic reaction.

Oh, God. How come I didn't know?

The words leap into my brain. *Anaphylactic shock.* Jesus, please no. He needs . . . he needs, what? An injection, adrenaline, is it? An ambulance? I feel a shout of helpless panic gathering in my own throat, of abject terror and thoughts scattering in every direction, *I should never have brought him with me, should never have let him come along today, please God don't let me lose both of my children, it's too cruel.* And then, down here below the desk, where Vincenzo can't see us—

—my son gives me a wink.

Just one. Very definite. A wink, like when he tries to wind his sister up or tell one of his silly jokes at the dinner table. For a second I wonder whether it's part of his convulsion, this reaction, or whether I've imagined it entirely.

Then he flashes me a mischievous smile and it's all I can do not to smile back.

He rolls backwards, full length onto the floor, clutching at his throat, making a horrible rasping sound like the death rattle of a sixty-a-day smoker. His eyelids are fluttering again as if he's about to pass out.

'Madam?' Vincenzo's voice is behind me. 'Does the child require medical attention?'

'Yes!' I shout it without turning around. 'He's severely allergic to whatever was in your bloody mints! Call an ambulance!'

One of the French ladies lets out a high-pitched squeal of alarm, another grips the edge of the reception desk as if she might collapse in sympathy. The third one clatters towards us in high heels, barking commands in French towards the staff.

I roll Lucas onto his side, into the recovery position, glancing up at the desk. Mariusz is nowhere to be seen and Vincenzo looks panic-stricken at the thought of a child expiring in the pristine lobby of his hotel.

'First aid kit!' I shout at him. 'Trauma kit, EpiPen, whatever you have, go and get it NOW!' To another hovering member of staff I shout: 'Call a bloody ambulance!'

The high-heeled tourist is talking to me now, a machine-gun flurry of rapid French I can't understand beyond repeated use of the word '*allergie*'.

I shout over my shoulder, 'Where's that bloody first aid kit?'

The French lady crouches beside us, surprisingly calm and unflustered, placing her index and forefinger on Lucas's neck as if she's checking for a pulse, still talking at me while she does it.

As staff either scatter in all directions or gather around my stricken son, I stand up quickly and dart around the reception desk as if looking for something to help him. The computer screen Mariusz had been working is black and I shake the mouse to wake it up, the monitor flashing back into life. There. *Guest Record Form. Name, address, email, date of birth, payment method.* I pull out my phone and snap three quick shots of the screen. There is no time to check whether the pictures are in focus.

Vincenzo is on his phone, talking fast, another member of staff beside him with a hand over her mouth, Mariusz hurrying from a side room carrying a red canvas first-aid kit.

I shove the phone in my pocket and run back around the edge of the desk. 'OK Lucas let's go! Let's go!'

He rolls over and scrambles to his feet, leaving the French lady open-mouthed in his wake. He ducks under Vincenzo's outstretched arm and I dodge around the grabbing hand of the doorman as we sprint, together, towards the big glass door.

'Madam!' Vincenzo's voice is a weirdly high-pitched shout, concern and confusion starting to give way to anger. 'Madam! Please stop! The boy!'

I grab Lucas's hand and we angle towards the door just as it slides open for another guest. And then we're out, back outside in the biting cold and still running as Vincenzo's shouts recede behind us.

24

We don't stop running until we're back on Kensington High Street. By then, my lungs are burning and my legs heavy, so we duck into a coffee shop and wait for a few minutes in case anyone from The Royal Pearl appears.

'That was *mad*!' Lucas says. 'Thought that bald manager guy was going to have a fit when I got up and started running.'

He tells me the idea came from a boy in his year who had a nut allergy and had suffered a reaction in the school dining hall in the summer term. A trip to the sick bay and the rest of the day off had been enough to put him right, Lucas says, but the episode had clearly made an impression on my son.

As the relief of escape subsides, a niggling worry takes its place. Creating a scene at the hotel had been reckless, possibly foolish – would the staff have followed us out, or were they still looking for us now? Would they call the police? Could they track us down another way?

I wait until we're safely back in the car before looking at the pictures I'd taken of the screen in the hotel. The first two are blurry and indistinct but the third one is pin-sharp and I pinch the image to zoom in on the name the room had been booked under. *S. Lawler*. My mind spins back to the postcard we'd found in Evie's bedroom, the postcard signed off with a single *S*. The address he'd given to the hotel is *220 Belvue Road, Northolt*. It's an Uxbridge postcode, not a part of the capital I know well, but the maps app on my phone says it's a ten-mile drive west that will take us close to an hour. A fresh bubble of euphoria makes my hand shake as I study the route. *We have an address. Evie might be there.* Even if she won't come home with us today, just to talk to her, see her, to know she's safe would be enough. For now, at least.

The date of birth makes him twenty-six – seven years older than Evie. In a way I'm relieved that he's not forty, or fifty or sixty, not some seedy older man who had hooked up with her on one of those awful websites. Although there can't be many twenty-six-year-olds who could afford to stay at The Royal Pearl.

But still, a stranger. And I was *assuming* it was a man. S. Lawler could just as well be female, I supposed. Either way, this was the person Evie had checked into the hotel with on the day she left campus, and several times before that too – assuming that it was the same individual each time. The name is not familiar to Lucas either.

We drive up and out of the car park and find a quiet side street where the 5G signal is stronger. I text Farley to ask if he can do me a favour, checking the name and address against the student records system or any other file he might have. I guess it was possible Lawler might have some link to the university, as a postgraduate student, a current or former member of staff. I send the details to my mum as well, in case she's heard the name before.

Lucas spends a few minutes on Google but can't nail down any likely matches among the first few dozen results.

'Do you think Evie might be living there?' Lucas gives up on his phone for the moment, plugging it into the car charger. 'If that's like, this guy's house?'

'Maybe,' I say. 'I hope so.'

'But if he's got a house, why go to a hotel? Especially one as expensive as The Royal whatever-it-was?'

'Good question. Only three reasons I can think of: either you've got more money than sense, or someone else is paying the bill.'

'And what's the third one?'

'That you're trying to impress someone.'

* * *

Lucas is distracted on the drive, fiddling with the radio, trying to find a song that he likes.

'Mum?' he says finally, switching it off. 'Are we going to get in trouble?'

'For what?'

'That thing back at the hotel.'

It's a question I've already asked myself, but there is no sense in having him worry too.

'I doubt it, Lucas.' I glance over at him. 'It's more bother than it's worth for them to get anyone else involved. And besides, I told them Evie was fifteen, so they're probably not in a rush to call the police.'

We're on the elevated section of the A40, giving a view down into the enveloping sprawl of west London. Below us, long rows of tightly packed houses, squat office blocks and shops roll by among the maze of streets. I try to imagine the place where S. Lawler lives, the kind of place you'd live if you were a man who could afford to stay at The Royal Pearl in Kensington. And it begged the question again: why check into a hotel if you lived barely ten miles away, in the same city? According to Lucas's quick study of Google Maps, 220 Belvue Road is a large building so I assume it's a set of apartments, a block of luxury flats with a couple of penthouses on the top floor.

Eventually, the map tells me to get off at the next junction and we take a slip road, down into some kind of industrial estate with a retail park at one end. Northolt just seems to be another of London's endless suburbs, each one blending into the next, and it's not quite what I expected. Nothing *wrong* with it, but not quite posh enough, somehow.

We follow the Maps app through more turns and junctions until it announces *your destination is on the left* and I pull up in a bus stop.

'What?' Lucas looks around, confused. 'He lives *here*?'

Belvue Road is a long, curving street with apartment buildings on one side facing small office units on the other. Number 220 is on the office side, a nondescript three-storey brick building with a small car park, sandwiched in between a self-storage company and the crowded forecourt of a van rental place.

'Maybe he works here.' I undo my seat belt. 'Come on, let's see if we can track him down.'

Lucas and I walk across the road, push open the door into a small glass-fronted lobby area, furnished with six plastic chairs like a GP's waiting room. A solid door on the far wall is closed, a keypad unit on the wall next to it glowing with a solitary red LED light. A short reception desk is manned by a bespectacled fifty-something man in a grey jumper, YFH Ltd embroidered in small green initials over his left chest.

He looks up with a smile as we approach.

'Hello, madam,' he says brightly, with the air of someone who's waited all day for someone to chat to. 'How can I help you?'

'I'd like to speak to Mr Lawler, please.'

He raises an eyebrow. 'Does he ... work here? One of the temps from the agency? Been a bit of a revolving door with temps recently.'

'Works here or lives here, I'm not sure yet.'

'No one lives here, madam, even though it feels like it sometimes.' He gives me a grin, rolls the chair to a monitor on the desk. After a moment tapping at the keyboard, he asks me to spell the name. 'Sorry, no one of that name on the staff roster at the moment.'

'You're sure? This is the address I have for him.'

'Ah. For him, or for his company?'

I frown.

'His company?'

'This place—' he indicates the small waiting room with a general wave of his hand '—YFH Limited – it's a registered office service, madam. Your Firm Here.' Seeing my frown, he adds: 'You're aware that every UK company has to have an official, physical address in the UK which has to be listed on the public register at Companies House?'

'Yes, I'm aware of that.'

He ploughs on as if he's not heard me.

'But a lot of people – if they work from home, for example – don't want their home address on the Companies House website for every Tom, Dick and Harry to find in ten seconds flat. So they pay us a small annual fee and use 220 Belvue Road instead. We handle any physical mail too: my colleagues in the back office will open, sort, scan and email it on to customers within—'

'How many?'

'I'm sorry?'

'How many companies use this place as their official, legal address?'

'Just over twenty-seven thousand, at last count.'

My heart plummets. Twenty-seven *thousand*. A needle in a haystack.

'And Mr Lawler runs one of them?'

He gives me an apologetic shrug. 'I've no idea, madam, but all of that kind of thing is confidential information, I'm afraid. Sorry.'

Back in the car we sit in silence for a minute, the windscreen slowly steaming up with our warm breath and obscuring the view of this grey London street.

'I don't understand,' Lucas says. 'What that man was saying. What does it mean?'

I let my head fall back against the headrest. 'You know when you were younger and you used to play pass the parcel at a party, you'd unwrap a layer, thinking it was the last one and you were going to get the prize, only to find there are lots more layers underneath? That's what this is. A way to keep people at arm's length.'

'OK,' my son says, wiping condensation from his window to look back at the brick office building. 'So it's like, a dead end. Isn't it?'

'Not necessarily,' I say. 'We just have work out how to peel back the next layer.'

EVIE

Five months earlier

Evie felt underdressed the moment she walked in: that feeling of being somewhere you didn't *quite* belong. She had 'borrowed' the outfit – a black scoop-neck blouse and black trousers, taken from the back of her mum's wardrobe – and bought a new pair of shoes to go with it, but she still felt like an impostor. As if someone was going to clamp a hand on her shoulder any minute and tell her she was in the wrong place.

Getting changed and doing her makeup in the train toilet had been awkward but she'd managed it; she just needed to remember to pick up her bag from the luggage place on the way home. Scott hadn't mentioned staying over, and she really wasn't sure what she'd have said if he had.

Opium was not easy to find – even with his directions – an underground cocktail bar tucked away in a Soho side street full of expensive gift shops and designer boutiques. It was warm and softly lit, with deep-backed sofas and a low pulse of drum and bass music – and Scott was already there, jacket off, standing up as she walked over to the corner table. Her self-consciousness disappeared as soon as he took her coat and kissed her softly on the cheek, one hand light on her elbow.

His crisp white shirt was open at the neck and he smelled *amazing*. Forest and sky and ocean, blended to an intoxicating mix.

'You look incredible,' he said. 'So good to see you again.'

A bud of joy blossomed in the centre of her chest. She was about to reply when she felt a hand on her shoulder.

'Hey.' A half-familiar male voice from behind her. 'Evie?'

She turned to face the newcomer, desperately hoping that she was wrong. That her memory was playing tricks on her.

It wasn't.

Because somehow, the muscle-bound figure of Colton Ryczek was there in the bar too. Of all the places in the city he could have been, somehow the American had walked in behind her. Uninvited. Same blond beard, dark blond hair gathered into the same topknot. Grey sweatpants, backpack and a skimpy Gold's Gym vest that showed off his bulk.

'Oh,' she said, the bloom of joy wilting, fading away. 'Colton. Hi . . . What are you—'

'So,' he said. 'How's it been going? How've you been? Thought I'd stay in the UK over summer instead of going back to the States, you know? So *lame* over there compared to London.' He had the same over-caffeinated, overpowering tone that she remembered from their first meeting. 'So I figured we could catch up over the summer and hang out but you've not been returning my messages? Or my calls – left you a bunch of voicemails for like, the last few weeks. You change your cell number?'

'No,' she said with a tight smile. 'Just been really busy with exams and everything—'

'There's so much cool stuff I wanted to show you, all these little corners of the city that most people never see, not even Londoners who live here their whole life. So much history and art and I figured we could get together one day. I can be your tour guide.'

'Colton, it's nice to see you but I'm actually just meeting a . . . good friend here for drinks.'

'What?' His brow furrowed. 'Who?'

Scott stepped forward.

'Hi.' He offered his hand. 'I'm Scott, Evie's boyfriend. Nice to meet you.'

Evie registered the word with a wash of sweet surprise, like sunshine on her skin. *Boyfriend.* The first time either of them had said it. But there was no time to enjoy the moment.

Colton snorted. 'What?'

Scott dropped his hand.

'We were going to have a quiet drink.' More pointedly, he added: 'Just the two of us.'

'Right. Only, she never mentioned you. Not once.'

'She never mentioned you either, my friend.'

The American took a step closer, squaring up to the taller man. 'I'm not your friend, dumbass.'

'How did you know Evie was here? Have you been following her?'

'None of your damn business.'

'It *is* my business if you're going to—'

Colton put out both meaty palms and shoved Scott hard in the chest, propelling him backwards until he collided with the arm of the sofa and pitched sideways onto his hands and knees. Someone on the next table gasped and all conversation in the bar seemed to stop as Scott hit the floor. Out of nowhere, a black-shirted bouncer appeared, twisting Colton's wrist up behind his back without a word and marching him towards the exit.

And then he was gone, shouting something unintelligible as he was escorted up the stairs.

Evie turned to Scott, who was getting gingerly to his feet, brushing dust from the knees of his trousers.

'God,' she said. 'Are you all right? Are you hurt?'

'Only my pride.' He gave her an embarrassed grin. 'It's fine.'

'That was mad. I can't believe he did that. You sure you're OK?'

Scott nodded. 'Strange guy, though. How do you know him?'

'He was the campus guide when I went to an open day at the uni. Showed me round for a few hours, somehow got my number off me and he's kept on messaging ever since. Calling me. Bit of a stalker, really.'

'Are you OK?' Scott touched her shoulder. 'You're shaking.'

'Just a bit of a shock.'

'The door staff won't let him in again.' He glanced towards the stairs, as if making sure. 'Come on, I think we both need a drink.'

* * *

Evie's hand shook as she sipped the blueberry mojito, the tall slender glass filled with crushed ice and lime. They had moved further into the depths of the bar, into a private area separated from the rest of the customers and by the time her drink was finished she felt the tension start to drain away, confident that Colton Ryczek would not reappear. Not tonight, anyway.

'Earlier,' Evie said, stirring the ice in her empty glass. 'What you said to Colton about us . . . being together.'

Scott held a hand up. 'Didn't want to be presumptuous, but I could tell you didn't like the guy and I thought it would get him to back off. Sorry if I overstepped the mark.'

'No, no, don't apologise.' She felt herself blushing, glad of the bar's low lighting. 'I liked it. What you said.'

Scott smiled, signalled for a waiter to bring two more drinks. Then he reached into his jacket and produced a slim black box tied with a black ribbon.

'What's this?' Evie put her glass down.

He shrugged. 'It's just a . . . a small thing. Something I thought you'd like.'

Inside the box, nestled in a bed of crushed black velvet, was the most beautiful bracelet she'd ever seen. A perfect silver circle that gleamed in the soft candlelight of the bar. She held out her wrist and he put it on her, his strong, warm hand holding hers.

'Platinum suits you,' he said. 'It really does.'

And just like that, it was as if they had not been interrupted at all. As if it had only been a couple of hours, rather than a couple of weeks, since they last saw each other face to face. They ordered snacks and the conversation flowed easily, effortlessly, about holidays and friends, work and home and family. Both Scott's parents and his older brother were doctors, he told her, and he'd felt a certain pressure to follow in the 'family business'. His father had never said he was disappointed – but Scott sometimes sensed it, even now.

'What about you?' he said. 'You never talk about your dad.'

Evie looked down into her glass. 'He died when I was young.'

'I'm so sorry.' He covered her hand with his. 'I didn't realise. It was thoughtless of me to ask.'

'It's OK. I never really knew him, don't really remember him at all. I think most of what I remember is probably stuff I've imagined in the years since, you know? What I would have liked him to be, rather than what he was.'

The waiter brought their snacks – delicate spring rolls, shrimp toast and rice crackers – and she steered the conversation into different waters.

'You've never actually told me what your job involves, Mr Mysterious.'

He shrugged. 'Civil service. Lots of spreadsheets and meetings. Very boring.'

She raised an eyebrow. 'Sounds like the sort of thing Jason Bourne would say.'

'Believe me,' Scott said, 'my job is a million miles away from Bourne. A *million* miles. Shall we get some more drinks?'

25

We park up in a nearby McDonald's, where Lucas and I spend a fruitless hour on our phones ploughing through the Companies House website in search of something connected to S. Lawler. But it won't let us combine his name and address in the same search, so each effort brings up thousands of entries, thousands of individuals, of companies set up or dissolved over the last forty-plus years. As I had feared, it was a needle in a haystack.

Finally, Lucas drops his phone into his lap in disgust.

'The website's rubbish.' Lucas wraps his arms around himself. 'Doesn't even make sense, keeps asking me to log in.'

'Let's go inside,' I say. 'Get a hot drink and warm up.'

Five minutes later we're sitting down at a corner table with a cream-topped hot chocolate and a steaming flat white when my phone chirps with a FaceTime call. *Incoming call from Craig Farley.* I prop the mobile against the wall and hit *accept*.

Farley's white-bearded face fills the screen and I'm surprised by how pleased I am to see him, this man who had been a stranger until a few days ago but had gone out of his way to help me. We run through brief pleasantries before I bring him up to date on where we are, what we've been doing. The office on Belvue Road that turned out to be a perfectly legal address for thousands of different companies.

'Yeah, about that,' he says. 'Thanks for sending the info over. Was going to ping you an email but I thought this would be quicker. Good news and bad news.'

He covers the bad news first: there was only one record of a former student called S. Lawler, from the mid-1990s – and that was a Siobhan Lawler who was now in her fifties, a lawyer living in Vancouver according to alumni records. Neither was he a current or former member of staff, contractor, or official visitor to the campus in any capacity that Farley could identify.

'OK,' I say. 'So what's the good news?'

'The good news is that I'm nosy,' he says with a smile. 'And I don't like questions without answers. I'm also a bit bored, with term being finished and most of the students having gone home.'

'We appreciate any help you can give us, Craig.'

'So . . . we have a duty of care to students when they're here, try to keep them safe, and it's part of my job to do the due diligence on contractors employed to work for the uni: construction people, maintenance, events, catering, anything that involves external workers coming onto campus.' He scratches at his beard. 'The uni pays for the enhanced access package offered by Companies House so we can check and cross-reference for bankruptcies, court judgements, legal issues et cetera.'

'And?' I lean forward, towards my phone's small screen. 'Did you find him?'

He nods. 'Found an S. Lawler listed as director of a company called Piranha Solutions Ltd, registered address at 220 Belvue Road. The date of birth info matches too – it would make him twenty-six years old. There's nothing about the company on Google at all, but I went through the latest financials and there was one thing in the asset listing that you might find useful.' He holds up a sheet of A4 paper. 'A business address. The *real* one.'

* * *

It's almost an hour and a half before we get to Ludlow Avenue, back into the city through stop – start London traffic all the way and rarely getting out of second gear. Lucas scrolls TikTok and Snapchat on his phone as we make our way through Chelsea, down to the river, past Battersea Power Station before crossing the Thames at Lambeth Bridge. The Maps app on my phone guides us east, past Waterloo and the South Bank, looping around Elephant and Castle.

A strange sense of paranoia creeps over me as I drive, a feeling that everyone, everything – every car and traffic light, every tailgating white van, every swerving Deliveroo cyclist and phone-fixated pedestrian – is conspiring against us. All of them working together to make this journey longer, slower, harder than it needs to be. The sense of frustration and paranoia curdles as we slog through traffic and it's not until I'm pulled up at a red traffic light on Borough High Street that it takes on a singular shape, a persistent presence behind me.

A low-riding black saloon, two or three cars back.

A front number plate so dirty that it's illegible, the windscreen virtually opaque with grime. It had been there earlier, I realise with an unpleasant jolt, when we crawled along Millbank. It had been there crossing the bridge, and it was still there now. Always a few cars back, behind us in the same lane. Never dropping away further or overtaking. I try to get a look at the driver but the windscreen is too dirty. Had it been parked up at Belvue Road too? I couldn't be sure.

The light goes green and I accelerate away hard, overtaking the car beside me and undertaking the one after that, nipping through the next traffic light as it turns amber.

The next time I check my rear-view mirror, the black saloon is gone.

Lucas glances up from his phone. 'Is it much further, Mum?'

'Just a bit longer,' I say. 'You ready to be my spotter? I'm going to need a sharp pair of eyes soon.'

It's gone five o'clock by the time we're finally heading up through Whitechapel and onto Mile End Road, choked with the ubiquitous London traffic and back-to-back red lights. It's quite a contrast with the conspicuous wealth of Kensington: takeaways and vape stores line both sides of the road, every pulled-down shutter smothered with graffiti. Pedestrians bundled up against the cold hurrying home along crowded pavements, hands thrust into pockets.

Google Maps directs us south off the main road and through a maze of side streets full of tightly packed post-war houses and a huge block of flats, until we finally emerge onto a long road running alongside the railway line. This is more of an industrial area, small warehouses and depots, workshops and storage yards. Only half a mile from the main road but much quieter.

'It's the next right turn,' Lucas says, studying the map on his own phone. 'Just up here. Ludlow Avenue.'

I make the turn, expecting to see a row of houses but it's more of the same: dark, windowless industrial units, only Transit vans and small trucks parked up at the side of the road. The street lights are far apart and struggle to illuminate the spaces in between.

'There aren't many building numbers.' Lucas gestures behind us with a thumb. 'But we passed sixty-something back there.'

'Can this be the right place though?' I pull over beside some kind of scrapyard and check my phone. But I hadn't made a mistake: this *was* the street address Farley had given.

'Just a little bit further, Mum.' My son buzzes his window down and peers into the dark at a dimly lit sign below a security light. 'This one here is ninety-three.'

Lucas counts the properties as we crawl further up the street, telling me to halt in the shadow of a huge warehouse. I can't see a sign, or a number, but Lucas is sure this is the right place. Through a large open gate there is some kind of car park, empty apart from a couple of vehicles pulled up close to the entrance. We sit and watch for a couple of minutes but there are no signs of life.

Lucas wipes condensation from his window. 'Surely he doesn't work *here*.'

'I'm going to have a closer look,' I say. 'D'you want to wait in the car? I'll just be a minute. Looks like it's shut for the day.'

'I'd rather come with you.'

We cross the road and walk through the gates, the chill of the evening air biting at our cheeks. It's walled on three sides into a kind of courtyard, signs in red and black stating CUSTOMER PARKING ONLY – CLAMPING IN OPERATION. The warehouse building is three-storeys high and has no windows, just a long, gently sloping ramp up to a recessed entrance lit by small spotlights. The sign over the door is a stylised graphic of a fire next to a single word: FLAME.

We climb the ramp up to the entranceway, where a double door has been propped open with a wheeled trolley stacked with crates of beer. Above us are the clear plastic hemispheres of a couple of cameras, looking down. From inside, a faint bass beat reaches us.

Then I understand: this place isn't shut for the day – it's just getting ready to open. Because 99 Ludlow Avenue is not an office, or a depot or a storage facility. It's not an industrial unit at all.

It's a nightclub.

26

I push the door that has been propped open with the cases of beer and Lucas follows me inside, into a dark corridor lit intermittently by coloured spotlights. On the right is a countertop recessed into the wall with empty racks of hangers behind it. The cloakroom. The pulse of music gets louder down the corridor until we push through another set of double doors at the far end, into a vast dark space split across multiple levels with dance floors, bars and a stage area, private booths high above us.

Flame nightclub is huge.

Everything – every surface, every wall, every staircase – is painted black and it makes the place feel much bigger on the inside than it looks from outside. Minimal lighting throws every corner into deep shadow – presumably they save the lasers and strobes and everything else until the venue is actually open. The stage is taken up by a DJ setting up behind a desk emblazoned with big fire emojis, but he's absorbed in his headphones and oblivious to our arrival.

A wide staircase leads to a bar that stretches the whole width of the left-hand side, a single member of staff unloading bottles into soft-glowing fridges.

'Hi,' I say. 'Wonder if you can help me?'

The bartender half turns to me, her eyes flicking over me and Lucas. She's wearing a white hoodie and baggy jeans, her blonde hair pulled into two high pigtails.

'Sorry, darlin', we're closed.' She slices open another cardboard box with a small blade and begins rapidly stacking bottles of lager into another fridge. 'Doors open at ten tonight.'

'I was actually looking for someone. A Mr Lawler?'

She shoots me another glance. 'Who?'

'Mr S. Lawler? Is he here?'

'You from the council?'

'No.' I take one of the printouts from my jacket, laying it on the bar. 'I'm looking for my daughter. This is her.'

The woman glances at the picture of Evie for perhaps a second, shaking her head. 'Can't help you, sorry.'

Abruptly, the booming music stops and this high-ceilinged, windowless place is plunged into echoing silence. The only sound the rattle and clink of glass as she continues to load bottles into the fridge in a six-high stack.

'Are you the manager of this place?' I say. 'Do you—'

'Me?' She snorts. 'Nah. I'm just here to fill glasses and take money.'

I put the printout back in my pocket. 'Is there a manager I could talk to? Someone who might be able to help?'

She jerks a thumb over her shoulder, pulls open the door of another fridge and begins filling it. 'Office is back there.'

At the other end of the bar is a black door marked PRI-VATE – STAFF ONLY. I'm about to knock when it swings open, a broad figure filling the doorway. He's in his late twenties with wide-set eyes and a thick neck, heavily muscled through his shoulders and chest. Despite the December chill he's in a short-sleeved white shirt, fabric straining tight against tattooed biceps.

I take an involuntary step back.

'Mr Lawler?'

'Nope,' he says. 'And we're closed.'

'I need to speak to him. It's urgent.'

He considers me for a moment, his eyes flicking briefly to Lucas beside me.

'Well, you're not Old Bill, are you?' He grunts. 'Unless it's Bring Your Brat to Work day. So who are you?'

'My name's Lauren Wingfield, my daughter is Evie Wingfield. Or you might know her as Evie Hicks.'

His eyes narrow. 'And who was this geezer you were looking for again?'

'Mr Lawler.'

He takes a step towards me, crowding me against the corridor wall. A sharp, sour smell radiates from him: testosterone and after-shave and a barely contained temper.

'Don't know him.'

His cockney accent is odd – almost convincing, but not quite. Like a public schoolboy trying to come across as a lad from the wrong side of the tracks.

I hold his gaze, heart starting to thud against my ribs. 'He's listed on the Companies House website as a director of a business operating out of these premises. Does that help?'

His thin lips spread slowly into a humourless grin, displaying a silver front tooth with a diamond stud embedded in it. 'Good effort,' he says. 'So who are you, really?'

'I've told you who I am, and why I'm here. Lawler was at a hotel with my daughter and he's a director of the company that runs this place. Now she's missing so I want to talk to him. Just tell me when he's here next and I'll come back, or you could give me his number?'

'Can't help you,' he says, jerking his head towards the exit. 'Way out's over there.'

'Not until I've spoken to him.'

He ignores me, turns to Lucas. 'What do you think, Harry Potter? Your mum wants to go into the office here so we can have a little chat. You don't mind staying out here for ten minutes, do you, while I give her what she's asking for?' He bends down, puts his big hands on his knees so that he's face to face with Lucas. Then he reaches up and plucks my son's glasses off his nose, puts them on himself, the round black frames ridiculously small on his wide, stubbled features. 'My friend Caz at the bar over there will give you a lemonade while you wait. On the house. So what do you reckon, Harry? Not going to cast a spell on me, are you?'

Lucas shrinks back and it takes a moment for him to find his voice. 'We just want to find my sis—'

'BOO!' The guy bellows it in Lucas's face. 'GOT YOU!'

Lucas stumbles back in shock, flinching against the wall. The guy gives a cackle of laughter but it's cut short as I grab a handful of his ear lobe and drag him backwards towards the door, away from my son.

'Leave him alone!'

'AHHH!' He jerks his head away, putting a hand to his ear. 'Ow! Crazy bitch! The fuck is wrong with you?'

He cocks a huge ring-heavy fist back and I brace myself for the blow, knowing that I'm half his size and too close to dodge away. Then, he drops the fist to his side, glancing over my shoulder. I follow his gaze. Behind us, the bartender has stopped what she was doing and is watching us, a bottle in each hand.

He swipes the glasses from his face and throws them into a corner.

'Stupid bitch.'

'That's me,' I say. 'And what's your name?'

'David fucking Beckham,' he says with a sneer. 'You owe me an earring. And a new shirt.'

There's a smear of blood dripping from his ear lobe onto his white shirt, more on my hand.

'I'm going to keep coming back here, until you tell me how to reach Lawler or I can talk to him. Or I can bring the police next time, if you like?'

'Good luck with that.'

'Or I could just stand on the street out there, telling every one of your punters that you and your mate are exploiting teenagers and . . .' I grope for the right words, for how to articulate something left unspoken until now. 'And trafficking underage girls.'

'Trafficking.' He grunts with amusement. '*Right.*'

'Maybe I'll even get some flyers printed up too. Put up Evie's missing posters right by the front door.'

'All right, calm down, love,' he says. 'Tell you what. Come back when we open tonight and I'll see what I can do, yeah? Me and you can have a proper chat. In private.' He points towards the corridor back to the main entrance. 'Until then, get out of my club.'

27

Lucas and I find a Pizza Express on Mile End Road and I book a twin room at the nearest Premier Inn while we wait for our food to arrive. Both of us are still shaky and wired from the encounter in the nightclub, adrenaline starting to drain away and leave a void in its wake.

Lucas is quiet, distracted, scrolling absently on his phone. Beside my glass of white wine, I have my phone out too – a clear violation of the strict 'no devices at the dinner table' rule that we normally observe at home. I'm trying to satisfy my curiosity about something Farley had said earlier today, some scandal at the university from five or six years ago. I have a vague recollection of the case and it only takes a couple of Google searches to find it.

One of the top tabloid results is '*Star prof in paedo probe*' but there are dozens of other variations too, page after page of results, comment pieces, analyses of his crimes. *A disgraced academic was today handed a fourteen-year jail term after investigators found thousands of child abuse images on computers at his home and workplace.* That was why the university's top brass were super-sensitive about bad publicity, Farley had said. But I couldn't see how there might be any direct link between this jailed professor, Alan Lovelock, and what had happened with Evie.

I call my mum, tell her what we've found today and explain that we're probably going to have to stay overnight in London.

'But where, love?'

'I've found a hotel.'

'Oh.' A pause. 'The two of you?'

'Yes, of course.'

'How's Lucas?'

'He's fine,' I say. 'He's good. Listen, Mum, could you nip over to mine tomorrow morning and put some food down for Bella? I put the cat feeder on for today but it will need refilling tomorrow morning.'

'Already done, love. I popped in earlier. The little furball's fine. Very chatty and vocal, as usual.'

Hearing my mum's voice is like a blast of reality, of normal life, and it makes me feel even more cut off and adrift here in this part of London where everyone is a stranger. We chat for a few minutes longer before I tell her I have to go.

'So we're not going home?' Lucas says quietly, after I've rung off. For the first time I notice that there's a crack in his glasses, a hairline fracture in the corner where they were thrown to the floor. 'We're staying over?'

I turn my phone face down on the table. 'I need to go back to the club when it's open, and it'll be too late to drive home then. We'll get toothbrushes and a few other bits from the Tesco Express. We can go home tomorrow and get your other pair of glasses, but it means you're probably going to miss another day of school.'

Under normal circumstances he'd be reluctant to miss school but he doesn't give any reaction, lapsing into silence again. I can tell he's still preoccupied with the confrontation in the nightclub.

'Are you OK?' I put my hand over his. 'After that guy . . . after what happened?'

He nods, but says nothing.

'Lucas?'

'Can't believe what you did, Mum. Thought he was going to hurt you.'

'He shouldn't have taken your glasses.'

His cheeks redden and he shakes his head. He still won't look at me. 'But he might have battered you. When I thought he was going to hit you I wanted to stop him, to mess him up so badly he'd never do it again.'

I've never heard him talk like this before, with such violence.

'Lucas—'

'But I couldn't do it, Mum.' His voice wobbles. 'I couldn't do anything, I was so scared and I just stood there like an idiot. Like a stupid coward.'

'You're not a coward, Lucas, and it's always better to walk away if you can. Besides, it's not your responsibility to look after me. I'm your mum, I'll look after us both.'

'*You* didn't walk away,' he says in a small voice. 'You pulled his *earring* out.'

'Not on purpose though,' I say, trying to give him a reassuring smile. 'Just gave his ear lobe a bit of a twist and it happened to be in the way.'

He doesn't smile back, just looks up at me with his big brown eyes. The same eyes that had first drawn me to his father when I was the same age as Evie is now.

'I don't want you to go back to that place,' he says suddenly. 'Not on your own. That guy was proper mad.'

'I have to. If we wait until tomorrow morning, it will be closed again.'

'Then I'll come with you.'

I give him a sympathetic smile. 'There will be bouncers on the door this time, they won't let you in because you're under eighteen.'

I do my best to reassure him that there will be less danger later, when the place is busy and there are more bar staff and clubbers and lots of potential witnesses. It's hard to tell whether he believes me or not. I'm not sure I believe it myself.

Our food arrives and while we eat, I make a list of things we need to buy for our impromptu overnight stay in London.

Two hours later I'm back on Ludlow Avenue.

And this time I'm alone.

28

My phone buzzes with another text from Lucas, the fourth since I left him in the twin room at the hotel with strict instructions not to leave and not to answer the door to *anyone* except me – and only when he'd checked through the peephole.

Have you gone in yet?

I type out a quick reply.

In a minute. Turn the TV off and get some sleep now. I'll be back soon x

He texts back a simple *OK* and I shove the phone into the pocket of my jeans.

From across the street, I watch the entrance to Flame for a little longer, as taxis start to drop off young people in their late teens and twenties, others arriving on foot in groups of three or four, some in larger parties of half a dozen or more. The boys are in baggy jeans and T-shirts, the girls in ridiculously short skirts and tiny tops. I want to offer them my coat, tell them to put on some proper clothes and warm up, get inside somewhere before they get hypothermia.

I shake my head. *God, I sound like I'm about ninety-five years old.* It's not that long ago since I was in their shoes, but it feels like centuries ago. Another lifetime.

This time of night is still early for clubbing, I know. At home, since Evie and her friends had started going to nightclubs when they were turning seventeen and could get fake IDs, they would still be at someone's house at this time of night – pre-loading with rosé wine and whisky sours and vodka shots, or 'pre-ing' as they called it, so they could spend as little as possible on expensive club drinks. A measure of insulation against the cold too, I guess. Judging by the excited chatter and shrieks of the young clubbers ahead of me in the queue, they've already been drinking for a few hours tonight too.

Maybe I'll see her here. Evie.

Perhaps I'll catch a glimpse of her wandering in with a group of new friends. Joining the queue with all the others for a night at this big East End nightclub. I study each group of new arrivals, scanning the girls' faces, studying the way they walk, their clothes, for a moment of familiarity. Waiting for one thing that clicks, that tells me the search is over, the one thing that says: *Yes. That's her. That's my Evie.*

But it's another needle in another haystack.

I lock the car behind me and join the queue on the long sloping ramp up into the building, feeling conspicuous in my quilted jacket and jeans, DMs and gloves. Even here, the pulsing music from within is fully audible. It takes twenty minutes in the freezing cold – surrounded by excited chatter and lads' banter and clouds of vape smoke – to reach the double doors at the top of the ramp, where two huge bouncers wait in black overcoats.

One of them, who must be at least six feet six and is so broad I'm not sure how he even fits through the door, gestures to me to lift my arms and scans me with an airport-style wand, front, back, sides, arms and legs. He gives me a strange look, just a beat of narrowed eyes, then waves me through to pay the £25 entry fee at the booth.

I head down the long corridor, past the cloakroom and through the next set of double doors into a blinding blaze of strobes and lasers and flashing spotlights in the main cavernous room. Not including our out-of-hours visit earlier this evening, it's the first time I've been in a nightclub in maybe twenty years and the first thing that strikes me is the sheer level of *noise*. The music is deafeningly, insanely loud, a hard pulsing mechanical beat, keyboards and a woman's vocals somewhere beneath it, so brutally loud it almost feels like it's inside my chest, my head.

The dance floor is already filling up. At the long bar on my left, the bartender from earlier is creating some complicated cocktails alongside half-a-dozen colleagues buzzing from fridges to customers and back again.

Waiting for my eyes to adjust to all the flashing coloured lights, I locate the door at the end of the bar, the one marked PRIVATE – STAFF ONLY. This time, however, there is a bouncer standing beside it. Like the one who had scanned me outside, he's also huge – with cartoonishly big shoulders that stretch the fabric of his black jacket and short, bleached-blond hair gelled flat to his angular head. Like the others, he's also wearing an earpiece with a coil of clear plastic flex that disappears into his jacket. As I approach, he holds up a big hand, shakes his head, says something I can't hear.

With some difficulty against the thudding music I explain to him that I'm here to see Mr Lawler, that I spoke to his colleague earlier and he told me to come back this evening. I end up having to lean in close to him, standing on tiptoes to talk right into his ear.

'Wait here,' he says, and disappears through the staff door.

I check my phone to see if there are any new messages from Lucas, but there is nothing. Meanwhile, the club is filling with ever more young people as the music seems to get even louder. There are a couple of female dancers on podiums raised above the main stage, a DJ behind his desk with one arm in the air to get the crowd going, the dance floor packed with a sea of moving bodies. I feel a shiver of anticipation at coming face to face with the mysterious Mr Lawler, running through what I will ask him first. Hoping that it won't be the man I met earlier.

But when the door finally opens, it's the bleached-blond bouncer again. He leans down, says something in my ear.

'What?' I say. 'Is he here?'

The bouncer leans closer. 'Mr Lawler's not here right now. Brandon said he'll probably be here around twelve thirty-ish or maybe one if you want to come back then.'

I check my watch: it's not even eleven o'clock. I can't cope with another ninety minutes of this frenetic, deafening noise, but I don't want to miss Lawler either.

'Really?' I shout. 'He's definitely going to be here later?'

'That's what the man says.'

He returns his gaze to the crowd, as if the conversation is over.

Back in the car, I switch on the engine and turn the heat up to maximum, rubbing my hands together. Lucas has not texted again so I assume he's asleep. It's been a long, strange day and I'm not surprised he's tired.

I need something to keep me occupied while I wait. I Google 'sugar daddies' and scroll through the first few pages of results. Every single website is profoundly alarming and grimly depressing in equal measure. Was it even legal? I guess there must be loopholes, grey areas in the law that allowed them to operate in the open. All the sites presented this unsavoury kind of arrangement as if it's normal, natural, perfectly understandable. Slick, professional-looking websites trying to give a shiny modern gloss to a vice as old as time itself: seedy old men who wanted to have sex with beautiful young women.

Which didn't explain why Mr Lawler was twenty-six years old.

Unless . . . unless he was procuring young women for others.

The thought makes my flesh crawl and I hit the phone's power button to switch the screen off, returning my attention to the street.

There is still a steady stream of taxis dropping off on Ludlow Avenue, pulling over into the gaps between the vans and trucks parked up for the night to disgorge more young clubbers joining the queue outside Flame. I watch as another Uber arrives, four young women piling out and tottering on high heels through the gates of number ninety-nine. As it pulls away, its headlights illuminate another vehicle parked up facing me, further down the street on the other side, just a brief flash of light but enough to see that this one didn't seem to be empty, locked up for the night. There is one – or maybe two? – faces just about visible through the windscreen. Just for a second, then the taxi's headlights move on and the car is plunged back into shadow.

I remember the black saloon from this afternoon, the car I thought had been shadowing us on the journey across central London. But this car – the one facing me fifty metres down this street – looks different, standing higher off the road. Dark grey or maybe navy blue, it's hard to tell, so far from the watery glow of the nearest street light. Was there someone inside? Sitting, observing? I slide down into my own seat a little, fear bubbling in my stomach, keeping my eyes on the parked saloon and waiting for the headlights of another passing taxi to wash over it again.

If they were watching me, two could play at that game.

29

I flinch awake with a start, my thigh jerking up painfully into the steering wheel.

The engine is still running, the air inside the car overheated and stuffy, the dashboard display telling me it's almost midnight. *Christ*, I've been asleep for more than an hour, a painful crick in my neck where my head's found an awkward angle against the headrest. I rub my eyes, switch the engine off and try to stretch some movement back into my arms, my shoulders. Maybe another half an hour, and then I'll go and see Lawler.

If he was even going to *be* there at all. It has occurred to me that the earring guy – Brandon? – might have just decided to string me along. That maybe I would go back in there at half past midnight and some other bouncer would tell me to come back in a couple of hours, and so on, and so on, until the sun came up and they closed for the night. Wasting my time as some kind of revenge for what happened earlier.

I'm seized by a huge yawn, feeling around in the door pocket for something to drink. There is an almost empty bottle of Diet Coke that has been there for a couple of weeks. It's flat but I drain the bottle anyway. Swallowing the last dull, coppery mouthful, I notice that the dark-coloured car I'd been watching earlier isn't there anymore. Perhaps it had just been picking someone up or dropping them off. My eyeballs feel like they've been bathed in grit and *God*, I'd kill for some coffee right now, a hot drink to—

A muffled noise reaches me from somewhere close by. I turn around, but the back seat is empty. The radio off. The street is deserted.

Then it comes again, a muffled noise. *Phone?* I tap my jeans pocket, my jacket, feel for the wireless charging point below the dashboard. Nothing. When the buzzing comes again, I realise it's coming from the passenger footwell, half fallen beneath my handbag. The noise of my phone's message alert must have been obscured by the idling engine up until now.

My heart lurches when the screen lights up and I see the display.

A string of WhatsApp messages and three missed calls. All from Lucas.

The three missed calls had come first, within the space of two minutes. Then the texts, stacked one on top of the other, the last one from only a moment ago.

I think someone's here
Are you back?
Where are you?
Someone outside room I can hear them
What shall I do?
PLEASE COME NOW MUM

There is a sick plunge in my stomach as my eyes run down the string of messages. The first missed call was eight minutes ago. *Oh God.* I stab the car's ignition button and then the handbrake, but a pinging alarm sounds with a message flashing from the dashboard – the seat belt sign – and I shout with frustration, slamming the buckle of the seat belt into its slot and shoving the car into gear. Stamping on the accelerator, I tear down Ludlow Avenue narrowly missing a parked van and flashing through the T-junction without stopping.

The phone is in my lap and I stab the icon to call Lucas back, but it just rings and rings.

'Please, Lucas! Pick up!'

I end the call then ring him again, steering one-handed through a long curving bend with parked cars on both sides, the engine screaming at high revs. A lone fox darts into the road in front of me, its eyes momentarily shining gold as they're lit by the glare of my headlights and then it's gone, scurrying away into the front garden of a house. On an abstract level I'm glad it's almost midnight and there are hardly any people around, only vaguely aware that this is a street I don't know, a part of London I've never visited, my route confused by the darkness of a midwinter night.

I'm one wrong turn away from being lost in the depths of this strange, vast city.

My son's number rings six times then clicks over to voicemail, his sweet untroubled tones a horrible counterpoint to the panic climbing up my throat.

'*It's Lucas, leave a message.*'

'Lucas!' I shout at the phone in my lap. 'It's Mum, I'm on my way back to the hotel now. Got your messages, I'm sorry, please call me back to let me know you're OK? I'll be there in a few minutes but whatever you do, don't open the door to *anyone* but me, d'you understand? No one but me.'

Stabbing the button to end the call I hope, pray, that I won't be too late.

The junction rushing up looks completely unfamiliar. *Which way which way? Think.* No time now to look at the Maps app, just have to go on instinct. At the last second I heave the VW into a right turn, then a left and another right before I see the lights of Mile End Road up ahead.

The breath is coming fast and hard in my throat, guilt squeezing my lungs like a vice. Lucas had been unsure, nervous about being left by himself in the room, on his own in the big city. It was his first night alone in a hotel, and I had told him I would only be a mile or so from him, five minutes away, and that there was nothing to worry about because no one was looking for us. And even if they were, they wouldn't know where we were staying. No one could get into the hotel without a keycard, and anyway there were at least a hundred rooms spread over three floors. I had told him—

I had told him it would all be fine.

And now he was terrified, alone, calling for my help. I had not been there for him. I had let him down, just like I'd let Evie down.

Please be OK, Lucas, please be OK just don't open the door—

Back on Mile End Road I swerve between a night bus and a black cab and blow through a traffic light doing 50 mph as it's turning red. Ahead, a police car pulls out of a side street, blue lights blazing on its roof as it comes towards me but it's too late to do anything now so I just keep driving, keep looking straight ahead and he flashes past on my right, siren wailing now, heading to some other emergency in some other place. Something more important than my reckless driving.

In my mirror, the blue lights recede. I push the accelerator pedal hard to the floor again, finally recognising the turn-off onto Heath Road and cutting across oncoming traffic to a cacophony of hooting horns and flashing headlights. Up ahead I can finally make out the purple sign of the hotel and when I glance down at the dashboard the speedometer is touching 60, dark lines of houses flashing past on either side, a skidding turn into the car park before I bring the car to a sliding halt right next to the front door.

I slam the car door shut, scrabbling in my handbag for the hotel keycard and pushing it against the sensor by the front door, every instinct screaming at me that this was all taking too long, that the hotel was too quiet, the car park half empty and whoever had been here was already gone, I was already too late.

Running past a pair of lifts I take the stairs two at a time up to the first floor, left down the corridor, counting numbers until

I come to room 116. Fumbling the keycard into the slot beneath the handle, remembering what I'd said to Lucas earlier in the restaurant. *I'm your mum, I'll look after us both.*

I open the door. Our room is in darkness. Silent.

'Lucas?'

I grope for a light switch and the main lights flick on, revealing the sparse family room as I had left it: wardrobe, desk, wall-mounted TV, two single beds separated by a small bedside table.

But both beds are empty.

Lucas is gone.

30

I slam the bathroom door back on its hinges, pulling the shower curtain aside as my heart drums painfully against my ribs.

'Lucas! Lucas?'

He's not in the bathroom. The wardrobe is empty too, just a folded-up ironing board and Lucas's coat still on a hanger from when we'd first arrived. His clothes are strewn over the armchair where he'd discarded them earlier, a tumbler knocked over at the foot of his bed, a dark stain of water soaking into the beige carpet. Was it definitely water or something else? The duvet of the narrow single bed is rucked up at one side, an imprint on the pillow where my son's head had been.

It was true: this was really happening. I had lost them both now. I had come to London in search of one child, and lost the other in the process. The man at the nightclub – had he told me to go back tonight simply to lure me away from my son? I had left Lucas vulnerable, exposed, alone. I should never have brought him with me.

It was my fault.

I swallow down the sob rising up my throat and reach for the landline telephone on the bedside table. *Dial 0 for reception.*

'Hello?' I say when a voice greets me at the other end. 'My son, he was here in the room and I think someone came in and took him. Have you seen him? He's twelve, about five feet tall, slim with curly brown hair and he's—'

'Please slow down, madam.' The voice is calm, steady. 'Can you give me your room number?'

'It's one-one-six, please help me find him, he's been taken out of our room and you need to alert everyone and get the police here now. Do you have cameras, CCTV?'

'We do. What's your son's name?'

Then: a sound.

A small rustling, shuffling sound from inside the room. Fabric moving against fabric. Against carpet.

'Mum?'

The breath catches in my throat. 'Lucas?'

His head appears from under the bed nearest the window, a mop of mousey-brown hair as he hauls himself out of his hiding place. He's barefoot, skinny in his T-shirt and boxers, with his mobile in one hand and glasses in the other. The man on reception is saying something else but I just apologise and hang up and pull Lucas into a tight hug, kissing the top of his head and for once he doesn't resist, hugging me back instead.

'Thought I'd lost you,' I say, biting back tears of relief. 'Thought you'd gone. Did someone try to get in? Did they knock on the door?'

'There were people outside,' he says into my shoulder. 'And I could hear them whispering. One of them tried the door handle and there was someone knocking, telling me to let him in. Kept on doing it and doing it.'

'I'm so sorry, Lucas, that must have been really scary.'

'So I just kept quiet and then I crawled under your bed, I messaged you and put my phone on silent in case they heard it ringing and knew I was in here, then I thought I didn't want the screen to light up so I put it flat to the floor. If they burst in I was going to do that thing where I call you and shout out details of what they look like and what they are wearing. Just like in that film.'

I pull him into another hug.

'You thought you were going to be kidnapped?'

'Like in *Taken*.'

'I'm sorry I left you, I shouldn't have done that. But you're OK, yes?'

He nods. 'Sorry, Mum.'

'You don't have to apologise, Lucas. You did the right thing, it's me that should—'

A sudden rising of male voices in the corridor outside our room, talking over each other in exaggerated stage whispers, shushing each other, a thud followed by more muffled noises.

Lucas tenses, pulls away from the hug.

I jerk a thumb towards the door. 'Is that them?'

He backs away, whispers a single word: 'Maybe.'

I creep over to the peephole in the door and peer through it.

31

The fisheye lens gives a weirdly distorted circular view of the first-floor corridor outside our room but I can see two middle-aged men loitering outside the room opposite, each of them wearing a garishly colourful Christmas jumper. One of them is trying and failing to fit a keycard into the slot beneath the door handle, bending over so his face is inches from the door and swaying like a sailor on rough seas. The other one is holding a pint of lager in each hand, his flushed face creased with barely suppressed laughter.

Not kidnappers. Pissed-up middle managers from an office Christmas do, I'd guess. Maybe they'd been here earlier and had just got the wrong room. I watch and wait until they've disappeared into the room, then hurry back downstairs to lock the car up for the night, telling Lucas not to answer the door to anyone. Once I'm safely back in the room, I lock that door too and swing the overnight latch to the left.

'Safe,' I say to Lucas with a smile. 'Let's both get some sleep now, shall we?'

* * *

It's strange, spending a night in the same room as my son.

The last time it had been just the two of us like this he'd been a baby, before I'd moved his cot into the little box room when he was six months old. There had been a handful of times since when we'd shared a family hotel room on holiday – but Evie had been with us, too. The three of us stopping off overnight en route to a campsite in Brittany or the Loire Valley. Thoughts of those old holidays usually bring a smile to my face, a warm pang of nostalgia, but there is no time for that today. There is only space in my heart for the here and now, for tonight, tomorrow. For my children, my blood, my life.

After I've turned the lights out, we talk in the dark. My son's disembodied voice in the single bed beside mine.

'Did you believe him?' Lucas says quietly. 'The American guy back at the university? Seemed like a bit of a weirdo to me. Not Evie's type at all.'

'Does she have a type?'

'Tyler, I reckon. The handsome boys, with longer hair. Skinny. And tall. She would never have dated someone like Colton.'

'So she *does* talk to you about this stuff?'

'Only once or twice. There was that time in lockdown when she was *really* bored.'

The strangeness of it, the strangeness of this day we've spent together, makes me feel closer to my youngest child than I have for years. And yet I feel further away from his sister than ever. Every step forward we take is more evidence of how hard she had worked to conceal her life from me over these past months.

I also know that I wouldn't have even got this far without Lucas's help.

'Thank you,' I say to him. 'For figuring out the thing with Evie's signature, the name she used to sign into the hotel.'

'It was the only thing in her notebook.' His voice is blurry and soft, as if he's halfway to sleep already. 'In the back pages. Like, there was nothing in the front but I knew she always kept her little notebooks clear at the front for proper stuff, boys and lists and parties.'

Now doesn't seem like the right time to ask how he knows what she'd normally write in her notebooks.

'If you hadn't figured out she was using her dad's name,' I say quietly, 'we would never have got that name and address for the nightclub.'

There is a long moment of silence, and I think he must have drifted off to sleep. It's been a long day, a difficult day. But then his voice finds me in the darkness again.

'Mum?'

'Yes, Lucas?'

'What was he like?' He pauses, the words hanging between us like some creature that can't venture out in the daylight, only at night. 'My dad, I mean?'

I'm momentarily thrown. A long time ago, I'd listened to a divorced friend who said she never criticised the father of her children in front of them. We've talked about his dad before, of course we have, but not for a long time. And I've sensed that some of his questions have always lingered, unanswered. Partly because I never knew him for that long myself. A brief, dazzlingly intense time that had burned as brightly as a supernova before he was taken away from me. A reconciliation some years later that had burned just as brightly before I lost him forever.

There are only a handful of pictures of us together and Lucas has a copy of my favourite somewhere, a shot of Declan and me on the big wheel at a fair on my eighteenth birthday. Candyfloss and big grins and coloured lights behind us, Declan still managing to look like the coolest guy there.

'He was . . . a free spirit,' I say. 'He didn't really like being told what to do. By anyone.'

Lucas considers this for a moment. I feel my eyelids growing heavy.

But then he shifts in his bed, a soft rustle of sheets as he turns towards me. 'What would he have done though?' His voice is soft, almost a whisper. 'If he was still alive and he was here now?'

The honest answer is that I don't know. If I had to guess, I'd say he would have already resorted to using his fists and would be sitting in a police cell by now. But perhaps here in the dark, in this strange room after this exhausting day, there is a better answer I can give.

'He would do whatever he had to do, Lucas. For your sister. For you.'

'I wish he was here, Mum.'

Tears prick my eyes as I stare up at the ceiling.

'Get some sleep now, Lucas. Love you.'

*　　*　　*

I sleep badly again.

In the snatches of rest I do get, my dreams are plagued with visions of someone else being in the room with us. A presence, low voices and heavy footsteps. A hooded figure at the foot of Lucas's bed, but when I flinch awake there is no one there, only the weak light from the corridor outside leaking under the door.

At 6.40 a.m. I climb silently out of bed to check on Lucas. He's still sleeping soundly, turned towards the window, the duvet hunched up around his shoulders. On the way to the bathroom I check the door. Still safety-locked with the latch in place. The overnight door-guard still flipped to the left, still engaged so no one would have been able to get in.

But someone *has* been outside. Something has been pushed under the door: a plain white envelope, sealed but unmarked. Which was weird in itself because I assumed this hotel was a paperless operation, pay on checkout and no need for invoices or receipts. Maybe it was an advert, a flyer? I take it into the small bathroom, clicking the light on and closing the door behind me. Squinting against the sudden brightness, I tear open the envelope and pull out a single piece of folded A4.

There are no words inside. Only two strings of numbers printed across the top of the page in bold black type:

51.41499226745905, -0.9409697147303053

I turn the paper over, check the envelope again, but there is nothing else written on it either. No name, no instruction. Just the numbers.

But I already know what they might be. As quietly as I can, I retrieve my phone from the bedside table and bring it back into the bathroom, pulling up a search page and carefully typing the digits in one by one. There is only a single result. *Map for 51.41499226745905, -0.9409697147303053.*

Above it, a Google map with a red pin dropped into its centre.

A red pin that marks the precise location of my house.

32

The walls of the bathroom seem to fold in on me as I stare at my phone.

I rub my aching eyes, pinch the screen to zoom in. But there's no mistake: the note put under our door last night contains the precise GPS coordinates for our house. The red pin looks like it's within a dozen yards of our front door.

We know where you live.

And they had found us here at the hotel too, they knew where we were staying even though we had checked in barely twelve hours ago. Maybe Lucas really *had* heard someone outside the door last night. A chill creeps over my skin. What else did these people know? Had our address come from Evie? God, what if whoever it was had forced her to tell them, forced her to—

'Mum?'

Lucas's voice reaches me through the closed door. I slip the note back into its envelope, and into the plastic Tesco bag of toiletries next to the sink. Perhaps I would tell him later. Or perhaps not – he was already freaked out enough by the events of yesterday and last night.

'Just coming.'

'I'm bursting.'

He darts past me, shooing me out and pushing the door closed as he lifts the toilet lid.

'You sleep OK?' I say through the door. 'By the window?'

'Not bad,' he says. 'What's for breakfast?'

* * *

The young hotel receptionist is sympathetic but not especially helpful. The front door, he says, is locked at eleven o'clock on weeknights and only accessible via keycard after that. But there's also a side door, he admits sheepishly, that gets propped open a lot by people smoking and vaping at all hours of the day and night. The only CCTV cameras are in the main car park and reception but only managers are allowed to access the footage – and his manager is not due on shift until 2 p.m.

'So,' I say, 'random people can just come in and wander around the hotel, is that what you're saying?'

'Not as a rule,' he says. 'Although we did have a Christmas party in last night and they got a bit . . . lairy. A few of them were in and out of the side door smoking half the night. Maybe one of them put the note under your door by mistake?'

'It's not a mistake.' I glance over into the hotel restaurant, where I've left Lucas loading up his plate with a second helping of bacon, hash browns and Danish pastries from the breakfast buffet. 'It was definitely intended for me.'

The receptionist says he'll talk to his manager at 2 p.m. and I leave my mobile number, in case they can shed any light on who left the note. Not that I'm particularly hopeful.

I get a flat white from the drinks machine and join Lucas at a window table in the sun-filled hotel restaurant, where he's chewing on a mouthful of bacon. As well as the fried food and pastries he also has a yoghurt, an apple, a banana, two pieces of toast, two small pots of honey and three different types of fruit juice arrayed in front of him. Starting to grow into his pre-teenage appetite, it seems.

'Bit hungry, love?'

He grins. 'This is *brilliant*. You can have, like, as much as you want.'

'Spare a piece of toast for your mum?'

He pushes one of the mini honey pots towards me and I start to unwrap a pat of butter.

We eat in silence for a few minutes, Lucas ploughing through his four-course breakfast as if he's not eaten since we left home. I shift in my chair to face more into the room, studying each of the other breakfast guests in turn. But none of them look out of place, none of them are paying us any undue attention or look as if they might be part of the over-muscled security team at Flame nightclub either.

All the same, I'm not going to let Lucas out of my sight today.

'So,' he says, drinking a glass of orange juice down in one. 'Are we going back to that nightclub?'

'It'll be closed now. Maybe later on.'

'What's next then?' He bites into a large Danish pastry studded with raisins. 'Are we going home today?'

I think of the note under our door, the coordinates for our house. The implicit threat. I don't want to worry Lucas more than he already is, but as soon as I get a chance to make a discreet call to the police I have to let them know about this latest development. It might even push them into taking Evie's disappearance more seriously.

'Soon,' I say. 'I think we need to go through Evie's stuff again first, the things she left behind at uni. There must be something else there, some kind of clue.'

While he eats, I call his school and tell them he's still not well enough to attend today.

When I'm finished, Lucas has stopped eating and is staring at his own mobile, his mouth set in a hard line.

'What is it?' I say.

'That idiot at my school, Jacob Jackson,' he says. 'He's done another TikTok about Evie, it's already had more than ten thousand views and rising all the time. Looks like this one's going viral.'

33

Lucas turns the phone around so I can see. Another video, this one incorporating clips of the school, of our street, Jacob in what looks like his bedroom and then walking and talking around the local area. Again, I'm struck by how natural this seems to him, how slick he seems on camera for someone who's eighteen at most.

'The mystery of Evie Wingfield's disappearance just keeps on getting weirder,' he says excitedly, filming selfie-style. 'After the Reading teenager vanished from her university campus it now appears that her *entire family* has vanished too. Her mother and younger brother, Luke, have also disappeared from the family home. I'm hearing all kinds of things from close friends, unconfirmed rumours that describe a turbulent family life at home.

'Other reports say that Evie had struggled with mental health issues for several years and there are even suggestions that money worries could be at the root of this mystery, that maybe the financial strain of paying for university in London just proved too much for this single-parent family. There are also questions being asked about why Evie's mum took so long – several *weeks*, possibly even a *month* – to report her daughter missing to police.' He smiles at the camera. 'Don't forget to check out my channel, like and subscribe for more videos and all the very latest updates on the disappearance of Evie Wingfield.'

Unconfirmed rumours. Reports, suggestions, questions being asked. No actual facts, no sources of this nonsense, no names – all of it just conjured out of the air, out of nothing. Take someone's heartache and anxiety and pain, repackage it as entertainment. As *true crime.* And the wilder the speculation, the more sensational the content, the more clicks and views and shares, the more money is made. If the occasional fact crept in as well, it was more by luck than by judgement. And by the time the truth has been uncovered he will have moved on to the next thing, or the one after that, without a backward glance. No consequences, no comeback. The only grudging positive was that at least it was getting the story out there, making more people aware that Evie was missing.

All the same, it's hard to tell whether a viral video would do more harm than good. I tap the screen to pause the clip and hand the phone back to him. I've seen enough.

'Thinks he's some sort of private investigator? He's not even managed to get your name right.'

'He's put the videos up on YouTube and X too,' Lucas says. 'And they're starting to get picked up and reposted by other people. Loads of them are putting their own theories in the comments on all his posts. Some of the things people are saying . . . they're horrible.'

'What sort of things?'

'Like . . . I don't want to say.'

'Tell me,' I say. 'It's OK.'

He won't look at me. 'Some people have put in the comments that it's your fault she's run away. That Evie was probably being abused and she's better off wherever she is now. Other people saying it's a scam or whatever for reward money or something.'

'Who?' I say. 'Who's saying that?'

He shrugs. 'Just people, I don't know. No one uses their real name, do they?' He pushes his plate away. 'Some of them are saying she died and we're covering it up.'

I put my hand over his. 'The internet is full of morons, Lucas. We're going to find your sister. Those people are wrong about everything. They're just trolls, sick, nasty people, and you've got to ignore them.'

'I know, Mum. But I thought I'd look in the comments in case there was anything useful, maybe someone has seen Evie. Do you think we should post about Evie on your Facebook?'

'I've not got tons of friends on there but it's probably worth a try.'

'Are you going to ring that lady again as well?' The number you called yesterday at the café?'

'Good idea,' I say. 'I'll try her again when we get back to the room.'

He eats a bit more of his breakfast but the TikTok video seems to have dented his appetite. After I've got another coffee from the machine, we head upstairs.

In the room, we pack up the few belongings we have into our backpacks and refill our water bottles from the tap. I sit in the arm-chair by the window and dial the number again, double-checking it's the right one, using Lucas's phone in case mine's been blocked. He reads out the number from the slip of paper that Farley gave me and I key in each digit slowly and carefully.

It rings out before going to voicemail.

I leave another message asking her to call me back, before Lucas and I do a final sweep of the room to make sure we've not left anything behind.

But as we're about to leave, there's a knock at the door.

'Who is it?'

'Can you open the door please?' A woman's voice.

Perhaps the young receptionist has found something after all, or been able to look at the CCTV? I peer through the spyhole, to see a woman standing in the corridor in a grey trouser suit, one hand still in the pocket of a long raincoat. She's in her thirties, at least a decade older than the receptionist, her unlined face framed by a neat bob. Maybe his manager?

'Who is it?' I say again.

'If you can just open the door please, Mrs Wingfield?'

I do as she asks and we face each other across the threshold for a moment. She's not alone – standing to the side, out of the view of the fisheye lens, there's a heavy middle-aged guy in a dark suit with a green quilted jacket over the top.

The woman holds up an ID badge, a crest, a photo.

'Lauren Wingfield?'

'Yes.'

'I'm Detective Sergeant Parry and this is my colleague Detective Constable Garcia.' Her face is emotionless, expressionless. As if she's done this many times before. 'Can we come in for a minute?'

And then everything is dropping, falling away, my stomach plunging into my shoes. My legs are suddenly made of water and it's only my tight grip on the door that keeps them from giving way.

The knock at the door.

The police officer.

The news that no parent should ever have to hear.

I pull in a shaky breath. 'Is it about Evie?'

'How about we come in for a minute?' Her voice a little softer now we're face to face.

I usher the two detectives in and retreat back towards the bed.

Parry looks around. 'Anyone else here with you?'

'Just my son.' I indicate the bathroom. 'He's in there.'

As if on cue Lucas appears at the bathroom door, toothbrush in hand, wiping his mouth with a towel.

'What's happening?' he says in a small voice. 'Mum?'

'The police,' I say. 'Why don't you come over here with me?'

Our conversation from breakfast is still fresh in my mind, the ugly comments of strangers relayed to me by my son. *Some of them say she died.*

'What?' I say to the officers, a painful tightness in my chest. 'What is it? Have you found her? Just tell me, please.'

Parry takes another step towards me. 'Lauren Wingfield, you're under arrest for ABH and assault. You do not have to say anything but it may harm your defence if you do not mention when questioned something which you later rely on in court. Anything you do say may be given in evidence.'

EVIE

Four months earlier

Something was different when they met again.

They'd had front row seats at a matinee performance of *Moulin Rouge* just off Piccadilly Circus, so close to the action that they were virtually onstage. With the music still ringing in her head and a huge, giddy smile on her face, they'd walked hand in hand through a maze of side streets towards St James's Square and a reservation at a discreetly expensive Japanese restaurant.

He'd ordered champagne to celebrate her exam results and by the time it arrived she was already wearing another new gift: a stunning platinum necklace that matched the bracelet he'd brought her the last time they met. She loved it – and told him so – but he was quiet during the meal. Subdued in a way she hadn't seen before. As exquisite dishes of blue fin tuna and Kobe beef were set down in front of them, Evie began to wonder if he was about to deliver bad news, if he was just waiting for the right moment.

Maybe this was it. Maybe he was ending it. Here, today. Maybe he'd decided that they couldn't carry on, that a seven-year age gap was too much or she was too young or lived too far away. Maybe he had got bored of her already. Maybe it had all been too good to be true, right from the start.

The thought of him breaking up with her opened an aching void in her chest.

Finally, as they waited for coffees to arrive, she couldn't bear it any longer.

'What's going on, Scott?' She held his gaze. 'Are you going to tell me what's bothering you?'

'Sorry,' he said sheepishly. 'Is it that obvious?'

'Is it me?'

His smile was warm, genuine. 'No, Evie. It's not you. I'm sorry, I just . . .'

'Stop apologising.' She put her hands flat on the table to stop them shaking. 'Just tell me, Scott.'

The waiter appeared with a tray, setting down two cappuccinos in fine white china cups. Scott nodded his thanks, waiting for the man to retreat before he continued.

'In my job, Evie, because of what I do, there are certain . . . sensitivities around it.'

'Sensitivities?'

'The service protocols require anyone with my level of security clearance or higher to follow specific rules.'

'OK.' Evie had no idea what he was talking about, but she nodded anyway.

'One of those rules states that I have to declare . . . relationships.' He gave her a shy smile. 'When they go past a certain point.'

'And what point is that?'

'When they're serious. When they become . . . close.'

Her stomach did a little flip. Perhaps this wasn't what she was expecting after all.

'It all sounds very James Bond.'

'Well,' he said, 'their vetting process is very thorough and it's going on all the time. On me, my colleagues, anybody new in our lives. They need to make sure we're not being targeted by agents of a foreign government who might try to compromise us, blackmail us.'

Evie put a hand on her chest, mock-serious. 'I'm not a Russian spy, Scott. Pinky promise.'

He gave her that dazzling smile but it faded quickly.

'I know,' he said. 'I know that.'

'But?'

'You said before that you felt bad, keeping us secret from your mother. Keeping her in the dark about me. About us.'

'Only sometimes,' Evie said. 'Not always.'

He was about to reply, then seemed to think better of it and took a sip of coffee instead.

'What is it?' Evie said. 'Are you going to tell me?'

He put his coffee cup back down in the saucer.

'The background check on your family turned something up, and I thought you should know. Maybe then you'd feel less guilty about keeping our secret.'

'Why?'

'Because your mother's been lying to you,' he said finally. 'For years.'

PART III

34

The cell at Bethnal Green police station is freezing cold and permeated with the flat, hard smell of industrial bleach.

It's tiled in blue and white, featureless and blank apart from a low bench, a thin plastic-coated mattress and a stainless steel toilet with no seat. I wrap the heavy grey blanket around my shoulders while I wait, the dull throb of a headache gathering behind my eyes. According to what I've been told by the custody sergeant, Lucas has been found a chair in the back office where other staff can keep an eye on him. We were separated after I was fingerprinted and had a DNA swab taken from my mouth, and all my subsequent requests to see him have been denied. Even though he should be safe inside a police station, it's not enough. I need to see him. To be sure.

Alongside that worry there had also been a measure of relief that I was *only* getting arrested. An initial rush of euphoria that Parry and Garcia had not been there to give me bad news about Evie, in fact they didn't even know who she was. For once, I was glad the police had no idea what I was talking about.

Part of me is almost pleased too that I finally have the attention of two detectives, despite the circumstances.

Nonetheless, it's more than two hours before I'm escorted out of the custody suite, through a series of secure doors and into a small grey-painted interview room. The two detectives are there on one side of the table, opposite a white-haired duty solicitor by the name of Critchlow with whom I'd had a brief chat earlier.

'Where's Lucas?' I say. 'Is he all right? He'll be worried.'

'Your son's fine,' Garcia says. 'He's in the squad room with one of the other officers. Barely looked up from his phone from what I've heard.'

'Can I see him?'

'Not right now.'

'Why not?'

'Your son's fine,' the male detective says again. 'He's perfectly safe.'

'When can I see him?'

'That depends.' He taps the table with a thick index finger. 'On how we get along in here.'

I glance over at Critchlow, the duty solicitor, but he is filling out a form in tight, spidery handwriting and doesn't even look up.

'There's a missing person's report,' I say. 'I made it on Saturday. It's got all the details about Evie, my daughter, I gave you the reference number so—'

'We'll get to that.' Parry turns on the digital recorder and goes through the formalities of stating time, date, place and who's in the room. Behind her, where the wall meets the ceiling, the red light of a camera blinks on. 'So first of all, Lauren, do you know why you've been arrested?'

'Not really.'

'You assaulted a man.'

'Did I?'

'Yesterday.' She flicks back a few pages in her notebook. 'On the premises of the Flame nightclub, Ludlow Avenue at around 6 p.m.'

'You've been misinformed.'

'So why don't you tell us what happened? From when you arrived, to when you left.'

I describe the events of yesterday evening in as much detail as I can, glossing over the part where I inadvertently pulled out the tattooed man's earring and finishing up with a description of the note that had been slipped under the door of my hotel room overnight – a clear threat to stay away.

'We've heard Mr Roper's side of the story, so why don't you give us your side.' Seeing my confused expression, she adds: 'Brandon Roper? The man you assaulted?'

'*Allegedly*,' Critchlow chimes in.

Neither detective even looks at the duty solicitor. Garcia says: 'What exactly did the victim say to you?'

'He said he couldn't help but maybe I should come back later, when they were open.'

Which was another lie on his part – because the 'assault' must have already been reported to police by the time I went back to the club at 10 p.m. So, presumably, he'd had no intention of helping me at all.

'And what did he say about Scott Lawler?'

'He was evasive at first, but it was pretty obvious he knew the name. I told him I'd found Lawler registered as a director of a company linked to that address, and he didn't deny it.'

Parry picks up the baton again. 'Why are you lying to us?'

The bluntness of her tone throws me for a second. 'I'm not lying. Roper is the one you should be arresting. He's an absolute dick.'

She raises an eyebrow. 'If that was an arrestable offence, Lauren, I'd have half of London down here in the cells. But why do you say that?'

'Have you *met* him?'

'Yes.'

'Then you know why.'

Garcia leans forward. 'You hit him because he's a dick?'

'I didn't hit him.' Which was *technically* true.

'You drew blood.'

'So he says.'

'Not just him,' Garcia says. 'We've got a witness, too.'

35

'Who?' I say. 'Who's your witness?'

'A member of staff.'

A reply catches in my throat, and then I remember: the blonde bartender in the white hoodie who had been filling the fridges with beer.

Critchlow puts a hand on my arm and says quietly: 'You don't have to respond to that, Lauren.' To the detectives, he adds: 'An employee of the complainant is hardly an unbiased witness, as you're well aware. She could easily have been coerced into making a false statement on behalf of her employer.'

Garcia throws him a patronising frown before turning back to me.

'Did you assault Mr Roper?'

'I just don't get it,' I say. 'All the crime in London, everything on the Met's plate right now, and you go to the trouble of finding me, arresting me for a slight misunderstanding? Two detectives knocking on my hotel room door before nine in the morning. This stuff must happen all the time in a nightclub. What makes me so special?'

'We had a complaint from a member of the public, Lauren.' Garcia's tone is patronisingly slow, as if he's speaking to a child. 'We investigated the complaint, and now we're speaking to you. This is how policing works.'

'How did you even know where we were staying?'

'Do you admit that you assaulted him?'

'I'm admitting nothing, I've done nothing wrong. I need to get out of here to find my daughter – she may have been kidnapped, trafficked, held against her will. That's the *real* crime here. That's what you should be investigating.'

'How about you tell us again what brought you to that address?' Parry laces her fingers together on the table. 'I'm assuming you weren't planning on going clubbing?'

I sigh with frustration: we are going round and round in circles. But I describe the journey anyway, from Queen Anne's campus to The Royal Pearl Hotel – glossing over the details of how we had tricked the staff – from there to Belvue Road in west London and then to the nightclub. A memory surfaces from that drive across the city.

'Did you follow me from there, yesterday?' I look from one detective to the other. 'There was a black saloon car that kept appearing in my rear-view mirror.'

Garcia shakes his head. 'Why would we have followed you?'

'You tell me.' I can feel a tension headache building, a vice squeezing my skull. Can I see my son now?'

He ignores my question. 'You've been arrested because you assaulted someone, Lauren. So you'd be well advised to cooperate with us, tell us what you discussed with Brandon Roper. In particular, everything he said about Scott Lawler, however insignificant it might have seemed at the time. Why don't we go over it again?'

* * *

We go back and forth like this for another hour.

As the time creeps towards noon, the hard plastic chair becomes increasingly uncomfortable against the small of my back, the air in the room slowly more stuffy and stale.

'When can I see Lucas?' I say for what feels like the tenth time. 'He'll be worried about me.'

'Not yet.'

Parry announces that she's suspending the interview, reaching over to switch the recording equipment off. To her partner, she says: 'Why don't you see if you can rustle up some coffees, Ed?'

He nods, getting up without a word and heading for the door. From my seat on the far side of the room, I watch him as he stops in the corridor. He looks first right, then left, then turns to his right and disappears from view. A moment later he's back, walking the other way instead.

A uniformed officer appears and Parry excuses herself too, after a quick whispered conversation at the door.

Critchlow, the duty solicitor, stretches and half turns in his chair to get a better look at me. He's a small man of around fifty, with a sharp, inquisitive face and the wiry build of a long-distance runner.

'So,' he says, producing a packet of paracetamol from his briefcase and putting the box in front of me. 'How do you feel, Lauren?'

'Tired of answering questions.' I nod my thanks and pop a couple of pills out of the blister pack, swallow them down with the last inch of water in my plastic cup. 'And confused about why they're making such a big deal out of this.'

'Probably better if you don't repeat the latter comment in the presence of those two fine officers of the law.'

'Do you mind if I ask you a question?' When he nods, I say: 'How long have you been doing this job?'

'Twenty-seven years, give or take.'

'All in this part of London? Called out as the duty solicitor, to sit in on these first interviews after an arrest?'

'Mostly, yes. East and south London, but we're spread pretty thin so I'll go wherever I'm needed.'

'You must know most of the police stations in this part of the city though.'

He cracks a sardonic smile. 'For my sins, yes. I know them all fairly well.'

'And most of the detectives.'

'I wouldn't say I'm on any of their Christmas card lists, but . . . yes, you get to recognise people. I suppose I'm on first-name terms with most of them, most of the major incident teams.'

'You ever come across these two before? Parry and Garcia?'

He thinks for a moment, shakes his head. 'Can't say that I have, no.'

'You've never dealt with them before?'

'It's possible they're new transfers in from another division, another force. But you'd generally pair a new face with someone who knows the area already, rather than putting two newbies together. Why do you ask?'

'Something about all of this just doesn't quite make sense,' I say. 'There must be dozens, hundreds of violent incidents in London every day. Stabbings, GBH, street robberies, gang-related crime. Why are they wasting their time on *me*?'

'Hmm.' Critchlow glances up at the door. The uniformed officer has stepped out into the corridor. 'You asked them earlier what makes you special, why they're expending so much effort on this.' He leans in, his voice softer. 'I think you might be . . . looking down the wrong end of the telescope, Lauren. Do you understand what I'm saying?'

I feel a dawning sense of recognition, the fog finally dispersing.

'I think so.'

'You still need to be careful.'

'Understood,' I say. 'But I have to get them to switch their focus onto Evie instead of me.'

'So what are you going to do?'

I glance towards the door. 'I'm going to call their bluff.'

36

Garcia returns with four black coffees in Styrofoam cups. He picks up the thread of the interview again, asking me in a loaded tone if I'd like to reconsider any of my previous statement.

'Now you've had a chance to think it over,' he says. 'I wonder if you'd like to tell us the truth now?'

I have to give him his due: he knows I'm holding something back. He just doesn't know what it is.

'I've told you the truth.' I take a sip of coffee. 'Now it's your turn.'

'How's that?' He gives me an amused look.

'Where are you based?'

'Excuse me?'

'Because you're not based out of this station, are you? You couldn't even find your way to the canteen for these coffees, had to ask someone for directions.'

The amusement on his face sours, sliding into a scowl. It reminds me of something my mum said to me a while ago, when I had lost my temper with a traffic warden who ticketed my car even though it was barely thirty seconds over time. *Angry middle-aged women make a lot of men uncomfortable*, she'd said. *Because they're not sure how to deal with you.*

'That's not how all of this works, Lauren,' he says. 'Questions come from our side of the table, answers from your side. Do you understand?'

'It just made me curious,' I say. 'Because if you're not based here, why have you picked up this case? Are you from another force? From outside London? Makes me think there's a lot more you're not telling *me*.'

Parry cuts in. 'Let's get back on track, shall we?' She clicks the top of her ballpoint. 'How did Mr Roper actually come to be injured yesterday? Who else did you see in the nightclub when you assaulted him? And who did you see later, when you visited for a second time?'

Critchlow says: 'I'd just like to remind my client that she's not obliged to answer your questions.'

I take a sip of the coffee, which tastes harsh and burned as if it's sat on a hotplate for several hours.

'Can I see your ID again?'

Parry fixes me with a penetrating stare. 'Listen, Lauren, if you want to spend the night here, you want us to get you booked into the magistrates' court for your first hearing tomorrow morning, you're going the right way about it.'

'But this isn't going to court, is it?'

Garcia grunts. 'If I had a pound for every time I've heard that, I'd be—'

'Let me just run something by you both,' I say, holding my hands up. 'You've met Mr Roper, yes? So if, hypothetically, he *did* come out on the wrong end of a little set-to like this, you really think a big pumped-up, tattooed-gym-lad bag of testosterone like him is going to want to go to court over this? That he'll want to stand up in public and tell everyone how he got schooled by some little woman who's literally half his size?'

Garcia regards me with the flat, cold eyes of a shark.

'So you're admitting that you assaulted him now?'

'Whether I admit it or not is irrelevant: Roper is never going to press charges, is he? The guy's ego would never allow it. Reporting this to you is just him firing another warning shot to get me to back off, just like the note under the door of my hotel room. And you're playing along with it, trying to put the wind up me to get as much leverage as you can. You're playing both sides off against each other. Why that is, I haven't figured out yet. But I reckon it's something to do with Lawler, and if that's got something to do with my daughter then I need to know what it is.'

Both detectives continue to stare at me across the pockmarked plastic table, and I wonder for a horrible moment whether I've overstepped the mark. Whether I've made a massive misjudgement that is about to take me further away from Evie, and Lucas, than ever before.

Parry announces she's suspending the interview for the second time, switching off the audio recorder with an irritated stab of her finger.

She stands, and Garcia follows her out into the corridor where their whispered conversation is too quiet for me to hear.

I glance at Critchlow. He gives me a half-raised eyebrow, but says nothing. He flips to the next page of his A4 pad where he's written two words in capitals, tapping them now with the point of his mechanical pencil.

BE CAREFUL.

I give him a nod of acknowledgement and it's not long before the two detectives return to the room and resume their seats. Garcia still has the angry flush in his cheeks, but Parry is calm, composed, and I sense a subtle change in the atmosphere between us. She repeats the mantra I've already heard: that Evie's over eighteen, and not what would usually be categorised as high risk – either to herself, or others. She's an adult, able to make her own decisions.

'How about you tell us exactly what happened with your daughter,' she says, restarting the tape. 'From the first moment you realised she wasn't where she was supposed to be.'

'You've read the missing person's report I filed on Saturday?'

She nods. 'We've accessed it on the system, yes. But we'd like to hear it direct from you.'

I take them through everything, from the moment I drove onto campus on Saturday morning until their arrival at my hotel room this morning. I've repeated it so many times over the past four days that it's started to feel fixed and unreal, like a story about someone else.

Parry looks up from her notebook when I'm finished. 'And what about . . . the two of you?'

'How do you mean?'

'How would you characterise your relationship with your daughter? Before she left for university.'

'She could be . . . rebellious sometimes.' This is something of an understatement, but I have to steer them away from the idea of Evie as a tearaway teen who's just had enough of living at home. 'She's always been quite strong-willed, all the way back to when she was a toddler. Always known what she wanted, had a very independent spirit.'

'And did she tend to keep secrets from you?'

I swallow down on the painful lump in my throat. 'Sometimes. But never like this.'

'You know,' Parry says quietly, 'it's not against the law to want some space from your parents.'

Garcia adds: 'Has it occurred to you that she might not *want* to be found?'

'She would never have kept this going for so long. A few days, maybe. A week. But not for this long, not voluntarily.'

'And you'd never heard her mention the names Scott Lawler or Brandon Roper before? How about Nicola Lawler? Eric Caruso?'

I describe my brief call to the number listed as Evie's emergency contact – a woman who had hung up on me and had not returned any of my messages.

'Could that have been Nicola Lawler?'

'She didn't give you her name?' He jots a note on his pad. 'What about Eric Caruso?'

I shake my head. 'There is someone else you should look at, though. His name's Colton Ryczek, he's an American postgraduate student at university with Evie.'

Parry looks up at that, her head cocked to the side, asks me to spell out the surname.

'You're sure he's American?'

'Yes, I've met him, spoken to him. Why is that important?'

'Doesn't matter,' she says. 'But why are you mentioning him now?'

'He was stalking her, following her. It just feels like, wherever Evie has gone, he's got something to do with it. He looks like he's pumped full of steroids and he's a very, very odd person.'

'No shortage of them.'

'Will you check into him? Please?'

She looks up, gives me a curt nod. 'We'll see where he might fit into the picture.'

'Thank you.'

Garcia picks up the thread again.

'So, at home,' he says, 'you never came across anything of Evie's that mentioned those other names? Diaries, notes, emails, messages?'

I tell them about the postcard we'd found in her bedroom, signed off with a single initial S.

'Whatever they're involved in,' I say, 'Evie has nothing to do with it. She's a good person, she's clever and kind and funny, she's never been in trouble with the police before and I just need to find her and bring her home. Please help me. *Please*.'

The two detectives exchange a glance.

'You're right about her police record,' Parry says. 'She's clean as a whistle. Evie's never been on our radar at all.'

'Until now,' Garcia adds.

* * *

By mid-afternoon I'm back in the cold blue-and-white tiled cell, the blanket wrapped around my shoulders again, pale strands of daylight from the single barred window leaching away towards dusk. A woman in the cell next to me is alternately retching and crying in long, hoarse wails of distress. A man, across the corridor, bangs on the door of his cell every few minutes, punctuating the noise with long volleys of angry shouting in a language I don't recognise.

Names from the interview run on a loop in my head as I scour my memory for any time I've heard them before this week.

Scott Lawler. Brandon Roper. Nicola Lawler. Eric Caruso.

Evie was involved in something. And I had to get her out of it before those people took her down with them.

I try to distract myself with practical issues – the most pressing of which is that I need to call my mum, to come and pick Lucas up if I'm going to be in here overnight. She hates driving in London but she's the only viable option, the only person I know who will definitely drop everything to make a three- or four-hour round trip into the city. Critchlow explained earlier that they can hold me here for up to twenty-four hours after my arrest, at which point they need to either charge or release me.

He leaves me with his business card before heading to another job, to sit with another newly arrested suspect at another police station across the river. I realise after he's gone that I never asked him what happens if I'm wrong – if I've totally misjudged this and I end up getting charged with assault or actual bodily harm and being remanded in custody for weeks, months, shuttled from one cell to another, trapped inside the system while the wheels of justice creak slowly forward. Could Parry and Garcia do that? Lucas could stay with my mum, but who would search for Evie?

Evie's never been on our radar at all.

Until now.

When the duty officer opens the viewing hatch in the door again to check on me, I plead with him to let me know that my son has had something to eat, to let me talk to the two detectives again, to give me an indication of how long I'm going to be stuck here.

Parry and Garcia don't respond to my pleas.

But ninety minutes later, they let me go.

37

I'm *released under investigation* according to the custody officer, which seems to mean that the potential charges are still hanging over me in case new evidence comes in or they take a different tack. I sign various forms and he hands back sealed plastic bags containing my car keys, cash, belt and coat. Parry leans against the reception desk, arms crossed, while I pull on my coat and re-lace my shoes.

'I need you to listen to me, Lauren,' she says. 'Just so we can be crystal clear on something.'

'I'm listening.'

'If you go back there, back to that nightclub or within a hundred yards of Brandon Roper, you'll be arrested again. Do you understand?'

'Got it.'

'I will personally see to it that you're held for the full twenty-four hours, at the end of which we *will* find something to charge you with. Believe me when I say this is for your own good,' she says. 'Back off, for your own safety. That's all I can tell you.'

'What about my daughter's safety?'

She hands me a business card.

'If we get any news on your daughter, we'll be in touch. In the meantime do yourself and your son a favour, and go back to Reading. It might be advisable to stay at your mum's for a few days.'

The detective sergeant disappears and returns through a side door a moment later with Lucas, who rushes over to hug me as if he's not seen me for a year. It's always a bit of a surprise now to have such a public display of affection and it feels so good to have him close to me again, to wrap him in my arms like I used to do when he was a little boy.

When he finally releases me from the hug, he hands back my bag, the purse and phone still inside.

'Are we going home now?' he says. 'That detective lady said we would be.'

'Let's get something to eat first. I bet you're starving.'

We head out of the police station, Lucas firing questions at me about the police interview, about what would happen next and whether I was still in trouble. I hail a black cab on Cambridge Heath Road to take us back to the Premier Inn. It's only when we're crawling in Friday afternoon traffic, some of the tension from the police station draining away, that I think to check my phone.

There is no call back from Evie's emergency contact number. But there are a lot of notifications on Facebook.

'I did a post on your account, about Evie,' Lucas says. 'Is that OK? I'm not on Facebook because it's for, like, old people, and it's not really the sort of thing you can put on Snapchat. Lowered your privacy settings too so that more people can see it and share it.'

'Good idea,' I say. He's posted a picture of Evie with a few lines of text, a description of her and a plea for anyone with information to get in contact with me by direct message.

'You've got a few DMs but I haven't read them yet.'

'How did you unlock my phone though?'

'Seen you draw your unlock pattern millions of times,' he says with a shrug. 'You should really set up thumbprint recognition, Mum.'

I only have 127 friends on Facebook, a mixture of family and old school friends, current and former work colleagues, some friends of friends plus a dozen or so where I have absolutely no idea who they are. I don't use it that often anymore and tend to lock down my privacy settings anyway to reduce the number of weirdos, stalkers and strange men commenting on posts. Since Lucas lowered my privacy settings though, I can see I already have more than two dozen messages and a string of new friend requests.

All the messages are variations on a theme.

God I'm so sorry hun hope you find her soon x

Sorry to hear this, will ask around to see if anyone's seen her xx

Saw this on TikTok it's awful hope you're OK. I'm sure your girl will be back with you soon x

Holding you and Evie in our thoughts and prayers tonight

None of them are of any material help in finding Evie; no one has seen her since September.

There are a total of twenty-eight new friend requests on my account and I don't recognise any of the names or avatar pictures. But this is no time to be discerning – I need to get as much information as I can, so I click *Confirm All* on the list of friend requests.

The cab drops us back at the hotel where I have to pay an extra charge for the fact my car's been stuck there all day. The receptionist is older than the young guy who was on earlier, and I have to ask all over again whether there is any CCTV footage from last night that might identify who put the note under my door. He duly explains that a) he's not had time to look at the footage, b) one of the two cameras is out of order and c) even if he did find something, he's not allowed to divulge such information to a third party without prior authorisation from the legal department at Head Office in Swindon.

He smiles the whole time while delivering this monologue, as if he's still hoping for a five-star rating on Tripadvisor.

* * *

Lucas picks at his food. It's early evening and half the tables are still empty in the restaurant, a generic American-style diner on Coborn Street offering a filling but unoriginal menu. I'd had nothing to eat since breakfast except a limp police station cheese sandwich and I couldn't face the drive home on an empty stomach.

'Not hungry?' I push my empty plate away and take a long drink of lime and soda.

He picks up a single chip and bites it in half. 'So *are* we going home?'

'The detectives said we should, yes. Do you want to?'

He shrugs his small shoulders. 'What about Evie?'

'It's just for tonight, Lucas. Then we'll get you to school tomorrow and I'll come back to London to do some more digging on Scott Lawler. The detective mentioned some other names too: Nicola Lawler and Eric Caruso.'

More than anything, I need to get Lucas to my mum's house, somewhere he can be safe. The paralysing fear of that moment last night, when I thought he'd been taken, has left its residue imprinted on me like the high-water mark after a flood. And I need to regroup, to think. To figure out what I do next. At least there are police involved now and I have their names, their numbers. It feels like some kind of progress.

'When are we going to go?'

'As soon as you've finished your dinner.' I flash a brittle smile. 'So at some point in the next six to eight hours, probably.'

He looks up, realises I'm joking and gives me a half-smile in return. But it fades quickly.

'We're not giving up, are we?'

'Of course not,' I say. 'Never. I'll never give up on your sister. Just like I'd never give up on you.'

He tears a piece from the top of the burger bun, dips it in ketchup and puts it into his mouth, chewing slowly.

'Just want to find her.'

'So do I, Lucas. More than anything.' When he doesn't reply, I add: 'What's the matter? You don't want us to go home yet, is that it? I suppose we could stay one more night, buy some clothes in the morning so we're not *too* scuzzy.'

He sits back in his chair, staring down at his lap.

'I have to tell you something, Mum.' It's not particularly warm in here but there's a flush creeping into his cheeks. 'I'm really sorry.'

'OK,' I say evenly. 'I'm sure that whatever it is, it's not as bad as you think.'

'It's *really* bad.'

A wash of unease creeps over my skin, the now-familiar sense of being kept in the dark by my children.

'Is it about your sister?'

'Kind of.' He finally lifts his eyes to meet mine. 'The thing is, I was *so* bored when you were in there, in that police station. It was hours and hours and *hours* and there was literally nothing to do, nothing to watch, nothing to read. No one to talk to. And so I was just on my phone basically the whole time.'

'You did that Facebook post about Evie on my account,' I say. 'That was good. You used your initiative.'

'It's not that.' The flush in his cheeks deepens to the warm rosy colour of a fully ripe apple. 'You promise you won't be angry?'

I'm about to say: *That depends.* That would be my response on a normal day, like the time Evie had reversed my car into a bollard barely a week after passing her test. *Promise you won't be angry,*

Mum? Or the sixteenth birthday party when her friends had played tennis with a dozen ripe satsumas in the lounge; or the year before that when she'd been caught with cigarettes in school.

But there was nothing normal about these past few days.

'I promise,' I say, 'that I won't be angry.'

He points to his phone, face up next to his half-empty plate. 'So I was just buzzing around online to, like, a million different websites for missing people and there's like a million different podcasts about it too. But they're all kind of the same. Then I was trying to guess Evie's passwords for her socials again, then trying to hack her email, then her WhatsApp, and none of that worked so I ended up going down some rabbit holes for a few hours.'

'I won't be angry if you can guess Evie's passwords,' I say. All normal rules of sibling privacy and respect had gone out of the window at the weekend. 'I'd be pleased, Lucas. Because it might help us find her.'

'So . . . then I thought, if only the lady on that number would call us back. The number the university man gave you? If only she'd call back and just talk to us for a bit, we could ask her how she knew Evie and maybe trick her into telling us where she lived, or something. But she's never going to do that, is she? So we'd have to be smart about it, get the info from her phone instead.'

'From her phone?'

'Like a . . . a location ping or whatever they do on *Hunted*? You know, that TV show where people go on the run and the hunters have to find them? So I was searching online for someone who could do that, a location ping. Someone we could pay to track this phone and find out where the lady was, where she lived. Then *we* could be the hunters, we could find her and maybe find Evie too.'

I reach across the table and give his hand a reassuring squeeze. By the way he'd been talking, I'd thought this was going to be something bad – something much worse than a few hopelessly naive searches on the internet.

'Oh Lucas,' I say. 'It's fine. I'm pleased you're using that big brain of yours to think of ways to help. But you can't just Google that sort of thing, love. Tracking someone's phone like that would be illegal. Not to mention impossible, unless you're the police, or MI5 or whatever. You can't just go online and buy a service like that.'

'But that's just it, Mum,' he says in a small voice. 'You can. If you're buying on the dark web.'

38

'You can get whatever you want on there,' Lucas says. 'Literally, anything you can imagine.'

'Not sure I want to imagine.'

He looks down at his lap. 'You said you wouldn't be angry.'

'I'm not angry. I'm just . . . I didn't realise you knew about those things. Don't you need some special software to get on the dark web?'

'Already downloaded it,' he says quietly. 'Ages ago. Forgot it was even still there until I was going through all the stuff on my phone this morning.'

He tells me the whole sorry saga. How he and some of the boys in his class had been at a sleepover in the summer and long after midnight one of them had been boasting about things he'd seen on the dark web. 'Pictures of real dead bodies and proper guns for sale,' Lucas tells me, 'and a video of this gang guy getting his finger cut off with a machete.' Which had spiralled in the way that things can with teenage boys until they were daring each other to download the dark web browser onto their phones, then to search for more and more outrageous things: drugs, stolen goods, fake driver's licences, stolen credit card info. And so on.

It's not all 'bad stuff', he tells me, just a place for all the hidden sites that can't be found through regular web browsers. Instead you have to use the Tor browser, which makes all web traffic anonymous as well as the people running the sites on there.

As he's telling me, I do a quick Google check on my own phone where the consensus seems to be that the dark web is not *just* for criminals and it's not illegal to visit – as long as you don't buy or sell anything dodgy. When I was his age, sleepover obsessions had been about Tamagotchis and Take That and – when we were a bit older – illicit vodka and Ouija boards.

'It doesn't matter,' I say when he's finished. 'If you didn't download anything, or try to buy anything. It's fine, it's OK. But probably best if you delete that browser now.'

He's still silent, and won't look at me.

'Lucas?' I say. 'You didn't download some sort of dodgy app, did you?'

'I had your bag with all your stuff in it, and I took the credit card out of your purse and . . .' He cuffs away a tear. 'I got scammed. I'm sorry, Mum.'

'Scammed?'

'Found a site that I thought could do the phone location thing. It looked proper, and it had, like, a four point six star rating from satisfied customers and I thought if we could just find out where that lady was, we could go and talk to her because she's never going to call us back, is she? But then I made the payment and gave the number and the site tells me to download a messaging app off the Apple store called Enigma, set up an account and the location ping would be sent there.'

'You set up the messaging account like they said?'

He gives a miserable nod.

'But there's nothing there. No message came through. And that was hours ago.'

'How much was it?'

He takes a big swallow of his lemonade. 'A hundred and ninety-nine pounds.'

On one level, I know I should be angry that he's gone behind my back, been conned by some internet fraudster, but instead I feel a strange sense of calm about it all. The whole thing is a pinprick, a minor inconvenience against the backdrop of everything that's happened in the last few days.

I log into my banking app and sure enough, £199 was debited from the credit card just before 1 p.m. today to an account called Jester Bear Ltd.

'I'm really sorry, Mum.' He sniffs. 'Just wanted to help.'

'Show me the website,' I say. 'The one you found.'

He taps and swipes at the screen of his phone, then hands it over the table to me. *FoneFinder*. The site is basic, a generic picture of an attractive glossy-haired blonde woman on a phone with some rudimentary graphics beneath, text couched in neutral language as if it's aimed at people trying to recover lost or stolen property.

Want to find your lost phone? Police can't help? For a one-off fee we can tell you EXACTLY where your missing phone is located – no questions asked. Don't bother with private investigators, WE can give you what you need because WE have people on the inside at all the major mobile networks – EE, Vodafone, 3 and Virgin – with access to the data YOU need. AND we give you a spread of data so you can spot patterns to help you locate your missing property. Find any mobile number, anywhere (UK only).

It gives a price list for various different options, alongside quotes from 'satisfied customers' that also look suspiciously generic.

FoneFinder looks like a stalker's paradise.

Or a lucrative scam taking advantage of the naive and the desperate.

39

Lucas continues to pick at his food. 'I'll pay you back,' he says quietly. 'From my birthday and Christmas money.'

'No, you won't.' I return the phone to him. 'You don't need to do that, Lucas. It's done now, already forgotten. And forgiven.'

It's not until we're back in my car that it fully hits me. My son – the Good Boy, the Rule Follower, the Venture Scout – had sat in a police station and tried to hire some sort of hacker on the dark web. He'd tried to procure a law-breaking act while a few feet away from people who would have arrested him on the spot if they'd known what was going on. Another lucky escape.

We stop for petrol at an Esso station on Euston Road. Standing in line to pay at the checkout, with Slade belting out 'Merry Xmas Everybody' over the speakers, I take my phone out and scroll through the new notifications on the Facebook post that Lucas put up earlier. It's been shared by twenty-six people and I have another forty-two friend requests – all of which I accept – plus dozens of messages of sympathy and support beneath the post, along with some spam messages linking to random pages or urging me to 'invest in crypto TODAY'.

Was any of it any use? A handful of direct messages had come through from friends and distant relatives asking if there's anything they can do; but most of them seem to be from new contacts who are complete strangers. I click through them one by one as I shuffle towards the front of the queue.

Hello, my dear, please consider this most courteous request to consider sending me a personal message at your earliest convenience so that we may discuss a fee for my services as a most esteemed private—

I hit *delete.*

hey my mum is a psycic and shes been on tv and everything finding missing peple she has a gift thats been in my famly for generashns and she could help you—

Delete.

Dearest one, you MUST learn to use the POWER OF PRAYER because our LORD AND SAVIOUR is the ONLY ONE who can bring your daughter back SAFELY—

Delete.

The cashier calls me forward and I tap my debit card to pay, reading and deleting another message from yet another internet chancer.

Back in the car, Lucas is frowning at his phone and barely registers me when I sit back down in the driver's seat. But as I start the engine, he puts a hand on my arm.

'Mum?' he says, still not looking at me. 'You might want to see this.'

'What is it?'

There is a honk of impatience from the driver behind me, so I pull my car away from the pumps and into one of the parking spaces at the edge of the forecourt.

'Remember that TikTok guy at my school? Posting all that stupid stuff about Evie?'

'Just ignore him, Lucas. The internet is overrun by idiots like him.'

'Yeah,' he says. 'I know. But the thing is, when we were at the police station, I was so bored and there was nothing to do so . . . I was watching his stupid videos again.'

'OK.'

'And reading all the stupid comments from other people.'

'Right.' I half turn in my seat to look at him. 'You didn't reply, did you? Tell me you didn't reply, love. There's nothing to be gained from it.'

'I was *so* bored though. So I started going through all the comments and a few were nice but most of them were the same, like, Evie going missing is our fault, or your fault, or it's a scam or a stunt or she's not even real. Like, *she doesn't exist.* And because I was bored I started firing back at a few of them, telling them they were wrong and they were talking crap.'

I check my watch; we really needed to get back on the road soon. Today had been a long day already and I wanted to get home to Reading, although I knew my own house wasn't safe now. We would stay at my mum's instead, take stock of everything and work out what to do next.

'Don't worry too much about it,' I say, handing him a chocolate bar for the journey. I can't imagine anything else he's going to confess will be on a par with him flushing money down the toilet of the dark web, but he seems quite worked up all the same. 'Just don't read the comments anymore, OK?'

'But there were a few that were *nice.* That said they were sure Evie would be all right and they were praying for her safe return, that kind of stuff. And one lady . . . she put up this comment.'

He hands me his phone, a text exchange on the screen.

So sorry to hear about this. I'm a mother in the same situation and know exactly how the family must feel. Sending thoughts and prayers for Evie's safe return xx

'I replied to her too,' Lucas says, swiping to another message thread on the phone. 'Asking her about, like, what had happened to her family and what else we might be able to do to find Evie. Stuff like that.'

He scrolls down the thread, to the stranger's reply.

I didn't mean to intrude, I'm not one of those crazy people who wants to involve themselves in other people's situations. Just wanted to show my support. I'm sure the police are doing everything they can. Good luck xx

I scroll back up to her first message, the words that made this one stand out from the rest.

I'm a mother in the same situation.

Her profile picture shows a middle-aged woman with short dark hair and glasses, cuddling a cocker spaniel; at the bottom one of those rainbow NHS logos with a 'Support our Heroes' caption that became popular during the pandemic. *Ruth Greenall.* She doesn't look the least bit familiar.

I scroll to Lucas's next message in the thread.

Anything you can tell us would be helpful. My sister was a uni student but she dropped out and didn't tell anyone. We only found out a few days ago and we can't find her. How old is your daughter? Did you get help from the police?

Ruth Greenall doesn't reply. The next message is from Lucas, an hour later.

Please talk to my mum? We're really worried about Evie and the police won't help

There is no response to this message either, and I assume that the pain is still too raw for this woman to open up to a stranger about her missing child.

After another hour with no reply, Lucas has repeated just a single word.

Please?

Half an hour after that – just a few minutes ago, in fact – she's finally given him a reluctant response.

OK. FaceTime?

40

Perhaps Jacob Jackson had served a purpose after all, if Ruth Greenall can help in some way.

The FaceTime call connects after the third ring. Ruth looks older than her profile picture, closer to sixty than fifty, her features drawn with tiredness. She seems to be in a kitchen, yellow and brown tiles on the wall behind her next to a small spice rack. We exchange awkward pleasantries and I thank her again for agreeing to talk to us.

She is hesitant at first, reluctant to share her own personal agony with a stranger. And as she slowly opens up, I wonder whether she is still clinging to hope by her fingertips, or whether she has already crossed the line from desperation to despair.

Her nightmarish experience has eerie parallels to my own.

Ruth's daughter was another smart young woman heading off to the capital who had cut off all contact after a couple of months, without warning. Cassie was slightly older than Evie – twenty rather than nineteen – and she was heading to a new job rather than to university, but otherwise our stories have a lot in common. A key difference was that Ruth had discovered the deception earlier, in late October, when she paid a surprise visit to her daughter on the way back from a shopping trip to the West End.

'I went to her shared flat,' she says, 'knocked on the door and this girl said Cassie had moved out weeks ago and she didn't know where she'd gone. The next day her phone went out of service, no email, the lot. Nothing more posted on her Instagram, no contact with her friends back home. And I've been looking for her ever since.'

'I'm sorry,' I say, feeling an eerie pulse of recognition. 'It was very similar with my daughter.'

It's been a long, tough day but the novelty of talking to a mother in the same situation – someone going through *precisely* the same thing as me – has given me a tentative burst of energy. I can hear in Ruth's voice, in her words, the same desperation that I've felt over the past few days. The same disbelief, an inability to understand what has actually taken place and why our children have been singled out like this. How they have – quite independently of each other – followed such a horribly similar path.

Farley had got a sense of it, I think, and so had the mothers of a couple of Evie's friends. But only in an abstract way – not like this. Not in the flesh-and-blood sense, the horrible wounded feeling as if a limb has been torn from your body and there's no way to stop the bleeding.

'I've been going out of my mind,' she says. 'Trying to work out what I missed, the signals, the clues, the build-up to it all. Don't know about you but somehow it feels like it was months in the planning, a long time coming. Doesn't feel like something she just decided to do on the spur of the moment one day.'

'Same with Evie,' I say. 'She'd split from her boyfriend at home, and not told me. She'd drifted from her friends as if she didn't have time for them anymore. It's almost like she'd been building this whole escape plan under my nose.'

'Escaping from what, though?' Ruth looks down, broken. 'I thought Cassie was happy. She *was* happy, I'm sure of it. She'd saved hard and she was looking forward to moving out and living in the big city and then . . .' She shakes her head. 'Then she was gone.'

We both sit in silence for a moment, interrupted by the squeak and hiss of brakes from a lorry pulling onto the petrol station fore-court behind me.

'So what are you going to do next?' I shift position in the driver's seat so Lucas can get a better view of my screen. 'Are you still trying to get the police interested?'

'I've tried,' she says. 'God knows I've tried but they've never really taken it seriously. With her being twenty, an adult, not an addict or what they regard as a vulnerable person—' she makes air quotes around these last two words with her fingers '—they've never made her a priority. To be honest, they've been bloody useless.'

'But if we go together, if we report them together, they might start to see they could be linked, right? Not just one isolated case but two, or maybe more, that's got to make the police sit up and take notice.'

She shrugs. 'Maybe,' she says. 'Anything's worth a try, I suppose.'

'Could we meet, maybe tomorrow? We could come to you.'

She leans back in her chair, away from the camera, and I can tell immediately I've gone too far, too fast.

'Well . . .'

'Or we could meet somewhere neutral? Somewhere in London? Wherever you like.'

The dashboard display says it's almost nine o'clock. Already creeping towards Lucas's normal bedtime and we were still miles from home in the middle of the city. Ruth and I make a plan to meet tomorrow at 10 a.m. A public place, open, busy – somewhere we can play it safe.

'I'll see you then,' I say to Ruth. 'And thank you. For this. It's a relief to talk to someone who's going through the same thing.'

* * *

There doesn't seem any point in going back to Reading now, when it will only take us further away from Evie. Not to mention the implied threat in the note that had been left under the hotel room door last night. If we keep moving, kept going from place to place, perhaps they wouldn't be able to find us again.

So instead I find another budget hotel, in Hackney this time, another twin room with two single beds side by side. It goes on the credit card again and I don't dare look at the balance. When I've got Evie back safe I'll take stock of how far into the red I've gone, but until then I just have to pray I'm not too close to my credit limit. Once we're safely in the room, I push the armchair away from the window and wedge it up against the door, before turning both locks into place. Then wash some of our clothes in the bath as best I can, leaving them hanging from the shower curtain rail to dry.

Half an hour later we're both in our beds, my limbs leaden and exhausted. I stare up at the ceiling, the only light in the room the ethereal glow from Lucas's phone as he scrolls and reads and two-thumb types.

'Time to turn it off now, love.' I stifle a yawn. 'You should get some sleep.'

He doesn't reply.

I turn my head to look at him. 'Lucas? Not more comments on the TikTok video, are there? Just ignore them.'

He's stopped scrolling. His face, lit ghostly pale by the iPhone, is slack with surprise.

'Can I borrow your phone for a minute, Mum?'

'What is it?'

I grope for the bedside table, hand him the mobile and he unlocks it deftly with my passcode pattern, then uses it to take a series of pictures of his own screen.

'What are you doing?'

He gives me his own mobile, some app that I don't recognise with a string of messages.

'Remember that FoneFinder site, the dark web thing from earlier on?' He leans up on one elbow now, a tremor of excitement in his voice. 'It wasn't a scam after all.'

'What?' I squint, the screen blazing bright in front of me. 'How do you know?'

'They've come back to me about that number I gave them earlier. Evie's emergency contact number from the university.'

The strange, unhelpful woman who had been reluctant to give anything away. Who had hung up on me yesterday, ignored my messages and screened my calls ever since.

But now we know where she is. Or at least, where she's been today.

There are a whole string of messages, ten or more, which have all landed in the last few minutes.

Location data for your phone as requested
Good luck recovering your property
Here are your pings!

The next message is just a long string of numbers and nothing else. As is the next one, and the next. A sense of unreality grips me as I scroll through this information that had been gathered illegally. Could this be traced back to us, to Lucas? How many laws had he broken? Were these messages even for real, anyway?

I scroll back up to the top of the thread, trying to get a sense of it.

Just as the first message disappears.

Each of the six messages disappears in turn, one after the other, replaced with two words: *message expired*. I hold the phone out to him, a lurch of panic in my chest at the sudden severing of this link to Evie.

'I didn't press anything,' I say. 'Honestly, they just disappeared. Where did they go?'

'It's OK, Mum,' he says. 'They're one-time messages, they show for sixty seconds then disappear. Like a security thing, I mean, the app is end-to-end encrypted anyway so it's sort of overkill. But that's why I needed your phone, to take pictures of each one.'

I look at the last six images in my own camera roll, feeling the stab of panic subside. Each of them is a shot of one of the expired messages, a string of digits like a . . . like the GPS location of our house. Timestamps show they were taken at the top of each hour, starting at 5 p.m. and going through to the last at 10 p.m., just a few moments ago.

The final messages are still there, still visible.

Last ping at 10 p.m. – most people at home then :-)
You won't hear from us again
Thanks for your custom
Jester Bear has left the chat

'What do you think?' Lucas says, his voice taut with excitement. 'Shall we have a look?'

I read out the first set of digits as he types them into his mapping app. While I call out the coordinates one by one, I wonder if the location will zero in to Flame nightclub. Or The Royal Pearl Hotel. Or maybe somewhere at the university, or even back home in Reading.

Lucas finishes typing in digits. He frowns, pinches the small screen to zoom.

'Well,' I say. 'Where's the lady with the phone?'

'Six pings over five hours.' He's still studying the screen. 'And the last five of them are in the exact same place.'

'Where?'

'Somewhere called Silvertown,' he says, looking up. 'Where's that?'

EVIE

Three months earlier

Evie perched on the side of the bed, steadying herself.

The hotel room spun slightly around her, champagne fizzed through her system and her ears still rang from the music in the nightclub. Flame was a world away from the poky little clubs in Reading, where she and Millie used to go with their fake IDs. This was a *proper* club, like one you'd see in a music video or a film, with podium dancers, multiple dance floors and literally *thousands* of people packed in across three levels. She had never been in the VIP area of a club before, either. Huge sofas, food on demand, buckets of champagne on ice – all provided by an entrepreneur friend of Scott's who'd gone to school with him but who hadn't actually turned up tonight. Brenton, was it? She couldn't remember.

Behind her on the bed, Scott kissed her ear, her neck, her back. Eased the bra strap down and kissed her shoulder, his stubble tickling her skin.

He stopped.

'Are you OK?' he said. 'Evie? You've gone quiet.'

'Just feel a bit woozy.' She felt foolish and naive, as if she was letting him down. 'Had a bit too much fizz, I think.'

He kissed her on the other shoulder.

'It's all right.' Scott's voice was deep and soft. 'Shall I get you a glass of water?'

'No.' She shook her head. 'Just want to lie down for a bit.'

'We can do that.'

She lay back and took deep breaths until the spin of the room subsided. Scott lay down beside her in his boxer shorts, pillows bunched beneath his head, just looking at her.

'It's OK,' he said. 'If you don't want to.'

'I do,' she said. 'Really, I do. Just a bit drunker than I thought I'd be. Sorry.'

'You have nothing to apologise for.'

'Could we just talk for a bit instead?'

He kissed her gently on the forehead and pulled the duvet up over both of them, made sure she was comfortable before turning out the lights. He told her about the private drama college he'd found in Hampstead, how he could help her with the fees. About his friend's parents, who owned a little flat in Hampstead, and would let her have it for mates' rates. How the college had close links with Elstree Film Studios to help students hoping for careers both in front of and behind the camera; an induction day coming up in early October, and how he'd love to go with her.

Scott made anything seem possible.

They lay like that in the darkness for a long time, face to face, hands clasped together under the sheet, laughing and teasing and whispering to each other about everything and nothing. He opened up too, about the heartbreak that he carried with him, the vulnerability that she had sensed right from the start. For the first time, he told her about his first real girlfriend, who he'd been together with through most of secondary school. How he had followed her to Leeds University; how he'd thought they would get engaged and married and have a family together. The devastation of losing her, in the summer after second year, to a road accident on a family holiday in Greece.

How he'd never believed he could be happy again, until he'd met Evie that day in Windsor. He told her things in the darkness of that hotel room that he'd never told her before, of secret scars, of dreams and hopes for the future, until the sky began to lighten with the first approach of dawn.

She was finally drowsing off to sleep when he said it.

The words so soft they were almost a whisper, like his last conscious thought before he drifted into sleep. The most amazing words she'd ever heard.

'I love you, Evie Wingfield.'

41

Ruth is late.

She texts to apologise as she fights her way into London from Hertfordshire amid throngs of Wednesday morning traffic. Mid-week is the most popular time to be in the office, I guess, most hybrid workers preferring to stay home on Mondays and Fridays. It occurs to me that Ruth coming from Hatfield represents another eerie parallel in our lives – another Home Counties commuter town well within the capital's powerful orbit. Close enough to feel the city's dark gravitational pull.

Silvertown has had to wait. It's on the river, near City Airport and the Thames Barrier, a lesser-known corner of east London that has seen better days, judging by what I've read online. Part of me had toyed with getting up before dawn and jumping in a cab to have a look at the place before meeting Ruth, but I wanted to see what she had to say first. It was only a few miles from last night's hotel, but east was the wrong direction.

Instead we've come west, to the wide open space and gently sloping parkland of Primrose Hill, looking out over an expanse of bare trees and the shining skyscrapers beyond. A public place. Safe. Normal.

Lucas hunches a little deeper into his coat on the bench beside me.

'You don't think she's just another weirdo, do you?' He's wearing his woolly gloves and a new Russian-style fake fur hat with flaps over his ears, a hasty purchase from Primark on our way to the Tube this morning. 'All the rest of the people who messaged you have been, haven't they? Like, maybe she's one of those internet copycats latching on, repeating all your stuff back to you?'

'She didn't seem weird, she seemed genuine. You saw her.'

I take his free hand in mine, give it a gentle squeeze of reassurance. But even as I'm doing it, I let my eyes wander over the people nearby. A middle-aged woman surrounded by a grey carpet of pigeons, all strutting and pecking as she throws out handfuls of bread from a plastic bag. A couple of young guys walking hand in hand along the path below us, their breath steaming in the cold air. A white-haired older couple on the bench nearer to us, both bundled up as if they're in the Arctic, sharing coffee from a Thermos. Squinting up towards the brow of the hill I can see a man alone on a bench, in a heavy leather jacket and scarf, wrap-around sunglasses and a baseball cap.

Something judders when I see him, like a needle skipping on a record. A memory drifting loose. The black baseball cap, no logo, pulled down low.

For a moment I think—

No, it can't be.

Or had he been behind the wheel of the black saloon on Monday? I raise a hand to shield my eyes from the low sun. Was he the one who had been following us?

'We should test her though,' Lucas says thoughtfully. 'The lady.'

'Test her?' I say, still squinting at the baseball cap guy. 'How?'

He takes a sip of his hot chocolate.

'Ask her something she wouldn't know if she was a scammer. Like, I don't know. Something she wouldn't know otherwise.'

I don't say it out loud, but I'm almost more scared that Ruth is telling the truth. Because if she is, then perhaps there is a pattern to these young women going missing. A pattern repeated across the capital, the modus operandi of someone who might have done this many times before.

The pattern of a predator.

'I'll ask her for ID,' I say, returning my gaze to Lucas. 'So we know she's for real.'

The day is sharp and clear, only a few defiant clouds against the winter-blue sky. Looking south-east towards the city I can make out the towers of Canary Wharf, Bishopsgate, the Barbican and the dome of St Paul's. The Shard standing proud, unchallenged, glinting like a blade in the hard December sunlight. I imagine Evie lost, desperate, alone among these gleaming towers of concrete and glass and steel. Somewhere amid the canyons and high-rises, the tunnels and tower blocks, the chaos and wealth and dirt of this vast city, my daughter was in danger and she needed me. She was lost, shipwrecked, far from home.

The ache in my chest is almost paralysing.

Where are you, Evie?

'Mum?' Lucas gives me a nudge. 'Is this the lady?'

He nods towards the path, where a woman is approaching with a cocker spaniel on a lead. She's small, not much more than five feet, and bundled up in a long belted coat and cream scarf, the strap of a shoulder bag looped across her chest. She's walking quickly up the hill, looking left and right, when her gaze finally lands on us and she angles towards the bench.

'I'm *so* sorry I'm late,' she says. 'There was an accident on the North Circular and traffic was snarled up all the way back to Mill Hill.'

She offers me her gloved hand and we shake, her grip delicate but firm. Up close, she looks like a librarian or a bookkeeper, with small, precise movements and sharp eyes. Wisps of blonde hair have escaped from either side of her bobble hat, framing her face. There is a sadness to her as well, a brittle tone to her voice that she does not try to disguise. Her dog is wrapped up against the cold, in a tartan winter coat, his tail swishing enthusiastically from side to side as Ruth takes in the view.

'And this is your son?' She raises a gloved hand to Lucas. 'Hello there, young man.'

Lucas pats the spaniel's head. 'What's your dog called?'

'This little rascal is Milo,' she says. 'And he just *loves* new people.'

Milo wags his tail harder as if in agreement, while Ruth takes a seat at the end of the bench.

'This is *so* strange,' she says. 'For weeks I've been talking to people who don't know what it's like to have a missing child, or look at me as if I'm mad, deluded. And now finally I meet someone who's living the same nightmare as me.'

'Thanks again for getting in touch, for coming to meet me at such short notice.'

'I'm just glad we found each other. It's been—' She breaks off, shaking her head. 'It's been awful to carry this alone for so long.'

'I'm sorry to have to ask,' I say. 'But I've had quite a lot of random people contacting me online about Evie since we put the appeal out there. Particularly on Facebook. Have you got any ID? Just so I can . . . be sure you are who you say you are.'

'Oh,' she says. 'I see. Of course, I totally understand – I've had the same kind of thing when I posted about Cassie. Nutters asking for reward money, saying they could find her if I just paid them a fee of a thousand pounds or whatever.' She plucks a chunky black purse from her handbag and unzips it, pulling a driver's licence out. 'Here you go. Cassie always takes the mickey out of my photo on there, so washed out I look about ninety-five years old.'

The licence gives her name as Ruth Valerie Greenall of Villiers Street, Hatfield, with a date of birth that makes her fifty-six.

I hand it back to her. 'Thanks, Ruth. My mum's a Valerie too.'

She smiles. 'Same here.'

She turns her phone towards me, a picture of a suntanned young woman with caramel-streaked blonde hair. The photographer has caught her mid-laugh, as if she's just been told a good joke. I can imagine her and Evie getting on well, being friends, having a good time together on a night out.

'That's my Cassie,' Ruth says. 'My daughter. Had a new job at an events company based in Battersea. But they said she just handed in her notice by email one day and never came back.'

Lucas strokes Milo's head. 'Does she have any brothers or sisters?'

Ruth shakes her head. 'Always thought I'd have four or five kids. But then . . .' She tails off. 'We ended up having to do three rounds of IVF so I was in my mid-thirties when Cassie finally came along. By the time we'd got the money together for another round, when she was still small, me and John had grown apart and, well, it just didn't happen.'

She repeats what she told me last night: how Cassie had vanished without trace from her job, her flat, her new life in London. All of her efforts in the last six weeks to track her daughter down, to find out where she went – or why – leading to one dead end after another.

We compare details, trying to work out if our daughters know each other somehow, if there is some hidden link between them. But aside from a handful of music festivals they'd both attended over the years, their orbits don't seem to have crossed at all. They both liked London clubs, drum and bass music, but then so did a million other young people. Evie and Cassie had grown up fifty miles apart in different towns, different counties, they were born in different years and liked different subjects at school.

They had grown up with almost nothing in common. Until now.

In broad terms, I describe to Ruth how we've tried to follow Evie's trail, first to the university, then the hotel in Kensington and the address in Northolt, the nightclub and a short stay at Bethnal Green police station. She studies me as I talk, nodding intently.

'Wait,' she says. 'Don't tell me. Was the hotel called The Royal Pearl?'

I stop mid-flow. 'Yes. How did you know?'

'It took me forever, but I eventually managed to get into Cassie's banking app and looked at all the transactions from around that time. There was one from the bar at The Royal Pearl dated three days after she quit her job, for twenty-seven pounds. I went down to the hotel, gave them dates and times and told them Cassie was missing. They said no, of course, gave me all the usual reasons, data protection, blah blah blah. But . . . I'm at that age now where I don't feel I have to put up with anybody's crap anymore. So I kicked off, right there in reception, demanded to see the manager, the records, shouting and cursing and causing as much fuss as possible.'

I look over at her with a smile. 'I know we've only just met, Ruth, but I can't imagine you kicking off at anyone.'

She grunts with amusement. 'Trust me. When you get to a certain age you suddenly reach this point when you don't care what other people think anymore, you just do not give a sh—'

She breaks off, with a glance at Lucas.

'What I mean is,' she says, 'you say what you think. You don't hold back, it's liberating in a way. Maybe it's the menopause. God knows.'

'So did they give you any information?'

Her shoulders slump. 'No. So then I begged. Pleaded. I didn't care what they thought of me. But they still wouldn't tell me how long she'd stayed, or who she was with. More importantly, who had paid her bill.'

'The staff aren't the most helpful, are they?'

'I ended up speaking to head office in Milan, then I tried to get the police involved, and when that came to nothing I even tried to get a job there to see what I could find out. But I didn't even get an interview. It was a stupid idea, really.'

'Hang on,' I say. 'Can we just rewind a second? The banking app – do you still have access to it now?'

'I can still get into it, yes.'

'So, you've been able to see where Cassie went from there, after she left the hotel? Where was the most recent transaction, is she still in London?'

Ruth swallows, gives Milo an absent-minded scratch between his ears.

'There weren't any more transactions,' she says quietly. All the fire of a moment ago seems to have deserted her. 'She hasn't touched her bank account since that day. Six weeks ago.'

42

I feel a shiver of cold fear, like an eel sliding through my body.

She hasn't touched her bank account since that day.

It doesn't need to be said out loud, and God knows Ruth must have thought about this every day, every hour since her daughter went missing. But if Cassie has not spent anything, not bought anything, not paid any money into her bank account, it couldn't be anything other than a huge red flag.

Either she had another account with a different bank, one that her mother didn't know about; or she had some other means of supporting herself. The memory of the Sugar Daddy websites returns, like a bad taste on my tongue. Perhaps she had just decided to drop out, to live off the grid, no cards – just cash. But how did you do anything nowadays without being able to tap and pay with a card? On the bus, the Tube, in every coffee shop and restaurant, almost everywhere wanted contactless payment.

Or perhaps she was being held somewhere against her will.

'Maybe your daughter lost the card?' Lucas says. 'Or it was stolen?'

Ruth gives him a sad smile. 'That's what I thought, at first. But she used Apple Pay on her phone for most things.'

'Evie's the same,' I say.

My fear is tempered with a powerful wave of sympathy for this woman. She had been a stranger barely twelve hours ago but now she feels as close as a best friend, the two of us tied together in our desperation.

'I talked to all of her mates from home,' Ruth says. 'Everyone I could think of, all of them in turn, trying to make sense of it. Hassled them until they were all sick of me. The only thing one of them said was that they thought a boy had been involved.'

'A boy?'

'Well, a guy, a man, however old he was, I never got any actual details. It was an assumption, more than anything. One of Cassie's friends mentioned in an off-hand way that maybe there was a man involved, but none of them knew for sure – just that she'd totally lost interest in the guys they knew and they couldn't work out why. But when I heard that, it made some kind of sense, if you can understand that? Growing up, she was always the kind of girl who threw herself into things one hundred per cent. No half measures, no lowering herself into a cold swimming pool an inch at a time if she could jump straight in off the high board. I'd always say to her, *Take your time, see if you like it and if you don't, it doesn't matter.* But she took after her dad in her attitude to things. Sport or hobbies or whatever it was – she never held back, always went at everything full on.'

'Sounds like my big sister,' Lucas says quietly.

'It does,' I say. My headstrong, naive, wonderful girl. 'All or nothing.'

'And it was the same with relationships. So if she'd fallen for someone, if he'd really turned her head, then maybe . . .'

I wait for her to finish but she just sits there, her lips pressed together in a hard flat line as if she's trying to stop the tears from coming.

'You think maybe she's gone to be with him?' I say quietly. 'Left her job and gone off with him somewhere, maybe travelling?'

She swallows hard. 'Yes. Maybe. I don't know, honestly I don't know. I just want to hear from her, to know that she's OK, to hear her voice again. Wherever she is, whatever's happened. Even if I don't see her face to face, just to know that she's all right. Not knowing, it's . . .' She shakes her head. 'It's like torture.'

Now the tears do fall and she turns away, wiping at them hastily with a gloved hand.

'Hey.' I dig out a packet of tissues from my handbag and hand one to her. 'We're going to find our girls. Both of them.'

Next to the tissues in my bag is the postcard with *The New Yorker* cover that Lucas had found in Evie's room. A fragment of poetry in flowing black handwriting on the other side. *Let me count the ways . . .* Signed off with a single S. No address, no stamp, so either it had come inside an envelope to stop me seeing it, or S had got it to Evie another way. I take it out and hand it to Ruth, explaining to her where it had come from.

'I think Evie probably forgot this, she'd perhaps meant to take it with her but it was tucked into a book. Did you find anything like this, among Cassie's things?'

She turns it over, shakes her head.

'Nothing personal, no.'

'The man who was on the booking with Evie at The Royal Pearl Hotel was called Scott Lawler. So I've assumed that he's S. He paid the bill when they stayed there; perhaps he paid for Cassie's too.'

She wipes her eyes. 'Both of them?'

'Maybe he's some kind of player.'

I ask her if she recognises any of the other people Parry mentioned to me. Brandon Roper, Nicola Lawler, Eric Caruso.

'Who are they?' she says. 'Are they missing as well?'

'Just some other names that have come up in the last few days.'

We lapse into silence as she studies the postcard more closely, lifting her glasses up to her forehead to examine the handwriting.

Up until the moment she sat down on this bench, I'd still been in two minds as to whether I would tell Ruth about the address, about the mobile we had tracked there. But considering it again now, I realise I've already made my mind up.

'We've got another lead,' I say. 'Another place to check out.'

She looks at me with hopeful eyes as I explain to her about the number Evie had listed as her emergency contact at university, but not the method Lucas used to trace it. Instead I tell her the address had been held by the university, and released to me as a favour by a helpful member of the security team.

'No idea where that even is,' she says. 'Do you think it's authentic?'

I shrug. 'We're going to find out. You're welcome to join us if you want to come.'

'When?' She frowns. 'You mean, today? Now?'

'Nearest tube is Canning Town but it's not that close, so we'll probably head back to the hotel from here to pick up my car.'

'Well, yes of course I would like to help you if I can, but . . .' Her small features crease with concern. 'Shouldn't we pass the information on to the police?'

'We're just going to take a look first. See what's there.'

'Or we could at least let them know that we're going? There's a detective that I've been in touch with, on and off. He's been utterly useless so far but maybe he could check if the address is in their records for any reason?'

'As long as you keep it vague,' I say. 'If he asks how we came by it.'

She sits up straighter on the bench, taking a deep breath.

'Not sure how much help I'll be,' she says. 'But yes, I'll come. Just to look?'

'Just to look,' I say.

We stand and she loops the strap of her handbag over her shoulder, plucking out her phone.

'We could meet there, if you give me the postcode? I'm only parked a couple of minutes away.'

'Sure,' I say. 'We'll get back over to Hackney first, pick up my car and hope it hasn't been clamped, then we'll head east to Silver-town and see you there.'

Lucas gives Milo another scratch behind the ears.

'Or maybe we could go together, to save time?' He looks from me to Ruth, and back again. 'In one car, and you can navigate, Mum.'

I shrug. 'It's not a bad idea, actually.'

'And one car is less conspicuous than two,' he says. 'Less . . . obvious.'

'What do you think, Ruth? Do you mind driving?'

'Well . . .' She looks as if she's trying to find a reason to say no, but can't think of one. 'My car's very small and it's such a mess.'

'We don't mind,' Lucas says. 'Do we, Mum?'

Ruth finally gives a reluctant nod of agreement.

'I suppose it'll be fine. But there's something else you should probably know.' She glances at Lucas, then back at me. 'Since I went looking for Cassie, since I've been going around asking questions, showing her picture everywhere, there have been times when I thought . . . I might have been followed. Never knew for certain but I just always had that feeling, you know? One or two men that I'd see repeatedly. A car following me in traffic, or parked across the street from my house.'

I remember the car that tailed me across London. The saloon that I'd seen again outside the nightclub.

'A black car, kind of low to the ground?'

She shrugs. 'Yes, maybe. Black or dark blue.'

'Me too,' I say. 'Did you notice anyone on your way here this morning?'

'No. But I thought you should be aware.'

We move towards the path, Ruth looping Milo's lead securely around her wrist. I take one last look at the towering buildings jostling for space along the skyline, at the walkers and tourists and workers on the benches and paths nearby, people taking time to enjoy the view.

The man in the black baseball cap is gone.

43

Silvertown is a part of London I've never visited, never even heard of it before. It's sandwiched between City Airport and the Thames, a mass of warehouses and industrial units, disused wharves and derelict spaces awaiting redevelopment. Ruth drives us there in her little electric Nissan, with me navigating in the front passenger seat and Lucas sitting behind us having made friends with the dog. Ruth had called her police contact as we walked to the car, leaving a message and asking him to get back to her urgently – without a reply so far.

We had made steady progress in stop–start morning traffic, through Camden, Shoreditch, Tower Hamlets, all the time pushing east, until we bypass the same towers we'd seen from Primrose Hill. Close up, they are looming giants that block out the sun, mountains of shining glass throwing mountainous shadows across everything around them. Eventually I see the first signs for the Royal Albert Docks, for Canning Town, Plaistow and Custom House, until at last we make a right turn onto North Woolwich Road and from there onto Factory Road.

Ruth pulls over beside a rusting chain-link fence and Lucas leans forward between the front seats to show us the map on his phone, a red pin icon dropped into the spot where the phone signal had been located. According to the satellite image, it's a large metal-sided building on a cramped lot. On one side it's bordered by a storage yard containing hundreds of long steel shipping containers, and on the other by some kind of huge industrial processing plant. The south side of the lot gives directly onto the broad brown depths of the Thames. Back in the day I guess it might have been some kind of warehouse for imported goods.

I summon the memory of a conversation from two days ago, the woman who had picked up when I called the number. Her accent had been bland, nondescript, if anything with a middle-class Thames Valley intonation. Nothing distinctively East London about it. And try as I might, I just can't seem to place her *here*. They just didn't seem to *fit*, her voice and this place. Perhaps Lucas had been right first time around: perhaps this was a scam after all. A randomly selected GPS coordinate to give to a gullible paying customer who could never complain and never ask for their money back.

A lorry roars past, so fast and so close that Ruth's Nissan rocks slightly on its suspension and Milo lets out a yelp of alarm. A cement truck follows close behind it, big drum turning. There is not much regular traffic on this road and it already feels conspicuous for the three of us to be here in this little electric car, so far off the beaten track where residents or commuters or tourists might normally be found.

'Up here a bit further,' Lucas says. 'Then it's another right turn, and the place is down at the end of that road.'

Ruth pulls back onto Factory Road and follows the directions, making a right turn into a dead-end street.

'I'm not sure about this,' she says, her voice suddenly taut with nerves. 'Am I supposed to just drive up and park outside?'

'There.' I point further down the access road. It had been a while since I'd been out on an active investigation at work, but I still remember a few tricks of the trade. 'If we pull in next to those wrecks we'll be able to observe for a bit without being seen.'

Among the debris of an abandoned lot is a forlorn row of junked vehicles. The nearest is a once-white Transit van turned rust brown, stripped of its doors, lights and wheels, weeds sprouting lustily through the cracked tarmac beneath. Ruth tucks the Nissan into the gap next to it, the little car almost hidden from the road now.

Lucas leans forward again.

'What are we going to do now, Mum?'

I release my seat belt. 'We're going to watch and wait for a little bit. And we're going to see what we can see.'

* * *

We watch for an hour.

No one arrives, and no one leaves.

Milo whines softly after a while and Ruth takes him out so he can relieve himself against the chassis of the old Transit. She stays low to avoid being seen and urges the spaniel back into the little Nissan as soon as he's finished, rubbing her hands together against the cold. She finds a packet of mint humbugs in the glove compartment and offers it to Lucas and me.

Ruth unwraps her own humbug and pops it into her mouth.

'D'you ever do one of those gratitude journal things?' She crinkles the plastic wrapper into a ball and settles back into the driver's seat. 'Read an article about it online somewhere once, don't remember where, but it seemed like a good idea.' When I shake my head, she adds: 'It's supposed to give you a positive mental mindset at the start of each day, or some such nonsense. You write down one thing every morning that you're grateful for.'

'Sounds like a good idea.'

She grunts. 'Found mine in a drawer, when I was turning the house upside down after Cassie went missing. Read the entries again and saw that I'd only kept it up for two weeks, finding something to write each day. *Two bloody weeks* before I ran out of things to say. How rubbish is that? I had no clue how good my life was. How much I had, how lucky I was that I had her and that she was happy and healthy and safe. I had no real idea until I lost it. Until I lost her. Ended up throwing that stupid gratitude journal across the room. What an idiot.'

'You're not an idiot, Ruth.' I put a hand on her arm. 'I was exactly the same. Blind to how lucky I was, how good everything was.'

We lapse into silence as a figure emerges from a fire exit on the first floor of the warehouse, manhandling something into the doorway before lighting a cigarette. It looks like a man in his thirties or forties, dark hoodie and jeans, average height and build.

'Wish we had binoculars or something,' Ruth says, as if she's glad to change the subject. She zooms in on her phone camera instead but he's a good hundred metres away and the picture she snaps is grainy and indistinct. 'Does he look familiar?'

I shrug. It's almost easier to see him with the naked eye, but still too far away to make out details. He leans on the railing, scrolling on his phone, the smoke of his cigarette coiling up and vanishing into the cold city air. The warehouse itself is three storeys high, its metal sides scarred with long, weeping tracks of rust that run from top to bottom. There are no windows and we can't see the front door from our vantage point, but we *have* got a good view of the only way in or out. Could Evie be here? Maybe held against her will?

We watch, and wait.

A small jet comes into land at City airport, engines whining as it drops out of sight below the line of buildings.

From somewhere nearer to us comes the soft, asthmatic shunting of a train slowing to a stop.

Ruth turns abruptly in her seat, tapping her forehead with the heel of her palm.

'I know what I was going to show you. God, I'm an idiot – *completely* slipped my mind.' She burrows into the shoulder bag on her lap. 'I did find something in Cassie's bedroom, but it wasn't a postcard. Her room's a tip normally, stuff piled everywhere. It was a bit better when she packed up to go to London but not much. When she went missing I decided to go through everything, every drawer, every pocket, every bag, under the bed, everywhere. Took me a while but I found these wedged way down in the side pocket of an overnight bag, underneath her bed.'

She hands me a couple of creased orange train tickets inside a small clear Ziploc bag. I hold them up as Lucas moves in to see. Return tickets from the end of June this year, from Waterloo to somewhere called Shelford Cross.

'It's in the middle of nowhere,' Ruth says. 'We've never been to that part of Sussex, we don't know anyone there or nearby, and as far as I know Cassie doesn't have any friends there either.'

'You didn't know she'd gone there?'

'Checked my diary and she'd told me she was out with a friend looking at flats in London. She was gone for the whole weekend. Of course, when I checked with the friend last month, they had no idea what I was talking about. It was all completely made up.'

'So you've been to this place? Shelford Cross?'

'A few weeks ago. Couldn't get the police interested so I got on the train myself. There's hardly anything there: two pubs, one of which has been closed since the pandemic, a couple of churches, a tiny village school, some houses and a few farms on the outskirts. Hardly anyone around. And there's nowhere to stay overnight, the pub didn't have rooms for guests so where did she sleep on the Saturday night before the train brought her back on Sunday? I talked to a few people, showed them Cassie's picture, but no one could remember seeing her. Mostly they looked at me like I was a bit mad.'

'I know the feeling.'

Lucas shows us the map on the screen of his phone.

'Near Brighton? Just looks like . . . yeah. There's literally *nothing* there.'

'Of course,' Ruth says, 'it could be a complete coincidence that she got a train out to this random little village. Maybe there was someone she knew from back in sixth form, or that she'd met online, but then why lie to me about it?'

'At this point,' I say, 'nothing feels like a coincidence.'

I try to put the pieces together, try to arrange them in an order that makes sense. These disconnected places that might have a link to Evie or Cassie – places they had been to or at least passed through. All unknown to me, to Ruth, until after our daughters had vanished into thin air. An upmarket hotel, a paid-for office address, an East End nightclub, a sleepy rural village miles outside London.

And this place too, Silvertown, perhaps another link in the chain.

Up on the fire escape, the smoker has finished his cigarette and disappeared back inside. But there is a slender, dark line between the fire door and the building itself.

I buzz down my window and squint over at it.

'I think we should get a bit closer,' I say to Ruth, without taking my eyes off the warehouse. 'What do you think?'

'Closer?'

'I've got an idea.' I open my door. 'Are you coming?'

44

'Lauren?' Ruth is still sitting in her seat, a look of surprise on her face. 'Is this a good idea?'

I lean on the open door of the Nissan, bending down into the car.

'You can stay here if you want. I'm going to have a closer look.'

'Isn't it trespassing?'

'If they ask I'll just say we're . . . I don't know. On our way to see a show at the O2 and got lost, got a flat tyre.'

She stares at me, then back towards the main road. 'No one gets lost nowadays, do they?'

'Thought you didn't give a damn anymore about upsetting people?'

'I don't.'

I glance at the rusted metal sidings of the warehouse. 'Well, I'm going to have a look.'

'Mum?' My son buzzes his window down. 'Can I come too?'

For a moment, my resolve weakens in favour of the urge to keep him close, to bring him with me. But surely that will expose him to more unknowns, more risk. More danger.

'You stay here, Lucas. I won't be long.'

I return my attention to Ruth, who still hasn't moved.

'Stay if you want. You can keep an eye on Lucas.'

'What are you going to do?'

'That phone is here so maybe the woman is too. Maybe I can find her.'

'Then what?'

'Talk to her. Ask her what she knows about our daughters: maybe Evie's working here and it's her boss's number? This place could just be a regular company, for all we know.'

Ruth casts a sceptical glance at the warehouse. 'I still think we should call the police. It doesn't *look* regular. It looks dodgy as anything, a knackered old warehouse on a dead-end street, in the arse-end of London.'

'OK,' I say, holding up a hand. 'Why don't you give your detective another try?'

She calls her police contact, Detective Sergeant Fuller, her face darkening as it goes to voicemail for the second time this morning. She leaves another message.

'Listen,' I say. 'Time is ticking and I can't sit around anymore. I'm going to take a closer look and if I'm not back in ten minutes, call nine nine nine.'

'No.' She opens her door, seeming to come to a decision. 'No. I'm coming with you.' Turning in her seat, she says to Lucas: 'Milo barks when he gets nervous. But he'll be calm if you stay with him, give him a bit of fuss. And he can look after you.'

The spaniel whines softly.

'We won't be long,' I say to my son. The niggling worry is still there, the memory of racing back to that hotel room when I thought he'd been taken. But I push it away. 'Ruth will lock the doors. There's a blanket here, you can tuck yourself behind the seats and hide under it, no one will see you. Got your phone?'

He nods uncertainly, holding up the mobile.

Once he's safely hidden under the blanket, doors locked, Ruth and I wind our way between the carcases of old cars and onto the access road. We cover the hundred or so metres to the warehouse forecourt at a brisk walk, side by side, dodging cracks and potholes in the ancient tarmac. There are no signs, no company livery, no markings or logos of any kind that I can make out. I can't see any cameras either. We angle right, past the fire escape and down the side of the building, but a corrugated iron fence bars the way down to the river only a few yards beyond. It occurs to me that while we had been watching the access road in, there might also be a jetty or a landing right on the river, at the back of the building. Another access point.

The blood thrums in my veins. A wild, fearful challenge that I haven't felt since I was a reckless teenager.

'Lauren?' Ruth is close beside me. 'What now?'

I indicate the metal fire escape up to the first floor.

Frown lines deepen across her forehead.

'I thought we were just going to *look*.' Her voice is a hoarse whisper. 'Find a window or something.'

'It's a way in.' At the foot of the fire escape I take out my phone and send Lucas a text.

You OK?

A moment later his reply drops in.

Yes are you coming back now?

I look back to the road. All clear.

In a minute

I switch my phone to silent and tell Ruth to do the same. The fire escape creaks with age as we climb it, up to the little gantry where we had observed the smoker ten minutes ago. As I thought, the door is not flush against the frame – the fire extinguisher he'd used to prop it open for his cigarette break is still there. I pull the door fully open and creep inside. There is a short, dimly lit corridor with a single solid door on each side. Both silent, both locked. The corridor turns left and ends in a narrow stairwell leading down. The air smells of damp and fried food and half-rotten wood.

'Wait,' Ruth hisses behind me. 'Thought I heard something.'

We both stand still, ears straining towards the stairwell, which presumably leads to the main part of the warehouse. But there is only silence. I nod towards the stairs and Ruth follows, breathing through gritted teeth. The stairs cut back on themselves down to the ground floor. Another pair of small rooms, presumably offices, are directly below the two locked rooms above. Both these doors are ajar.

I listen at the left-hand door before pushing it open all the way to reveal some kind of workshop, two tables in the centre set up with clamps and tools of all kinds, soldering irons, fine wire and laptop components strewn across both. Circuit boards and dismantled mobile phones litter both tables, along with lots of other electronic kit. Along the side wall is a rough wooden sideboard, like the breakfast bar of a kitchen, with plug sockets all the way along. Each of the sockets – and there are ten at least – has a four-way extension plugged into it.

And attached to every single plug is an iPhone. I tap the screen of the nearest one to wake it up and the display comes to life with a generic screensaver overlaid with a standard set of apps. There is no passcode to unlock it, no request for a thumbprint ID.

The screen shows twenty-three missed calls, all from the same number. Fourteen voicemails, a stack of unread messages.

I tap the next one and the one after that, both of which are switched off. The next one, though, comes to life – and again unlocks without asking for a thumbprint or anything else. Eighteen missed calls, eight voicemails.

Ruth taps another screen. 'Why aren't they ID protected?'

I shake my head. 'Maybe they never leave this room. Or there's more than one person using them, so they can't go on a fingerprint.'

'So *many*,' she says under her breath.

'Do you see all the missed calls?' I point at the screen of the nearest phone. 'Maybe the number I've been calling is one of these phones?'

I take my own mobile from my pocket and call up the list of recently dialled numbers, my thumb hovering over the green *dial* button.

Ruth's eyes bulge with fear. 'Are you mad? What if someone hears it?'

'Just one ring,' I say. 'I have to know.'

She glances back towards the corridor, a hand over her mouth. I press *dial* and put the phone to my ear, a long silence as the call connects. If the woman answers, I'll offer money to her in exchange for information about Evie, I'll tell her to name her price, I'll beg her to—

At the other end of the wooden sideboard there is a soft buzz as an iPhone lights up with an incoming call.

A number shows on the screen.

My number.

Oh my God.

With trembling hands I end the call, my brain scrambling to work out what this all means. The information Lucas had bought from the dark web had been right on the money: the location was correct. The phone was here, among all these others. All these identical phones with stacks of missed calls.

My eyes meet Ruth's, and I can tell that she's thinking the same as me.

'So many phones,' she says again, as if in a daze.

I point to them. 'What if each one of these means another missing girl? Another missing person?'

I pick up the phone that rang, opening it up and tapping one app after another. WhatsApp, Messenger, iMessage, email. All empty.

Nothing personal on the phone at all, no photos, social media accounts, no calendar entries, nothing to indicate the owner. I lay it back down on the workbench. Why had Evie had this number listed as her emergency contact, instead of me? Why this random mobile among a couple of dozen others, in a run-down warehouse in this East London backwater?

The door opposite opens into an office, tatty carpet and a blank whiteboard, a desk strewn with paperwork amid three laptops, all open. The desk is a mess of papers, printouts, two A4 envelopes spilling bound stacks of money into the mess. A two-inch wedge of twenty-pound notes tied tightly together with rubber bands. Euro notes in the other envelope, tens and twenties tied tightly together in fat stacks. Thousands upon thousands. Half concealed beneath one of them, my eyes are drawn to the angular black metal shape of—

A gun.

45

'Jesus,' Ruth breathes beside me. 'Is it real?'

A chill touches the back of my neck. 'No idea. It *looks* real.'

'We should go,' she says, a hand on my forearm. 'Call the police. This is mad.'

'But what if she's here?' I say. 'What if they're both being held here? They could be spirited away long before the police arrive.'

I move a couple of the money stacks to reveal the pistol fully, staring at its chunky black grip, the smooth curve of the trigger. For one mad second I think about picking it up, just for the weight of it in my hand, the dangerous potential, maybe a way to take control of this situation. The power to bring my daughter home.

No. Not like this.

I back away from the desk, the gun, the money, returning to the corridor with Ruth close beside me. She looks petrified.

There is a third door, which looks like it leads out onto the main warehouse floor. We stand beside it, listening for any sound, before I pull it open very slowly.

The sight that greets us seems so out of place, so incongruous, that I stop and stare as Ruth peers over my shoulder. Five gleaming black Mercedes four-by-fours parked very close to each other side by side, none of them with numberplates. They're shiny clean, absolutely pristine: none look as if they've done more than a handful of miles.

My phone is still in my hand and I select the camera, taking a couple of pictures of the cars. It occurs to me that I should go back and take pictures of the money in the office, the phones, the gun – but then I see there are three messages from Lucas which have arrived while my phone's been on silent. Three questions I have not answered.

What's happening Mum?
Are you on your way back?
Are you OK?

I send a single thumbs-up emoji in reply and take a picture of a dozen pallets next to the cars piled high and covered with tarpaulins. Lifting the edge of one of the tarps reveals stacked cartons of two hundred cigarettes, hundreds of them shrink-wrapped together into a huge cube. I don't recognise the brand; a foreign name, maybe Eastern European.

No signs of life. No sign of the guy who had come out for his cigarette break, or the woman who had answered the phone when I called it two days ago. The warehouse is huge, dimly lit by a handful of strip lights in a ceiling matted with cobwebs. There are no windows here either; no natural light at all. We keep moving. More pallets are loaded in stacks two and three tall, too high to see over. Shrink-wrapped brown cardboard boxes that have symbols on them in another language I don't recognise. Maybe Chinese or Korean. This place is like a maze.

Somewhere outside on the river a passing boat blasts its horn.

'Ruth?' I say over my shoulder. 'Look – some more offices here.'

She doesn't reply.

'Ruth?'

I turn to see her terrified face, eyes bulging wide.

A tall man has one large, tattooed arm around her neck, the other gripping both wrists together in front of her. He is holding her close, as if embracing her from behind.

His face is a skull.

The grim reaper.

My stomach loosens in terror even as I see that it's a black bala-
clava printed with dirty grey bone, a sharp jaw, grinning teeth, a
black shadow where the nose should be. A death's head mask with
only a pair of dark eyes visible through a narrow slit.

The sound of a familiar voice jerks me back around to the
front.

'Hello again, Lauren.'

Another black-clad man, another death's head balaclava. But
the size of him, the height, the voice, is much more familiar.

Brandon Roper.

His heavy frame slips into view in front of me, blocking my way
forward.

Suddenly there is another man on my right, and a fourth
emerging from among the pallets on the left. Anonymous in
black jackets and jeans, each with an identical mask as if we've
just stepped into some circle of hell populated by the living dead.

Or walked into a trap.

A fifth man emerges through the stacked boxes in front of us,
the heels of his brogues clicking on the concrete floor. He's also
masked but is not dressed like the rest of them; instead he's in a
long navy overcoat and scarf, a soft grey polo neck and dark blue
jeans. He's fit-looking but slim, not a gym-heavy thick-neck like
the black-clad men. He comes close enough to me so that I can
smell his aftershave, something musky and dark, his pale blue-grey
eyes visible through the slit of the mask.

'Phone.' He holds a gloved hand out.

'What is this place?'

'I'm not going to ask again. Phone.'

Behind me, the guy holding Ruth releases her wrists, digs her
phone out of her handbag and switches it off. She gives a little gasp
of pain as the arm across her neck pinches tighter.

With a pang of regret that I didn't take the gun from the office a few moments ago, I hand over my phone. He checks the screen briefly before handing it to Roper, who switches it off.

The man in the overcoat considers me for a moment, then Ruth. Studying us both with cold, intelligent eyes. He moves closer still, until he's mere inches away from me.

'I want to show you two something, because I don't think you appreciate who you're dealing with. Let me explain.'

He snaps his fingers and one of the other masked men hands him a stoppered glass tube, the size of a large cigar. A clear, colourless liquid inside. He holds it up, shakes it in front of my face.

'The skin dissolves first,' he says. 'Then the layer of fat beneath, eyelids, lips, nose cartilage, tendons, it'll burn your eyeballs right out of their sockets. Secondary thermal burns will even eat into your bones. An *extremely* vigorous chemical reaction. It's like burning alive.' Beneath the mask, it looks like he's smiling. 'Inhale the vapour and it starts dissolving your oesophagus, your lungs.'

'Please,' I whisper, shrinking back. 'We don't want to—'

'Three parts concentrated sulphuric acid mixed with one part hydrogen peroxide. You know what they call it?'

I shake my head, a knot of terror lodged tight in my throat.

'*Piranha solution.* Honestly, that's what it's called. Because the way it works is so violent, the agony so excruciating, it's like the feeding frenzy of a pack of piranhas. Imagine that, Lauren. People beg for death, in my experience.' He pauses, blinking slowly. 'Just want to make sure you know who you're messing with. Do you understand now?'

I nod quickly, remembering the company name that Farley had dug up from the Companies House website. *Piranha Solutions*: the double meaning is horribly clear.

I try to speak again but he puts a finger on my lips.

'No, you still don't understand, Lauren. But you will in a minute.' He leans closer, whispering into my ear. 'Thirty-seven Woodstock Close, Newbury. Your mum's got some lovely hanging baskets by the back door, hasn't she?'

46

My heart lurches in my chest.

'That's . . . how do you know that?'

'Trust me, it's really not difficult to find this stuff out.'

'Please, she doesn't know about any of this,' I say. 'Leave her out of it, don't hurt her.'

Turning to Ruth, he says: 'Ninety-two Belfry Avenue, South Hatfield. Your sister should really get a proper lock on that side door, it pops open easy as you like. Anyone could get in while she's sleeping.'

Ruth whimpers with alarm behind me and I realise what is now obvious: *he's enjoying this.*

He stands back, seemingly pleased with the impact of his words.

'Don't suppose I need this mask anymore.'

He hands the glass tube to one of his men and pulls the balaclava up and over his head, dropping it to the floor and using both hands to smooth his hair back into place.

He looks like a model, one of those men who's so beautiful it's difficult to take your eyes off him. *Scott Lawler*, I think to myself but don't dare say out loud. He's in his mid-twenties, with chiselled cheekbones and neatly trimmed stubble, dark-blond hair swept back and shaved down to a skin fade at the sides. A beautiful, terrifying man wielding ugliness as a weapon, the threat of acid to disfigure, blind, maim anyone who gets in his way. Surrounded by these dead-eyed men in their skeleton masks, as if the acid has already burned their flesh to the bone.

Roper nods to one of the other men, who produces a handful of plastic zip ties from his jacket and proceeds to cinch one tight around my wrists, then another around Ruth's, with a speed and efficiency that suggests he's done it many times before. He pushes Ruth forward so she's standing next to me, then moves to one side.

'Now, Lauren, you asked me what this place is. You've snooped around, you've seen it. What do you think it is?'

For a moment I can't find my voice, my throat is so dry.

'I don't know,' I say, swallowing hard. 'I don't care, we just want our daughters back. Both of us.'

'And how do you think I can help with that?'

'I know you took Evie to a fancy hotel in Kensington,' I say. 'Ruth's daughter too. You convinced Evie to drop out, Cassie to quit her job, isolate both of them from their parents, their friends. Did you tell them you were in love with them, was that it?'

He ignores my question. 'This is a problem for me, Lauren, because you've been inside my business premises now and you've seen lots of ... *commercially sensitive* aspects of my operation here.'

'I'll never tell anyone,' I say. 'I swear.'

'On Evie's life?'

Roper snorts like his boss has just said something funny.

I look from one man to the other, a fresh shiver of cold dread washing through me. 'Yes. I'll never tell a soul as long as I live.'

'I wish I could believe you,' he says, his face crinkling with a charade of concern. 'Really, I do. It would be so much easier. But life just isn't like that, is it? And if I told you where they might be, how do I know you won't—'

Ruth takes a step towards him. 'Please!'

He considers us both for a moment, this impossibly good-looking man with the cold, calculating eyes of an alligator.

'OK,' he says. 'I don't know how to break this to you, so probably better to just get it over with.' He doesn't show a flicker of emotion. 'Your girls? They're gone.'

47

The plunge of fear and helpless anger is so powerful it almost knocks me off my feet.

'What do you mean, *gone*?' Ruth says. 'Have you sent them away?'

He shrugs, the shoulders of his fine lambswool overcoat rising.

'In a manner of speaking, yes.'

Ruth gives her bound hands a frustrated shake. 'What have you done with her? Where's my Cassie?'

Lawler claps his hands together, the sudden noise making me flinch.

'OK,' he says, as if coming to a decision. 'You want to see her? I'll take you to her.'

To one of the masked men, he says: 'Get the boat ready.'

The man nods and disappears through a rear door without a word.

Turning to another of the men, he says: 'We'll take Mrs Wingfield first, I think. Check her for ID.'

The guy pats me down thoroughly, taking my purse and shoving it into his own jacket pocket.

'A boat?' I say. My mind flashes to an image of Lucas, alone in the car outside. 'Where are we going?'

The guy ignores my question. 'Give me your rings,' he says. 'Your jewellery.'

'Why?'

Even as I'm asking it, a pulse of dread shivers down my spine. *No ID. No personal effects. So it's harder to identify you.*

Fear ripples through my stomach. *We have to get out. We have to find a way out of here. But first I have to know the truth.*

'Where is she?' I say, hearing the quiver of fear in my voice. 'What have you done with Evie?'

Lawler spreads his hands. 'You said you want to be together? That's one thing I can do for you.'

I look from face to face as I try to ease the delicate silver band off my finger. Lawler watches me, his cover-model features as blank as a waxwork. Roper looks as if he just wants an excuse to hit someone. Ruth is crying next to me. One of the other black-jacketed men is removing big barbell weights from a pallet, six steel-grey discs the size of dinner plates clanking together as he shoves them into a dirty brown sack.

I'd inherited the silver ring from my grandmother a few years ago, and taken to wearing it on the fourth finger of my left hand as a first line of defence against unwanted advances from creepy men.

It still won't come off.

'Get on with it,' Roper snaps. 'Unless you want me to do it for you?'

He steps forward, towering over me and taking a rough grip on my hand, yanking at the ring with his big fingers. I flinch as the metal bites into flesh bunched painfully against my knuckle. He pulls harder, swearing under his breath until blood leaks from torn skin and I grit my teeth because I won't cry out in front of him, won't give him the satisfaction—

A small, high voice echoes off the metal walls of the warehouse.

'Get back! Get away from her!'

I turn around, heart leaping into my throat, even though I already know who it is.

Oh, no. No, no, no.

Lucas.

My son has come up behind us. His cheeks are pale, his eyes wide with barely controlled terror.

With both hands he clutches the black pistol.

All the men freeze, all stopping what they're doing to look at this small frightened boy brandishing a semi-automatic.

'Let her go!' he shouts. 'Untie their hands and let them both go!'

'Lucas.' My voice cracks. 'What are you doing?'

He swallows, eyes wide with terror. 'It's OK, Mum.'

The gun looks freakishly large in my son's hands as he waves it in Lawler's direction. Roper lets go of my fingers, the silver ring still in place, and takes a step towards him.

'Well now,' he says, his voice full of bravado. 'If it isn't the Pound Shop Harry Potter again.'

'Get back!'

'Or what?'

'Let them go,' Lucas says, pointing the pistol at Roper's broad chest. 'I mean it.'

None of the men move. Except for Roper, who takes another half-step forward until he's only a few feet away.

'So, what you going to do?'

'I said get back!'

'What's it going to be, Lucas?' His eyes flash with a wolfish smile. 'Top boy with a Glock now – going to shoot all of us, are you? Every single one of us?'

Lucas raises the gun to point at the big man's head.

'No, Brandon.' His finger curls around the trigger. 'Just you.'

48

Time slows to a crawl.

Lucas's finger tightens on the trigger.

Roper's face slackens beneath the mask.

For a second the words are locked in my throat, my voice paralysed with fear. My sweet, innocent son is about to kill a man in a room full of people. A room full of witnesses. An act that will change everything, forever.

'Lucas!' I gasp. 'Don't! Don't do it!'

'Why not?' Lucas says. 'He hurt you. He deserves it.'

'Listen to your mum, kid.' All the bravado has drained away from Roper's voice.

The gun shakes in Lucas's hand. 'You hurt her.'

'Apologies for that, mate,' Brandon says, taking a step back. He's nodding rapidly, his hands up high. 'Just put the gun down, yeah?'

I hold my hands out to him, telling him to cut us loose, but he shrugs an apology as if he doesn't have a knife on him. Lucas keeps the gun up as he moves closer to me, asking if I'm OK. He gestures to Ruth to come closer.

'Let's go,' she breathes. 'Let's get out of here.'

'Wait.' I turn to Lawler, who is regarding the whole scene with a look of detached interest. 'When you said you were going to take me to Evie, what did you mean? Where is she? Where were we going to go?'

'You'll never know now.'

'You bastard.'

He spreads his hands. 'My offer's still open. Get your boy to put that gun down and we can have a proper chat. A civilised chat. I'll tell you everything you want to know, Scout's honour.'

Lucas switches his aim to point the pistol at Lawler. 'Tell us where my sister is. I don't care if I have to shoot you.'

'You're not going to do that, little man.' He flashes a smile full of perfect white teeth. 'If you were going to shoot anyone, you'd have done it already – but that moment has passed. I'm right, aren't I?'

His words from just moments ago, still bouncing like a sick echo in my head.

Your girls. They're gone.

I need to ask the question but my mouth won't make the shape of the words. They rise up my throat like a fist and lodge there, stuck fast. Words I can't bear to speak out loud.

Is she dead?

Is Evie dead?

My son tells the men to get on their knees instead, and all of them comply – except for Lawler. He stays standing, arms crossed casually over his chest in a silent challenge. I tear my mind from the unspoken question by trying to figure out how we can leave here without them catching us. Any of these men would be able to outrun us even if our hands weren't bound, and Ruth has at least twenty years on the oldest of them. We won't even make it back to the car unless we have a head start.

'Thank you, Lucas,' I say quietly. 'But you were supposed to stay in the car. And ring the police.'

'I did,' he says, the gun wavering slightly in his hands. 'And I waited, but nothing happened. I reckon they thought I was a prank caller. So I came in to find you.'

I strain my ears for the sound of sirens, of screeching tyres and running feet, of rescue, from somewhere outside. But there is nothing. Only the white-noise rumble of traffic up on the main road, the distant blast of a boat's horn far up the river.

The zip ties. The masked man who restrained us had a pocketful of them. Enough to tie their ankles and give us time to get out of here.

I turn to tell Lucas as a dark shadow looms up behind him, creeping between the stacked pallets.

A man.

Two men.

Both in black jackets, one behind the other. The first – in a bala-clava – is within striking distance, a long curved blade glinting in his hand. But as he raises the knife, the second man grabs him and slams his masked head against the side of a pallet *bang-bang-bang* until he folds to the concrete like a broken puppet. The knife clatters to the floor.

The second man materialises out of the shadows behind us, both palms up to Lucas as if to say, *It's OK. Stay calm.* My son levels the gun at him anyway, eyes wide, finger curling tight against the trigger again.

'It's OK,' the man says. 'I'm a friend.'

He takes off his baseball cap and sunglasses so I can see his face properly for the first time. We lock eyes and I feel a powerful shock of recognition, as if I've jumped into an icy plunge pool.

It's the man I'd seen at Primrose Hill. The man in the BMW. The man who'd been following us.

It was . . .

'Hello, Lauren,' he says, his voice deep and strange and yet familiar, like an old song I've never quite forgotten. A stranger I have known half my life.

It couldn't be.

It was impossible.

The dark brown hair that used to be long is now cropped close to his scalp, a new scar visible behind his right ear. His shoulders seem broader beneath the black leather jacket and the stubble is new too, as is the heavy blue ink of a Celtic tattoo climbing the side of his neck.

But the eyes. The eyes are the same.

Lawler stares at the newcomer. 'What the fuck are you doing here?'

Lucas is staring desperately over his shoulder at the man, the gun swinging wildly back to Lawler.

'Mum?'

'It's OK, Lucas.'

'What's going on?' he says. 'Who's this guy?'

The newcomer picks up the curved knife dropped by the bearded man and Lucas swings the gun suddenly back onto him. A second of terror where I think it's all about to go horribly, horribly wrong—

Then the stranger reverses it so he's holding it by the blade, the handle extended to me. I grip it awkwardly with my cuffed hands and use it to quickly slice through the zip ties restraining Ruth, before she does the same for me.

I take the knife back from her and turn to face Lawler, who is still there with his arms crossed and not a hair out of place.

'What you said about Evie,' I say, 'What did you mean? Where is she?'

He gives a small shrug, but says nothing.

'Tell me!' I shout. 'And how many girls have you taken?'

'A gentleman never tells.'

'I'm going to find her!' I point at him with the knife. 'Then I'm going to find you!'

He smiles at that, a flash of genuine amusement in his eyes.

'Good luck,' he says. 'And watch out for piranhas.'

Sprawled on the floor at our feet, the knifeman groans and stirs. He tries to push himself upright, a string of blood dangling from his mask.

'We have to go – now,' the stranger says. He holds out a hand to Lucas, his palm open. 'Let me take it from here, Lucas. I'll look after this lot while you three get clear and away.'

Lucas lowers the pistol slightly.

'Mum?'

'It's OK, Lucas,' I say. 'Do as he says. Give him the gun.'

'Why?'

'We can trust him.'

'But *why*?' His desperate brown eyes flick back and forth between us. 'Who is he?'

I swallow hard on a dry throat. Finally facing the lie that I had planted so long ago, a lie that had started for what I thought were all the right reasons. A lie that was finally about to be unearthed.

'He's someone I haven't seen for a long time, Lucas.' I hold my son's gaze. 'He's your dad.'

EVIE

Two months earlier

She had almost turned around and gone back.

Right at the last moment, when she was standing across the road from the old church hall, waiting for a gap in traffic. She had surprised herself with a sudden thought that maybe she should just leave it, just head back to the Tube and go home, forget this place and move on with her life. But . . . she was *here*. And turning around, walking away now? That was not her style. Not at all. After all, what did she have to lose? Scott's revelation about her dad had left her with too many questions, too much that she wanted to know. Did he remember her? Why had he been hiding all these years? Why had her mum said he was dead?

She put her sunglasses on and crossed the road, making her way around the side of the church and its empty car park. At the single-storey hall, a blue-and-white sign beside the door read NEXT STEPS, the name of the place she'd been given. In smaller print beneath it were the words NO APPOINTMENT NEEDED – ALL WELCOME.

The main door was propped open and it led into a small low-ceilinged hall, the scuffed parquet floor set with small round tables and plastic chairs. A catering hatch housed large urns for tea and coffee and an office door at the far end was closed; the whole place had a tired, institutional smell of dust and floor polish and stewed tea. A couple of men sat alone at their own individual tables, one in his early twenties in a bright orange puffa jacket, the other close to fifty. Both had their arms crossed and both gave Evie a curious look as she sat down at an empty table in the corner.

It was a weirdly warm day for October, the air muggy and still, and she felt a trickle of sweat under her denim jacket as she perused a discarded leaflet with the Next Steps logo on the cover. Just as Scott had told her, it was a charity that advised ex-offenders on work, benefits, getting somewhere to live, helping them get back on their feet and reintegrate into society after their release from prison. At the far end of the hall, the office door opened and a man walked out folding a sheaf of papers in half. The guy in the orange puffa jacket stood, went through the door and shut it behind him. Fifteen minutes later, the older man followed suit, taking his turn in the office.

Evie waited, her heel tapping the floor with a low thrum of nerves. She kept the big square sunglasses on.

It was only when the older man finally left that another figure appeared at the door, in blue jeans and a black polo shirt, leaning around to scan the almost-empty waiting area. He was tall and strongly built, with broad shoulders tapering to a slim waist. His dark hair was clipped short at the sides, the pattern of a Celtic tattoo at his neck.

'Hi,' he said. 'Do you want to come through?'

Evie stood up and walked toward the office, the butterflies in her stomach fluttering faster with every step. She had planned out what she was going to say a dozen times but now, as he gestured to her to sit down, she found that her mind had gone completely blank. Adrenaline pumped, as if she was about to take the toughest exam of her life.

He sat down and pulled a fresh form from a tray on the desk. 'First time here? I don't think we've met.'

'No,' Evie said. 'I mean, yes, it's my first time here.'

'Why don't you start by telling me what you need, what I can help you with? Have you been out long?'

'I'm not . . .' She stopped. 'Not here for that. Not for me.'

'You're here for someone else? A brother, a boyfriend?' He gave her a nod of encouragement. 'It's all good, I can still help.'

'No . . . I came to see you.'

'Me?' He stopped writing, looked up at her again. 'Why's that?'

'You don't recognise me, do you?'

He frowned. 'Should I . . . ?'

She took off the sunglasses and folded them into her shaking hands. Looked up at him, heart thundering in her chest. Watched as his expression started to change, his eyes widening, recognition breaking through like a shaft of sunlight on a cloudy day.

He dropped the pen, right hand rising to his mouth.

'Evie?'

PART IV

49

Lucas is silent in the back of the car as we thread our way through the streets of south London. I try to talk to him, leaning around from the front seat, but he won't engage. He just stares angrily out of the window, cheeks flushed, his face set in a deep frown.

We'd made it back to the Nissan at a dead run, not daring a look over our shoulders until we were back in the car and pulling out of there as fast as we could, Milo yapping with frantic excitement in the back seat. Fearing every second that a group of angry men would spill out behind us and give chase, or an SUV with blacked-out windows would roar around the side of the building and block off our escape. But to my immense relief, we make it back out onto the main road without challenge.

It's all I can do now to focus on the road ahead and behind, to give Ruth directions while fighting the simmering tide of emotion that threatens to overwhelm me. A tide that I have pushed deep down inside for too long, too many years, feelings I thought I'd never have to wrestle with again.

Declan Hicks.

He was part of the past. He was *in* the past. What the hell was he doing here, now, today? Turning up out of nowhere, a man I had given up for lost so many years ago? A man who had let us down so many times but was living his own life now, a free man, crashing back into our lives as if he'd never been away?

Too many questions; but no time for them now.

Following Declan's whispered suggestion before we left the warehouse, we take the Rotherhithe Tunnel under the river and make our way to the car park of South Bermondsey train station to wait for him. Less than ten minutes after we arrive, his black BMW swings around the entrance in a big U-turn, his headlights flashing twice to indicate it's safe and there is no one tailing him. We follow him onto the Old Kent Road, then south towards Peckham. Ruth had suggested we could stay at her house tonight, but it's a long way out – and we had to assume Lawler's men already knew that address.

I keep a close eye on the traffic behind us, in case we're being followed, trying unsuccessfully to get Lucas to talk to me. He must have a thousand questions but steadfastly refuses to engage.

Ruth calls her sister in Hatfield, tells her to pack a bag and go to stay with a friend for a few days. Or better still, a hotel. She tells her that she can't explain exactly why, only that some very dangerous people know where she lives and it's to do with Cassie. I call my mum at the same time, urge her to do the same until finally, reluctantly, she says she'll call a local B&B to see if they have any rooms.

'Please, Mum,' I say. 'They have your address and they're really, really bad news.'

We both ring off and sit in tense, impotent silence for a long moment. Weighing the risks against each other. The threat against a sister, a mother, balanced against our missing daughters. The emotional weight of loved ones set against each other, on either side of the scales.

Ruth keeps her eyes on the road.

'We should call the police as well,' she says eventually. 'Tell them about the warehouse. Tell them what he said, all of it.'

'And you really think they'll believe us? I'm on their list already for the wrong reasons and that detective you've been talking to won't even take your calls.'

'I just think we have to—'

'For all I know there are men waiting outside my mum's house *right this minute*, and all she has to do is answer the door, go out into the garden or walk down the street, and she gets a face full of acid.' I shiver. 'God. I can't bear to think of it.'

'So what do you suggest?'

'Let's at least talk about it first,' I say. 'Maybe Declan will have other ideas.'

'Are you sure about him?' She indicates to follow the BMW as it peels off left at a junction. 'You're sure we can trust him?'

'I don't know,' I say honestly. 'But we wouldn't have got out of that warehouse without him.'

'How did he even find us?'

'I think he's been following Lucas and me for a couple of days.' I describe how I'd seen his car shadowing us several times. Perhaps there had been other instances too – when I hadn't even seen him at all. 'I've no idea how he got onto us in the first place. He doesn't have my number, or home address, or anything.'

I had no idea he was even out. It's on the tip of my tongue before I stop myself, along with a dozen other thoughts, a dozen angry questions. I would tell Ruth sooner or later, but we needed to get where we were going first, so I could talk to Lucas.

Then work out what Scott Lawler meant when he'd talked about Evie and Cassie.

Ahead, Declan's black BMW sticks strictly to the speed limit, driving smooth and steady as we follow. I hadn't realised how old his car is until now, how beaten up, as if it's been knocked about and patched up more than a few times in its long life.

Ruth glances up at the rear-view mirror before her eyes return to the road ahead.

'It's really none of my business,' she says. 'And tell me to get lost if you like, but . . . I take it you and Declan have not been together for a while?'

I stare out of the window. It's been a long time since I've been to this part of London and I wonder idly if any of our old places are still even there. His little flat over the betting shop on Rye Lane; the Chestnut pub on the corner; the club on the high street. The places where we had burned so fiercely for a few short months. Before everything changed. Before Evie.

'No,' I say. 'Not for a long time. Not since before Lucas was born.'

She lowers her voice. 'He didn't want to be involved?'

'He didn't really have much choice in the matter.'

We drive on in silence, pulling up to the BMW's bumper at a red traffic light. I turn around in the passenger seat, looking at Lucas in the back seat. Milo has his chin in my son's lap, Lucas stroking the dog's soft fur absently even as his eyes are still fixed on the window. Staring without seeing.

'Lucas?' I say. 'Are you hungry? We'll get something to eat soon, OK?'

He shrugs, once, continuing to look out at the traffic.

I put a hand on his knee. 'We could get McDonald's? Would you like that?'

'Whatever.' He still won't look at me. He takes his phone from his pocket, stabs the screen and begins angrily scrolling.

I turn back to face the front, guilt blossoming in my chest. He is right to be angry. I have lied to him. A lie that had been easier than the truth, better than the truth, safer. Sometimes a lie was necessary to protect those you loved most in the world. Deep down I'd always known that I would have to have this conversation, to answer for my deception. Just not today. Especially not while Evie was still out there.

The light goes green and we pull away, Ruth keeping the little Nissan close to Declan so no other cars can cut in between us.

She opens her mouth to speak, then seems to think better of it.

'What?' I turn towards her. 'It's OK. You can say it, I don't mind. I'm sure I've heard it before.'

'It's just that . . .' She gives me an awkward half-smile. 'I suppose I wouldn't have put the two of you together. As a couple.'

'My dad said the same,' I say. 'Back in the day. Although he was much, much more blunt about it.'

'They didn't get on? Declan and your father?'

I laugh, but it dies quickly in my throat. 'You could say that.'

The BMW indicates right off the main road, waiting for a gap in traffic before turning into a long terraced street. It slows and pulls in, Declan waving out of the window to point out another space further down the road. Gesturing for me to stay in the car, he walks up and down the street for a minute, checking both ways and both sides, before disappearing into a narrow two-up two-down with a navy blue front door.

After a minute he emerges again. Gives a thumbs up and beckons us in.

Ruth unclicks her seat belt. 'You're sure about this?'

But Lucas is already opening the back door and crossing the road towards the house, Milo's lead clutched in his hand. I get out and follow, leaving Ruth's question unanswered.

The house is small and tidy, a front door opening right into the lounge that has a small sofa, an old gas fire and a TV stand in the corner. A kitchen at the back with a folding table and two chairs. Declan points out the bathroom, a door beyond the kitchen. The furniture is homely but well looked after, the sofa covered with blankets, the walls plain but for a few large black-and-white prints, framed photographs of trees and parks and churches. No people. A small porcelain Buddha sits cross-legged on a book-shelf. A barbell leans against the wall, weights as big as hubcaps stacked next to it.

Lucas goes through to use the bathroom and the three of us are left in the small dining area where a window looks out onto a small fenced-in garden. Milo scratches at the reinforced back door and Ruth goes out with him.

Declan and I are left alone in the room. Unasked questions hanging between us, a million unspoken words, the air suddenly filled with them like moths gathering around a flame.

This man. This ghost from my past. A ghost I thought I would never see again.

50

The silence is thick between us. There are so many conflicting emotions all competing for the same space in my head. A small measure of relief is among them; but also anger. Fear. Confusion. Heartache. It has been twelve years since we last spoke, since I last saw him across a courtroom on a day I've tried so hard to forget. Nineteen years since we first met. Half a lifetime.

And now he's back.

'What the hell, Declan?' I stare at him, with no idea where to start. 'What the hell?'

'I'm sorry,' he says simply.

'What are you sorry for?'

'Everything.'

'For cutting off all contact?' I put my hands on top of my head, as if I can keep a lid on the fury inside. 'Dropping out of our lives like we didn't matter? Dropping out of my life?

'You're right, it's—'

'You know for a while I genuinely thought you were dead? It was like you'd vanished off the face of the Earth. And then when I found out you weren't, I was so angry I just decided to tell the kids that anyway. I made up a story because it was so much easier. Cleaner. You have no idea how angry I was. I still am.'

He looks down at the faded lino of the kitchen floor.

'I was ashamed,' he says quietly. 'Thought they'd be better off without me.'

'And yet one day you decided to follow me across half of London, stalk me, drop on me and Lucas out of the clear blue sky?'

'I can explain.'

'And what do you expect from us, Dec?' I gesture towards the bathroom door, at the far end of the kitchen. 'What do you expect from your *son*?'

'Nothing.' He shakes his head. 'I don't . . . expect anything from you. Or him, or Evie. I know I don't deserve anything and I'm not asking, either. I just want to help. I screwed up everything so badly before. I was an idiot.'

I consider him for a moment. So much about Declan is different. But so much is the same, too. His voice is the same. The way he stands, the set of his shoulders, the dangerous economy of his movements. The way he looks at me. And yet there is still the niggling doubt in my mind, an echo of what Ruth had said in the car barely twenty minutes ago. *You're sure we can trust him?*

'How did you even get out of that warehouse?' I say, my anger already starting to burn itself out. I feel suddenly exhausted. 'With all of those men there?'

'Herded them into one of the offices at the back, snapped the key off in the lock. Won't have held them very long, but I guess it was long enough.'

'Thanks,' I say through gritted teeth. 'For helping us.'

He shrugs. 'It was nothing.'

I'm jittery, the last of the adrenaline draining away, and I can't believe how calm he is.

'It wasn't nothing,' I say. 'You saved us.'

He takes something from his jacket pocket and hands it to me. My purse.

'You know they're going to come looking for you, Lauren, don't you? These aren't the sort of people you can just walk in on like that, humiliate on their home turf. They won't let it go. And you've seen too much.'

'I can't stop,' I say. 'Not with Evie still out there somewhere.'

'I know.'

'Will you help us?'

'I will if you—'

We both turn as the bathroom door unlocks and Lucas emerges, walking slowly through the kitchen. He joins us but hovers uncertainly by the back door. Still unwilling to stand next to me, but reluctant to be too close to Declan, either. Three points of a triangle, all of us equally distant from the other. It is the first time, I realise, that the three of us have been alone in a room together. The first time we've occupied the same space: mother, father and son breathing the same air. The weirdness of this moment makes it feel like some kind of strange, surreal fever dream.

Declan breaks the spell.

'Why don't you and your mum sit down in the lounge for a minute,' he says. 'I'll make us some tea.'

*   *   *

'I don't understand,' Lucas says for the third time. 'You said my dad died in a car crash before I was born. But all this time he was alive and he was here. In London.'

He sits at the other end of the small sofa to me, clutching a glass of water. Declan had brought me a cup of strong tea and then retreated back to the kitchen without being asked.

'I'm so sorry, Lucas. I thought it was for the best, for you and your sister.'

'But why did you lie?'

'To protect you.'

'From who?' He shakes his head. 'Didn't he want us? Evie and me?'

'It's not as simple as that.'

'Has he got another family? Is he someone else's dad too?'

'No.'

'Then why?'

I lean over to put a hand on his but he shakes it off, shrinking away against the edge of the sofa. I've never seen him like this, so angry and upset, all of it directed at me – and completely justified. For years I've told myself that I would share the truth with him, one day, perhaps when he was eighteen and I could lay everything out and let him decide what to do with the information. But in the end it had just been easier to push it away until another day, file it away at the back of my mind.

'Your dad and me . . .' I pause, trying to find the words. 'We got together when I was very young. When we were *both* very young. I was eighteen, in my first year at university and your dad was only a couple of years older. He just . . . he wasn't like anyone else I'd ever met. We'd not been together that long when I got pregnant with Evie, so I dropped out of my course and came home.'

'Is that why you always give Evie such a hard time about exams? About uni and working hard and all that stuff?'

I blink. 'Do I?'

'Yeah.'

'Since when do I give her a hard time?'

He frowns as if this is a stupid question. 'Since forever, Mum. But I still don't get why you and him didn't stay together.'

I shrug. 'We just couldn't make it work, with him being in London and me being back with my parents in Reading.'

'Why didn't he just move in with you and Grandma and Granddad?'

'It wasn't that simple, Lucas. Your granddad Roy, he really didn't like Declan. Not at all, and neither did your grandma. We had a lot of arguments about it. So many rows.'

'But *why* didn't they like him?'

I try to summon those feelings from back then.

'He was different,' I say. 'Different to the boys at my school, different to anyone I'd met before. He didn't really care what anyone said, or what people told us we should be doing – including your gran and granddad. He had this group of mates, all south London boys and they were so cool, they sort of lived their own life on the edge of everything. They didn't live by the rules that everyone else did.' I lower my voice. 'I was in love with him.'

And then I got pregnant, and everything started to go wrong.

Even as I'm saying it, it feels like I'm talking about someone else. It feels like a different life, a different century, a different universe.

Lucas blushes harder, shaking his head, and I can tell he doesn't really follow what I'm saying.

'But you could have got married,' he says again, like a statement. As if it's obvious. 'If you were going to have Evie.'

'We couldn't.'

'Why not?'

I take a breath. 'Because then your dad went to jail.'

51

This stops my son in his tracks. He looks up at me for the first time since we arrived here.

'Jail?' He forms the word slowly, as if it's the first time he's ever said it. 'Why? What did he do?'

'It doesn't matter now, Lucas, it was a long time—'

'*What did he do?*' His voice is louder now. 'To get sent to jail?'

Dredging up the memory is like returning to a place I thought I'd left behind forever.

'He got involved in a fight outside a bar, not far from here,' I say. 'Another group of lads jumped him and his friends as they came out. One of your dad's mates was stabbed and your dad stayed with him when everyone else ran, he stayed waiting for the ambulance but the police got there first. One of the lads they'd been fighting was knocked out and because your dad was there, he got arrested and charged. He got two and a half years.'

Lucas is shaking his head as if he's struggling to take in all this new information, trying to make it tally up with the carefully measured fiction I have given to him.

'How old was I? When he went to jail?'

'You weren't around yet at this point.'

'So . . . you got back together again, when he got out?'

'We tried to make a go of it again,' I say. 'Your sister was a toddler and I was back trying to pick up my degree again at the local college.

Me and your dad were together, on and off for a bit longer, but he ended up getting back in with his old friends and getting in more trouble. Really serious trouble this time. By the time you came along he was on his way back to prison to serve a much longer sentence.'

'For doing what?'

'That's a conversation you need to have with him, I think.'

'Can't believe you lied about it for so long.'

'I'm sorry, Lucas. It's no excuse, but . . . I thought it was for the best. When you were born all I could think about was you following in your dad's footsteps, falling in with the wrong kind of people. Getting in trouble. I wanted to make sure you didn't go down a path like that, you or your sister. He'd cut off all contact with me anyway, so I made up a story to answer your questions.'

He stares at me. 'That's why you're so strict with Evie, about her going out and stuff.'

'I didn't want her to make the same mistakes I did.'

'Is that what we are?' His cheeks are flushed a deep red now. 'Mistakes?'

'No,' I say quickly. 'I didn't mean it like that. You and your sister are the best thing that ever happened to me.'

'Then why have you lied to us our whole lives?' His eyes brim with tears. He hardly ever raises his voice to anyone, let alone to me. But his voice now has a harsh, strident edge that I've never heard before. 'And how do I know you're not still lying now?'

Before I can answer, Declan's voice makes us both look up.

'Your mum did the right thing.' He appears in the doorway, depositing a plate of digestive biscuits on the side table in front of us. 'I know it must be hard to get your head around, Lucas, but she did it to protect you. I was involved in some bad things . . . with some bad people back then, and I would only have dragged you down. All of you.'

'Didn't you want to . . . see us? Hear about us, what we were doing, me and Evie?'

'I thought your mum was better off without me,' he says. 'That you and your sister would be better off too, and anyway I couldn't bear the thought of you visiting me, seeing me locked up, stuck in that stinking prison. My first day sitting in that cell, I just thought you'd be better off if I was dead, and that's why I never replied to any of your mum's letters, never let her visit, never even told her when I got out. I broke it off, broke your mum's heart.' He gives his son a smile. 'I wish now that I hadn't done that, but here we are. And looking at you I reckon she's done a hell of a job since that day.'

'So it's true?' Lucas says, staring up at him. 'That you were a prisoner?'

'Yes,' Declan says simply. 'All of that is true. But it's not who I am now.'

'I still don't understand.' Lucas is crying now, swiping angry tears away as they start to fall. 'All this time I was always jealous of my friends who had their dads there, even the lame ones, because they'd still do stuff with them and talk to them, take them places, help them with homework. But I knew I could never have that because my dad was dead. Except that was all a big fat lie, wasn't it, Mum?'

I hold my hands up. 'Lucas, I—'

'I hate you!' The words erupt as he stands up from the sofa. 'And I want to go home!'

He marches out through the back door and slams it hard behind him.

52

I'm about to go after him when Declan puts a hand on my arm.

'Leave him for a bit,' he says. 'He just needs time to think before you talk to him again. Get his head around things.'

I shake his hand off with an angry flick, moving towards the back door.

'I'm not letting him out of my sight,' I say, peering through the kitchen window. 'Not now, after everything that's happened. And I don't think *you're* in a position to hand out bloody parenting advice, thank you very much.'

'You're right,' Declan says quietly. 'But I don't mind going out there for a bit to keep an eye on him.'

Lucas is perched on the edge of a mossy wooden bench against the side wall, phone in his hand but staring off somewhere else. His words are still here in the house with us, hanging like smoke. *I hate you*. He's never said that to me before. His sister has, several times over the years – she'd written it in her diary too. But never Lucas. Never my sweet boy. Never those particular three words, sharp like scalpels.

I watch him through the back window instead, torn between the urge to go and comfort him, protect him, and to make sense of what else we've discovered today. For all the angry intensity of being in the same room as Declan again, of talking to him, introducing him to his son, it is still Scott Lawler's words that loom larger than everything else. Careless, callous words. A mocking echo that won't leave my head.

Your girls? They're gone.

I refuse to believe it. I know Ruth feels the same. The two of us clinging to each other for solidarity, for our sanity. For hope. Lawler had spent time and money grooming Evie, drawing her deeper into his web, so there had to be a reason for it, didn't there? A purpose other than violence?

In the garden, Lucas stands and glares towards the house. He sees me and Declan, the two of us side by side, and he scowls and turns away, rolling a football out from under the bench instead. He begins to kick it angrily against the old wall at the back, a percussive *smack* of leather on brick in the darkening space.

Declan reaches for his jacket, on a peg by the back door.

'I'll go and sit with the boy.'

But Ruth is coming through the door, shaking her head.

'Not sure he wants to see either of you pair just now,' she says with a raised eyebrow. 'Me and Milo will keep an eye on him. I need a ciggy anyway. And it seems like you two have quite a lot to talk about.'

She calls the little dog to heel and they both head back out into the garden, where Lucas gives them a brief glance before continuing to kick the football. She settles on the bench and produces a cigarette from her handbag.

Declan picks at a loose thread on the cuff of his sweatshirt.

'Listen,' he says. 'I understand that you're angry. I get it. I've got no excuse for what I did and I can't go back to make it right. But if you want my help now, I'm here.'

I want to hate him. The flame of my anger had burned so hot for so long, I'd imagined what I would say to him so many times if I ever saw him again. Because even though more than a decade has passed, I still find myself thinking about him from time to time.

I still see him in the children – Evie has his colouring, Lucas his eyes, his cheekbones.

I want to hate him. But somehow I can't. And in any case, that's an emotion for another day. For now, in this moment, there is no time or space for anything apart from finding Evie.

If we're not already too late.

'Yes,' I say finally. 'OK. Ruth and I need whatever help we can get.'

He nods slowly, moves past me into the narrow galley kitchen.

'First, can I get you another drink? Tea?'

'Have you got anything stronger?'

'None in the house, sorry,' he says. 'Don't touch it. Not anymore.'

He makes more tea anyway and sets it down on the fold-out dining table. A large cat appears at the bottom of the staircase, entirely black apart from a white bib under his chin and two white feet. He jumps up onto a windowsill by the back door and bristles at the sight of Milo in the back garden, regarding the interloper with luminous yellow eyes.

'This is Elvis,' Declan says. 'In theory he lives here, but mostly he just does what he likes. Comes and goes as he pleases.'

'Sounds like someone I used to know,' I say, hearing the note of bitterness in my voice.

He gives me a mournful smile, as if he can't argue with the jibe.

Our son is still kicking the ball against the wall outside. *Smack. Smack. Smack.*

'You can all stay here tonight, if you want.' Declan opens a cupboard and takes out a bag of cat food, fills a silver bowl for Elvis. 'I'll take the sofa; there are two bedrooms upstairs.'

'Thank you,' I say. 'But we need to talk about what we do next.'

'If you want my opinion, Lauren, we should get the police involved. We can't do this on our own.'

'No police. Not yet.'

'I really think you should—'

'Too dangerous,' I say, before he can finish. 'Did you hear what Lawler said? He's got my mum's address, Ruth's sister too. And if police arrive on his doorstep now I just know we'll never see Evie again.'

'I know I don't get a vote on this, but if it was up to me—'

'No,' I say, cutting him off again. 'You don't get a vote. And no, it's not up to you.'

'All right.' He sips his tea and glances out of the back window, where Lucas and Ruth are bathed in the white glow of a security light. 'OK. But there's something I need to tell you about Evie. About how she came back into my life.'

EVIE

Six weeks earlier

It still felt like a dream. To be waking up here, not the little flat in Hampstead but in a huge suite of this five-star Kensington hotel again, with Scott in the bed beside her. This extraordinary man who could surely have any woman he met but had somehow chosen her.

And last night . . . She smiled to herself. Last night had been as amazing as she'd hoped it would be. She had told him how she felt, for the first time.

She had told him she loved him.

Evie touched a hand to her ear lobe, felt the small, perfectly cut diamond. Still there. She hadn't dreamed it. She felt the smile growing wider. She hadn't dreamed *any* of it but that was what it felt like – one long waking dream. Like she was flying, soaring, a constant sense of euphoria, the best drug you could ever imagine. The best high you could ever hope for.

Was this what love felt like? Was it possible that every morning could be like this one? She never wanted to leave this place.

She climbed out from under the duvet and went over to the La Spaziale espresso machine, getting out coffee pods and cups as quietly as she could so as not to wake Scott in the big king-sized bed. Maybe she'd wear the earrings when she went home at Christmas, when she'd explain everything to her mum. But until then, she would keep living this new life, exploring all of its wonderful possibilities for herself. She'd covered her tracks quite well, she thought – had even changed her emergency contact number at the university, just in case some random admin person there called it by mistake, told her mum that Evie had dropped out. Anyone who rang it now would get through to Scott, and he would just pass on a message to her.

The guilt about lying to her mother had faded almost to nothing since she'd found out the truth about her dad. The lie her mum had told about his death right from when she was a little girl. When all this time he'd been very much alive, in prison, and now a free man again.

Scott had made that happen – had given her the truth, like a priceless gift.

Her dad had seemed like a part of the dream too, at first. A man she'd only ever seen in a couple of creased old photographs, suddenly come to life and living in the same city as her. It was like living in one house your whole life and then discovering another door, another room, another wing you didn't even realise was there. Declan – she was still a way off calling him *Dad* – was not like she remembered him at all but much quieter, calmer, more serious somehow. In a good way.

Scott had been as good as his word, putting a deposit down for her first semester fees at the private drama college in Hampstead and even helping her out with the flat. Family money, he'd said. An inheritance that he'd never quite known how to spend. She'd only been at the college for a few weeks but it was everything she'd hoped for. It was exhilarating and joyful and challenging and *fun* – it was everything that her law degree was not. Scott had helped her to realise that she had to pursue her own path in life, to make her own choices. Rather than have them imposed on her by her overprotective mother.

Evie knew she would have to tell her mum the truth sooner rather than later, and definitely before the end of term in December.

But not yet.

53

We sit in the darkening lounge as Declan lays it out for me. He describes how Evie had appeared at the old church hall where he works, the drop-in centre for ex-offenders. How she had simply turned up and introduced herself, completely out of the blue.

Finally he breaks off, swallowing hard. His jaw is tight, the emotions of that autumn day still writ large on his face.

'I was . . . yeah.' He shakes his head. 'Completely gobsmacked. Couldn't believe it.'

But it was not like some TV reunion, he says. No tears or hugs, no crying or wailing. They had talked for a bit, ten minutes or so, and then she'd left with a vague suggestion that she might come back.

'Thought I'd dreamed it,' he says. 'Like I'd banged my head or something and hallucinated the whole thing. And even if I hadn't, she was never going to come back, was she?'

But it had seemed, he says, like a second chance. A chance to get to know the daughter he had barely seen for the first eighteen years of her life, who had only just started primary school when he was sent to jail for the second time.

'We just talked. I listened. I wanted to hear about everything from back then. All the things I'd missed.'

I sip my tea. The urge for a large glass of wine is still strong but this will have to do.

'How did she find you?'

'I'll get to that.'

They had met for coffee three times, just the two of them. Each time she would turn up at his work at the end of his Monday shift and they would walk to a little greasy spoon.

'Did you get her number?'

He shakes his head. 'I gave her mine but she preferred to keep it offline. Thought she might give me her number eventually but I wasn't going to push it. She wouldn't even let me pay for the coffees – she had this gold Amex credit card like it was nothing special.'

'That can't be right,' I interrupt him. 'She doesn't have an Amex card. I told her she couldn't have a credit card until she got a full-time job.'

He raises an eyebrow. 'Yeah. She talked about you. Your rules. Your plans for her degree, her life.'

'*My* plans?' I say. 'No – she wanted to do it. She wanted to study law, she worked really hard on her A levels.'

He lets that go without comment. The first couple of times they'd met were great, he says, but the third time she seemed edgy as if there was something else going on. When she got up to leave, he had asked if she was going to come again next week. She'd been evasive and he'd offered to walk her to the bus stop, wanting to finish the conversation. Fearing that she might never return.

'She wasn't catching the bus back to uni,' he says. 'I walked with her down to the common and there was this sports car parked on the double yellows. A powder-blue Maserati with tinted windows. By this point Evie's sort of shooing me away and I stand there across the street as she goes over and gets into the car. There's some flash-looking geezer in shades behind the wheel and he drives off with her in the passenger seat. And that was the last time I saw her.'

'How long ago?'

'A few weeks,' he says. 'Since then, she hasn't been back to the centre. I knew something wasn't right with her that last time, so

I tried to find her again. Went up to her uni but she wasn't there. She'd mentioned this guy she'd met but never said his name, like it was some big secret, but that he was this businessman and he owned all these nightclubs and other places. They were really serious together and she was proper smitten, you know? Nights out in London, theatre shows, fancy restaurants, a trip to the south coast.'

Declan says the one thing that she had let slip was that he'd take her for weekends at this five-star hotel in Kensington. He had taken to driving over there on his days off to see if she might appear again.

'The Royal Pearl?'

'That's the one.'

'So you were looking for her too. And that's where you saw us?'

He nods. 'I wanted to see her again, just to make sure she was OK because she'd been so edgy the last time we had coffee. Then all of a sudden I see you and the boy rock up, marching into this hotel and I knew something was really, *really* wrong.'

I think back to my confrontation with the staff at The Royal Pearl. It's only two days ago but it feels like a month.

'So anyway,' he continues. 'This bloke she's met, the one with the Maserati? He's the reason she came looking for me. She got my work address from him.'

'Why would he do that? And how did he even find you?'

Declan looks down at his hands, the knuckles callused and thick. Fists clenching and unclenching on the table.

'I had a feeling there was something off about the boyfriend, and when I clocked the flash car the pieces started falling into place.'

'What do you mean? What pieces?'

'The reason she's in trouble,' he says quietly. 'The reason she's missing. I don't want to sound like a massive narcissist, or whatever you call it. But I think it's because of me. It's my fault.'

54

I put my cup down carefully on the table between us.

'How can it be your fault, Declan? You've not seen her in years.'

'It's not a coincidence, that she's got together with this particular guy. They didn't meet by chance.'

A chill creeps over my skin.

'Then what is it?'

'Revenge.'

He takes me through it slowly, carefully, a story that I've never heard. A story that had started one night more than a decade ago, when we were together again, when I was pregnant with Lucas and I thought we'd got our lives back on track. He had been approached by a guy he knew from the neighbourhood, who'd been in prison with him that first time. Declan was told he was going to do someone a favour: he would provide an alibi for a man he barely knew. An alibi to say they had been together, driving a truck to Manchester, on the night of a brutal double murder in south London.

'I refused,' he says with a shrug. 'I didn't want to get back into it, into that life again. I had you, and Evie, I had everything I wanted. I was going to stay clean.'

I think back to it, to that brief span of time after his release from the first prison sentence. We had been happy, or so I'd thought. He'd promised to put everything behind him, to start again, and for a time I'd really believed that we could make it work.

'The guy I was supposed to provide an alibi for,' Declan says. 'He ended up getting convicted of that double murder, got thirty years. His name was Robert Lawler.'

Declan keeps talking, staring into his mug of tea as if he doesn't want to meet my eye.

A week later they'd come for him, he says. Lawler's men – to punish him, torture him, make an example of him before disposing of his body somewhere it would never be found. But instead, Declan had killed one of them in the confrontation that followed before managing to escape. It was this crime – a conviction for manslaughter – that had sent Declan back to jail for the second time, propelling him out of our lives for good.

Until today.

I try to process this new information, try to make sense of it. To understand a new emotion softening the hard edges of my anger.

'They kept a lot of the details out,' he says. 'When I was on trial. A lot of the background was withheld because of other investigations that were still ongoing, undercover stuff, other prosecutions that were coming up. Legal reasons, I didn't really understand it all at the time.'

'So, Robert Lawler,' I say. 'The man who got thirty years in prison because you wouldn't lie for him – Scott is his son?'

Declan nods. 'Son and heir.'

'You should have told me all this,' I say. 'At the time.'

'Didn't want to involve you in that world, that life.' He sighs. 'I knew any family I had on the outside would be at risk, anyone who came to visit, anyone I wrote to. They tried it on with me a few more times, when I was in Belmarsh.' He lifts his sweatshirt, revealing an ugly criss-cross pattern of scars across his torso, around to his back. More livid scar tissue up his left arm from the wrist to the elbow, the skin burned or scalded. 'Then I got moved to Whitemoor after a few years and things calmed down. I thought it had gone away, but . . . they don't forget. They don't forgive.'

'You think this man *targeted* Evie, to get revenge on you?'

He rubs absently at the scar tissue on his arm.

'I think that's part of it, yeah. He wanted me to know, so he found out where I worked and gave her the address, knowing that she would come looking for me. It was a taunt. His way of saying, *Screw you. I can get to you, to your family.* You saw how much he was enjoying himself in that warehouse.'

'But there must be a reason why she's cut off contact with me. She's obviously in danger.'

'All I can tell you is he's the worst kind of bad news,' Declan says. 'Even worse than his dad. We need to find her and get her away, fast.'

He sketches out what he knows of Evie's boyfriend, what he's heard over his years in prison and from other former prisoners. The Lawler family owns a string of legitimate businesses and properties, including Flame nightclub, but the real money is made under the table. And the contents of the warehouse, the contraband cigarettes, the cars – that was only a sideshow.

'Their number one moneymaker,' he says, 'is drugs. Import and distribution.'

My heart drops. I describe the office we'd found with rows of identical mobile phones plugged in and charging. The interview under caution with Parry and Garcia, who had taken such a keen interest in Brandon Roper's complaint – and then simply let me go.

Declan unfolds a map of Greater London onto the table and with a pencil, circles the locations we know. The university up near the M25, near the Hertfordshire border; The Royal Pearl in posh west London; a registered office address that had led us to Flame nightclub in the East End; the warehouse in Silvertown beyond Canary Wharf. And now Peckham, here in south London, where Evie had walked back into her dad's life one day.

She was the link, but how did all the other pieces fit together?

He taps the map thoughtfully with the pencil. 'The hotel, the registered address, the club, the warehouse – basically they're all cut-outs, aren't they?'

'Meaning?'

'They're all one or two steps removed from Lawler's personal life, separated like a firewall, so he can keep his business at arm's length. But where does he actually *live*? A house, an apartment block, a mansion, a bloody castle for all we know. Maybe that's where Evie is.'

'Do you think any of your contacts might know?'

Declan looks doubtful. 'A guy like him, he'll want to keep that sort of information on the down low. I could ask around. But first we need to get you and the boy something to eat.'

He stands, gathers our empty mugs and moves into the kitchen to refill the kettle.

Elvis jumps down from the windowsill and disappears through the cat flap in the back door. A moment later, Milo begins to bark in the garden with short, insistent yaps deadened by the double glazing. I stand up and look out of the back window, where Lucas and Ruth sit side by side on the wooden bench. He seems to be showing her something on his phone, both intent on the screen. The dog and cat face each other across the narrow garden, Milo straining at his leash while Elvis regards him from the top of a wheelie bin.

It's only when I root through my bag for my phone charger and plug it in at the wall socket by my feet, that I realise I haven't switched it out of silent mode from earlier, when Ruth and I were creeping through the warehouse. As I'm switching the sound back on, I notice there's a missed call from an unknown number. A text to let me know a voicemail has been received.

I dial the voicemail number and the robotic voice kicks in. *You have one new message.* I'm so preoccupied with Declan's story, with his sudden reappearance in my life, that I'm only half listening as I the voicemail starts to play.

And then nothing else matters.

Nothing else exists.

Just me and the phone in my hand.

Because when the message clicks in it's the sound I've been desperate to hear, the one that means everything. The most beautiful sound in the world.

My daughter's voice.

55

My heart clenches as I listen, the words hushed and hurried as if she is frightened of being overheard or discovered.

'Mum? It's me.' She sounds out of breath and there is no background noise at all, no echo, as if the call has come from inside a small, cramped space. 'This might be my last chance to call and I just wanted to say . . . I'm sorry. For everything. For not telling the truth and for all the times we argued. I wish I could turn back the clock and do it all differently but I can't. I'm so sorry for lying to you, Mum. I have to go now, I don't know who else might be listening in and it's not my phone or Cassie's so don't try calling back. But I'll always try to keep my eyes on the horizon, just like you told me, Mum. I love you. And Lucas too, tell him . . .' She breaks off, her voice hitching into a sob. 'Just tell him.'

Then she's gone.

The message ends and I find that I'm whispering her name. Tears are wet on my cheeks, heart crashing painfully in my chest. For a long moment I can't say anything else. The only sound I can hear is Milo barking at the cat, a constant yap of noise from the back garden. I play the message again and focus on every word, drinking in every syllable of my daughter's voice. I call the number back, listening to a long dial tone as it rings and rings in my ear.

Pick up. Pick up, Evie.

The call is not answered.

'Declan!' I call into the kitchen. 'Declan! You need to hear this.'

He hurries in holding a sheaf of takeaway menus and I play the message back a third time for his benefit, turning the volume up. I want to listen to it again and again and again, just to hear her voice, but I have to talk to Lucas first. To share the message with him, and Ruth too.

Declan looks thoughtful. 'When did she call?'

'About an hour ago,' I say. 'My phone was on silent.'

'Well that's good, right? That she's back in contact.'

'She sounds so scared.'

More gently, he says: 'But she's alive, Lauren. And scared means she knows she's in trouble, she knows she needs help. She's not lying anymore.'

'I know,' I say. 'I just . . .' Tears threaten again, my throat thickening with the thought of Evie lost, alone, making a desperate phone call that goes unanswered. 'Why would she say it might be her last chance to call?'

'Maybe she has to give up her phone, Lauren. Or maybe she's getting on a flight?'

'But why?'

'The thing she said about the horizon,' he says gently, ignoring my question. 'What do you think she meant?'

I feel dizzy, light-headed, as if I've stood up too fast. 'I have no idea.'

'Are you OK?'

I stagger, grabbing for the chairback. 'Yes. Fine. I need to talk to Lucas. He found someone who could track a phone before, maybe we can do that again.'

Declan puts a steadying hand on my arm. 'I mean, are you *really* OK, Lauren?'

I don't have the headspace to think about that question now; there is too much else going on, too many other thoughts spinning and colliding inside my head.

'I feel a bit . . .'

'Have a seat,' he says. 'You look exhausted, you need to look after yourself.'

He fans out the takeaway menus on the table between us.

'You need to eat something,' he says. 'And then we'll sit down and talk. We'll listen to the message again and figure out what to do next. What does Lucas like to eat?'

I flick idly through the folded leaflets – Chinese, Indian, Thai, fish and chips – not really seeing them.

'I should never have brought him along,' I say. 'It was a mistake. I've got to get him out of this, Declan, away from these people. Back there at the warehouse . . .' I shake my head at the memory. 'He could have killed someone with that gun.'

'Probably not,' Declan says. 'The safety catch was on.'

A faint pulse of relief, at least, that Lucas had been held back from catastrophe.

'What did you do with it?'

'The gun?' He shrugs. 'Bottom of the Thames.'

It's only now, as the last of the daylight fades outside, that I realise I can no longer hear the sound of Milo barking outside. Nor can I hear the sound of a football kicked against the wall. Lucas must have got cold, or bored, or both. I stand and head past the foot of the steep stairs, into the kitchen. Empty. The bathroom door stands open, only darkness within.

I open the back door and step out into the cold evening air, a blinding security lamp illuminating every brick, stone and blade of grass in brilliant white light.

But the small garden is completely abandoned, the back gate swinging open.

Lucas is gone.

EVIE

Four weeks earlier

The staff at The Royal Pearl Hotel had started to recognise her.

Evie exchanged polite small talk with the reception manager as he checked the booking and handed her a keycard to their usual suite. She'd asked Scott a few times if she could come back to his Docklands flat, but he'd said the whole block was being renovated and it was an absolute mess of dust and noise and building work. The hotel was much nicer, he said. At least until the renovations were finished in a month or two.

He'd told her to meet him there – that he had a surprise for her. It was all very mysterious. Evie let her mind wander as the mirrored lift ascended to the top floor. Perhaps something in the West End? He knew she loved shows and musicals and there were so many she still hadn't seen. Or maybe a trip, a weekend away somewhere? That would be lovely too, but if she was honest she was happy enough to be here with him, just the two of them. As long as they were together.

She let herself into the suite, hoping he might already be there waiting for her. Everything inside was pristine and perfect – as it always was – but there was no Scott. The room was the same as always, except for a laptop on the desk, a cable curling up to the TV above it. She opened a can of Diet Coke from the minibar and went to the window, to look down on the street below. People coming and going. Expensive cars. Expensively dressed people. A cute little

Italian café across the square, the front window already lit up with multicoloured fairy lights for the approaching festive season.

The electronic buzz of the door lock sounded and she felt her heart lift as the door opened.

But it wasn't Scott.

Instead, it was a heavily muscled man of about thirty, with wide-set eyes and a thick neck. He was in jeans and a black puffa jacket that accentuated the broadness of his build.

'Sorry,' Evie said, an electric pulse of alarm shooting up her spine. 'I think you might have the wrong room.'

But there was a keycard in the man's hand. He hadn't forced the door.

'Evie, right?'

'How do you know my name?'

'Scott couldn't make it,' he said. 'Sends his apologies. I'm Brandon, I work for him.'

He extended a big hand and Evie took it in an awkward shake, not knowing what else to do.

'Why isn't he here?' She tried to make sense of this stranger being here in his place, already judging whether she could dodge past him and get to the door first. 'Is he all right?'

'Yeah, he's all right.' Brandon went to the laptop, opened it, entered a passcode. The screen on the TV flickered into life. 'Just a bit tied up this afternoon.'

'What are you doing?'

'Why don't you have a seat, Evie?'

She stayed where she was, arms crossed tightly over her chest. 'Why?'

He shrugged. 'Suit yourself. Just think you'll want to sit down when you've seen this, that's all.'

'Seen what?'

He didn't reply. Just tapped at the keyboard on the laptop. A video file appeared on the screen of the big wall-mounted TV.

Brandon hit *play*.

And the world stopped.

The video was of a couple having sex in a hotel room. A big bed, the sheets kicked all the way down, close-ups of everything, the man's face pixelated out but the woman's face clearly—

Oh God.

Oh no.

No. No. No.

She felt the tears, hot on her face. Her throat was clogged with horror, with fear, with disbelief. With betrayal.

She took her hand away from her mouth.

'What is this?'

'This?' Brandon studied the scene playing out on the TV. 'This is you, love.'

'Turn it off,' she gasped.

'Already? There's like another hour of it to go yet.'

Here. In this room. In this bed. There must have been cameras . . . everywhere. Hidden.

'Turn it off!'

He tapped the keyboard and the video froze on a close-up of her face, eyes closed.

'What do you think?'

Bile was rising in her throat.

'What do you want?'

'I'm going to make you an offer.' He leaned in closer to her, his bulk towering over her. 'Because we're at a fork in the road here, Evie. One of two things is going to happen in the next fifteen minutes. You can walk away if you want, I won't stop you, I swear. But by the time you get on the Tube this video will have been sent to every single contact in your phone book.' He points at her mobile on the desk. 'And yeah, we've downloaded all of them. All your friends, your family, aunties and uncles and grandmas and cousins. Everyone from school, college, uni, employers. It'll be uploaded to all your social media accounts, every single one of them, then blasted out on a load of other bot accounts we've got set up for this sort of thing, enough to make it go viral. *Then* it'll be uploaded to YouPorn and about fifty other porn sites around the world. So it'll be out there forever, basically. You'll be *famous*.'

Evie felt as if she was falling off a cliff. Nothing left but the impact.

'Please,' she said. 'Don't.'

'You don't want that, do you?'

She shook her head. Her voice had deserted her.

'Neither do I,' said Brandon. 'Neither does Scott, really.'

'You're not his friend,' she said. 'A friend wouldn't do this.'

'The good news is there's a way you can stop all of that happening. You can choose the other option, make sure this video doesn't get out there on the internet for everyone to see. Protect yourself. Your future.'

Through her sobs, she forced the word out.

'How?'

'Very simple,' Brandon said. 'You're going to go on a little trip, and we'll see how you get on. You work for us now.'

56

Ruth is gone too. My stomach drops with a sick plunge of dread.

'Lucas?' I call his name over the fences to my left and right. 'Lucas? Ruth?'

The football is there, abandoned in shadow next to an over-grown hedge. Not just a hedge, I realise now, but plants that have grown thick around the frame of an old gate, the wood green and split with age, a heavy rusted bolt pulled back. The gate stands open a few inches. I pull it open all the way and step through, batting away hanging creepers that flicker at my face. It leads out to an old back alley that runs behind this row of terraces and the gardens of the next street. Dozens of wheelie bins are lined up on both sides, alongside fox-torn bin liners spilling out their contents.

I call Lucas's name again up and down the alley, trying to keep the high note of panic out of my voice. Hearing only my son's words just as he had slammed the back door barely half an hour ago.

I hate you and I want to go home.

I want to go home.

Home.

Perhaps he was punishing me, trying to frighten me, for what he'd discovered today. For the lie I'd told about his father for so many years. An angry, emotional reaction to a traumatic dis-covery. A totally understandable reaction, in hindsight. Perhaps

Ruth had followed him, gone after him, taken Milo with her as she tried to persuade him to come back.

But how far could he have got already? He had no money, no cards, no ticket. Did he even *know* the way home? He'd never been to this part of London before.

'Lucas!'

Black sacks of rubbish are pushed against the wall, humps of shadow in the dark alley. It's only when I get a bit nearer that I see the piles are uneven, the shape is wrong, the outline of a small foot, a shoe lying on its side, a trouser leg—

Oh, no.

Please God no.

As I crouch down another blinding-white security light clicks on and I squint against the glare, at a motionless form lying next to the dustbins like so much discarded rubbish. Ruth is lying face down on the cracked tarmac, one arm tucked awkwardly under her body. I roll her over gently, fresh blood smeared around her mouth and leaking from a cut at her temple.

'Ruth?' I check her breathing. 'Can you hear me?'

Her eyes open slowly, painfully. Battered and bruised like this, one cheek smeared with dirt, hair tangled and her clothes wet from the alley, she looks ten years older. She turns her head away from the glare of the light, her forehead creasing with pain, a groan escaping her lips.

'Unhhh . . .'

'Ruth, are you all right? Can you sit up? Where's Lucas?' She blinks, lifts a hand to the blood on her temple, but doesn't reply. 'What happened, Ruth? Where did he go?'

She mutters something inaudible, wiping blood from her mouth.

'What?' I say. 'What was that?'

'I'm sorry,' she says with another groan. 'Took me by surprise. Did . . . did Milo come back?'

Declan steps out into the alley, his eyes darting left and right.

'What's going on, Lauren?'

'He's gone,' I say. 'Lucas has disappeared and Ruth's been attacked.'

His face darkens with alarm.

'*Gone?*'

'Can you help her into the house then go around the front, see if he's there?' I nod towards the end of the alley. 'I'll check this way.'

He hoists Ruth up easily with one strong arm, walking her quickly back inside.

I fumble for my mobile, calling Lucas's number as I run down the alley. Waiting for the call to connect as I shout his name, ignoring the stares of an elderly lady peering through a gap in her net curtains. The number doesn't ring, but just clicks straight into voicemail.

'It's Lucas, leave a message.' *Beep.*

'Lucas?' I press the handset tightly to my ear. 'It's Mum, where are you, love? Call me back as soon as you get this.'

I tap *end* and redial his number straightaway. Voicemail again.

The alleyway joins onto another street that looks identical to the one where Declan lives. To the right, it winds away in a long curve, two rows of tightly packed cars and more of the same narrow ter-raced houses. To the left are the lights and bustle of a main street, a shopping street.

I shout my son's name into the dark but there is no movement under the watery street lights, no shadows detaching themselves to move closer.

Which way?

Left or right?

The phone is still in my hand. I'm about to run towards the main road when I have a better idea, pulling up the Find My app and jabbing the list to select Lucas's iPhone. I had done the same with Evie's phone so many times but had never felt the need with Lucas. He was normally such an easy boy, he never pushed boundaries or broke rules.

The map loads, zooms in, and I squint at the blue pulsing dot to figure out where it is in relation to me, which direction he's headed.

The blue dot seems to be stationary.

It's just behind Ellis Road, halfway down the street.

With a sick lurch of panic, I realise it's within metres of where I'm standing now. Which means his phone is either right here, or . . . this was its last location before it was turned off.

Shit.

Switching on the torch function, I flash it desperately around the alleyway: brick walls, wooden gates, more bagged rubbish. Milo is there, sitting obediently by a pair of wheelie bins. When I shine the light on him he barks once, his small eyes twin points of glowing amber, then trots off back towards the house as if nothing has happened.

But there's no phone. No Lucas.

57

I turn left and run towards the main street, dodging around a dog walker and a mess of traffic cones. The street is busy with crawling traffic and jostling pedestrians. It's fully dark now and most of the people are taller than Lucas, blocking my view with their big coats and bags and bobble hats. A trio of pensioners are waiting to cross at the lights and I step in front of them, showing them a picture of Lucas on my mobile, asking if they've seen him in the last few minutes. They all shake their heads and one starts to ask me something but I'm already turning away to ask the next person, and the next, before moving on to show his picture to a queue of bemused people waiting at a bus stop. More shaking heads.

I run down the street, slaloming between shoppers bundled up against the cold, ignoring curious looks as I shout Lucas's name over and over again. Praying to catch a glimpse of his unruly mop of hair, his slim figure somewhere up ahead, looking in a shop window, standing at a bus stop, sitting on a bench. Or at least the high-vis uniform of a police officer on patrol. But I don't see either.

Except—

Wait. *There.* The glimpse of a dark jacket, a small-shouldered frame, phone in hand as he walks. Oblivious to everything else around him, focused on the small screen of his mobile.

'Lucas!'

I step into the road, holding up both hands against the furious horns and screeching tyres of oncoming traffic, hurrying between cars until I'm on the other side and he's there, *thank God*, he's there almost within touching distance. Running up behind him, I put a hand on his shoulder and come around to face him, to embrace him, to catch my breath and tell him—

The boy looks up from his phone and gives me a startled glance. 'What?'

Not Lucas. Younger, smaller. Someone else's son.

The man beside him has also stopped. To me, he says: 'What the hell are you doing?'

'Oh.' I take my hand away. 'I . . . I'm sorry, I thought . . .'

'Josh?' he says to the boy. 'Do you know this lady?'

The youngster shakes his head.

'I'm sorry,' I say again. 'I thought he was my son, I'm looking for him.' I bring up the picture again on my phone but the man is already leading his son away, looking at me as if I'm demented.

I stagger backwards as people move around me on the pavement. A desperate, whirling terror spins like a vortex in my chest.

Both of them.

I've lost both of them.

I've been stupid and careless and now they've both been swallowed up in the darkness of this vast city.

The breath is still heaving in my lungs, cold air stinging my cheeks.

Declan appears beside me. 'Checked the street all the way to the end, gardens as well. No joy.'

I put my hands on my hips, breathing hard. Terror and anger and pure molten panic swirl in my stomach. I wheel around and put a hand on Declan's broad chest, pushing him back into the road. '*You* said you weren't followed from the warehouse! You said your place would be safe!'

'I'm sorry, Lauren,' he says. 'We'll find him, OK?'

'Is it you?' I have a sudden vision of him sharing a prison cell with one of Lawler's goons back in the day, getting friendly, getting on the payroll. The whole story he'd told me earlier some elaborate fiction, all misdirection so I would drop my guard. 'Are you part of it? Working with them?'

'No, Lauren. I'm not.'

'So how do you afford that house, two years out of jail?'

'It's a rental,' he says. 'Comes with the job.'

'They knew we were coming at that place in Silvertown,' I say as the realisation hits me. 'They were waiting for us, masks on and ready. And they knew we were here, too, they knew Lucas was here.'

'Not because of me,' he says, with a shake of his head. 'I swear.'

I let out a sigh of frustration and check my phone again, but there's no reply from my son. *Of course not – it's still switched off.* Not even five minutes since we'd realised he was missing but half an hour, at least, since he'd first gone out into the back garden. How far away was he now?

'I'm going to call the police.'

I'm tapping the third nine into my phone's keypad when the display switches to show an incoming call.

An unknown number.

'Mum?'

'Lucas!' The relief in hearing his voice is overwhelming, the same rush of pure joy I'd felt with Evie's message a few minutes ago. 'Where are you? Are you OK?'

'Mum?'

'Lucas?' I say again. There's a background hum at his end, as if he's in a car. 'Can you hear me? The signal's not good. Tell me where you are, we'll come and get you.'

A muffled cry is followed by deeper voices, a strangled silence, then the static crunch of a phone being passed around.

'Hello?' I push the phone harder against my ear. 'Can you still hear me? Lucas? Are you there?'

The silence draws out for five long seconds. Ten.

Then a man's voice is in my ear: an unruffled London baritone that I don't recognise.

'Here's how this is going to go,' he says. 'You'll go back to the house on Ellis Road. You won't stop on the way, you won't talk to anyone or make any phone calls. You're not going to try tracking this handset, and most important of all, you're not going to contact the police. You'll be back in that house inside the next sixty seconds and then you'll wait for a call. Do you understand, Lauren?'

'Yes,' I gasp. 'Please just—'

'Good,' the voice says. 'Because otherwise you'll never see your boy again.'

58

We run all the way back to Declan's house.

I'm panting hard by the time we're in his kitchen again, half bent over with my hands on my knees, chest burning with the sudden exertion. Declan's shoulders rise and fall as he gets his breath back. I turn the mobile's volume to maximum, clutching it in my hand and willing the stranger to call again.

Ruth is slumped in a chair, holding a balled-up tissue to the cut on her forehead, staring at us both as I tell her what's happened in a garbled rush. She tries to stand and reach for me, but wobbles on shaky knees and collapses back into the chair instead.

'You need to take it easy,' I say. 'Just sit for a few minutes, OK?'

'Don't worry about me,' she says, pale-faced. 'Just a silly bang on the head.'

'What happened? What did you see?'

She blinks hard. 'Milo got out and we both went through the gate to look for him. Before I realised there was someone there, I just got this colossal whack on the side of my head. It was like . . . there were men there, waiting for us. Next thing I knew, you were saying my name and I was lying face down in the alley.'

'You're sure you didn't see anyone? Did you see who took Lucas?'

'Sorry.' She shakes her head slowly, eyes brimming with tears. 'This is all my fault, Lauren. I was there with him, I should have . . . I'm sorry.'

Declan paces the small kitchen beside us. 'I'm so *stupid*,' he says, smacking his palm against the worktop. 'Should have seen this coming.'

'None of us saw it coming, Dec.' I stare at my phone, dark and silent in my hand. 'Not even me.'

'But it was obvious they were going to look for leverage, we'd seen inside that warehouse so they were never going to just let it go. They needed a way to put pressure on you, stop you going straight to the police with what we'd seen. And they found one.' He slaps the worktop again. 'I should have realised they'd try something like this.'

Ruth regards us both with wide, jittery eyes.

'I'm so sorry,' she says again. 'Surely there must be something we can do?'

Declan indicates my mobile. 'How about Lucas's phone, have you ever tracked it before?'

I explain my previous efforts but try again anyway. This time I select the Snapchat app on my phone, tapping the map icon. Once again, it shows his last known location as right here, around the back of Declan's small house.

'No joy,' I say. 'Whoever's got him is way ahead of us. They must have known we'd try.' I drop my mobile back onto the table. 'Damn!'

Ruth looks agitated and seems to have retreated into herself. 'Can I make a suggestion?'

'Of course.'

'Perhaps now is really the time we *should* call the police? I know the caller said not to but then they would say that, wouldn't they? They're trying to scare you into a corner when the police might actually be our best—'

'We're not calling the police.' It comes out with more venom than I'd intended. 'We're going to do whatever they say to get Lucas back. To the *letter*.'

'These people,' she says. 'You know you can't trust them, Lauren. You can't believe a word they say.'

'They have my baby boy,' I say. 'They took my daughter. And I'll do whatever they say to get them back safe.'

She looks to Declan, as if for support, and plucks her mobile phone from her handbag.

'Look, I'm going to call the police anyway, so technically it won't be you, will it? Those detectives have all kinds of amazing techniques for finding people like this, all the kind of things we can't—'

'Nobody's calling anyone!' My shout echoes loud inside the small kitchen. 'No police! No calls! Do you understand?'

Ruth flinches back in the chair, hand still clutching her phone. Slowly, she lowers it back into her handbag.

'All right,' she says in a small voice. 'Sorry. I get it.'

Declan taps the table. 'Let's just see what they say first, then decide what we're going to do next.'

The three of us lapse into an uneasy silence, the only sound the occasional car passing slowly on the street outside. Every minute or so, Declan comes over to look at my mobile. But the phone's screen remains stubbornly dark.

Eventually, Ruth speaks up again, her voice so quiet it's almost inaudible. 'What if they don't call back? What then?'

'They'll call,' Declan says.

'How do you know?'

'They've got leverage now, they'll want to use it for their own benefit. Maximise it while they can.'

Leverage. That's what he is now, my son. My shy, quirky, clever boy, who likes skateboarding and *Stranger Things*, who is loyal and funny and has always been in the shadow of his big sister. He is collateral, something to be bargained with, a piece in a game whose rules I still don't understand.

The truth hits me then, the truth of what I've done. The danger I've exposed Lucas to, the very same danger that has already taken his sister away. The horror of it comes rushing up fast, as if a huge black void has opened up at my feet and I'm standing right at the edge. Nothing to hold onto, nothing below me at all but cold, black emptiness.

All the remaining strength drains from my limbs and I lean heavily on the back of a chair.

'What have I done, Declan?' Tears prick at my eyes. 'I was blind to it all, what was going on with Evie. And now I've dragged Lucas into it too and he'll be so scared. He'll be terrified. What if . . .' The breath catches in my throat. 'What If I've lost them both?'

59

Instead of replying, Declan crosses the small room and enfolds me in his arms in a gesture that is both utterly strange and achingly familiar at the same time.

My first instinct is to push him away. To tell him he's crossing a line that I swore we'd never cross again. But the warmth of his touch brings so many memories rushing back. The prison years have made him broader, harder than he was then but the feel of him is the same, the sense of him, the careful strength of his hands on my back. Enough to hold me up, to support me, protect me. Enough to protect all of us.

'Listen to me,' he says, his words a quiet rumble through his chest. 'We are going to find them, OK? We're going to get them away from those people, whatever it takes. I promise. We just have to keep our heads, be smart.'

We stand like that for a moment longer in his silent kitchen and I close my eyes, drinking in the calm confidence of his words.

'I'm sorry,' I say, half into his sweatshirt. 'For not telling the kids the truth about you. I was young and angry and scared, and I thought it was the right thing to do back then. And once I'd said it, I couldn't take it back. Couldn't unsay it, so I just let them believe it was the truth.'

He rubs my back. 'No, Lauren, it was me. I put you in an impossible situation. But whatever you said, it's in the past now. Neither of us can change what's happened, and there's nothing to be gained from going over it again. But what we *can* do is change the present, the here and now, today, tomorrow and the days that come after.'

I withdraw from the embrace, forcing myself to take a step back, a step away from him.

Ruth hands me a tissue and I wipe the tears hastily away.

'The man on the phone,' she says carefully. 'Did he mention anything about the girls, about Cassie or Evie?'

'No,' I say. 'But there's something else you need to know. I was about to come out and tell you when they took Lucas.'

She gives me a look of alarm.

'What is it?'

'A voicemail,' I say. 'Evie called earlier, left a message. And she mentioned Cassie, by name.'

'Is she OK?' Her voice cracks. 'Is Cassie OK?'

I unlock my phone and select the voicemail. 'I don't know, but it sounds like they're together.'

I play the message for her twice before we lapse into an uneasy silence broken only by her sobs, her hands clasped tightly together as if in prayer. She seems broken, almost folded in on herself, and she dabs at her tears with a fresh tissue. Declan says he'll try a few of his next-door neighbours instead, to ask if they saw anything – or anyone – in the back alley. He promptly disappears out through the kitchen door, the security light illuminating the garden behind him as he goes to the gate.

Ruth and I stare at my phone, lying dark and unresponsive between us. She's just starting to say something else when the first notes of my ringtone sound and the screen flashes into life. *Unknown caller.*

In my haste I almost stab the decline button, my finger slipping across the screen.

'Hello?' I say quickly. 'This is Lauren, Lucas's mum.'

A long moment of silence. Rustling static. The stirring of breath.

'Are you alone?'

It's a different voice to the one I heard before. Unemotional, almost artificial, as if all the rough edges have been smoothed out.

I glance up at Ruth, whose hands are still clasped in front of her

'Yes,' I say. 'Can I speak to Lucas?'

He ignores my question. 'Have I got your full attention, Lauren?'

'Yes. I'm here.'

'Because you've created a big headache for me and a lot of changes to my plans. But now you're going to put it right.'

'Whatever it is,' I say. 'I'll do it.'

'I'm going to give you some instructions now and they're extremely important – for both of us. You still following me?' When I answer, he says: 'First: some ground rules. If you're recording this, stop the recording now. If you're writing it down, stop now. If you're trying to share this conversation with anyone else, stop now. If you break any one of the rules, little Lucas goes into the sea a mile off the south coast inside a ventilated body bag loaded with enough steel plate to take him straight to the bottom. He'll still be alive when he hits the water but it'll be a mercy compared to what a litre of piranha solution will do to little Evie. Do you understand?'

I swallow down on a pulse of nausea clawing its way up my throat.

'I understand.'

'Good girl.' He explains what he wants, setting out each step in detail as I make mental notes and reiterate the key points silently to myself. 'You'd better make it convincing, Lauren, make it the performance of a lifetime. The lives of both your kids are going to depend on it.'

EVIE

Three weeks earlier

Evie didn't know exactly where she was. Just that it was a cellar, a basement, somewhere underground in east London, close enough to the Thames to hear boats chugging by at night. Traffic noise, planes sometimes, filtering through a narrow strip of frosted glass that provided the room's only natural light. It made the little Hampstead flat seem like a palace. The walls were damp, flaking brick, as if it had been converted from a storeroom or coal cellar and the space was tiny, even smaller than her student room at university.

God. That seemed like a lifetime ago.

She sat in the chair in the middle of the floor, facing front as she'd been told. Scott stood behind her with his back to the wall, arms crossed.

'Let's go over the ground rules again, shall we?' His voice, his presence, the pungent smell of his aftershave filled the cell-like room. 'Who do you speak to?'

'No one.'

'Who do you trust?'

'No one but you.'

'Rendezvous?'

She recited the details she had learned by heart: date, place, time. A first name.

'What do you say if you get caught?'

Evie eyed the rucksack by the door, new hiking boots beside it and a waterproof hanging above on a hook. All packed and ready for tomorrow.

'I say a friend asked me to carry some Christmas gifts home for her family. They were already wrapped and I didn't look at them.'

'And what happens if you say anything else?'

She looked down at the dirty stone floor.

'You release the video. And you hurt my family.'

'Correct.' He leaned down, held the screen of his mobile close to her face.

She glanced at it, instantly felt the bile rising in her throat.

He grabbed a handful of her hair, forced her head back around. 'DON'T look away!'

She made herself look again, feeling the grisly image burning its way into her brain, knowing she would never be able to unsee this picture of agony and acid-scorched flesh.

'I understand,' she gasped. 'I get it. I won't say anything.'

'She was one of ours,' Scott said, gesturing at the screen. 'One of our originals. Thought she was smarter than us, thought she could get out. So we had to teach her a lesson. Her dad too.'

'I'll do whatever it takes,' she said. 'Just leave my family alone.'

He finally put the phone back into his pocket.

'I've got faith in you, Evie. When it comes to lying to your mum, you're already an expert. And your dad ... Well, you can forget about that waster.'

Brandon's large frame filled the doorway, blocking the dim light from the corridor. He twisted the cap off a bottle of beer and handed it to Scott.

'We're all set upstairs, boss. Anything else you need me for?'

Scott took a swig of the beer. 'We need to schedule a couple more social media posts before she heads off. Have you got her phone?'

The bigger man produced an iPhone from the side pocket of his combats, typed the passcode and selected the Instagram app. He chose a picture from the gallery and held the screen up to her.

'Didn't post this one yet, did you?'

It was a picture from the student union bar in Welcome Week at the university. Evie shook her head, praying that he wouldn't check back and see that she *had* posted an almost identical shot in October, right at the beginning of term. Watching as Brandon methodically cropped the picture, typed a short caption with his big thumbs, added some of her usual hashtags, scheduled a time and date to post it to her account.

'Oh,' Scott said. 'You're going to call her next week as well, on the thirtieth. Once you've made your first little trip. After that, we'll just keep it to texts until she comes to pick you up.'

'Then what?' Evie had a sudden, ridiculous thought that maybe if she did what they asked for the next few weeks, if she cooperated and came back OK and didn't get caught, then maybe they would just let her go. Back to her family. Back to her life.

But one look at Scott's dead-eyed grin told her she was being hopelessly, stupidly naive.

'Well,' he said. 'Mummy comes to pick you up from uni and we terminate your phone contract on the same day. Email too. All she knows is that you're gone. Run away to live your own life, do your own thing. And you want nothing to do with her anymore. With all the shit you've put her through over the last few years, she'll be glad to get shot of you.'

Evie felt tears threaten again. 'She won't believe I've just left everything without saying goodbye. She'll come looking for me.'

'She wouldn't be the first.' He patted her cheek. 'And she won't be the last.'

60

Detective Sergeant Parry regards me over the rim of a large white coffee mug.

It's only thirty-six hours since we sat opposite each other in a police interview room but she looks as if she's barely slept. Dark shadows crowd beneath her eyes, her skin ghost pale, the blouse beneath her jacket slashed with creases. I suppose I look the same. Neither of us, it seems, have been able to find much rest since we parted company at Bethnal Green police station.

Within twenty minutes of making a call to her this evening there had been a large SUV idling in the street outside Declan's house, a heavy knock at the door from the driver and a summons to an unknown address where I could tell Parry what I had learned, face to face at an anonymous black-fronted building in Vauxhall. Fifteen storeys of dark glass but no sign, no name, no logo above the heavy front doors. A line of anti-ram barriers along the pavement outside and a pair of armed police officers inside the only clues that this was not the corporate head office of a bank or a tech company.

The driver had pulled into an underground car park and escorted me up to a windowless fourth-floor room furnished in soft greys and blues, a sofa and an armchair, a table, a water cooler in the corner. The discreet plastic eye of a small camera mounted over the door.

'Tell me again,' Parry says. She had been reluctant, at first, to meet me at all this evening – until I told her why. Now her face is taut with expectation, or even excitement. 'Tell me exactly what your daughter told you, using the words she used. In your own time.'

I take a second to gather my thoughts. *The important thing is to keep it simple and straightforward. Don't embellish, don't deviate – that's the way you get caught out.*

'Evie called me,' I say, following the script in my head. 'She said she'd been away, out of the UK, but she'd be coming back tomorrow. She said she was getting the Eurostar from Paris and it would arrive at London St Pancras at 3 p.m., she asked me to meet her there. She said she had to give something to a friend when she arrived but after that, she wanted me to take her home, back to Reading. She said she was sorry for everything that had happened and she'd never meant for it to end up like this.'

I shift my weight on the edge of the sofa, unable to hide the nerve-jangling fear that has burrowed its way inside me since Lucas was taken. Parry sips her coffee in the armchair while Garcia is at the table, making notes, both of them wearing lanyards with the three-letter acronym *NCA* beside the logo of a white crown on a black background. The sofa and armchair arrangement in the corner feels oddly homely for a building like this, a comforting contrast to the hard angles and tinted glass that seems to characterise the rest of the place. I suppose that's precisely why this furniture is in here.

'And that's all?' Parry says. 'She didn't say what she'd been doing? Where she'd been, with whom? Or what she had to give to the friend when she arrived?'

'No,' I say. 'It sounded like she was in a real hurry and she was speaking in a kind of whisper, like she didn't want to be overheard. Right from when I answered the call she said, "Don't talk, Mum, just listen, I can't explain now but I really need your help." I was just so happy to hear her voice and I had a million questions but she cut me off before I could say anything else.'

I stop, take a breath, aware the narrative is starting to run away from me. *Keep. It. Simple.* I had to stay steady on the tightrope – give them enough to pique their interest without tripping myself up. In any case, there were only three key pieces of information I needed to convey: St Pancras International Station; Eurostar from Paris; arrival tomorrow at 3 p.m.

Garcia looks up from his notepad. 'You're absolutely certain of the time and place?'

'Yes, she made me repeat it back to her.'

'And you're going to be there, are you?'

I frown at him as if this is a trick question. 'Of course. She's my daughter.'

'How did she sound?'

'Scared.' I look down at my lap. 'Petrified, actually. Never heard her so frightened before.'

Parry's tone is gentler now, almost soothing.

'I can't imagine how difficult all of this is for you, Lauren.' She gives me a small, sad smile. 'It must be unbearable.'

'It is. But it's not as if I have a choice. I'm her mother.'

'You'd do anything for her.'

'Yes.'

'I'm sure I'd do the same.'

A beat of silence between us.

'How old are yours?' I take a sip of my coffee. 'Your children?'

'Twelve and fourteen,' she says, her expression softening. 'Two girls. Couldn't imagine one of them being missing, out of reach, out of contact. Let alone involved with something like this.'

She holds my eye for a moment longer and I get a powerful sense that in another time and place, in another life perhaps, we might very well have been friends. Neighbours. Saying hello at the school gate, chatting on the sidelines of a kids' football pitch on a Saturday morning.

But not today.

Today I only have one job: to get her to believe me.

Parry leans forward in her seat.

'Did Evie say anything else? Anything at all?'

I look from one detective to the other.

'She told me not to tell anyone, begged me not to tell the police.'

'And yet here you are.'

'Yes,' I say. 'Here I am.'

Layers of deception, one over the other.

I'm aware that lying to these detectives must also be a criminal offence, that I'm digging a hole for myself by deliberately misleading them. A charge of wasting police time, perhaps, or perverting the course of justice. But I also feel detached from it, remote, as if it's someone else in this small room rather than me. Someone who follows the rules, does the right thing, trusts the system to protect her family. Rather than a desperate, terrified parent playing for the highest stakes imaginable.

'So are you going to arrest me again?' I glance towards the door. 'Like you did the other day?'

Parry shakes her head.

'You need to understand,' she says. 'We have to keep up appearances, do you see? This is a delicate operation at a very sensitive stage. If one of their people makes a complaint of criminal conduct, we log it, process it and respond in the standard way. As if they're just regular citizens and there's nothing else going on. If we deviate from standard procedure *in any way* they could get a sniff of how close we are, then they could get spooked and change their plans, change everything. Disappear. And we'd have to start again from scratch.'

'Right,' I say. 'I just wondered if Lawler had a few friendly police officers on the payroll, ready to do his bidding.'

Garcia gives me a strange look, the silence spinning out between us for a long, uncomfortable moment. He glances over at his partner, then back at me.

'I'm going to pretend you didn't say that. And probably better if you don't repeat it to anyone else in this building.'

'Why?'

'Because your daughter's fate is hanging in the balance here,' he says carefully. 'And we're your best hope of lenient treatment for her when the dust settles. We're your best hope of getting her back.'

I nod, unsure what to say in response. Wondering if he has an inkling of how far that is from the truth.

'For what it's worth,' Parry says, 'you've done the right thing in coming to us, Lauren. The smart thing, and I respect you for that.'

'Have I?' I give a defeated shrug. 'I don't even know why you're interested in her, what you think she's involved in. Is she in a lot of trouble?'

'What do *you* think she's involved in?' The detective sergeant cocks her head to the side. 'If you had to guess?'

I think back to my instructions, what I had been told to say and what I had been told should not be mentioned under *any* circumstances: Lucas's kidnapping, the warehouse at Silvertown, the involvement of Ruth's daughter, Cassie.

'Christ, I honestly have no idea, which is one of the most terrifying things of all.' This, at least, was partly true. 'But me coming here and talking to you, it'll make it better for her, right? It's something in her favour, helping you with all this?' I gesture at the room around us. 'Whatever *this* is. Are you going to tell me? I don't even know what building we're in.'

Parry considers me for a moment. 'You've heard of the National Crime Agency?'

I shrug. 'I suppose so. You go after . . . people smugglers?'

'Among other things. But the task force we're part of has a different focus.'

'A focus on what?'

'Fentanyl.'

61

So there it is. Out in the open now, clear and unambiguous: *drugs*.

Specifically, a synthetic opiate called fentanyl, the detective tells me. A drug that has become a scourge of American cities and is already gaining a foothold in Europe.

'Fifty times more potent than heroin,' Parry says. 'A hundred times stronger than morphine. Less than one-hundredth of a gram is potentially fatal, which is why it's so easy to overdose.'

She recites the grim litany of this man-made drug. In the US, fentanyl kills more than 70,000 people a year – much higher than the death toll from guns in one of the most heavily armed societies on earth. It could be sold and taken in pill form, which meant no messy needles, no cooking up, no injecting. It could also be smoked by users whose veins had already collapsed from addiction to other drugs. It was typically made from chemicals mass-produced in China, which made it easier and quicker to manufacture than heroin or cocaine, which relied on cultivation of poppies or coca plants.

One kilogram of pure fentanyl, she tells me, has the potential to kill half a million people.

'It's incredibly lucrative and it's coming to the UK next,' she says in a tired monotone. 'Most of it's arriving via legal entry points from Europe. We're just trying to hold back the tide.'

Several organised crime groups are competing to establish themselves as the main supplier for the UK, she explains, using different routes, different methods of transport, different types of courier to evade law enforcement. All these groups trying to innovate, develop new techniques to open up the UK as a fresh, untapped market for fentanyl.

Lawler's taunting words to me were making a new kind of sense. *Your girls? They're gone.* Because they *had* gone – abroad, gone off on some twisted journey to bring this poison into the country, to make a rich criminal even richer.

I look from one detective to the other. 'Evie would never willingly get involved in anything like that. She must have been coerced, blackmailed.'

'Quite possibly.'

'So does it make sense, what I've told you? Bringing it in on the Eurostar? You don't seem surprised.'

'It makes a certain amount of sense,' Parry says. 'We know Lawler has a network in France, contacts, affiliates. Bulk shipments generally arrive in North Africa and are broken down into smaller consignments for distribution north through Spain, France, Italy, east into the Balkans and so on. We have some pretty good intel that your daughter has been in France recently, we just weren't clear on her return route.'

'But now you know.'

'So it would seem.'

She stands up from the armchair and goes over to confer with Garcia, the two of them speaking in low voices, their heads close together. She leans forward against the table, rolling her neck as if to loosen the muscles. When she speaks again all the softness has left her voice and she's back to the brittle matter-of-fact tone I'd heard when we first met.

'Where's your son, Lauren? Lucas, isn't it?'

'Back home with my mum.' I swallow, leaning into the lie. 'It was all a bit much for him on Monday, being stuck in that police station.'

'So he's not staying with Mr Hicks at his residence on Ellis Road?'

'No.'

She plucks a sheet of printed paper from a folder open on the table. 'I'm assuming you're aware that Hicks has convictions for assault, ABH, manslaughter?'

'Yes,' I say. 'I know.'

'Presumably you also know he was also a known associate of people involved in the importation and supply of class B drugs, prior to his manslaughter conviction?'

I try to keep my face neutral, to keep the surprise from showing. *Drugs? Why did Declan not mention this earlier?*

'I know what he did,' I say instead. 'But he's still the father of my children.'

'And you separated after he was sent down for the second time, is that right?'

I shift in my seat. 'He's not the same man he was back then.'

Parry raises an eyebrow at this but doesn't pursue it further.

'By the way,' she says. 'You said Evie contacted you by phone? Can you show me?'

I pull up my phone's call history and show her, thinking back to the last instruction I'd received from the stranger an hour ago. *In five minutes' time you will receive a call from another unrecognised number. You will accept the call and say nothing. Do not hang up until the caller does. When they hang up, you will call the number back twice. You will wait for it to ring out both times.*

The detective points a slim index finger at the screen. 'Whose number is that?'

'Don't know, I'd never seen it before.'

Garcia cranes forward to look at the call list.

'You didn't get through when you tried to call her back?'

'It wasn't answered. I thought maybe she'd bought a cheap pay-as-you-go, or borrowed someone else's phone then switched it off after she called.'

To her partner, Parry says: 'See what you can get from that number will you, Ed?'

Garcia takes a picture of the screen, stands and heads out into the corridor without a word.

'So what happens now?' I say. 'I mean, what happens tomorrow?'

'We'll take a look at the train. It's possible your daughter won't be travelling under her own name but we'll check anyway.'

'She took her passport from home,' I say, nodding. 'You're not going to arrest her, are you? She's been manipulated, exploited by someone else to do this, whatever it is. This is not my Evie, it's not who she is. She's got her whole life ahead of her.' I realise I'm rambling, going off the script, and any misstep could see this whole deception blow up in my face.

Stop talking. You've done what they asked.

'We'll just have to see what happens tomorrow,' Parry says. 'Play it by ear. But like I said, you did the right thing, bringing this information to us. The right thing for Evie, too.' She stands up, a signal that we're finished, and I follow suit. 'I'm going to need your phone.'

'No.'

'No?'

'It's the only way Evie can reach me.'

For a moment, Parry looks as if she might be about to arrest me again, throw me in a cell, confiscate the phone. But then she seems to think better of it.

'Contact me immediately if she gets in touch with you again. For any reason.'

'Will I see you at the station tomorrow?'

'No,' she says. 'But we'll see you. Oh – and there's one more thing.'

I stop. 'Yes?'

'The name you gave us, Colton Ryczek, the postgrad at your daughter's university? I checked him out and he came back clean. No hits on the system, no convictions, no red flags.'

Once again, I swallow down the guilt at the pack of lies I've just told her.

'OK. Thank you.'

The same tall driver escorts me back downstairs to the underground car park and I ask him to take me to the budget hotel in Hackney where Lucas and I had stayed last night. My VW is where I left it, a yellow-and-black penalty notice tucked under the windscreen wiper. I screw it up and throw it into the back seat.

It's only when I'm safely back at Declan's house in Peckham that I dial the number from earlier tonight. It's answered after one ring, the same male voice as before.

'Speak.'

'It's done,' I say.

'And?'

'We're good. I'm pretty sure they bought it. All of it.'

62

I've focused so hard on making the lie believable for Parry and Garcia that I almost believe it myself. The fantasy of standing on the concourse at St Pancras Station, of seeing a train arrive and Evie getting off, of watching her in a crowd of travellers moving nearer to the barrier. Seeing her smile, the laughter in her eyes, and being able to pull her into a hug for the first time in months. To hold her close and forgive her, and ask for her to forgive me, to link arms as we walk out of the station without looking back.

Instead . . . what did we have? Evie, Lucas, Cassie, all missing. All out there somewhere beyond our reach. I had asked the caller on the phone, begged him to let me talk to Lucas or at least to know that he was OK. But he had simply hung up without answering.

All the way here, on the way to pick up my car and the silent drive south back across the river, I had wrestled with an impossible dilemma.

I could do as the caller said, follow his instructions to the letter: go to St Pancras tomorrow and play out his lie to the end. Knowing that my daughter won't be on the train. But hoping it will save my son. Or I could keep going down the road I've been travelling since Saturday morning. Keep pushing to find her, to unravel this whole thing, almost certainly putting Lucas in even greater danger.

Or perhaps I had lost them both already and just didn't know it.

I push the thought away and walk through to the kitchen, where Declan and Ruth are deep in conversation. Milo lies curled on the lino floor between them, fast asleep.

Declan looks up when I walk in. 'How did it go?'

'OK, I think. As far as I could tell, they believed me.' I look at Ruth, an angry bruise starting to darken the skin around her right eye. 'They think the girls are being used as couriers, bringing drugs into the country.'

She looks as if she's been hit again, a hand rising to cover her mouth.

'*Drugs?*'

'Parry and Garcia work for the NCA,' I say. 'National Crime Agency. Google says it's like . . . the FBI or something.'

I describe my conversation with the two detectives, trying to fill in the blanks in our knowledge and sketch out what might happen tomorrow.

Declan nods thoughtfully. 'So St Pancras is going to be full of cops tomorrow ready to swarm the three o'clock train from Paris when it pulls in?'

'I think so.'

'Which means that's the one place Evie and Cassie definitely *won't* be. Police will probably cover the earlier and later trains as well, just to be sure.'

'Then . . . what? The girls lie low for a bit longer and come back to the UK next week? The week after?'

He shakes his head. 'Not when Lawler has gone to the trouble of taking Lucas, blackmailing you to put the police off the scent. No point creating a big diversion unless you're going to use it. The girls will be back in the UK tomorrow afternoon but via a different route, to a different place. I'd put money on it.'

'And would you bet their lives on it too?' As soon as the words are out, I wish I could take them back. 'Sorry, I didn't mean it like that. I just mean, we have no idea where they're going to be.'

'But if we can figure it out, then maybe we can meet them, intercept them before they make the delivery. Or before they get caught. Then we have the drugs and we trade them for Lucas.'

I put my hands up. 'But there must be a *hundred* places they could arrive.'

'Not necessarily.'

*　　*　　*

Declan orders in two pizzas from the takeaway down the road and folds out the little dining table to make space for the three of us.

I haven't eaten since breakfast and it's only when he opens the first pizza box that I realise how hungry I am. Judging by Ruth's reaction she feels the same way, and the three of us eat in silence until only a couple of slices are left. Declan clears the plates away when we're done and goes to the sink to fill the kettle.

Ruth dabs at her mouth with a square of kitchen roll and mouths to me: 'How are you doing?'

'I'm OK. You?'

She shrugs, peering around me to check we're not being overheard.

'What do you make of all that?'

'My head's still spinning, to be honest.'

Declan brings us each a cup of strong, dark coffee. The table cleared, he unfolds an OS map of southern England and spreads it across the table between us, then plugs in a battered laptop that looks older than Lucas. Ruth produces an iPad from her shoulder bag, along with a notepad and pen.

As we sip our coffee I tell them about DS Parry's interest in Declan's crimes from a dozen years ago. The fact that he was a 'known associate' of people in the drugs importing business. He had insisted back then – and says so again now – that he was only ever on the edge of it, never directly involved, a peripheral player caught up in something much bigger. But whatever the truth is, we need him to draw on that background now.

'I know you've left all of that behind,' I say. 'But you need to think like them again, like you're in that world. You want to get couriers back into the UK without getting caught – how do you do it?'

'It's been a long time.'

'I know,' I say. 'But where do we start?'

'Things have changed a lot since then.' He looks down at the map. 'A lot of the loopholes have been filled, I reckon. But then . . . you've also got a lot more attention on people smugglers now, small boats crossing the Channel – that's all you hear about in the news. A lot of government time, energy and money goes on stopping those small boats. Drug enforcement can't really compete, hardly makes the headlines by comparison. So there's bound to be new gaps where mules are getting through.'

'Mules?'

'Sorry,' he says. 'Couriers. There was a bloke I was padded up with in Whitemoor for the best part of a year, he got nicked at Gatwick with three kilos of cocaine in his suitcase.'

Declan relates what he learned from his erstwhile cellmate over many long months on twenty-three-hour lockdown in prison. That couriers usually travelled alone or in pairs and would not have a handler with them, not even a name or delivery address written down, certainly not a phone number, in case they were caught. They would simply be told to go to a rendezvous in a public place at a particular time and date. If they were not paid volunteers then coercion, blackmail and threats of physical violence could be used – or a combination of all three.

I shiver at the thought of Evie being mistreated like this, remembering the phone message and the strain in her voice.

Ruth clicks her ballpoint pen. 'OK. So if they're coming back tomorrow, what else do we know for certain?'

'That they *won't* be on the Eurostar,' I say.

She makes a note on her pad. 'All right then. Let's start from there.'

63

The three of us agree that we can probably rule out central London as a whole, since Lawler will be steering well clear of St Pancras.

'Or maybe not just central London,' Ruth says, 'but all of it? The whole city. If they go through the Eurotunnel by car, they come out at Folkestone and that's well clear of London. Cassie passed her driving test in the summer. Maybe they've got hold of a vehicle?'

Declan looks sceptical. 'Given that we know the Eurostar story is just a diversion, I'd give the tunnel a wide berth if it was me. Even though the car train stops at the coast rather than going into London, why take the risk? Parry might decide to deploy a team down to Folkestone as well, just in case.'

'So, then . . . a flight? Tons of flights from Paris Charles de Gaulle. She could come into Gatwick, Luton, Stansted?'

'Could be,' Declan says. 'Or London City Airport – it's right on the doorstep, barely half a mile from the Silvertown warehouse. Virtually walking distance from the terminal. In other circumstances, it'd be a great location, but . . .' He tails off.

'But what?'

'I'm not convinced by that either. Just not feeling it.'

'Why not?'

'The warehouse,' he says. 'It's probably their secure depot for the drugs before distribution, right? They've clearly got other dodgy gear in there. Maybe they use the nightclub as well. But Lawler has to assume both those places might be compromised.'

'Why?'

He points at me. 'You've turned up at both and they can't be sure what else you've said to the cops.'

'So, a different safe house, then? A different airport?'

'Feels like airports are going to be too risky at this stage. A lot of security, a *lot* of technology, even if the girls are travelling with false passports they could get picked up by facial recognition – it's always airports that use the top-end technology, the latest stuff. That's how my old cellmate got picked up. And there are a lot of bottlenecks in the layout, by design. A *lot* of chances to get caught.'

Milo wakes up, stretches, and looks up at his owner with large, hungry eyes. Ruth produces a small packet of dry food from her bag and puts it down in a dish by the back door, the spaniel crunching into it almost as fast as it comes out of the packet.

'What about a lock-up?' she says. 'Like, a garage? Or one of those storage units you can rent by the month?'

Again, he looks sceptical. 'There's a lot of risk in leaving the drugs somewhere they could be found, ripped off by someone else. I think they're going to want to keep a close eye on the shipment. Also they might need to chemically process it, cut it, dilute it so it's ready to be sold – better to have somewhere quiet to do it, low profile, where they're not going to be disturbed. And the sooner they can cut it to the right purity, the quicker they start selling.'

Ruth strokes the dog's head as he eats. 'So, somewhere like a laboratory?'

'Wouldn't need to be that sophisticated. As long as there was space, storage, basic facilities. Privacy.'

He types something on his ancient laptop.

'They're making a lot of noise with this diversion,' he says, without looking up. 'With you spinning them a line about St Pancras.'

'That's the whole point, isn't it? Noise? A distraction?'

'It feels like . . . if the bluff is a flash train from Paris belting through the Channel Tunnel at a hundred miles an hour, the actual truth is going to be . . . the opposite of flash, if you know what I mean.'

'Like what?'

'Like something low-key, boring. Invisible.'

Elvis, his large black-and-white cat, emerges through the flap in the back door and casts a suspicious stare at Milo. He pads into a corner under the kitchen worktop, circles carefully before his long body convulses once, twice, three times and he retches up a large black furball and some dark, half-digested creature onto the lino.

'Elvis, mate,' Declan says, 'you're supposed to be sick *outside*.'

The tomcat ignores him, disappearing around the corner with his tail aloft.

To us, Declan says: 'Sorry, he's always catching birds and what-not. They don't seem to agree with him.'

He goes to clean up the mess, apologising again.

But I'm not listening to him anymore. Something has clicked in my tired, aching brain; a blur moving into sharper focus. I pick up my phone, dialling into voicemail to listen again to the message Evie left.

Ruth gives me a quizzical look. 'What is it, Lauren? Are you all right?'

'Just give me a second,' I say. 'I think I've remembered something.'

64

I put the phone on loudspeaker as the message plays again, Evie's trembling voice filling the silence.

Mum? It's me. This might be my last chance to call and I just wanted to say . . . I'm sorry. For everything. For not telling the truth and for all the times we argued . . .

We listen to the whole thing again, just a handful of sentences barely thirty seconds long, an apology that sounds like a farewell. But perhaps it was something else too.

I wish I could turn back the clock, Evie says, *and do it all differently but I can't. I'm so sorry for lying to you, Mum. I have to go now, I don't know who else might be listening in and it's not my phone or Cassie's so don't try calling back. But I'll always try to keep my eyes on the horizon, just like you told me, Mum. I love you. And Lucas too. Just tell him.*

Ruth is still looking at me. 'Lauren? What is it?'

'"Eyes on the horizon",' I say, repeating the phrase. 'When I first played this back earlier I thought it meant she'd try to be careful, you know? Like, keep her head up and look after herself?'

'Sounds like a song lyric to me,' Ruth says. 'Or is it a . . . What do they call it? A meme? One of those things teenagers say to each other?'

'No, it's not that,' I say. 'It's not that at all.'

Declan points at my phone. 'She said it was something *you* told her.'

'I've told her a million things, never thought she actually listened to any of them. When she was twelve or thirteen we went camping in France. Lucas must have been . . . five? Six? Evie was ill on the way there.'

The memory pierces me like a shard of broken glass. For months after, Lucas had been sure to remind his big sister of that infamous, nauseous journey with a chant of 'Eyes on the horizon, remember!' followed by a full-cheeked mime as if he was about to throw up.

'Car sick?' Ruth says.

'No,' I say. 'She's usually fine in the car. She was sick during the ferry crossing, and on the way back too. We spent the whole time out on the passenger deck because I'd said the best thing she could do was keep her eyes on the horizon. Something to do with your inner ear and how it deals with motion.'

Declan is nodding. '"Eyes on the horizon". She's telling you how she's coming home.'

'On the ferry.'

Despite everything I feel a small, hopeful smile on my lips. This slim chance, this coded message meant only for me, my child reaching out from across the sea.

But the rush of endorphins quickly subsides as reality takes hold again.

'Which one, though?' I say. 'There must be a dozen places you could get a ferry to, up and down the coast.'

Declan is looking at me with a new intensity.

'True,' he says. 'But maybe we can narrow it down.' He taps the map at a series of places where land meets the sea, pale blue dotted lines across the English Channel indicating ferry routes to and from the Continent. 'I reckon we can forget about the ones up north, the crossing would take too long and it's too far away from their base of operations in London. So we discount Liverpool, Newcastle, Hull.'

I point to the Suffolk coast. 'What about . . . Harwich?'

'Not if Evie's in France,' he says. 'The Harwich ferry comes from Holland.'

'Maybe Plymouth?' Ruth indicates the screen of her iPad.

'Hmm.' Declan rubs at the scar behind his ear. 'Hell of a long way from London though. Where do they sail from?'

She squints at her screen. 'Roscoff? Wherever that is.'

'Arse end of Brittany, like, four hundred miles from Paris.' He shakes his head. 'I just can't see it. What's left?'

'Dover, Portsmouth, er . . . Poole?'

'Poole's a bloody long way as well. Dover or Portsmouth seem more likely. Closer to London.'

I peer at the map. Portsmouth to the south-west of the capital, Dover to the south-east. *Were we supposed to toss a coin?*

'Dover,' Declan says, 'is the nearest spot to France by sea. Twenty-one miles. Big and obvious, more passengers than all the other ports combined. But it's also where most of the small boats try to cross, the asylum-seeker boats. Which means a lot of eyeballs on that bit of the coast: Border Force, Customs, National Crime Agency. Quieter in Portsmouth, for sure.'

I scan the map, my heart sinking as I spot another alternative.

'What about this one?' I say. 'Newhaven?'

Ruth peers in closer. 'Didn't even realise there was a ferry that went there.'

'Goes to and from . . . Dieppe.'

She types on her iPad, raises an eyebrow. 'Huh. Says here Newhaven is the closest ferry port to London. And Dieppe the closest one to Paris.'

I tap a finger on the OS map, on this unassuming corner of East Sussex. It's a small port nestled between two much bigger neighbours – Eastbourne and Brighton – directly south of the capital. Well served with A-roads feeding up into London like arteries.

Ruth pushes the iPad aside, frowning down at the map again.

'Something is ringing a bell here,' she says. 'Sussex.'

'What about it?'

'Cassie went there. A few months ago, before she disappeared. Perhaps she went there to visit *him*. Lawler.' Her eyes rove over the contours of the map for a long moment before she clicks her fingers, a smile of realisation brightening her face. 'Remember those old train tickets I found in Cassie's bedroom. Waterloo to . . . that place neither of us had ever heard of?' She digs into her bag, roots around, comes out with one of the creased orange tickets. 'Shelford Cross. It's too small for this paper map. Let me try on the iPad.'

She lays the tablet flat and brings up a map of the south coast, zooming in near Brighton, then east to Newhaven, then inland, spreading her thumb and index finger to zoom in further. The smaller roads appearing between the villages, old Anglo-Saxon placenames emerging as she goes in closer.

'There,' she says, turning the device to show me. 'Look.'

I peer at the digital map, mostly green, streaked with blue and grey capillaries, rivers and streets. More grey at the crossing point of three roads, denoting a village of perhaps a hundred houses, a handful of farms and a train stop so small it barely merited the name.

'Shelford Cross,' I say. 'This is the place on the ticket?'

Ruth zooms out again, showing the location of this small settlement relative to its surroundings.

It's about three miles from Newhaven.

None of us speaks for a moment.

'OK,' I say finally. 'That's definitely low-key.'

Declan rubs his jaw thoughtfully. 'Just inland from the ferry port, maybe ten minutes' drive. But still basically the middle of nowhere so they can offload fast and quiet. Totally under the radar. Compared to Dover, Newhaven's small fry, just a backwater.' He's nodding now. 'It makes a lot of sense.'

I Google ferry crossing times for tomorrow. 'There's one here that leaves Dieppe at noon local time—'

'And gets to Newhaven at 3 p.m.?' Declan raises a questioning eyebrow.

'Yes,' I say. 'Three o'clock arrival.'

'Just when Parry and Garcia and all their colleagues are going to be waiting at St Pancras.'

Ruth leans back in her chair, her face pale.

'So this is it? This is the place?'

Declan nods slowly. 'I reckon it's our best shot.'

There is a sudden plunging in my stomach, a sensation of dropping in free fall as if I'm on a theme park ride.

He puts a hand on my arm. 'You OK, Lauren?'

'I'm all right.'

'What is it? You look as if you're going to faint.'

I take a deep breath. 'We're only going to get one chance at this, aren't we? One shot. What if we get it wrong?'

He opens his mouth to reply, then seems to think better of it. But he doesn't need to say it. *If we get it wrong, they'll be gone. Maybe forever.*

Instead, he says: 'I don't think we're wrong, Lauren. I think this is it. Everything we know says this is the place.'

'But somebody will be waiting for them, won't they? To scoop them up when they step off that ferry and hand over the drugs and then . . . God only knows what they'll do with the girls.'

He taps a long index finger on the map. *Newhaven.*

'Not if we get to them first.'

EVIE

Five days earlier

The first two trips, she'd gone on her own, come back on her own. Small packages, small amounts. She didn't ask what was inside the Christmas-wrapped bundles and they didn't tell her either.

For the third trip they had decided to mix things up a little: pair her with another young woman, change the route, increase the load. A pair of female backpackers going on holiday together attracted less attention than a solo traveller, Evie supposed. It was also, she suspected, a case of her showing the ropes to a new recruit. *This is how we act. This is where we go. This is how the pickup is done.*

The other woman's name was Cassie.

She was pretty, petite, with a heart-shaped face and long dark hair. Kind eyes. Scared eyes.

It was hard to talk freely because they knew they were being shadowed, followed, by at least one of Lawler's people. To make sure they stuck to their instructions, didn't get any stupid ideas about grabbing a gendarme on the street, asking for help.

You won't see them, but they'll always be there. Watching you.

At least that's what Evie had been told. Was it true? Impossible to tell. But it was enough to keep her looking over her shoulder, to keep her scared, off balance.

She and Cassie stood side by side on the ferry's passenger deck, leaning on the rail, watching the chalk-white cliffs near Beachy Head recede into the distance behind them. The sea was a churning, bottomless depth, the frigid December wind whipping their hair and biting their cheeks.

'How did you meet him?' Evie said. 'Did he have the dog with him?'

Cassie answered quietly, keeping her eyes straight ahead. 'Yeah. Lulu. She just came trotting up to me, sat down with her tail wagging. Then he appeared and we got talking, he was—'

'Going to visit a dog trainer?'

'Yeah,' she said miserably. 'And I had his number because I'd called the one on the dog's tag. So I got back in touch.'

'Same,' Evie said. 'Exactly the same with me.'

'Have you done *this* before? To France?'

'Third trip. You?'

'First,' she said, her voice catching in a sob. 'They sent me up north a few times but nothing like this. There was a video, they were going to blow up my life. What are we going to do?'

'What they tell us to do.' Evie found a packet of tissues in her pocket, held it out to the other woman. 'At least for now.'

She decided not to tell Cassie about the other message she'd received two days ago. A little reminder – in case she was starting to forget – of who held all the cards. It was a photo of her little brother walking to school in his uniform, thumbs hooked into the straps of his backpack, chatting with his friend Yusuf as if he didn't have a care in the world. The picture looked like it was taken from inside a car, further down the street. Whoever took it was holding a stoppered glass bottle full of clear liquid in their other hand, the black-and-yellow warning symbol denoting *corrosive substance* clearly visible. The text beneath it was chillingly simple.

Next time we burn him.
Remember what's at stake.
Do your job.

Her heart ached at the thought of Lucas at the mercy of these people too. They could get to him at any time if she stepped out of line. In case that hotel video going viral was no longer enough of a threat.

Cassie checked over her shoulder again. 'What if we get stopped? At customs?'

Then we're screwed, Evie thought.

But instead, she said: 'They won't stop us. Just imagine you're going on holiday. Be calm, act natural.' She forced herself to smile. 'It'll be OK.'

PART V

65

Newhaven ferry port is quiet.

Beside us, the river Ouse flows dark and fast towards the sea. Out beyond the breakwater, the English Channel is a choppy grey-white mass that stretches to the horizon, a biting December wind carrying the tang of saltwater and burned diesel.

We find a spot at the back of the car park and pull both cars in next to each other. The ferry terminal is a squat two-storey building of weather-beaten white panels, the front entrance facing us where foot passengers will emerge. From here, we also have a good view towards the Channel and will be able to see the ferry approaching from a few miles out. Evie and Cassie should be on board now and I wonder absently if she's seasick again today just like when she was younger. It looks like it might be a rough crossing.

Declan, Ruth and I had set off from London before dawn to head south to the coast, arriving mid-morning with enough time to grab something to eat before we settled down to wait for the ferry to arrive. Declan had driven his own car, with Ruth and I following behind in her Nissan. With a couple of hours to kill, she reclines the driver's seat and tells me she'll try to take a nap. Milo dozes, oblivious, on a blanket in the back seat.

I get out and walk around to Declan's BMW. He's hunched into a heavy leather jacket with the collar pulled up against the cold and greets me with a nod when I get into the passenger seat beside him.

From a flask in the footwell, he pours out a cup of steaming sweet tea and hands it to me.

'How's Ruth doing?'

I sip the tea, welcoming the jolt of sugar. 'Tired. She's trying to get forty winks before the ferry arrives.'

'Good idea,' he says. 'And how are you doing, Lauren?'

'I'm OK, I think.'

He'd insisted on being in place by 1 p.m., so that we would be in situ well before Lawler's men arrived. We sit in silence for a while, watching the comings and goings. There are a few lorry drivers, a handful of foot passengers and one or two staff members, but on the whole the place is not busy. I don't imagine December is a very popular time to be crossing to northern France for holidays.

I finish the tea and hand the cup back.

'Dec?'

He keeps his eyes on the terminal building. 'Yeah?'

'What if we *are* wrong?' The thought has been nagging at me all morning, all the way down to the coast, the creeping fear that we might have made the wrong choice. That what had seemed so clear, so logical in Declan's small kitchen last night might turn out to be the wrong call in the cold light of day. 'What if it's not here, not this ferry? What do we do then?'

'We won't know for sure until three o'clock,' he says calmly. 'But I don't think we're wrong. Everything points to this. Here. Today.'

'What I mean is . . . it's not too late to call Parry, is it? She could send some people here too, or have people waiting at Dover and the other ports just in case, so we cover all the options. We make sure our girl is safe and then, the police have negotiators to help us get Lucas back, right?'

Declan is shaking his head. 'We can't have Parry here. Or anywhere else.'

'Why not?' I say. 'It would be a kind of insurance, wouldn't it?'

'Because Evie and Cassie would be nicked for drug trafficking, what they call a category one offence which means at least a seven-year stretch, and probably banged up on remand for the best part of a year before it even gets to trial. And worse than that, all the drugs are taken as evidence, so we have nothing to bargain with – no leverage with Lawler to get our son back safe.'

Our son. He's never said that before. The words hang there, awkward and heavy between us. Despite all the time that has passed there is still a link between us that can never be broken. Our kids.

I stare out towards the Channel. 'So we just let them have the drugs? We hand everything over?'

'Whatever the girls are bringing into the country,' he says, 'that's our bargaining chip. We trade for Lucas. Everyone gets what they want.'

'But . . . all that poison going out into the world? Maybe thousands of doses of Fentanyl. That could be thousands of people at risk, lots of them Evie's age or not much older.'

'That's Parry's job. Not ours.'

'I know, but—'

'Look, the clock's ticking. When the girls are safe, when Lucas is safe, we can talk to the NCA and tell them everything. Give them a better chance to stop that fentanyl before it gets to the street. But not yet.'

He was right, and I knew it. It was the devil's bargain, but I suppose all of us were hard-wired to put the safety of our own children before others. To put our own family, our own blood, before everything else.

'You're right,' I say.

He lets the silence spin out for a long moment before he speaks again.

'I've only met my son once,' he says, his voice low. 'I've failed him his whole life. Not going to fail him again now.'

I put out my right hand and he takes it, the grip of his large, callused palm surprisingly gentle.

'I'm glad you're here, Dec.'

'Me too.'

'How many men do you think Lawler will send to meet the girls?'

'I'm thinking probably two, a driver and a minder. Three if we're unlucky.'

'And what do we do about them?'

'Let me worry about that.'

*   *   *

We watch, and wait.

Slowly, Declan opens up a little more, telling me about his time in prison and his life since, his role at the ex-offenders charity and the satisfaction he gets from helping former prisoners get back on their feet. The novelty of having a place of his own. He's keen to hear everything I can tell him about Evie and Lucas, about what they're like and how they get on with each other, about school and friends, their hopes for the future.

'I came to your house once.' He says it quietly, like a confession.

'What?' I turn in my seat to stare at him. 'When?'

'About a year after I got out. Sat outside trying to work up the courage to knock on the door.'

'How did you even find out where I lived?'

He shrugs. 'Had time on my hands, and most people aren't that hard to find these days. Anyway I sat there for a few hours, then you pulled up with Evie and Lucas in the car, and you're all chatting and joking and laughing with each other as you go in the house. A really tight unit. You looked happy. And I didn't want to screw that up. Didn't think I had any right to suddenly turn up out of the blue. So I bottled it.'

I put a hand on his arm. 'I had no idea, Dec.'

'It's all water under the bridge.'

We have so much to catch up on and ninety minutes vanishes before I know it. We're still deep in conversation when he stops, points through the windscreen.

'Not long now,' he says. 'Look.'

In the distance beyond the breakwater, powering steadily through the winter sea towards us, is a yellow-and-white ferry. It's broad and tall, towering over the waves and growing slowly bigger as we watch. It seems almost too big to fit into this small harbour but it continues to plough on as straight as a die into the estuary, dwarfing the low buildings on the quayside.

I check my watch. Ten minutes to three.

'Right on time,' I say.

'And so are they,' Declan says, inclining his head towards the car park's entrance.

Turning, I see a dark Mercedes saloon with tinted black windows peel in through the gates, stop at the far edge of the car park and reverse into a space next to the chain-link fence. In each of the car's front seats there is a man in dark clothing. As the Mercedes rolls to a stop, the passenger door opens and one of the men gets out, pulling a packet of cigarettes from his overcoat pocket.

He is thickset, bearded, dark bruising around his left eye. The last time I saw him he was wearing a mask but I still recognise the shape of him, the turn of his head, the way he moves.

One of the men from the Silvertown warehouse.

Declan gives a grunt of satisfaction.

'Well, Lauren,' he says. 'It looks like we were right.'

DS PARRY

DS Parry checks in with her team again, hailing each of them on the radio to confirm they're in position.

They're deployed in plain clothes around the Eurostar arrivals gate at St Pancras International Station, split into two teams: two pairs within fifty feet of the gate, with another pair at each end of the concourse in case the girl tries to bolt. She also has mobile units full of uniformed officers parked at the front and back of the station as well as an armed response vehicle on standby in a side street. All have been briefed this morning, issued with pictures of the suspect and a description of the drugs she's thought to be bringing in: six kilograms of high-grade fentanyl with an estimated street value of more than half a million pounds.

Parry herself is in a glass-fronted coffee shop further down the concourse. A laptop is open in front of her, showing a live feed from a wireless camera pointed at the arrivals door.

'Has anyone got eyes on the reception committee?' she says, checking her watch. 'They must be in place by now.'

'Negative.'

'Negative.'

'Sorry, boss. None that look likely.'

Parry curses silently to herself. It will be much cleaner, much quicker, to take the girl here along with whoever is going to meet her off the train. And there *had* to be someone meeting them, surely? Someone other than Lauren Wingfield, whose car had been tracked with ANPR to a multi-storey nearby. Scott Lawler would send at least two of his men to make sure the girl didn't have second thoughts. And it would be much more satisfying to have a couple of them in the bag as well by the end of the day.

'Sandhu?' Parry says. 'How about you?'

Detective Constables Sandhu and Wood are part of a small crowd watching a teenager on one of the station pianos who has been bashing through an enthusiastic medley of Queen songs for the last ten minutes.

Sandhu does another quick scan of his surroundings.

'I've got ... maybe one, possibly? White male, five ten, grey overcoat. Sitting on a bench facing the arrivals door.'

Parry pans the camera around on her laptop until she finds the man, who is cramming the last bite of a sandwich into his mouth. He checks his watch and gets quickly to his feet, cheeks still bulging as he chews, hurrying away towards one of the escalators with a suitcase in tow.

'That's a negative,' Parry says with a sigh. She looks up to the vaulted ceiling of the station high above, a latticework of curving steel beams. 'You still got eyes on Lauren Wingfield?'

'She has her back to us,' Sandhu says. 'But yes.'

'OK. Stay on it, not long now.'

Garcia talks discreetly into his radio beside her. 'Roger that,' he says. 'Keep me updated.'

Parry takes a hurried mouthful of lukewarm coffee. 'Any activity on that number Evie Wingfield used to call her mother last night?'

'Still switched off.'

The calls to Lauren's phone had been traced and triangulated to an unregistered pay-as-you-go in Paris's 10th arrondissement, within 500 metres of the Eurostar terminal at Gare du Nord station. They had been monitoring it ever since in case another outgoing call was made, to trace Evie's progress on her journey home. Parry was quietly hoping the teenager would do what most others would do in her situation: text or call ahead to say she was on her way. To check her mother would be there to meet her.

Assuming the phone belonged to her at all, of course. It might have been borrowed, stolen or purchased just for that single call and then discarded. But was Evie Wingfield savvy enough to be that careful? She was barely out of secondary school, a frightened teenager, an amateur. It didn't seem likely.

A voice in her ear relays a report: the train had arrived, slightly ahead of schedule. The passengers would be processed, funnelled through the usual customs checks and then out onto the main concourse where the target could be identified, subdued if necessary and plucked from the crowd. The customs boys, too, had their instructions to ensure the target wasn't pulled in for a random bag check in one of the side rooms. She would be allowed to stroll right through without a whiff of trouble – until she reached the concourse.

The voice in her ear says: 'Passengers starting to disembark now, boss.'

'Stay sharp everyone,' Parry says on the all-team channel. 'Let's get this done.'

She feels a pulse of excitement at the thought of having Evie in custody within the next ten minutes, a few other suspects with a little bit of luck. *This* was what she had joined up for. This sort of day made all the other stuff worthwhile. All the bureaucracy and bullshit, all the things she'd missed with her daughters – the school plays and sports days and everything else.

The first passengers emerge through the international arrivals exit: a young couple who march out pulling wheeled suitcases and turn left to head straight for the Underground. The door swings shut and then opens again on a group of secondary school students all chattering excitedly in French; behind them comes a family of four and then it is just a general melee of big groups, small groups, more families and young travellers, a few business people in suits, all milling and mixing and heading off in different directions.

There is no sign of Evie Wingfield.

Seconds tick by slowly. Minutes crawl. More passengers, an almost continuous stream of people now.

Parry checks her watch: approaching ten past three. This was taking too long. She asks for her team members to check in with updates, receiving another chorus of negatives.

'Have any passengers been held up?' She hates the uncertainty in her own voice. 'Anyone who's been stopped in the disembarkation area and still hasn't come through yet?'

One of her team says they'll go to check. But the flow of arriving Eurostar travellers is already slackening and slowing until they're only coming through in small groups: an elderly couple, a family with two small red-faced children in pushchairs, a quartet of twenty-something lads who look as if they've been drinking since breakfast.

'Has anyone got eyes on the target? *Anyone?*'

Even though she already suspects what the answer will be.

To DC Garcia next to her, she says: 'I've got a bad feeling about this.'

She shuts her laptop and hurries out of the coffee shop, breaking into a run as she heads down the concourse and dodges passengers in her path. Garcia calls to her from behind but she doesn't slow down.

Even from a distance, she can see Lauren's cream coat as she moves away towards the staircase.

Alone.

'Lauren Wingfield!' Parry ignores the looks of startled onlookers. 'Stay where you are!'

The woman doesn't stop, but doesn't speed up either. When Parry reaches her, bundled up with a scarf and hat against the cold, she grabs her by the shoulder and spins her around.

'Where is she? Where's your daughter?'

The woman takes off her sunglasses.

Parry feels her stomach drop into her shoes. She hadn't thought to issue pictures of Lauren Wingfield too. Her car had been tracked here with ANPR, which meant she would be here, too, just like she said.

Valerie Wingfield stares back at her.

'I'm sorry,' she says. 'Who are you?'

'Where's Evie now?'

'I honestly have no idea, officer. Lauren wouldn't tell me.'

Parry feels her cheeks start to burn. Either the courier's travel plans had been changed at the last minute, or . . .

Or she'd been played. Tricked. Which meant Evie was never going to be on this train at all.

She bites down on a curse and reaches for her phone.

66

We watch as Lawler's men settle in to wait. The heavyset man leans on the front bumper of the Mercedes, smoking one cigarette after another, his eyes never leaving the ferry terminal's front entrance. He has a mass of purple-black bruising down the left side of his face from the encounter at the warehouse. The other man – the driver – stays in the car. I had half expected to see Brandon Roper doing this job but perhaps it was beneath him to be escorting drug mules. Particularly if he was Scott Lawler's second-in-command.

Declan turns towards me. 'You ready?'

'I'm ready. Just tell me again what I need to do.'

'As soon as we have the girls,' he says, 'we leave quietly. Remember to keep to the speed limit, drive nice and steady like we've just picked up our daughter and her friend from their holidays. We don't want to attract any unnecessary attention. I've got a mate in Brighton where we can crash overnight. I'll make the exchange with Lawler and bring Lucas back. OK?'

'OK,' I say. 'I just want for all of it to be over. To have them back. Both of them.'

The cross-channel ferry looms even bigger now, a mountain of floating steel halted at the quayside. On our left, long-distance lorry drivers who had been chatting and drinking coffee are starting to disperse, climbing back up into their cabs, restarting engines, ready to roll forward into the belly of the big ship for the return trip to France. The wind has picked up, a chilling onshore breeze that makes the Union Jack flag on a nearby warehouse whip and snap.

'Lauren?' There is a subtly different tone in his voice. 'Before we do this, I . . . need to tell you something.'

'What?'

'I lied to you yesterday.'

I turn in my seat to look at him properly.

'About what?'

Instead of answering, he leans over and pops the glove compartment open, moving a blue plastic bag out of the way to reveal what lies behind it.

A black pistol.

'About this,' he says, lifting it out. It looks like the gun from the warehouse, the one Lucas had picked up before Declan took it. He grips the gun now in his right hand and I flinch back against the car door, all the certainty of the last few hours disappearing like smoke in the wind.

Had everything been leading to this? Had Ruth been right? Was trusting this man a terrible mistake?

My heart begins to thud painfully against my ribcage.

'Dec,' I say quietly. 'What are you doing? You said you threw it in the Thames.'

'Yeah,' he says. 'Sorry. I probably should have. But I thought you might need it. Just for today.'

I let out a gasp of relief. 'Me? *God* no.'

'These guys, the ones we're dealing with, Lauren, they don't mess around.'

'I know that,' I say.

He checks something near the gun's trigger guard, depresses a small stud with his thumb and withdraws a chunky rectangle of plastic from inside the grip. It's about the size of a small TV remote but is topped with the dull brass shape of a bullet, with more bullets stacked tightly beneath. Declan studies it briefly, seemingly satisfied, then pushes it back up inside the grip with a metallic *click* and covers the gun with his left hand.

'You've got to understand something, Lauren: these people are *totally* ruthless. They don't care that you're basically just a bystander, that you're a mum, that your kids are caught up in all this and none of you want to be part of it. So you need to be able to protect yourself, if it comes to it.'

'Not with *that*,' I say.

'Just hold it for a minute,' he says. 'It's OK, the safety's on.'

I take it from him, feeling the solid, tempting power of the gun in my hand. A dangerous weight full of deadly potential.

'I'm not going to shoot anyone, Dec.'

'You probably won't have to,' he says. 'Just point it at them, that should be enough. Then you get the girls and get the hell out of there as fast as you can.'

A police patrol car cruises slowly past on the street beyond the chain-link fence, but Declan doesn't turn towards it. Doesn't miss a beat. The patrol car keeps going, turning away and out of sight. Just routine.

'I can't.' I hand it back to him.

'You're sure?' He holds it out to me again, butt first. 'Better to have it and not need it, than need it and not have it.'

For a second I think about taking it from him. Then common sense wins out.

'I'm sure,' I say. 'Probably just shoot myself in the foot by accident anyway.'

He frowns, and is about to put the pistol back in the glove compartment then seems to think better of it. Instead he tucks it into the waistband of his jeans, lifting his shirt over the top of it.

'Dec?' I put a hand on his arm. 'You're not going to shoot anyone, are you?'

He shrugs. 'Not unless I have to. You'd better check Ruth's awake. I'll bring the girls out to my car, you and Ruth can follow in hers. We get to Brighton, then we negotiate. If we get separated for any reason, I'll meet you at the Marina.' He reaches under the driver's seat and puts a pair of brass knuckles into his jacket pocket.

'Won't be long.'

We both climb out of the old BMW, closing the doors quietly. I walk quickly to Ruth's Nissan and get into the passenger seat; she's blinking sleepily and sipping from a bottle of Diet Coke.

'It's happening,' I say to her quietly. 'Evie and Cassie are going to be here any minute. We need to be ready to leave soon.'

She sits up straighter, rubbing her eyes. We both watch as Declan walks casually across the car park, angling towards the back, the landward side where he won't be so easily seen by the men in the Mercedes. He loops around so he can come at them from behind and I hold my breath as he closes in. His right hand goes into the pocket of his jacket but the movement is subtle, normal. Nothing to draw attention to the weapon concealed within. The heavyset man is still leaning against the bonnet of the Mercedes, his hand cupped around a Zippo as he tries to light another cigarette.

Declan approaches from behind and at the last moment the man turns in surprise, only to meet a clubbing punch from the brass knuckles that knock him to the floor.

His colleague flings open the driver's side door with a shout of alarm and a wide-bladed knife gripped in his hand, advancing on Declan and thrusting the weapon forward. Declan sidesteps one lunge, then another, feints left and then brings his brass-knuckled right fist around in a savage arc that snaps the man's head sideways. He collapses backwards onto the concrete, already out cold.

With a quick scan of the car park, Declan retrieves phones from both men and hauls them around to the back of the big Mercedes, pops the boot, and heaves them inside one at a time. With that done, he locks it before pocketing the keys.

The whole thing takes less than sixty seconds from start to finish.

Declan turns, brushes himself down and checks again that no one else in the car park has witnessed the confrontation. Then pockets the brass knuckles and gives me a casual thumbs up.

All clear.

I let out a heavy breath and watch as he begins a slow, casual walk towards the terminal as if he has all the time in the world.

Ruth turns to me, open-mouthed. 'Holy crap,' she says quietly. 'Your ex doesn't mess around.'

My phone rings, the display showing DS Parry's name. I reject the call – but a moment later she tries again.

Ruth glances at the display as I reject it for the second time.

'She must have just realised,' she says. 'That you've stitched her up.'

'I bet they're all furious.'

She shrugs. 'That's their problem.'

The first of the passengers come through the sliding glass doors of the terminal building. A man on his own in a green parka, pulling a large, wheeled suitcase. A couple in their seventies, with backpacks and hiking gear. A group of middle-aged men; a family with three small children; another guy travelling solo and having a loud conversation on his phone as he emerges from the terminal.

And then, finally, I know for sure that we've come to the right place.

Because she's there, at last. Walking through the sliding glass doors and out into the fading December daylight.

Evie.

67

My heart feels as if it's going to burst out of my chest.

It is the first time I've seen my daughter in the flesh in almost three months.

She seems so much older, taller, more adult than I've ever seen her before, walking out of the terminal with a big rucksack on her back, a yellow waterproof coat zipped up tight and heavy walking boots. I don't recognise any of her clothes but she looks every inch the keen backpacker, home from Interrailing around Europe with a friend dressed in much the same way. The girl next to her is shorter and seems dwarfed by her bulky rucksack; her dark wavy hair tied back in a loose ponytail. To the casual observer, they look like good friends who have spent a few weeks relishing new experiences, new travels, but are tired and hungry all the same – in need of a bath and some home-cooked food.

It's a very convincing disguise.

The only thing that gives them away are the expressions they wear. Not the relief of returning travellers, looking forward to home comforts and a good night's sleep. Instead they look tense. Uncertain. Their eyes darting this way and that as they emerge. Not only from the stress of getting through customs unchallenged but also the fear of what awaits them here, now, after they're picked up and relieved of their deadly cargo. Both of them, presumably, recruited and groomed in the same way, by the same man.

I had been googling it last night, wired with nerves and caffeine and unable to sleep. The technique was as old as they come: young women lured into what they thought was a loving, romantic attachment with an alpha male who showered them with gifts, compliments and attention. All the while, the man is manipulating the victim, telling her he loves her, to the point where she honestly believes they are in a serious and committed relationship. The man would also find ways to distance their victim from friends and family, isolating them from normal support networks – so that when the exploitation starts, they are more vulnerable. More likely to fall victim to the lies and manipulation, to the coercion and threats to take part in criminal activity. Threats that often descended into blackmail and violence.

All of this flits through my mind as I watch my beautiful, kind, clever daughter walk slowly out of the terminal. I've let her down so badly. I have put too much pressure on her, put all of my own expectations onto her, punished her when she acted out and pushed her away in the process. So much has happened in her life in the last few months that I didn't know about, that I've only started to discover in the last few days. I make a silent promise to her, to myself, that I will *never* let it happen again. That I will never make her feel as if she can't tell me the truth.

As I watch, Declan closes the distance between them, the light already fading as dusk approaches. Evie sees her dad, frowns, slows her pace, looks around in confusion as if she's expecting someone else. He stops, exchanges a few words with the two of them and turns to point over towards me. I hurriedly step out of the car and raise a hand in greeting.

Evie's expression changes when she spots me. Uncertainty blending into genuine, open-mouthed shock at the sight of me standing by Ruth's car. Shock folding into relief, and relief into hope.

Both Evie and Cassie start to hurry in our direction, threading their way through ranks of parked cars with Declan bringing up the rear.

My throat thickens as they approach and I urge them to hurry up with a rapid wave of my hand. It seems impossible, unbelievable, that this nightmare might soon be over, that I had brought one child back from the darkness and would soon be able to reclaim the other. It feels like the most precious gift in the world, like a second chance. Like redemption.

My thoughts turn to Lucas, to where he is at this moment. To the trade we will make for his safety, using the contents of the rucksack on his sister's back. To have them both back with me, back at home, the three of us. *And not just three anymore*, I remind myself. We were four, now. And we had a chance to mend some long-broken bonds.

A white van roars in through the car park gates.

Another van follows close behind it.

Both of them skid to a halt in front of the terminal building.

With Declan urging them on, the girls break into an awkward run towards me, encumbered by their heavy packs.

Declan, however, stays where he is.

'I'll hold them here,' he calls to me. 'While you get clear.'

He turns around and starts threading his way back through the parked cars to where the vans have pulled up.

'Declan?' I shout. 'We can all—'

Over his shoulder, he shouts one word: 'Go!'

Evie and Cassie hurry towards me and I wave them desperately forward.

'Come on! Quickly!'

Behind them, dark-jacketed men are starting to emerge from the vans. Two, then three, then a fourth. One of them opens the front passenger door to jump down and Declan lunges forward, grabs the door and slams it against the guy's arm twice, then the side of his head. The man folds to the concrete, blood already pouring.

Two more men appear from the Transit, coming at him from both sides.

The gun, Dec, I think. *Show them the gun.*

But still, he doesn't reach for it under his jacket, even as more men appear. Then I see why: a stream of children climbing out of a minibus just beyond them. If bullets start flying they'd be right in the firing line. Instead, Declan ducks a punch and throws one back that lands with a heavy wet *smack* I can hear from where I'm standing. Then he is struck from behind, staggers, turns and floors his attacker with a wild uppercut.

But still more of them are coming, a ring of men closing in on him.

I tear my eyes away to see if we still have a way out. Because we're parked in the back row, our lane of the car park is clear all the way to the exit.

'Open the boot, Ruth!' I shout towards her. 'We can still make it!'

Evie and Cassie finally reach me, panting from the sudden sprint, their eyes wide with fear. I take the pack from Evie's shoulders and heave it around towards the boot as it pops open.

'Mum?'

'Get in, Evie,' I tell her. 'Your friend's Cassie, right?'

The other girl nods, handing me her rucksack.

'Your mum's here,' I say, hefting her bag into the boot. 'Jump in behind her.'

She says something which I can't make out. Over her shoulder I see Declan fall, get back to his feet only to be knocked down again.

Cassie is still standing there, peering into the car.

'Get in!' I say, slamming the boot shut. 'We have to go *right now.*'

'What's going on?'

'What do you mean?'

'I mean . . . that's not my mum,' she says. 'My mum died when I was eleven.'

Ruth switches off the engine and pulls the keys from the ignition.

'Welcome to Newhaven, girls. Let's all go and say hello to my wonderful son, shall we?'

68

They separate Evie and me, bundling her into the back of one van and me into the other.

I'm shoved to the bare metal floor opposite Cassie instead, our phones taken, hands zip-tied in front of us. My last sight before the doors are closed is Declan being hauled, bloodied and semi-conscious, into the back of the other van as Evie pleads with our captors to be careful. Then the doors are slammed shut and two men climb into the front, the van pulling quickly away.

There are no windows in the back of the Transit, only a little light that filters through from an observation panel in the cab up front. Cassie and I face each other in the gloom, bumping and swaying as the van makes its way through Newhaven and out into the countryside beyond.

'I'm sorry,' I say. 'She said she was your mum. I trusted her.'

Cassie nods, miserably. She's pretty, with a heart-shaped face and thoughtful eyes.

'She lies like her son,' she says. 'That's what they do, it's *all* they do.'

'Are you OK? Are you hurt?'

She ignores my question. 'They're not going to let us go, are they?'

The thought has been playing on my mind ever since the attack at the ferry terminal, the planning involved, the fact that 'Ruth' has been quietly manipulating everything since she first got in touch. We already knew too much for them to let us go.

'I don't know, Cassie.' I don't have it in me to lie to her. 'But wherever they're taking us, we have to find a way out.'

* * *

It's only a short journey, a few miles, but the daylight is almost gone by the time the van pulls to a stop. We sit and listen as more vehicles arrive and park, doors open and slam shut, men shout to each other before their voices start to recede.

It's another fifteen minutes before the doors of our van are flung open and we're hauled out. We're at some kind of farmhouse, a rambling old stone building at the end of a long gravel driveway, hidden from the road by a screen of trees. There is nothing else around us but hulking barns, machinery, a tractor and trailer, a handful of cars – and fields in every direction. Off in the distance there is a blaze of light at the corner of one ploughed field: some kind of big farm vehicle with spotlights attached. One of the men shoves me in the back and we carry on through a broad stone doorway and into the house.

He pushes Cassie and me down onto a bench seat in the big kitchen, our backs against the rough brick wall. Declan is already here, his face a mass of blood, head lolling, Evie half holding him upright. I stand up and move towards her too, to reach out to her, just to touch her even though my hands are still tied in front of me, but one of the men grabs my shoulder and shoves me roughly back down again with a muttered curse. I mouth to her, *Are you OK?* and she nods back, shooting a worried glance at Declan who seems to be slipping in and out of consciousness.

The timber-beamed kitchen has floor tiles of dark, rustic red and an Aga, as well as an open fire roaring in the hearth with Milo curled on a rug in front of it next to a brown Labrador. On a big oak table in the centre, the two rucksacks have been emptied out, clothes, toiletries, shoes discarded at one end while at the other end lies the reason we're all here. The *real* reason.

The fentanyl has been shrink-wrapped into six densely packed blocks, each about the size of a house brick and laid side by side. The little blue pills bulge from the packaging, packed tightly together – there must be thousands of doses in each block.

Nicola Lawler – 'Ruth' – sits at the table typing on her phone while Scott, her son, leans against the worktop with a self-satisfied look on his handsome face. Brandon Roper is there too, a bottle of beer in his hand, as well as two other men in blue surgical gloves making some kind of chemical mixture on the worktop.

'Where's Lucas?' I say. 'Where's my son? Is he here? Is he all right?'

Scott waves my question away. 'He's all right, Lauren. For now.'

'I just want to see my boy. Please.'

'You will.'

'Why don't you let the kids go?' I say to Ruth. 'As one mother to another, please let Evie and Lucas and Cassie go. Declan and I will stay, do whatever you want. But let the children go.'

She ignores me.

'Sorry,' Scott says. 'It doesn't really work like that, I'm afraid.' He picks up a walkie-talkie from the table and clicks the button, as if our conversation is already over. 'Eric? Can you send someone over to the annexe, get the furnace up to temperature? And then can you get yourself down to the bottom field and make sure Jez is doing what he's told? Take someone with you who can handle the JCB.'

Through the kitchen window, I can make out the headlights of the big farm vehicle lumbering across a ploughed field.

'Scott,' I say. 'Please. This is insane.'

'No. It's just business. Isn't that right, Mum?'

Nicola glances up at him with a smile.

'Just business, love.' She nods. 'Your dad would be so proud of you, if he could see you now.'

I struggle against the zip tie biting into the skin of my wrists.

'I swear to God,' I say. 'If you've hurt Lucas, if you've done anything to him, I'll—'

'You'll what?' Scott turns to me with a wolfish grin. 'Call the police? Have another chat with Detective Sergeant Parry? I think your credibility with her is less than zero right now.'

The heavyset man walks in holding a surgical dressing to his jaw, a murderous expression on his face. The last time I'd seen him, Declan was heaving his unconscious body into the back of the Mercedes. But now, it seems, the boot is on the other foot. The man cocks back his fist and punches Declan hard on the side of the head, knocking him to the floor. He starts to kick him in the stomach.

'Enough!' Nicola says. 'Don't you dare make a mess of my kitchen, Jason.'

The man stops abruptly, before his boot can connect again. He approaches the older woman and speaks quietly, respectfully, gesturing at his face, at Declan lying on the floor. But she shakes her head, saying something back to him that has the hard-edged tone of an order.

She indicates Evie with a casual wave of her hand.

'Be quick,' she says. 'We have a lot to do tonight. And if she gives you any trouble, just shoot her.'

69

The heavyset man hauls Evie roughly to her feet and begins to drag
her by the arm towards a hallway leading off to another wing of the
farmhouse.

'Leave her!' I shout. 'What are you doing with her?'

Nicola holds a hand up, a look of faint irritation on her face.

'He's going to take her to your son. Show her that he's still alive.'
She goes back to typing on her phone. 'Anything to stop your
bloody *whining*.'

My daughter is silent, her head down, as the man pushes her out
through the doorway.

'Evie—'

But then she's gone.

'By the way,' Nicola says, 'in case you didn't notice we're quite
a way from the next house here. Half a mile from the main road,
almost a mile to the village. No one's going to hear you so if you're
thinking about screaming and shouting, don't bother.'

As best we can with our hands tied, Cassie and I help Declan
back up onto the bench. He murmurs his thanks, more blood
leaking from his mouth.

'So what now?' I say, trying not to think about Evie, alone with
a violent stranger. 'What are you going to do with us?'

Scott gestures at the tightly packaged pills of fentanyl on the
table. 'Do you know what this is?'

'Poison.'

'Users call it the f-rush,' he says matter-of-factly. 'Apparently it's like an out-of-body experience, euphoria like you've never known before. Better than heroin, better than crack, better than crystal meth. And the best thing of all? As soon as you come down, the brain immediately starts craving another hit, so the demand for product just keeps going and going.'

I stare at him. 'Assuming the first hit doesn't kill you.'

'Yeah.' He picks up one of the tightly-wrapped packages of blue pills, studying it with an air of satisfaction. 'We'll probably break these down, cut them with something cheap before distribution. More money to be made that way too. It's the new gold rush, Lauren. The best, latest thing – and your daughter has helped us to get in on the ground floor. Easier to smuggle, too, 'cos small amounts are so powerful. This is like investing in Apple shares way back in the eighties. Getting in early because the share price is only going to go up, up, up.' He puts the package of pills back on the table. 'Only one more thing to find out before we start to get a return on our investment.'

'I'll tell you whatever you want to know, just let the—'

'No,' he says, cutting me off. 'Not from you. Well, not *exactly*. The thing is, these pills are supposed to be extremely high purity but we need to test that before they're sold on. And you know the best way to test them, don't you?'

I swallow, scrambling to keep up with the change of tack. 'You have . . . a lab set up in one of those barns?'

He snorts. 'A lab? No. *You're* my lab, Lauren. You and Declan here, and your kids, and Cassie. All different shapes and sizes, which is even better. Best way to find out if the dose is a little *too* powerful, if you get my meaning. We're going to have a little clinical trial, right here, right now.'

I think back to web searches I'd done on fentanyl this morning, on the drive to Newhaven, sitting in a car next to a woman I'd thought was my friend. *Each dose carries a high risk. The amount required to create a narcotic effect is only slightly below the dose that can trigger unconsciousness, breathing difficulties and heart failure.*

A chill creeps over my skin.

'And what if we overdose?'

He shrugs. 'Then we'll know for sure they have to be cut with a little baking soda to reduce the purity. More profit that way too.' Turning to the man in the blue gloves, he says: 'Open up a fresh pack, there should be some five hundreds in there.'

The man gives him a nod, reaching for one of the plastic-wrapped bundles and taking it to a large steel mixing tray on the kitchen side. He takes a small blade from the knife block and begins carefully cutting away the masking tape.

'Five hundred micrograms,' Scott says, matter-of-factly. 'Half a milligram – it's all you need. That's the beauty of it.'

70

I watch the man slicing into the bundle, cutting through tape, making careful incisions like a surgeon slicing into flesh. Each tiny dose inside a probable death sentence.

Everything is moving too fast.

I need to slow this down, need time to *think*. To work out how we can escape this place.

'Why did your mum get in touch with me in the first place?' I shift my gaze to the woman I'd first known as Ruth. 'To keep us away from the police?'

Nicola doesn't look up from her phone. 'I knew I had to keep an eye on you, Lauren, as soon as you started poking around and making trouble. Easiest way to do it was just to make contact, find out what you knew and feed it back to my boy. As long as I could be sure you'd end up here, it was all good. A little nudge here, a little suggestion there. Can't take credit for the train tickets though, that was Scott's idea. We knew we were probably going to have to tempt you down here to Shelford Cross sooner or later. Nice and quiet here, you see. Lots of space, lots of privacy. The sort of place where people disappear, never to be seen again.'

'You told your people to take Lucas,' I say. 'When we were at Declan's house. Lucas was in the garden with you and then all of a sudden he'd vanished, while I was talking to Declan and you were supposed to be keeping an eye on him. You told them where we were instead.'

'He nearly got away, actually.' She studies a fingernail. 'Slippery little bastard, isn't he? Clouted me one when I grabbed him. It was lucky for him I was in a good mood last night, otherwise I might have had the lads give him some payback in that alleyway.'

'Speaking of payback,' Scott says. 'It's about time we got down to business. Isn't it, Declan?'

Declan tries to raise his head, squinting with the one eye that is not already swollen shut with bruising.

'It's me you want,' he says through bloody lips. 'Not them. Just me. You want revenge. Fair enough, let's get on with it.'

'Fair enough?' Scott stands up, fists clenched. 'FAIR ENOUGH? You want to talk about my dad rotting in jail until he's an old man? A thirty-year stretch and still with years to do, all because you wouldn't be a stand-up guy? Is that FAIR? Is it?'

The man in the blue surgical gloves cuts the plastic-wrapped package in two, a mass of pills spilling out onto the steel tray. He comes over and places a pill in my hand, then does the same to Cassie. He fills a mug with water from the tap and places it on the bench between us.

I stare down at the tablet, an innocuous blue disc in the middle of my palm. The size of a paracetamol with the letter *M* stamped in the centre.

'I'll take one of your pills,' Declan says, pain in his voice. 'Instead of them. It's not about them, it's me you want.'

'You *made* it about them when you put my dad away.' He flashes a malevolent smile. 'But I'm not going to make you take a pill. I've got something much better in mind for you.' He comes around the table and for a moment I think he's about to hit Declan, who is bound both at the wrists and ankles. But instead he does something much worse.

He pulls a pair of thick black rubber gloves from his back pocket and snaps them on. Then a white surgical mask that he pulls over his mouth and nose. From a padded box on the worktop he takes a clear glass bottle with a yellow-and-black warning label on the side. The bottle has a wide neck and contains perhaps a pint or a little more.

Inside is a clear, colourless liquid.

The terror comes then, bright and hot, all the strength draining from my arms and legs.

Scott unscrews the cap, holding the bottle at arm's length.

Cassie whimpers beside me, an animal noise of dread in her throat.

'Don't need to tell you what this is, do I?' His voice is muffled behind the mask. 'You're about to get a taste anyway.'

Declan shrinks back against the rough stone wall, away from the open bottle, but there is nowhere for him to go.

'Do what you have to do,' he says, holding the other man's gaze. 'But let Lauren and the kids go.'

Scott gives a slow, amused laugh.

'It was worth it, bringing your little girl in.' He moves the bottle closer to Declan's face, tilting it so the oily liquid sloshes inside. 'Not just for the fentanyl, but for all the time I was with her. Making her fall in love with me, holding her trust in the palm of my hand, taking her to bed and knowing I could destroy her life any time I wanted. It was *delicious*. Having the power of life and death over her, like I have over you now.'

'Just leave her—'

One of the men balls up a dirty rag and shoves it roughly into Declan's mouth.

Scott holds the bottle above Declan's head. Even from a few feet away, the terrifying industrial stink of the acid burns the inside of my nose.

'This is for my dad.' Scott nods towards me and Cassie. 'And I'm going to make them watch. So they know what's coming.'

Declan shakes his head vigorously, eyes bulging, words swallowed by the gag.

Scott tips the bottle further, the liquid almost at the mouth now and ready to cascade down onto unprotected skin.

'You're going to wish you were dead, mate. You're going to be begging for it, begging me to put you out of your misery.'

My wrists are still zip-tied together, but I flip the pill from my right palm into my left to turn it over. The number *500* is stamped on the other side.

So small, and yet so deadly. The root of so much suffering.

I raise the pill to my mouth and look across at Cassie, who is doing the same. Her eyes are huge, fresh tears on her cheeks. *Hide it under your tongue*, I want to say to her. *Whatever you do, don't swallow it.*

Scott looks over, his handsome face twisted with sadistic glee.

'Well go on then,' he says to us. 'What are you waiting for? Trust me, when your ex starts screaming, you'll be glad you're floating away on a cloud of—'

He's interrupted by a flat, hard *crack* from somewhere else in the house. Even in here, surrounded by the thick stone kitchen walls, the sound is unmistakable.

A gunshot.

71

The sound of the shot is like a bolt of terror right to my heart. There is nothing but silence in the moments after, no voice crying out, no shout of pain, no plea for mercy.

No Evie.

My eyes fill with tears and then I'm shouting, screaming her name, standing to move to the doorway before Roper shoves me back down onto the bench, his heavy hand gripping my shoulder like a claw.

Scott nods to one of the men at the worktop, a bald guy with a black goatee. 'Go and see what the hell Jason's playing at, will you? And if he's made a mess, I will *not* be pleased.'

The bald man strips off his blue nitrile gloves and walks quickly out to the hallway.

'Where's Evie?' I say. 'What was that shot?'

'Shut up,' Scott says. 'Shut up just for a minute, will you? You're doing my head in.'

'If she's hurt, I swear I'll—'

'You'll do nothing, except what you're told.' He brandishes the acid-filled bottle again, clearly enjoying the terror on our faces. 'Which is to take that pill and then watch a man burn inside his own skin.'

He settles the mask securely over his mouth and nose again.

'Now, Declan. Where were we?'

Declan meets his gaze, breathing hard through his nose, the gag still firmly in place.

Scott looks at me. 'Shall we give him half a dozen pills before I start? Send him on his way?'

Declan turns, shaking his head. Our eyes lock for a second and I see all his determination there, battling with the fear. Sorrow too. And regret.

Scott slaps him to get his attention again.

'No pills?' he says. 'You want to feel every last second of it? Fine with me, because I'm going to enjoy this. I've been looking forward to it for a long time.'

He tips the bottle again and the acid is millimetres from the lip when the bald man with the goatee – the one he'd dispatched a moment ago – reappears in the doorway. He's walking backwards, with his hands up at shoulder height.

He backs all the way into the kitchen.

Evie appears in the doorway. Her cheek flames with a livid red mark, a trickle of blood smeared beneath her nose.

She's holding the gun Declan showed me earlier.

Lucas is behind her, eyes wide with fear.

A paralysing terror clutches at my chest, squeezing the air from my lungs.

'Lucas!'

'Mum?'

Roper lunges for the other doorway but Evie turns and fires in a single motion, splinters of wood exploding from the door frame next to his head. He flinches away from the impact and puts his hands up, stepping back into the kitchen.

'Evie,' I gasp. 'What are you doing?'

She doesn't take her eyes off the four now seated at the long wooden table. 'I got us into this, Mum. And I will get us out of it.'

Scott turns to Roper. But there is no fear in his eyes, only irritation. 'You don't learn, do you, Brandon? How many times have you been told to search them before you bring them on site?'

'I *did*,' Roper says, a defensive tone in his voice. 'Searched her when we put her in the van, I swear.'

'And did you search her dad too?'

'Of course,' Roper protests with a shrug. 'We took the knuckle-duster off him, but he was out of it, anyway. He was no threat, he was half dead.'

'But he was carrying as well.' He shakes his head. 'And she's taken it off him while they were in the back of the van together. You absolute *moron*.' Evie gestures at him with the gun.

'Put the cap back on that acid and put it back in the box. *Slowly.*'

He grins, and for one horrible moment I think he's going to hurl it at her. But then he does what he's told, stoppering the bottle and laying it back in the padded box.

'Put the gun down, love. I've got a dozen blokes on this farm, you've got no chance.'

Evie levels the weapon at him. 'No. We're leaving.'

Scott leans forward, tanned arms on the table. 'Tell you what, Evie. You hand the gun over, I'll let you and your brother leave. And your mum, OK? That's fair, isn't it? We've got something special lined up for your dad, so he'll have to stay.'

Evie spits on the floor at his feet. 'No.'

'How about I let you take Cassie too?'

'How about I've got a better idea.' She nods towards the pile of pills. 'You wanted this stuff so badly, you should be the first to enjoy it. Take a pill.'

'I don't think so,' Scott says. 'Not my style.'

'A pill or a bullet. It's up to you.'

Roper lowers his hands slowly.

'You're out of your depth, love.' He takes a step towards her and she swings the gun his way.

'All right, how about you go first,' Evie says. 'Go on, Brandon. Which one do you want?'

'I think I'll have that gun instead.'

She grips the pistol in both hands and slowly, calmly, takes aim at his leg.

'A pill.' Her voice is very quiet now. 'Or a bullet.'

'Big gun for a little bitch,' Roper sneers. 'You best put that down, love, before someone gets—'

His left kneecap explodes in a spout of blood, the gunshot incredibly loud against the kitchen's low ceiling.

A high-pitched scream bursts from Roper's mouth and he staggers back against the worktop, dropping to the tiled floor as he clutches his shattered knee.

'Well, Brandon?' Evie says. 'Do you want to keep playing?'

'You shot me!'

'I did.'

'Psycho bitch!'

He screams a string of obscenities, blood pulsing through his fingers as he writhes on the floor.

Evie shifts her aim, her voice still eerily calm. 'I'm going to shoot your other knee unless you take a pill, Brandon.'

'All right!' His voice cracks and he begins to drag himself awkwardly across the flagstone floor, leaving a dark red slick in his wake. He reaches up for a blue pill from the steel tray, sending dozens of others scattering in all directions. With a final terrified glance at Evie he dry swallows it down, opening his mouth to show her it's gone.

She turns the gun towards Scott.

'And now it's your turn, *love*.' The word drips with sarcasm. 'Unless you want your mum to take one next?'

*   *   *

Three minutes later, Evie and I hold Declan up as we stumble across the courtyard towards the big Mercedes, the farmhouse door locked behind us. Cassie leads Lucas by the hand, both of them running ahead, hitting the car's remote to unlock it with a beep and a flash as they throw open doors and scramble inside. We heave Declan bodily into the back seat and then for a moment, just a moment, Evie and I are face to face, both of us breathing hard, her face streaked with blood in the moonlight.

I pull her into a desperate hug and suddenly there are tears hot on my cheeks, my heart filling, bursting, singing with joy. *My daughter. My girl. I finally found you, and I'm never going to lose you again.* She hugs me back, holding on tight and I want to stay like that forever, but there is a shout from the dark fields behind the house, and we pull apart.

'I'll drive,' she says, her voice thick. 'You need to make some calls.'

I'm climbing into the back seat as she raises the pistol and fires three times – *crack crack crack* – high into the farmhouse windows, dropping cascades of shattering glass before aiming more shots at the tyres of the van parked alongside us.

She throws herself into the driver's seat, hits the ignition button and stamps on the accelerator as her door is swinging shut. The first figures are emerging out of the gloom behind us but we're already moving fast, tearing down the driveway as the big car's headlights cut through the blackness, a spray of gravel in our wake. Evie and Cassie sit up front, me and Lucas in the back with Declan tucked in between us. The drive curves through the grounds, dark ploughed fields on either side. No lights behind us. No one in pursuit.

Evie flashes through the gates doing sixty and blasts out onto the main road back towards the coast.

Once I'm sure we're clear and away, I dial Parry's number and put the phone to my ear.

72

TEN DAYS LATER

Declan is already there when we arrive.

We've arranged to meet on neutral ground, roughly halfway between my house and his: a little country pub near Egham called The Crooked Billet. It's warm and homely, a seventeenth-century coaching inn with heavy oak beams and a log fire roaring in the hearth. He's found a corner table for the five of us and stands up as we approach.

'Wasn't sure you'd actually come,' he says. 'It's really good to see you again, Lauren.'

I gesture at Evie and Lucas, who are already shrugging off their coats. 'Couldn't have kept these two away if I'd tried.'

Declan moves closer and there is an awkward moment as neither of us knows quite what to do next, what's appropriate in the circumstances, before he leans in to give me a chaste peck on the cheek. He's clean shaven, in a white shirt that looks new, his face still dark with bruises from that terrible day at Newhaven. He goes to the bar to get a round of drinks in – although my mum is the only one who asks for anything stronger than Diet Coke – as we settle around the table.

Both children are nervous. I can tell by the way they both stare at Declan's back as he stands at the bar, ducking his head to avoid the low beams. Lucas is wide-eyed with awe while his sister seems to be studying her father, her eyes following every move as if he might disappear again at any moment. He brings the drinks back to the table two at a time, takes a seat opposite and holds up his pint of Coke in a toast to the children, to me and my mum.

'Well, I know I'm a bit late,' he says, 'but Merry Christmas anyway, hope you had a good one and you're all doing OK.' He smiles at Evie and Lucas.

The conversation is slow at first.

But gradually it picks up, as questions are traded back and forth. Declan asks about Cassie, who's stayed in touch with Evie and will come to visit us in the New Year. The two of them are helping each other to process what they went through, helping each other to heal. Every so often I see Lucas gazing up at his dad, studying him, as if he can't quite believe he's real. Then Declan will look over, catch his son's eye, and Lucas will give him an uncertain smile. I have to remind myself that this is only the third time they've met. By contrast, Evie and her father are quickly at ease with each other, almost casual, bantering as if they've known each other all their lives and barely ever been apart. In truth they are very much alike, father and daughter, both of them impulsive and generous and quick to smile.

It feels right that he's back in their lives, but I don't *need* him. Not like that. Not anymore.

After twenty minutes, Lucas plucks a menu from the next table.

'Can we actually get some food, Mum? I'm *starving*.' He and his sister pick from the sandwich menu and I go to the bar to order. The pub has filled up and the lone barman is busy pouring drinks for a large group that has just arrived. While I'm waiting to be served, my phone buzzes with a text from Craig Farley at the university, a belated Merry Christmas and good wishes for next year. I type a quick reply, telling him Evie and I would like to pay one last visit to Queen Anne's – so both of us can thank him in person for his help.

I turn back to look at my little family tucked around the corner table: four of us that have now become five.

As well as the bruises from that day, Declan had cuts and cracked ribs and a concussion, but doctors have told him none of the damage is permanent. We've all agreed to let him into our lives slowly, as we get to know each other again. The main thing right now is that he can build some kind of relationship with his children, which seems to be what all three of them want. All I can think of is that it's the first time I've sat down for a drink with him in more than a dozen years and it's been very weird, almost surreal to see him like this, to introduce him to my mother again after so much time has passed.

Details of the armed police raid on the farm at Shelford Cross and the discovery of the drugs have been all over the media for the last few days. More than a dozen arrests – so far – and the biggest haul of fentanyl ever seized in the UK. More seizures of goods at a warehouse in London's East End, and at a nightclub that's been shut down until further notice. Two men at the farm hospitalised with gunshot wounds, although both are expected to pull through. The weapon has not been found, and it won't be either. I made sure of that – this time it really *did* go to the bottom of a river.

On the quiet, DS Parry has confided to me that two of those arrested – I don't need to ask which two – were close to death by the time NCA officers swooped in and broke down the farmhouse door. Overdosing from a single tablet of high-purity fentanyl and only saved by the quick-thinking action of paramedics, who administered naloxone to pull them back from the brink. Despite everything, I'm glad no-one died that day. Four others were zip-tied and unable to offer any resistance when the police arrived. Scott Lawler, his mother Nicola, Brandon Roper and the rest of those arrested are being held on remand on drug trafficking and supply charges, plus kidnapping, extortion and GBH for what will no doubt be a huge trial next year. Parry has assured me that the whole organisation has been dismantled, all the leaders rounded up, but I won't feel completely safe again until they're convicted and put behind bars for good.

The farmhouse and all the buildings and fields around it are still being treated as a giant crime scene, combed for more drugs and weapons. The police have already discovered more than six million pounds in cash on the site in multiple currencies, as well as a make-shift laboratory set-up in one of the barns with the capacity to cut and process thousands of doses of fentanyl a day. Enough to flood the streets of every town and city in Britain.

Our names are being kept out of it, thank God. Including Evie's, after the discovery of the compromising footage from the hotel room, clear evidence that she was coerced and enough to persuade the CPS that a prosecution would not be in the public interest. Parry has assured us that the footage will be destroyed in due course.

It seems the NCA is only too happy to take all the credit for breaking up one of the biggest drug-smuggling rings in the country.

Lucas is still not sleeping well, still nervous with strangers. The trauma of his kidnapping will take time to fade, I know, but he has all of us around him now to help him through it. He seems to have discovered a shared love of Marvel movies with his dad and it sounds like they're already planning a cinema trip in January.

Evie is definitely leaving her law degree behind and has applied to a drama college in Manchester instead. It's a big change of direction but I can tell just by looking at her face, by the way she talks about it, that it's the right choice. I'm glad she's following her heart. And I'm learning to step back and let her do just that. To let her live her own life, find her own path. In a funny way, taking that step back has brought us closer than we've been for a long time.

Next week will be a brand-new year. A new start for my daughter, a new guardian for my son. A new parent for both of them.

Declan glances up from his drink and gives me a slow smile, the one that dazzled me all those years ago. The one he gave me in a crowded bar when I was eighteen that made my stomach do a little flip.

Maybe the new year will bring a second chance for all of us.

Acknowledgements

Like most of my other books, *The Daughter* grew out of a 'What if?' scenario: an idea that popped into my head while I was driving to collect my daughter after her first term as a student. For the record though, Queen Anne's is a fictional university – eagle-eyed readers might remember it as the setting for my second novel, *29 Seconds*.

A few readers might also recognise the named halls of residence in the early chapters: New Orchard, Selincourt, Lodge, Maynard and Chesney. These were all halls at Westfield College, University of London, where I was a student quite a few years ago. Sadly, Westfield merged with another institution and no longer exists as a separate entity, but I have many happy memories of being a history undergraduate in that leafy part of north-west London.

I'm indebted to my friend Rachel Redford, who helped me to understand the way that universities monitor student attendance and the procedures for checking up on individuals who are not engaging with their degree course in the usual way. Any errors are, of course, mine.

I have drawn on insights from *The Reverse Opium Wars*, a feature by Stephen Gibbs and Keiran Southern in the *Sunday Times* magazine, March 2024. Their excellent article outlined the terrifying rise of fentanyl and the deadly toll it is taking in the USA and other countries.

Thanks as ever to my editor, Sophie Orme, and to the team at Bonnier Books including Blake Brooks, Holly Milnes, Eleanor Stammeijer, Georgia Marshall, Rachel Johnson and Isabella Boyne.

The Daughter is my ninth book for Bonnier (with a tenth on its way) which seems both wonderful and unbelievable at the same time. It doesn't seem so long ago that my debut, *Lies*, was being published and working with such a great team really does make all the difference.

I'm grateful to my agent, Camilla Bolton, for her usual insight and expertise in all things book-related. Also, to her colleagues at the Darley Anderson Agency including Jade Kavanagh, Georgia Fuller, Francesca Edwards, Shanika Sterling, Sarah Brooks, Rosanna Bellingham and Helen Dudley. And to Sheila David at Catapult Rights who continues to champion my work for adaptation to the screen.

Thanks, as always, to my wife Sally and my children, Sophie and Tom. We moved house at the beginning of 2024 and were settling into our new place while I was writing this book. I'm pleased to say that I have a new writing cabin too, and I have a feeling there will be plenty more stories that begin in that particular corner of the garden.

A quick mention for the surfing boys – Ken, Jim, Joe, Julian, Mark, Ollie and Simon – for many good 'plot idea' sessions in various pubs in Croyde, Braunton, Georgeham and other beautiful parts of North Devon over the years. I'm (fairly) sure that a few of those ideas have made it into print one way or another – cheers lads.

This novel is dedicated to my Dad, Mike, who celebrated his 85th birthday this past year. Some of my earliest memories are of him reading stories to me and my brothers when we were growing up – and I'm sure those early stories helped to inspire a love of books, reading and writing that has stayed with me ever since. He has always helped and encouraged me in whatever I wanted to do and continues to be an inspiration in every way. Thank you, Dad, for everything.

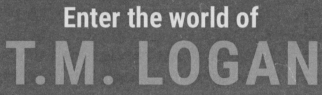

Hello,

My daughter was a first-year student at Cardiff University when the idea for *The Daughter* first popped into my head. This was a few years ago, one December day when I was driving south down the motorway to collect her at the end of term. It was the first time she'd lived away from home, the first time she'd had a measure of independence – but it still felt like a safe environment, lots of first year students all living together in halls of residence.

It's a three-hour drive from Nottingham to Cardiff and a strange thought occurred to me as I got closer to my destination: *What if Sophie isn't there when I arrive?* Quickly followed by: *What if no-one in her corridor knows her? And then she stops answering her phone?* I knew these thoughts weren't entirely rational, but once they started circling in my head I couldn't shake them off. Needless to say, I was very pleased when I arrived at her room that day and Sophie opened the door . . .

That was the starting point for the novel you're holding in your hands now. I would come back to the idea in one way or another over the next few years each time I drove to Cardiff and then – with my son, Tom – to Bath. So my children have contributed in their own way to the creation of this story!

My next thriller will be coming out in early 2026 and if you'd like to be the first to hear more about it, you can join my free Readers' Club at www.tmlogan.com. Just click on the yellow 'Sign up' button, it only takes a moment and I promise I won't spam you with lots of emails.

My publisher, Zaffre, will keep your information private and confidential, and it will never be passed on to a third party. I'll get in touch every so often with news about my books, cover reveals, competitions and more. When I have news, members of my Readers' Club are always the first to know – so sign up if you'd like to become a member (you can unsubscribe at any time).

And lastly, a quick favour . . . if you have a minute, please do rate and review *The Daughter* on Amazon, Goodreads or any other e-store, on your blog or social media accounts, talk about it with friends, family or reading groups. Sharing your thoughts and views helps other readers, and I always enjoy hearing what people think about my books.

Thank you again for reading *The Daughter*, I really appreciate it.

Best wishes,

Tim

Read more from
THE MASTER OF THE
UP-ALL-NIGHT THRILLER

T.M. LOGAN

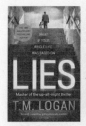    

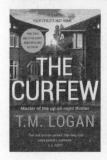   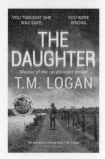